VISSI D'ARTE

A Story Of Love And Music

By the same author:

EUMERALLA – Secrets, Tragedy and Love

THE DOLL COLLECTION – a crime novel

VISSI D'ARTE

Joanna Stephen-Ward

Popham Gardens Publishing

Popham Gardens Publishing

November 2012

Reprinted with minor revisions August 2009

This addition November 2012

ISBN 978-0-9545857-0-9

EAN 9780954585709

Popham Gardens Publishing
www.publishingforyou.com
e-mail: enquiries@publishingforyou.com

Please visit the author's web site at:
www.joannaauthor.co.uk
for more details of this book and the story behind it.

Author's Note

Vissi d'arte was inspired by **Gertrude Johnson**, the founder of the National Theatre in Melbourne. The character **Harriet Shaw** is loosely based on the achievements of Gertrude Johnson, but Gertrude was far kinder, more humorous and artistically adventurous. Her personality and character were nothing like Harriet's.

The rest of the characters are fictional and are not intended to resemble real people, either living or dead.

The National Theatre as described in *Vissi d'arte*, is the real National Theatre, but the events therein are of my own making. The National Theatre did not move to St Kilda until 1972, but for the sake of the story line, I have taken the liberty of having it resident there in 1968.

Those wishing to know more about Gertrude Johnson can read *National Treasure – The Story of Gertrude Johnson and the National Theatre* by **Frank Van Straten**, a Victoria Press Publication, published by the Law Printer in 1994.

Acknowledgements

Thanks to the members of the *Richmond Writers' Circle* for their support and constructive criticism, especially **Owen Adams, Gerry Ball, Rebecca Billings, Suzanne Bugler, Tim Byrne, Feola Choat, Peter Clark, Alan Franks, Harry Garlick, Nancy Godwin, Mike Gordon, Annie Morris, Richard Rickford, Mike Riley, Alison Smith, Susan Wallbank,** and **Owen Wheatley.**

Special thanks to **Nancy Godwin, Laurelei Moore, Susan Paice, Susan Wallbank** and **Jenny Webb** for taking the time to read the whole manuscript and give me valuable feedback and encouragement.

Early in 2009 I posted *Vissi d'arte* on *Authonomy*, a website for writers run by a major publisher. Over 300 members commented on the manuscript. I am extremely grateful to them all for their helpful comments and support.

This book is dedicated to the memory of
Gertrude Johnson
My Inspiration.

For my husband **Peter**, with love and thanks.

In loving memory of my wonderful father
Carlyle Stephen

VISSI D'ARTE

A story of love and music

Part One

OVERTURE

January 1968 — January 1969

Chapter 1

'Of love bereft,
this life is torment.'
The Force of Destiny – Verdi

January 1968

Branches torn from the chestnut trees blocked the entry to Lichfield Road. Nicholas found a gap and squeezed through it. Snow crystals hit his face and drove into the gap between his coat and scarf as he carried his suitcases up the icy footpath. Only the thought that he might be in Australia in a few weeks cheered him. The blizzard almost obscured the elegant house he had inherited, but did not want. Kew, with its botanical gardens and tree lined streets was too suburban for Nicholas. He preferred the frenetic atmosphere of Chelsea where he had lived for seven years. Tomorrow someone else would take his place in the crowded attic flat.

He stood at the gate, daunted by the responsibilities facing him. The house had belonged to his family since 1890, and to sell it seemed wrong. Gusts of wind caught the hem of his coat, hooking it over the jagged end of a fallen branch. He disentangled himself and walked up the path to the front door. It was the first time he had been in the house alone. He took a deep breath, expecting to smell the Chanel perfume his grandmother had worn, but her scent had not lingered. Unprepared for the stale air, he felt bereft. He dumped his cases at the foot of the staircase.

Letters scattered over the black and white tiled floor of the hallway raised his hopes. He looked for an airmail envelope, but there was nothing from Australia. Most of the others were electricity and gas bills addressed to his grandmother. His letters were from people in the drama company, begging him to return.

His grandmother's money gave him the luxury of not having to find another job in a hurry. As he pulled off his scarf, he saw a shadow through the stained glass panels on the front door. He opened it. "Hello, Tanya."

She held up a shopping bag. "I've bought you a moving in present. I bet you forgot all about food."

He kissed her cheek. "You're right. Thanks."

She began to unbutton her orange coat.

"Leave that on till I light the fire."

She shook the snow from her hat and hung it on the coat stand. After putting the food in the kitchen, he led her into the drawing room.

"What a fabulous house."

Underneath her affectionate manner, he detected tension. 'She's going to tell me something about Sally,' he thought.

The fire was set and there were logs on the hearth and a box of kindling and newspapers. With his cigarette lighter he lit a stick and waited while the paper caught fire. When he stood up, he saw Tanya looking at the portrait over the mantelpiece. It struck him that, as well as the house and antique furniture, he also owned all the photos and portraits of Harriet.

"Is that your mother?" she asked.

He shook his head. "Her sister. Well, that's what she's reputed to be."

She looked puzzled. "But?"

"I'm not sure." He frowned. "When I was a child, every time my relatives looked at her photos or this portrait, they'd gaze sorrowfully and sigh. Actually, for years I thought she was dead. I was twelve when I discovered she lives in Australia."

"What happened?"

He shrugged. "No one would tell me. They said she had gone to Australia because she wanted to start her own theatre."

"Sounds plausible. Are you sure you didn't dream about the sighing relations?"

"Positive. I have vivid recollections of family gatherings. They'd stand in front of her portrait and then say, 'What a tragedy'."

2

Tanya burst out laughing. "I can't believe people stood in front of a portrait moaning like a chorus in a Greek … " She was too overcome with laughter to continue.

"It didn't happen like that." In spite of his exasperation the image amused him. "Why did I think she was dead? She had an amazing life here. She sang leading roles at Covent Garden." He went to the piano stool and took out the scrap book his mother had kept when she was a child. "Look through that."

As Tanya scanned the newspaper cuttings, he could see she was impressed.

She nodded. "It's strange she gave all this up. Australia's not the cultural centre of the world, is it? If I was as famous and feted as she was – I see what you're getting at." She pulled a face. "I bet it was something to do with a man."

"I doubt it. She never married."

Tanya poked him in the ribs. "Then it's definitely something to do with a man. Damn men. Are you going to make me a cup of tea?"

"Do you trust a man to make you a cup of tea?"

"I'm so desperate I'll trust anyone – even you." She started to follow him out of the room, then paused and looked back at the portrait. "Nick? Maybe … um … no."

"What? Tell me."

"She might have been – you know. She might have preferred women."

That had never occurred to him. "What makes you think that?"

"It's unusual for her not to have married. People keep secrets because there's shame attached. Maybe there was a scandal and that's why she went to Australia."

He shook his head. "Millions of women were left without men after the First World War."

Tanya took a photo off the grand piano. "Not a woman like her."

"You're a feminist, but you're going on as if marriage is the ultimate achievement for a woman, and if they don't marry there's something wrong with them."

"Nick, in those days marriage was the ultimate achievement for a woman. For too many women it still is." She picked up another photo. "She's got – I don't know how to describe it. Nothing as crude as

3

sexiness. It's not the superficial thing of walking into a room and men staring at her. Just looking at these photos, I feel I want to know her. When did she go to Australia?"

"Forty years ago."

Tanya went back to the portrait. "She's old now."

He nodded. "In her seventies."

"She looks a lot like you."

"Yes. That's why … " Not wanting Tanya to think he was obsessed by Harriet, he hesitated.

"Go on."

"I've often wondered if she's really my grandmother. It's possible – she was twenty when my mother was born."

Tanya whistled. "In those days it would have been disgraceful. I bet that's the secret. Now where's my tea?"

He didn't move. "You want to tell me something about Sally, don't you?"

She blushed. "I'll tell you when we're having our tea."

'She's getting married to that bastard,' he thought, determined to act nonchalantly when Tanya got round to telling him.

In the kitchen, while she unpacked the shopping, he switched on the fan heater and filled the kettle.

She took off her coat to reveal an orange velvet caftan that she wore over a black polo neck sweater. "Come back to the theatre, Nick. We miss you."

He lit the gas. "No one's indispensable and I've – "

"You are." She cut up the fruit cake. "You're a fantastic director. No one we've interviewed has been any good. If it'll make any difference, we'll get rid of Sally."

"No, Tanya. If she no longer loves me, it's my bad luck, not hers."

"You're too honourable, Nick," she said, pouring milk into the cups.

"Okay, stop fandangoing around. Tell me about Sally." Seeing her reluctance, he said, "I suppose she's getting married."

She shook her head. "The opposite. She knows she made a terrible mistake."

He couldn't hide his surprise.

"She wants you back. Would you have her?"

4

Thoughts of Australia receded. He pictured Sally erasing the loneliness of this house. "We'd have to talk. I wouldn't start where we left off. I'd have to make sure I could trust her again. Fidelity's important to me. Getting engaged is a serious commitment." He felt a ripple of optimism. "But, I'd be willing to give her a second chance."

"Hell and buckets of blood. Now I'm going to have to tell you. She asked me not to, but you've got to know. She had an abortion."

Horrified, he stared at her. "Was it mine?"

"She didn't know if it was yours or his." She touched his arm. "Sorry, Nick."

"God." He felt chilled. "Are you sure she had an abortion?"

"Yes. She asked my advice – "

He pushed her hand away.

"Stop looking at me like that. I begged her not to."

Roughly pulling out a chair, he sat down. "Do you want to come and live here for a year? I'm going away and I'll need someone to look after the house."

"What? I couldn't afford to rent this place."

"I don't want any rent. You'd be doing me a favour."

"Where are you going?"

"Australia. Harriet's got a theatre company with schools in Melbourne."

"When did you decide this?"

"About thirty seconds ago."

"I know you're upset, but it's a bit drastic isn't it?"

"It's not that sudden. When Sally broke our engagement I wrote and asked her if I could have a job."

"Doing what?"

He shrugged. "Anything. I haven't heard from her yet."

Tanya wrinkled her nose. "My cousin's just come back from Australia. He said Melbourne's fifty years behind the times. You'll hate it. You know what? *Hair*'s banned."

"I'll shave my head then."

She slapped his arm. "The rock opera, you idiot."

"I know. Why's it banned?"

"The nude scene I suppose."

He shrugged. "I've got to get away – I can't stop thinking about

5

Sally. Nothing's certain yet. Harriet might not offer me anything, but will you come and live here if she does?"

She smiled. "I'd be crazy to refuse. This kitchen's bigger than my bedsit."

When Tanya left, he rummaged through his suitcases. When he found the photos of Sally, he took them into the drawing room and threw them on the fire. Unable to watch them burn, he took a book of Chopin Preludes from the bookcase and went to the piano, but his hands were so cold his fingers lacked dexterity.

The stereo he had bought his grandmother for her last birthday was in the alcove near the window. He lifted the lid and saw an old 78 record on the turntable. It was one of Harriet's. Turning out the light, he opened the green velvet curtains and stood by the window scarcely aware of the crackles as the stylus cut into the grooves. Harriet's soprano voice filled the room, its brilliance preserved for over forty years by early recording technology. The melancholy song from Handel's *Semele* suited his mood. Pressing his finger to the glass, he watched a fragment of ice turn to water and slip down the window.

When the song ended he put on a Rolling Stones LP and sat in the armchair by the fire gazing at the flames. Desperate to do something constructive, he found his pen and sat on the sofa making notes about starting a new theatre company. Modernize Shakespeare? Update the language? He thought about the party scene in *Romeo and Juliet*. Have Beatles and Stones music playing on the stereo?

He tossed the pad and his pen aside. Nothing could distract his mind from Sally and the abortion. Thoughts that the baby might have been his tormented him. Banging his hands on the arm of the chair, he stood up and looked at Harriet's portrait. It had been painted when she was twenty-six, the same age as he was now. The artist had captured an expression that was a mix of humour, dreaminess and determination. Rage and grief had resurrected his desire to know if she really was his grandmother. They had the same striking good looks with high cheekbones, straight noses and wavy hair that was almost black. Fashionably long, his fell past his ears. In all the photos round the house, Harriet's hairstyle depended on what role she was playing. His brown eyes were the same almond shape as her grey ones.

His grandmother had kept a journal since she was fifteen. When he was doing a project about the war at school she had allowed him to read some. He went to the cabinet where she had kept all her journals. Originally he intended to skim through them to discover what had happened to Harriet, but his grandmother's accounts fascinated him. Sometimes a year might only occupy a few pages, whereas her frantic writing during the First World War had taken up fifteen volumes. The entries about his mother's birth in 1914 scotched his theory that Harriet was really his grandmother.

> *I am expecting a baby. As Harriet is twenty, we feel shocked, afraid and delighted.*

Her next entry was a few weeks after his mother's birth.

> *We have another beautiful daughter and have named her Charlotte. Harriet is elated. This baby has two mothers!*

The journals were out of order, but the covers were numbered. It took him an hour before he found anything significant.

June 1924

> *We have just come home from seeing Harriet off to Australia. We pray she will rebuild her life and find happiness. Today was the culmination of the worst two years we have ever endured. When it was time for us to go ashore, Charlotte clung to Harriet and refused to leave. We had to drag her down the gangplank. People looked at us disapprovingly, thinking she needed discipline. If they had known what she had been through, they would have been kinder. On the quay we held the streamers that were our last link with Harriet. As the ship pulled away they broke and disintegrated in the churning water.*
> *Writing in my journal is cathartic. For two years it has helped keep me sane. Charlotte never talks about what she saw that night. I pray she has forgotten most of it. Her*

7

nightmares are less frequent now.

His anticipation grew as he searched the volumes covering the twenties. One book ended with an account of Harriet's performance as The Queen of The Night in 1922. He looked for the next one, but there was nothing until three years later. Four consecutive journals were missing.

He read on, looking for some reference to a tragedy involving Harriet. There was nothing specific, just oblique comments that, had he not been looking for them, he would have thought unimportant. He decided Harriet's refusal to come to England for his parents' wedding was significant. His mother had often told him about her big sister, who, in spite of her busy life as an opera singer, had made time to play games, take her for walks and give her piano lessons. Their relationship, in spite of the miles separating them, was still close. Harriet wrote once a week, phoned four times a year and had always taken an interest in him.

Fuelled by coffee and toast, he spent all night reading. When he could find nothing he went back to the books covering the twenties. Instead of scanning them, he read them carefully, and realized there were large gaps in the dates. An inspection of the bindings showed fragments of paper, confirming his suspicion that pages had been torn out. When he finished the last journal, faint sunlight was leaking through the curtains.

Deciding the other journals had been hidden, he went up to the attic. A bare bulb hanging from the ceiling cast its harsh light through the cobwebs. Among the pieces of furniture and boxes was a metal trunk. Convinced the missing volumes were inside, he undid the rusty clasps and lifted the lid. A smell of mothballs wafted out. Inside, wrapped in tissue paper, lay a wedding gown and three bridesmaids' dresses, one of which had been made for a child. At the bottom of the trunk he found a pile of wedding invitations. They were not for his mother's wedding, as he had thought, but for Harriet's, who was to have married Doctor Andrew Walters in Saint Anne's Church on Kew Green in July 1922.

Part of the mystery was solved, but a broken engagement did not warrant the secrecy. 'Was she abandoned at the altar? Did she discover he was a bigamist? It might have been her fault. Maybe she fell in love with someone unsuitable and disgraced herself.'

He considered Tanya's suggestion. Recalling the snippets of conversation from his childhood and the writings in the journals, he concluded the misfortune had been Harriet's. If the engagement had been broken because she had been discovered in a compromising situation, the sympathy would have been with Andrew. 'Maybe the engagement wasn't broken,' he thought. 'He might have died or been killed. But why keep it a secret?'

In spite of a thorough search, Nicholas could not find the journals. That his grandmother might have destroyed them increased his interest. He found Harriet's letters, but his excitement died as he read them. All she ever wrote about was her theatre. The only time she became enthusiastic was when she discovered a promising new singer. Not once had she mentioned the past or told her mother she missed her. Her clinical writing was at odds with the girl of twenty who had been thrilled about her sister's birth.

When he went downstairs there was a pile of mail in the hall. Among the bills were his Australian visa and a letter from Harriet. After explaining that the reason for the delay in replying had been the illness of her opera director, who had been ordered to rest, she asked Nicholas if he would like the job. Excited by the opportunity to direct opera, he was grateful to Harriet for her trust. As he read her letter he realized he would be too busy to brood about Sally, because he would also be teaching drama to the opera school students.

She gave him details of his salary and enclosed a brochure about the theatre. His interest in Harriet had mainly concerned her past, but as he read the brochure, he realized how far-sighted she was. Although her chief love was opera she had founded a theatre and schools for opera, ballet and drama. The schools were part-time with classes held in the evenings and at weekends, so gifted people from all walks of life could participate.

When he read the opera season was in May, he felt a sense of urgency. Going to the bookcase he pulled out the scores of *La Traviata, Trittico, The Marriage of Figaro* and *Romeo and Juliet*, pleased he knew them by heart.

Three days before he left for Australia his parents came from Wiltshire to stay with him.

"I'm pleased you've had your hair cut at last – you looked like a hippie," said his father.

His mother hugged him. "I'm thrilled you'll be working with Harriet." Then she looked round the room at the overflowing ashtrays, dirty cups and piles of books. "It didn't take you long to create chaos."

It suddenly struck Nicholas that his mother could have taken the journals before he moved in. He waited until they were having dinner before asking questions.

"Why didn't Aunt Harriet and Andrew Walters marry?" he asked as he poured mint sauce over his roast lamb.

His mother looked startled. "How did you know about him?"

"I found the wedding invitations. What happened?"

She put down her knife and ran her finger along the pattern on the handle. "She changed her mind."

"Why? I know there was a tragedy."

"You theatre people are fixated with tragedy," scoffed his father. "You've been smoking marijuana, like all you arty types."

Nicholas was about to protest. Then he realized his father was making inflammatory statements to create a diversion. "If I want to get high I listen to Beethoven or opera," he said calmly. "I don't take drugs – and you know it." He stared at his mother. "Where are the journals?"

She looked guilty.

"Nicholas, the subject's closed," said his father. "And don't badger your aunt with insane questions when you get to Australia."

The next morning Nicholas took the journal into the kitchen. His mother was alone washing the breakfast dishes.

He found the page and read it aloud. "Do you remember what you saw?"

Vigorously scrubbing the porridge saucepan, she said nothing.

"What did you see? Where did you see it?" He decided he was asking the wrong question. "Who did you see?" he asked instead. "What were they doing?"

He heard his father come in. Before Nicholas could stop him, he took the book and ripped out the page, tore it up and threw it in the bin.

His mother handed him a tea towel. "Do something useful, Nicholas." Her voice shook. So did her hands.

10

Later, he retrieved the pieces his father had torn up, and sellotaped them together. He packed the page with the scores he was taking with him.

'I'll find out what happened when I get to Australia,' he vowed.

Chapter 2

'See there, what venom flashes from her eyes!'
Parsifal – Wagner

Nicholas pushed his trolley through the excited crowds at Tullamarine Airport, looking in vain for his aunt. An hour later he went into a phone booth and dialled her number, but there was no reply. He debated whether to catch a taxi to Harriet's house or stay at the airport in case she was stuck in a traffic jam. Most of the passengers had left, and the airport was almost deserted. He sat down and took out his cigarettes.

A young woman with a tear-drenched face and rings of mascara under her eyes hurried up to him. "Are you Nicholas Forrester?" she asked breathlessly.

He stood up. "Yes."

"Hugh's just died. Harriet's at the hospital. We were leaving to meet you when they rang."

He guessed Hugh was the director who had been ill.

Tears poured down her face. "He had another heart attack."

"I'm so sorry," he said, wondering who she was.

She wiped her eyes and walked towards the exit. Grabbing his trolley, he followed her. When he stepped outside, the searing heat engulfed him. He squinted against the glare of the sun. As they walked across the car park he noted with surprise that the majority of cars were British. She unlocked the boot of a black Wolseley. He stacked his suitcases in and got into the front seat, wincing as the hot leather burned through his trousers. The girl put on her sunglasses and wound down the window.

The drive from the airport was conducted in silence. She was a tense driver who concentrated on the road and other vehicles as if expecting them to crash into her. Sweat dampened his clothes and he hoped he didn't smell. Disconcertingly, she made no attempt to point out sites of interest as they drove through a city he presumed was

12

Melbourne. He wondered if she would be annoyed if he asked her who she was. Glancing at her serious profile, he decided she would. The wind blew locks of her blonde hair out of its chignon.

Fifteen minutes after they left the city, she pulled into a small street and parked the car. Dramatically, the tension left her. She pushed her sunglasses up on top of her head. "Harriet found you a flat – she thought you'd feel more independent on your own. Her house is a five minute walk away."

He took his cases out of the boot. "That was very considerate of her."

They walked up a path edged with hydrangea bushes that were drooping in the heat.

"It's half a house really." She took the keys out of her handbag and opened the front door. "If you don't like it you can look for another one. It's furnished so the furniture's awful. It's clean though – Harriet's cleaning lady did it specially."

He was pleased to see that among the dull fifties furniture in the front room was an upright piano.

"That's a present from Harriet," she said.

He saw that her eyes were an unusual colour. 'Gold,' he thought. 'No. More like amber.'

There were two bedrooms, and a kitchen that overlooked a bare garden with brown grass. As the girl had promised, the flat was clean and smelled of pine disinfectant.

"You must be exhausted. Get some sleep," she said, after she had shown him where everything was. "I'll ring you tomorrow."

He walked to the door with her. "I'm sorry, but what's your name?"

"Phillipa Matthews."

"Harriet's secretary?"

"Yes."

He smiled. "Her letters described you as wonderfully efficient, so I'd imagined a middle-aged woman with grey hair pulled back in a bun."

She looked amused, then, as if ashamed of her frivolity, her face became sombre. Nicholas opened the door for her and watched her walk down the path. Trying to cool down the flat, he opened the windows, but minutes later the place was invaded by flies. The front and back doors had fly screens so he left them open, but there was no breeze to relieve the humidity. He found a can of fly killer and sprayed it around the flat.

Exhaustion overwhelmed him. He went into the bedroom and was about to undress when he saw someone walking down the street. Used to bedrooms that were upstairs, he felt exposed. He closed the curtains and took off his sweat soaked clothes. In the bathroom were cakes of soap, a bottle of shampoo and towels. Accustomed to baths, he found the shower invigorating. The water was so soft he kept dropping the soap. After cleaning his teeth, he got into bed between cotton sheets that smelt brand new. Just before he fell asleep, he realized he didn't know his new address.

Christ Church was full and, as the organ began to play 'Nearer my God to Thee', there were feeble attempts to sing, but most of the opera singers' voices had deserted them. During the vicar's tribute, the sobs of the congregation increased. Nicholas sat with Harriet and Phillipa, wishing he could comfort them but, being a newcomer, he felt that any physical gesture would be too intimate. Since his arrival three days ago, Harriet had been so grief-stricken she scarcely acknowledged his presence. He had always felt that he was confident and able to manage most situations, but he had no idea how to behave towards Harriet and Phillipa. He wondered if this was because he was in strange territory or because he didn't know either of them.

The Victorian sandstone church, located in the once grand but now dilapidated suburb of St Kilda, had some of the most beautiful stained glass windows he had seen. Rich jewel colours in ruby, sapphire, amethyst, emerald and topaz blazed as the sunlight shone through them. The cathedral where he had been a choirboy had stained glass windows, but they had been too high to appreciate. 'These are just the right height,' he thought.

At the end of the service Harriet took Phillipa's arm and they walked towards the door. In the cemetery, he found himself standing opposite them. The severe black of mourning suited neither. Harriet's face was grey, and Phillipa's unflattering straw hat, hurriedly bought,

14

obscured her golden hair. The rest of the mourners stood limply in the scorching heat oblivious to the flies that buzzed round them. His grandmother's burial had taken place on a freezing morning with slanting sun glinting on the snow. He thought that the heat and flies robbed this occasion of its dignity.

After the service, everyone went to Harriet's house in East St Kilda. Melancholy people stood around in groups. Although some looked at him curiously, no one introduced themselves. When everyone else had left, Phillipa closed the curtains.

"I should have married him," said Harriet. Warily, as if she had been too revealing, she wiped her eyes.

Nicholas went into the kitchen and filled the kettle, thinking that the act of making tea would make him useful. He hadn't realized there had been more to Harriet's relationship with Hugh than friendship. Wondering if his mother knew, he lit the gas. He could hear their conversation clearly.

"What are we going to do? I can't go on without him."

"You've got Nicholas," Phillipa said.

He was depressed by the lack of conviction in her voice. While he looked for the teapot he heard Harriet blow her nose.

"Oh, Phillipa, can you see another director having the relationship with the cast and students he had? No one will be as dedicated as Hugh. The theatre was his life."

Nicholas imagined the pessimism etched on Harriet's face.

"It's you, Harriet," said Phillipa. "You inspire devotion. He did it for you."

Nicholas couldn't find the tea, and decided that to ask would be intrusive. He turned off the kettle, quietly left the house and walked to his flat, thinking that coming to Australia was the worst decision he had ever made.

He woke the next morning covered with mosquito bites. Trying to shake off his feelings of displacement, he had a shower. As he washed his hair he imagined the humiliation of being compared unfavourably to Hugh. "He's not as good as Hugh ... Nicholas is too young ... He's never directed opera ... It's only because he's Miss Shaw's nephew that he's here at all ... "

15

Aware that many of his teaching methods would have to be modified, he had intended to rely on Hugh for advice about teaching drama to opera students. He dreaded his first opera rehearsal. He had no one to turn to for help or friendship. His aunt was a wreck and he felt incapable of attempting to restore confidence.

Finishing his shower with a blast from the cold tap that made him gasp, he dried himself and decided to go for a walk. He searched through his wardrobe, but even his summer clothes were too thick for this climate. As soon as he was dressed he felt hot again. The thought of food made him feel sick so he went down the hall intending to play the piano. By the front door was a note.

Dear Nicholas,

I didn't want to wake you with a phone call. Please forgive me. I was so upset I didn't even welcome you. Will you come and have lunch today? I'll expect you at about 12.

Aunt Harriet.

The walk to her Victorian house in Hotham Street took five minutes, but when he arrived his shirt was wet with perspiration. Her front garden was a mass of bushy shrubs and tall native trees that provided a screen from the busy street. When she opened the door he was amazed by the change in her. Her back was straight, her ice-blue linen suit was immaculate and her face bore no traces of the ravages of the past few days. Her white hair was flatteringly styled and her dark grey eyes were only slightly red. Like his grandmother, she smelt of Chanel perfume.

Pleased that she had overcome her unhappiness, he lost his awkwardness and kissed her cheek. For the past few days she had been so submerged by grief that he had been unable to think of her as the daughter of his grandmother. Now he felt a strange sense of blurred identity. Physically, she resembled his grandmother, but there was a dramatic difference in her expression. The only photos he had seen of Harriet had been those taken before she left England. The woman who accepted his kiss had lost her radiance and humour. Ruthlessness, determination and another expression he could not define had replaced

16

it.

"Come inside before all the flies invade." Unlike the quaver of yesterday, her voice was steady. She closed the fly-screen door.

He followed her down the hall into the back room. Decorated in yellow and grey with a Chinese rug covering the polished floor, it overlooked a garden full of mature trees, colourful shrubs and rose bushes. Yesterday the house had been full of people and he had hardly been aware of his surroundings. Now he saw that the mantelpiece, desk and grand piano were crowded with familiar photos of his grandparents, his parents and himself. Photos of his mother as a baby, a toddler, schoolgirl, bride and mother, had their own special place on a mahogany table. Suddenly, it occurred to him that the part of his grandmother's journals about his mother's birth might have been a clever deception, written to hide the fact that Harriet had given birth to Charlotte. Were disputes about his mother the reason she had left England?

He walked over to the fan. "Is it always this hot?"

"In summer it is. Didn't you bring any summer clothes with you?"

He nodded. "I'm wearing them."

"Oh dear. You'd better go shopping." She handed him a glass of water in which a slice of lemon and ice cubes floated.

He grimaced. "I hate shopping."

"Take Phillipa. She enjoys it."

A movement on the wall caught his eye and he saw an enormous spider. Stifling an exclamation of fright he stepped backwards.

Harriet smiled. "It's a huntsman. They look terrifying, don't they? Don't worry, they're harmless."

Embarrassed by his reaction he said, "It looks poisonous enough to kill ten elephants," he said as he looked at its brown furry legs.

The doorbell rang and Harriet went to answer it. He shuddered as the spider ran further up the wall. "Don't you dare go on the ceiling and fall on my head," he muttered, watching its progress. He walked to the other side of the room. It reached the ceiling. He gritted his teeth as it began to crawl across. "Keep away from me."

Harriet came back with Phillipa, who smiled shyly at him. She wore a white sun dress, which accentuated her golden tan, and her pale blonde hair was loose and just touched her shoulders. Like Harriet, she

17

looked much better.

Harriet and Phillipa went into the kitchen. Nicholas glanced round the room. The spider had gone. 'Where the hell is it?' he thought.

They returned carrying plates of salad and a jug of iced water.

"We'll have lunch and then we'll show you round the theatre," said Harriet.

He followed them into the dining room, noticing that it was furnished in the same Victorian style as his grandmother's house.

Gauging that talking about the theatre would ensure there were no uncomfortable silences, he asked, "Does the theatre have government funding?"

Harriet passed him the salt and pepper. "No."

"How do you manage?"

"Ticket sales and patrons," Harriet replied.

He was surprised. "You actually make a profit?"

Harriet nodded. "Apart from providing training and opportunity for gifted singers, ballet dancers and actors, my aim is to make money for the theatre. I'm often criticized for doing only popular operas, but I choose operas that will fill the theatre. I exclude anything discordant or unknown. There's no point in putting on a little-known opera, however good, and playing to half-empty houses."

Nicholas, who had been looking forward to directing some modern operas, was disappointed. He hoped he could persuade her to change her mind.

Harriet refilled her glass. "Everyone must receive their wages, all the bills have to be paid and what's left goes back into the theatre. Drama's different – they can afford to experiment. If a play's well written with a good plot, the audience will enjoy it, because they understand the medium. The critics often attack me and say I lack imagination, but the drama company holds an annual competition for new playwrights – that was my idea."

She spoke with passion and Nicholas caught a glimpse of the young woman from the old photographs.

After lunch, Harriet drove them to St Kilda. Unlike Phillipa, she was a confident driver. Phillipa was a tense passenger, and he wondered what had caused her aversion to cars.

The theatre was much larger than he expected. "You must have a lot of rich patrons," he said as they walked across the foyer to the marble staircase.

"Yes," said Harriet. "We have banks, factories, department stores, insurance companies as well as individuals."

As they showed him round, Nicholas realized the extent of Harriet's achievement. Originally a cinema, it had been built in 1921 with seating for three thousand. The stalls had been converted into studios of various sizes, each equipped with mirrors, a piano and ballet bars. The foyer, lounge and dress circle, which had ornate plaster mouldings, had been refurbished to their original state. The stage, dressing rooms and orchestra pit had been built over the studios. As Harriet and Phillipa gave him a tour, he felt excited. Nothing enthralled him more than the atmosphere of a theatre, even an empty one. He was interested to discover that the studio theatre was called a theatrette. In the air conditioning, he felt comfortable for the first time since his arrival in Melbourne.

"What do the patrons get in return?" he asked as they went into Harriet's office.

"Free advertising," said Harriet.

Phillipa took a programme out of a drawer and handed it to him. It had a burgundy cover, gold lettering and good quality paper.

"That's from the drama season," said Harriet. "They have full-page advertisements in all the programmes for opera, ballet and drama. There's a board in the foyer listing the names of our individual patrons."

He turned the expensively-smelling pages. "This must cost a lot."

"No. The printers are patrons," said Harriet. "Their advertisement's further on."

"You're a great businesswoman."

"I have to be," she said, seeming pleased.

The austerity of Harriet's office surprised him. He had expected it to be large and personal like her house, but it was small with a plain desk, chairs and filing cabinets.

Harriet opened her diary. "Nicholas, I'm auditioning a girl tomorrow. I think you should be present. Hugh used to play the piano for auditions, but the pianist from the ballet school is standing in till we can find a replacement."

"I can play reasonably well. I'd be happy to be your pianist."

"You'll have to be very good. People who audition are nervous enough without having their accompanist fumbling his way through an aria."

"Okay. Audition me now."

They went into a studio and he played the overture to *The Force of Destiny.*

Harriet smiled. "You've got the job."

Nicholas winced as the girl screeched the first line of 'One Fine Day'.

Harriet stood up. "Stop!"

The voice shuddered to a halt.

"You sound like a train going through a tunnel. Nothing I can do will make you sound any different. It's a matter of biology. You either have good vocal cords or you don't. You don't. There are many charlatans around who'll take your money and tell you that you have talent. I hope you believe me because it will save you money and embarrassment."

When the girl left with tears streaming down her face, Harriet turned to Nicholas. "Unfortunately I hear many voices like that."

Nicholas was appalled. "Did you have to be so brutal?"

She looked surprised. "Someone has to tell them. I could lie, but why feed their useless dreams? I have an excellent reputation. There are only a few good singing teachers in Melbourne and I'm one of them. Incidentally, one's an old pupil of mine. The rest ruin voices by overworking them. They're screeching teachers not singing teachers."

He closed the lid of the piano and stood up. "If you were a doctor telling a patient they were dying, would you be gentle or brutal?"

She looked annoyed. "That's different. There's no room for sentimentality in the theatre, Nicholas. You should know that."

"I'm talking about compassion," he protested. "You're shattering dreams."

"I shatter dreams that have no foundation, but I fulfil dreams that do," she said coldly. "It might have sounded cruel to you, but it's better to be honest."

"Not as honest as that. Your formidable reputation could turn nervous singers away from you and straight to these bad teachers.

20

Indirectly, you might be ruining voices."

Harriet's expression was stony.

Nicholas was frustrated that nothing he said was making an impression on her. "What if that poor girl was so distraught she killed herself?"

Harriet flinched and he stared at her in alarm.

He knew he had gone too far. "Aunt Harriet, I'm sorry."

She ignored him and left the theatrette.

That night he wrote letters to his parents and Tanya telling them how much he was enjoying himself. He knew he could never have the same relationship with his aunt that he had enjoyed with his grandmother. Unlike her mother, who had welcomed differences of opinion, Harriet's attitude was rigid. He imagined her reaction if he told her about Sally's abortion. His feeling of loneliness was so acute he almost wept.

♪   ♪   ♪

Brushing away the swarms of flies, Nicholas explored his new surroundings with Phillipa in the sultry January heat, and tried not to brood about his quarrel with Harriet the day before.

"St Kilda was one of the early suburbs of Melbourne," Phillipa told him as they walked along the Esplanade, looking at the crowded beach. "It was affluent once, but most of the mansions and large houses have been divided into flats and neglected by their tenants and owners."

The area depressed him, and the brown grass added to his feelings of alienation. Fitzroy Street, where they caught a tram to the city, was more prosperous with cafés and continental and Jewish shops. The tram clattered up St Kilda Road, which was wide and lined with elm trees. Its elegance made him feel more optimistic. When they arrived in the city he was impressed by the clean streets and gracious arcades, but regretted that many Victorian buildings were being demolished. Skyscrapers towered over their graceful neighbours.

"Are there any good pubs round here?" he asked.

"I don't know. Why?"

"I'm hungry and thirsty, and it's lunch time."

Phillipa's indignant expression puzzled him. "What's wrong?"

"Respectable girls don't go into pubs."

"Really? Everyone goes into pubs in London. You couldn't have looked more outraged if I'd suggested we visit a brothel."

She blushed.

He hid his irritation. "Where do people have lunch in Melbourne?"

"Cafés or restaurants. Only rough girls go into pubs."

He wondered how long he could survive in this city where the only hint of modernity was the miniskirt which, he was relieved to see, was worn by most young women. Phillipa, whose dress fell modestly below her knees, was a rare exception. As they had lunch in a café in The Royal Arcade, he resisted the temptation to tell her that he understood why Melbourne had a reputation for being fifty years behind the times. He felt empty. Unhappy about his relationship with Harriet, he needed to confide in someone, but knew it would be unfair to involve Phillipa.

After lunch she took him to Myers, a large department store in the main shopping area of the city. The shop assistants were the most helpful he had ever come across. Phillipa, obviously enjoying herself, bustled him from one department to another. She insisted that he try on the jackets and trousers before buying them. The fabrics were much lighter and more comfortable than his present summer clothes. In the changing room he grinned when he saw himself in Bermuda shorts and socks. Instead of laughing, Phillipa advised him to buy five pairs.

"But I look ridiculous – like a man pretending to be a schoolboy."

"Rubbish." She gestured at two men standing nearby. "Do they look ridiculous?"

"No," he admitted. "But they've got suntans."

Phillipa picked up the seven short sleeved shirts he had chosen. "You'll get one soon."

"Okay, but if I get laughed at … "

"You won't." She looked at his legs. "Well, not once you've got a tan."

Back in St Kilda, they walked through the grounds of the church in Acland Street, where Hugh's funeral had been held. Nicholas heard the organ playing Saint-Saëns. "Can we go in?" he asked. "The organ symphony's one of my favourites."

It was a cloudy day, and darker inside than it had been on the morning of the funeral. He inhaled the scent from the flowers decorating the church.

Phillipa stroked one of the white ribbons tied to the end of the pews. "There's going to be a wedding."

The organ thundered before launching into what Nicholas thought was one of the most celestial pieces ever written. Uplifted by the music he leant against a pew and gazed at details of the window opposite.

"Do you go to church a lot?" asked Phillipa.

"Not much now – I like to sleep-in on Sundays. What about you?"

"I attend weddings and funerals only," she replied shortly.

"What about Christmas?"

She looked scornful. "Christmas celebrates the birth of a man who tried to make the world a better place. He failed miserably, ended up dying a hideous death, and people have been fighting about the way he should be worshipped ever since."

Her expression, he realized with a jolt, was the same as Harriet's. It was the expression that, two days ago, he had been unable to define. It was held in check, but it was there. "Phillipa, who do you hate?"

"God."

"Why?"

The hatred in her expression changed to despair and she turned away. Trying to think of the best way to help her, he watched her walk towards the back of the church. He thought she was going to leave, but she stopped and stared up at a window. While he contemplated the reason for her hatred, the sun came out and shone through the stained glass, throwing shafts of colour over her.

'A boyfriend or brother killed in Vietnam?' he wondered.

The sunlight faded and the church became darker.

He walked over to her. "Phillipa?"

Still staring at the window, she took a deep breath. "When I was a child, all I ever wanted for Christmas was a baby sister or brother. I gave up when I was ten and asked for a puppy instead. My mother asked me why I didn't want a baby sister or brother any more. I said I'd given up. That night when my father came home from work they told me that my mother was having a baby near Christmas. I was so excited. Mum let me choose the cot and pram and I helped decorate the baby's room. My sister was born on Christmas Eve. Ten days later my father and I went to collect them from the hospital. We were hit by a drunk driver on the way home. They were all killed."

He didn't know what to say. 'Sorry' was an inadequate word. Her stoical determination not to cry made him feel futile. If she had wept it would have been natural for him to put his arms round her, but she looked defiantly at him. He put his hand out to touch her shoulder.

She stepped backwards. "Don't give me sympathy, or I'll start crying."

He spoke at last. "Would that be so wrong? You were crying the first time I saw you."

"That was different – Hugh had only just died."

He had a vision of Phillipa the little girl, thrilled by her baby sister. He imagined her skipping out to her parents' car looking forward to getting home and inviting her friends to see the baby. He turned away. If she wasn't going to cry neither could he.

"Nick, do you believe in God?"

Her question was unexpected. Composing himself he turned back to her. Wanting to ease her bitterness, he thought for a few moments before replying. "I think about God as the leader of the force for good and the devil leading the forces of evil – like in *The Magic Flute*. Sometimes God wins, sometimes the devil does." Mindful of her desire not to weep he was careful to keep his voice neutral. Although he wanted to touch her, he kept his hands by his sides. "Your family was killed by a man who'd had too much to drink and then drove his car. He was tempted by, and succumbed to, the forces of evil."

"Why didn't God stop him?"

"Perhaps because he couldn't. Evil is powerful and inviting." He saw her considering his views.

She stared at the pew as if memorizing the carving embellishing the post. A few moments later she looked at him. "Thanks," she whispered as the organist played the final notes.

He looked towards the chancel. A girl sat in the choir stalls, with one leg resting inelegantly on the book rest. The organist's bored daughter, he supposed. He heard the murmur of voices, then the organist began playing 'Hear my Prayer'. Thinking that Phillipa needed to be alone, he went up the stairs into the gallery at the back of the church. The music paused before 'Oh for the Wings of a Dove', and the girl stood up and began to sing. Her voice had the purity of a choirboy's, but sparkled with colour.

Nicholas was enthralled. 'A crystal shot with prisms,' he thought.

When the anthem finished, Phillipa ran up the stairs. "What a voice," she whispered excitedly. "We'll bring Harriet to hear her sing one Sunday. She's obviously in the choir – she was probably practising her solo."

As they walked back to the theatre, he tried to think of a way to heal the rift with his aunt. Since their argument yesterday there was a coldness between them that he hated. In retrospect, he realized he had been judgmental. Harriet had a successful opera company and school, and many pupils to whom she taught singing. Phillipa was devoted to her. The wardrobe mistress had been with her for twenty years, despite repeated offers from The Australian Opera. More money and prestige withstanding, she stayed with Harriet. Nicholas had known his aunt for less than a week, but had judged her harshly and provoked a quarrel.

As soon as he got back to the theatre, Nicholas went into Harriet's office. "I'm sorry about yesterday, Aunt Harriet. What you said about her voice was true, but I can't endure any more sessions like that. Her face haunted me."

She looked mollified. "I've been thinking too. I made myself remember my first audition and how I would have felt if the things I say had been said to me. How can I soften the blow?"

"Cut out the insults. Explain that their voices are not good enough for opera. Talk about other aspects of the theatre – drama or stage management. Be sympathetic."

"I've got a better idea. You talk to them." She smiled wickedly. "I'm sure you'll do very well."

"Thanks, Aunt Harriet," he said ruefully.

Then Nicholas told her about the girl he and Phillipa had heard in the church. "We thought you could go along one Sunday and hear her sing. She was phenomenal."

"A lot of people have great voices, but not all of them want to be opera singers. If she's interested, she'll come to me."

"Are you sure? She might go to one of those screeching teachers you told me about."

"Yes," she said thoughtfully. "How old was she?"

He shrugged. "It was dim in the church. Why?"

25

"I don't take students till they're seventeen. You must have some idea. Was she ten – older, younger?"

"Older. Sixteen – maybe seventeen. You won't be sorry."

"I hope not, Nicholas. I hate wasting time."

Chapter 3

'Cast your idle hopes away.'
Così Fan Tutte – Mozart

Natasha tried to concentrate on the geography lesson, but the hot classroom faded as her imagination transported her to London. After throwing herself off the Castel Sant'Angelo, she jumped off the mattress and heard the applause of the audience. The curtains of Covent Garden opera house parted and she stepped forward.

"Natasha!"

Startled out of her daydream, she tried to look attentive. "Yes, Miss Bremner?"

"Repeat what I just said."

Natasha looked at the blackboard. "Low pressure areas." She knew by the giggling that her guess had been wrong. She felt her face turning scarlet.

"Come here."

Aware that everyone was staring at her, she stumbled between the rows of desks. When she reached the front of the class she looked at the sea of faces and found the one she sought. Immediately she was comforted by her sister Jacqueline's look of sympathy.

Miss Bremner folded her arms. "Why weren't you listening?"

Natasha looked out of the window at the leaves of the peppercorn trees and concentrated on the words of Tosca's aria.

"I suppose you were dreaming about George Harrison."

"Who?" asked Natasha.

The class laughed hysterically, and she remembered that he was a member of The Beatles.

"Don't be insolent," said Miss Bremner when the laughter stopped. "Your parents pay a great deal of money to send you here. The way you're going you'll have to repeat this year a third time."

Natasha felt the anticipation in the room. Enraged by the reference to her poor scholastic abilities she decided to give her audience the fight it wanted. "I'm going to be an opera singer – that's what I was dreaming about."

"You're seventeen, Natasha, it's time you grew up and stopped having fantasies."

"It's not a fantasy. My choirmaster said I had a better voice than Melba."

Miss Bremner sneered. "Girls, we have a star in our midst. Perhaps we should ask for her autograph."

"You should," said Jacqueline.

"Stand up, Jacqueline Howard. How dare you interrupt?"

"You asked a question and I'm answering. Get Natasha's autograph now, she'll be too busy to give it to you in ten years' time."

"You two are going to be busy after school – doing detention."

Natasha was aghast. "I can't. Not today – I've got an audition with Harriet Shaw."

"You haven't the fortitude to be an opera singer. You're a drifter. You'll probably become one of those dreadful hippies as soon as you leave school. It won't take much – your hair's such a mess you almost look like one now. Go back to your seat."

Natasha returned to her desk, shaking with rage. When the bell rang to signal the end of the lesson, instead of going to their history class, she and Jacqueline went into the cloakroom.

"What am I going to do, Jacqui? Miss Shaw will think I haven't bothered to turn up. She'll think I'm unreliable."

"Just go – I'll tell the old bag you were ill."

Jacqueline stood in the empty classroom, watching from the window. With relief she saw Natasha run out of the gate. She heard footsteps in the corridor and sat down.

"Where's Natasha?" Miss Bremner asked as soon as she entered.

"She was ill – she's gone home."

"You're lying."

Jacqueline smiled. "She is – she was vomiting."

"Get that insolent grin off your face. Tell your parents I want a note confirming her illness tomorrow." She picked up a piece of chalk and wrote, *I must not be rude and interrupt in class*, on the blackboard.

"Write that one hundred times. Neatly – or you'll do it all again."

Jacqueline filled her fountain pen. *Natasha Howard is going to be a famous opera singer*, she wrote.

In the scorching heat, Natasha waited anxiously for a tram. Normally she would have walked the mile to the theatre, but the temperature was a hundred and two degrees. Her uniform, damp with perspiration, clung to her body.

"There won't be any trams for ages, dear," said a woman, struggling with two bags of shopping. "There's been an accident and a truck's stuck across the line."

Natasha shrieked and tore down Wellington Street. At St Kilda Junction she dodged the heavy traffic and ran in front of a tram, ignoring the driver as he rang the bell furiously at her. She ran without stopping until she reached the theatre. Breathing heavily, she flung herself at one of the doors. It swung open. She fell inside and lay sprawled on the floor. Books fell out of her schoolbag and her collection of coloured pencils rolled over the tiled floor. As she crawled round, gathering up her scattered belongings, she heard someone walking towards her. Looking up, she saw a woman with white hair.

"Can I help you?"

Natasha shoved an exercise book into her bag. "Oh, yes please," she gasped. "I've got an audition with Miss Shaw and I'm late."

The woman smiled. "Natasha Howard?"

She scrambled to her feet. "Yes."

"I'm Miss Shaw, and you're five minutes early."

Jacqueline put down her pen and looked at her watch. It was four o'clock. 'Natasha will be at the theatre now,' she thought. 'One day we'll be invited to open the school fete or sing at a fund raising concert. Miss Bremner will ask us for our autographs and we'll refuse. We'll tell the papers how horrible she was.' She pictured the headlines: *Young singers were tormented by a cruel teacher at school.*

"Have you finished?"

"No, Miss Bremner."

"Don't think about the time then, because you won't leave here till you have. How much have you done?"

"Not much."

"Then hurry up."

Jacqueline assumed a guileless expression. "But it's got to be neat – it won't be if I hurry."

"Keep writing, Jacqueline."

"Yes, Miss Bremner." As she wrote, her thoughts turned to her own audition the following week. 'I'll never do it,' she thought. 'I'll make a fool of myself. How can I get out of it?' She remembered the nightmare she'd had last night in which Miss Shaw had told her she sounded like a frog.

Miss Bremner's voice cut into her thoughts. "I know you're not very bright, but you shouldn't take this long. How much have you done?"

Jacqueline counted her lines. "Eighty – I think – it could be more. I lost count – it could be less. I'm not very good at counting."

"Bring them here."

"But I haven't finished."

"Bring them here!"

With deliberate slowness, Jacqueline gathered up the sheets of paper.

"Hurry up."

She walked to the front desk and handed over the pages, watching Miss Bremner's expression turn to fury.

"You insolent, disobedient girl!"

"What?" Jacqueline tried not to laugh. "It's my best writing."

Miss Bremner pointed to the blackboard. "I told you to write that."

"I did." She widened her eyes. "At least I think I did – did I leave a word out? Did I make a spelling mistake?"

Miss Bremner thrust the pages at her.

Jacqueline looked at them as if confused. "Natasha Howard is going to be a famous opera singer. Oops, I've given you the wrong pages – here, these are the right ones."

Miss Bremner snatched them.

"My parents taught me it was rude to snatch."

"Go home, you – you horrible girl."

Jacqueline walked to the back of the classroom. In the doorway she paused. "Miss Bremner, Natasha's going to be a famous opera singer."

She ran outside wishing she had the confidence to add, 'and so am I.'

Nicholas felt a stab of pity as he handed Natasha a glass a water. Her dark red hair was greasy and dishevelled and had come loose from her plaits. Her face, which was smothered in acne, was crimson and clashed with her hair. Below the hem of her fawn uniform her knees were covered in scabs. She looked more like a starving waif than a budding opera singer. 'She doesn't look as if she can sing one note, let alone a whole aria,' he thought.

She took the glass, thanked him and gulped down the water.

"Do you enjoy school?" asked Harriet.

"I hate it. I'm only there because my parents won't let me leave. They say I need a proper job in case I don't make it as an opera singer, but I'm hopeless at lessons. The only thing I can do is sing."

As they walked down the corridor to the theatrette, he dreaded Natasha's disillusionment. 'She might be a good character actress,' he thought. 'She's got a lively personality and an arrestingly ugly face. I wonder if she'd be interested?'

"What are you going to sing?" Harriet asked when they arrived at the theatrette.

"'Vissi d'arte'."

'She'll never get through it,' he thought.

Harriet smiled. "The last girl who sang that for her audition wanted Nicholas to chase her round the theatrette to put her in the mood. But I think you've run far enough today."

Natasha giggled and handed Nicholas her score. Prepared for a weak voice quivering with the effort, he waited while Harriet walked to the back row and sat down. When Natasha sang her first notes his spirit leapt in recognition. It was the girl he and Phillipa had heard a week ago in the church. As her exquisite voice floated on the top notes, tears distorted his vision. He blinked them away. To play a wrong note in the middle of her aria would be sacrilege. When she finished, Nicholas imagined the effect her voice would have on an audience.

He saw that her body was rigid with tension.

Harriet walked towards them, and as she stopped in front of Natasha, Nicholas saw her stunned expression.

"In all my life I've never heard a voice like yours." Her voice was

31

husky. "You made me cry."

He heard Natasha give an anguished squeak. "My choirmaster told me I was – I wanted to be an opera singer," she howled.

Harriet, looking startled, put her hand on Natasha's skinny arm. "You will be. You can sing."

Natasha looked at her in confusion. "But – you said I made you cry."

"Yes. Because your voice is so – pure and … "

"Oh, Miss Shaw. You'll teach me? Really?"

"Yes, really."

Natasha wiped her eyes with the back of her hands. "And I can go to opera school in three years time and everything?"

"Yes. Provided you show commitment."

"I will, Miss Shaw, I promise. I won't be like I am at school – I'll practise really hard."

"No. Don't practise at all until I tell you," said Harriet. "Being a good singer is not about how hard you practise. Singing is about thinking. You'll see what I mean when you have your first lesson."

Natasha laughed. It was a joyful gurgle that made Nicholas want to laugh as well. "My parents won't believe me – they have to nag me to make me do my homework."

Harriet took her diary from the top of the piano. "When would you like to come? Four-thirty or six o'clock on Thursdays and six o'clock on Tuesdays are free, or what about Saturday morning?"

"I've got piano lessons Tuesdays, I'll come on Thursdays."

Harriet pencilled in her name. "Before your first lesson buy *The Melba Method* and read the introduction."

"Yes, Miss Shaw." Natasha picked up her bag. "My twin sister's got an audition next week."

"I hope her voice is like yours," said Harriet.

"No, it's not," said Natasha as she ran out of the theatrette.

Harriet closed her diary. "That's a shame."

Richard Greythorn arrived at the theatre half an hour early. On the way to the washroom to change his sweat soaked shirt, he tried to forget his colleague's taunts and the laughter that had followed. "Hey, everyone, Spotty's got an audition – must be for Frankenstein."

He pushed open the door. 'When I'm an opera singer ...' He saw his reflection in the mirror and his confidence drained away. Because he had gone to the beach at the weekend and fallen asleep in the sun, he looked even worse than usual. 'What am I doing? Humiliating myself. Miss Shaw will look at me and – and what?' Balancing his briefcase on the basin, he opened it and took out his razor. 'She'll be polite and ask me to sing and then tell me I'm not good enough.' Switching on the razor, he navigated it over the mounds of acne on his sunburnt face.

Taking off his shirt, he splashed his face and arms with cold water. The boil on the back of his neck throbbed. After spraying himself with deodorant, he took the white shirt out of its packaging and put it on. The stiff new collar touched the boil which hurt when he moved his head. As soon as he had put on his tie, the boil burst. Cursing, he grabbed a handkerchief and held it to his neck. "Why didn't the bloody thing explode before I'd put my shirt on?" he muttered. He gently squeezed the area and felt the pus pouring out.

When he was sure the suppuration had stopped, he turned round and saw to his relief that his hair covered the patch of blood on the collar. He combed his thick blonde hair which, although washed that morning, was already greasy. 'At least I'm not going bald. My acne will clear up one day.' He looked at his watch. Soon his future would be decided.

The thought of being an opera singer had not occurred to him until he was asked to sing at a friend's wedding three months ago when he was twenty-two. He sang 'Panis Angelicus' in the church and at the reception he was besieged with requests to sing.

Later in the evening the bride's uncle approached him. "Have you ever thought of being an opera singer, Richard?"

"No."

"You should. Go to Harriet Shaw and in ten years you'll be singing leading baritone roles with The Australia Opera."

Clutching his score of *Rigoletto*, he went down the corridor. 'Her uncle was probably drunk,' he thought.

The door of the theatrette opened and a girl with red hair, whose face was almost as marred by acne as his own, ran out. He jumped out of the way to avoid a collision.

She laughed. "Sorry."

"That's okay."

She did a jig of glee. "Miss Shaw's going to teach me." She grabbed his arm and he tried not to wince at the assault to his sunburn. "Have you got an audition now?"

"Yes. Will you wait for me? We can go and have coffee in Acland Street." He was amazed that he had asked. Girls laughed at him, so he avoided them, but her friendliness had made him act impulsively. Expecting a refusal, he was surprised when she tossed her bag on the couch.

"Okay."

"No. I couldn't bear it if you heard me fail. Wait for me in *The Scheherazade*. If I haven't turned up by half past five you'll know I haven't made it."

She slung her bag over her shoulder. "See you there. Good luck."

He stared after her.

The door of the theatrette opened. A man looked at him and smiled. "Richard Greythorn?"

He picked up his briefcase. 'Please let me do well,' he prayed.

Richard left the theatre with Miss Shaw's praise turning over in his brain. Hoping the girl had waited, he ran up Acland Street to *The Scheherazade*, which had delicious looking continental cakes displayed in the window. He saw her as soon as he opened the door, and went over to the table, beaming at her. She beamed back. In front of her was a slab of chocolate cake sandwiched with cream.

He sat opposite her. "Is that good?"

"Yummy."

He looked at the menu. The smell of coffee and chocolate and pastries overcame his resolution to resist rich food and he ordered cappuccino and a slice of coffee gâteau. After comparing their audition experiences, she asked him where he worked.

"Treasury Place – I'm a public servant."

She poured her vanilla malted milk into a glass. "Do you like it?"

He grimaced. "The people at work tease me because I've got pimples."

"Stupid half-wits." She slid her fork into the cake. "Why don't you leave?"

"I was thinking about starting my own business, but now Miss Shaw's accepted me, I'll stick it out. I know it's not forever now. The money's good, the work's easy and I've got a terrific view of the gardens from my desk and ... " The waitress brought his order. He waited for her to leave before continuing. "Anyway I'd still have pimples and people somewhere else would tease me."

"Don't worry about it – I don't." She grinned. "You should hear the things I get called at school – fungus face – skeleton."

He was so used to the girls at work who were obsessed with their appearance, that her attitude astonished him.

She scooped up a blob of cream with her finger and licked it. "Mum says the acne will clear up and Dad says it's what you are inside that counts. Beauty fades, but character endures – well that's what he reckons."

He noticed her eyes were the colour of spring leaves and very large like a cat's. Unusually for a redhead, her lashes and eyebrows were black. Her eyelashes were the longest he had ever seen. He realized that without the acne she would be attractive. The knowledge made him shy again. He wanted to say something profound, but his mind went blank. 'Don't be a fool,' he thought. "Do you have any brothers or sisters?" he asked.

"A twin sister."

He sipped his coffee. "Are you identical?"

"No. Jacqui's got black hair and blue eyes. She's much better looking and she's voluptuous." She pulled a piece of icing off her cake and put it in her mouth. "Her skin's beautiful, but she deserves it. She doesn't eat too much chocolate."

He looked at her generous expression. 'So different from the calculating girls at work,' he thought.

"Do you have any brothers or sisters?" she asked.

"Four brothers and three sisters. My parents wanted a girl – I was the fifth boy and they were disappointed. It was different for the first four – they were born close together, but there was a six year gap between me and the fourth one. I'm the only one interested in opera and classical music – I never felt I belonged. As soon as I started working I moved into a flat in Prahran so I could play opera without anyone moaning."

"How did you become interested in opera?"

"A friend at school came from a musical family and he introduced me to it. I remember going to his place for the first time. His mother played the piano and his father sang 'Celeste Aida'. Suddenly I had a sensation of belonging somewhere." He finished his gâteau. "When are your singing lessons?"

"Thursdays."

He was disappointed. "I won't see you for ages, mine are on Tuesdays."

"Are you going to the opera season in May?"

"Yes."

"So are Jacqui and I – we might see you then. If not, we'll see each other when we start opera school."

The thought that he would not see her for three years dismayed him. "Miss Shaw has Christmas parties so we'll see each other then," he said.

She looked at her watch. "Eek! My parents will think I've failed my audition and thrown myself under a tram." Opening her bag she took out her purse.

"I'll pay," he said.

"No, no." She threw some money on the table. "That should be enough." She jumped up and grabbed her bag. "Bye."

Richard wanted to catch her up and ask her out, but the cashier was infuriatingly slow. By the time he went outside she had disappeared. "I don't know her name. Why didn't I introduce myself? I'm such an imbecile."

Chapter 4

'I lament and I sigh and I tremble with terror'
Orpheus and Eurydice – Gluck

'I wish this tram would crash,' Jacqueline thought. 'I could fall over and pretend I've hurt myself.'

Natasha grabbed her arm. "Come on, we're here."

Jacqueline was terrified. Her uniform was crumpled and she had run her sweaty hands through her black hair so many times it stood on end like a hedgehog's bristles.

"Jacqui, it will be over soon," Natasha coaxed as they walked to the side door. "Miss Shaw will recognize your voice is truly great."

"How? I'll croak like a frog. What if I'm sick all over her?"

Natasha grinned. "Don't stand too close to her. Jacqui, please try. Remember? We're going to sing at Covent Garden together."

Jacqueline sighed. "I'll be your dresser or manager, or sweep the stage or something."

Natasha dragged her towards the back door. "I'm not going to Covent Garden without you. Think about Miss Bremner – think about her asking for our autographs and imagine the satisfaction when we refuse. Go on. I'll wait out here."

She moaned. "I can't, I can't – I feel sick."

Natasha opened the door. "You can. Even if it's just to spite Miss Bremner." She pushed her inside.

As the door closed behind her, Jacqueline wished she could escape. She heard someone walking quickly down the corridor and froze. Seconds later a girl looking fresh and cool in a green and white striped dress appeared.

"Hello, can I help you?"

Jacqueline swallowed, trying to lessen the strangling tightness in her throat. "I've got an audition with Miss Shaw at four-thirty," she stammered. "I'm Jacqueline Howard."

The girl's friendly expression turned to concern. "Are you all right?"

She shook her head. 'The audition hasn't begun and I've made a fool of myself already,' she thought.

"It's this dreadful heat. Come to my office. I'll get you some water." She opened the door and pulled out a chair. "Sit down. I'm Phillipa, Miss Shaw's secretary. You can't sing if you're not well." She pulled the diary across the desk. "I'll arrange another time for you."

Jacqueline shivered. "I feel sick because of the audition. I'm petrified."

"Miss Shaw understands people get nervous – "

"It's not her," Jacqueline interrupted. "It's auditions. I can sing really well if I can pretend I'm someone else, dressed up in costume and everything, but I'm awful at auditions. I went for the part of Ruth in *The Pirates of Penzance* once, but my legs shook so much I nearly fell over. I couldn't sing, I just croaked. The way they looked at me – I was humiliated."

Phillipa looked at her thoughtfully. "Hang on." She disappeared and came back with a glass. "Quick, drink this, all in one gulp, it'll make you feel better."

Jacqueline took the glass and swallowed the contents so fast she almost choked. She shuddered violently and her eyes watered. "What was that?" she spluttered.

"Brandy. Take three deep breaths. Fortunately, you're early. Miss Shaw's not here at the moment."

Five minutes later Jacqueline felt calm and colour had returned to her cheeks. Phillipa led her into the washroom and watched while she combed her hair and washed her face. Then she ushered her to the couch outside the theatrette and Jacqueline sat serenely until summoned for her audition. She did not remember much about her rendition of 'Che Faro', from *Orpheus and Eurydice*, but she would never forget Harriet Shaw's words of praise.

"You have a beautiful and unusual voice. Good contraltos are rare. You have the added advantage of a long range."

In a daze she wandered down the corridor, opened the back door and stepped outside. She saw Natasha running towards her. Needing to steady herself, she leant against the wall and shut her eyes.

"Jacqui," she heard Natasha say anxiously.

She opened her eyes.

"Jacqui, what happened?"

"I did it," she whispered. "I did it."

The next day they went to a florist and spent all their pocket money on a bouquet of flowers for Phillipa. With it they sent a note inviting her to dinner.

With a pleasurable sense of anticipation, Harriet arranged the props she would use for Natasha's first singing lesson. For her to be so impressed by a student at an audition was unusual. It had not only been Natasha's voice, but her personality, which erupted out of an ugly little face.

When Harriet opened the door, Natasha jumped off the chair, knocking her school bag onto the floor. "Hello, Miss Shaw," she said eagerly.

"Come in, Natasha. Did you have a good day at school?"

She picked up her bag. "I got into trouble for daydreaming again. I used to get upset, but I don't care any more – not since you said those fantastic things about my voice. I was imagining I was at Covent Garden and having masses of curtain calls like Joan Sutherland."

Harriet remembered the words of a director at Covent Garden: "If you go wrong – go gloriously wrong." That was Natasha. She was gloriously and unashamedly wrong. The acne, the greasy, untidy hair and the crumpled beige uniform. It was all wrong. But her honesty and enthusiasm rose above everything and made what was wrong endearing rather than irritating. She closed the door. "That's not dreaming, that's looking into the future, and if you do as I say you might have more encores than Joan Sutherland."

Natasha pulled the *Melba Method* out of her bag. "I read the introduction – it was terrific!"

"What impressed you most?" Harriet asked, hoping Natasha's zeal would never wane.

"The first line. It's easy to sing well and difficult to sing badly."

"This is your first singing lesson, but you won't sing one note. Does that surprise you?"

"Not now I've read what Melba says about practising. I thought I'd have to practise for hours every day – so I was flabbergasted when she said that beginners should only do five minutes."

Harriet sat down and gestured at the other chair. "Today and for the next eight weeks, we're going to talk about the mechanics of singing. These will be the most important lessons you'll ever have, because your understanding and adherence to the rules will secure your future as an opera singer. But I'm not going to sit here lecturing you. Tell me what happens when a house is built."

Natasha looked surprised. "Bricks are put on top of one another."

"What happens first? Before the bricks are laid?"

"The foundations are dug," said Natasha.

"Yes. Before the bricks are laid the most important thing is prepared. Without foundations, the house, however well built, will collapse. What do you know about foundations?"

Natasha appeared flummoxed. "Nothing much."

"When you auditioned I told you that singing is about thinking, and that's what I'm making you do. Now, tell me what you know about foundations. Anything at all."

Natasha gazed thoughtfully at the brandy balloon on the piano. "You can't see them."

"Well done, Natasha. That's the answer I wanted." Harriet knew by her expression that Natasha was not used to praise. "Why do you think I'm talking about foundations?"

Natasha seemed hesitant.

Harriet smiled. "Come on – use that imagination of yours."

"The one that's always getting me into trouble?" she asked wryly.

Harriet nodded. "I promise you it won't here. I'll actively encourage it."

"I think you're likening foundations to breathing," she said slowly. "because you can't sing or do anything without breath. You can't see breath and you can't see the foundations of a house."

Harriet was delighted. "Clever girl. Yes." She stood up. "Without breath control your voice will be erratic and wobbly, but with it your singing will be effortless. Breath is the foundation of the voice. You already have a beautiful voice and we're going to work together to make it stronger, more agile and completely under your control. Not the control of your nerves, health or emotions, but the control of your brain."

She picked up a tumbler of water from the piano. "The voice must be like this." She gave Natasha the brandy balloon and poured the water from the tumbler into it. "Able to go anywhere, fill any shape and soar to the heights like a fountain. Imagine your voice is liquid. It can trickle, gush, drip or pour out gently. Sometimes it will be like water, sometimes like honey. But it will be nothing unless we work on your breathing and make the muscles that control your diaphragm strong."

Natasha looked fascinated and Harriet was pleased. Some pupils wanted to start singing immediately and were disenchanted by their first lessons. "I'm going to ask you not to sing for eight weeks. This is important. Do you understand why?"

"So that by the time my breath control is right, I'll have forgotten any bad habits I have that might strain my voice?"

"Correct. There's an understandable impulse among the young and eager to practise hard. Once the vocal cords have been damaged, they can never be repaired. Never." She sat down and smiled. "Now, we're going to talk about your acne."

Natasha blushed. "I eat too many chocolates."

"I have a cure which will get rid of them in eight weeks and you can eat as much chocolate as you like."

"Golly, that sounds too good to be true."

"It's not easy. It entails drinking a gallon of water a day."

Natasha's eyes widened in horror.

"A gallon's only eight pints so that's sixteen half pint glasses a day. Get a mug or a glass, work out a timetable and stick to it. By as early as next week we'll see an improvement. Now stand in front of the mirror."

Natasha looked wary and Harriet saw she was prepared for ridicule. "Your posture is excellent," she said reassuringly. "You have a lovely straight back. I predict that in a few years' time, you'll look elegant. You may never be beautiful, but you'll be striking. Beauty is unimportant, it's charisma and presence that count. Take Maria Callas for instance. Many of the women and men who have changed the world have been plain. Napoleon was short and fat and Anne Boleyn was apparently plain." She frowned. "And personally, I think Wallis Simpson is grotesque. Now I'll give you some breathing exercises for

41

your homework."

She took a tape measure and wound it round Natasha's hips. "Look in the mirror and take the biggest breath you can."

Natasha took a huge breath.

"Relax. Now, tell me what you think was wrong."

"My shoulders rose and I made a lot of noise."

"Right." Harriet adjusted the tape measure. "Now think of a deep contented sigh, and imagine you're breathing through your back instead of your nose."

After a few seconds Natasha looked at Harriet in awe. "It works."

"Yes." She looked at the tape. "And you took in more breath. I know you have a good imagination, because most of my pupils struggle hard with that exercise, but you did it effortlessly the first time." She took a candle from the top of the piano, lit it, and held it in front Natasha's mouth. "Take a deep breath. Then let it out slowly."

Natasha took a deep breath and expelled it. The candle went out immediately.

Harriet lit it again. "The object of this exercise is to keep the candle alight all through the expulsion of your breath. This time, imagine you're in a situation where you can scarcely dare to breathe."

Natasha tried again, and the flame remained lit until halfway through.

"Much better. Aim for the candle to be alight when the last bit of air has left your lungs." That's all for today." She handed Natasha a sheet of paper. "Here's a summary of this lesson for you to study. I'll see you next week."

Natasha's eyes shone with fervour. "That's the best lesson I've ever had. You didn't shout or get cross. I can't wait for next week."

"I enjoyed teaching you. Remember the water."

"I will, Miss Shaw. I will."

"Wake up, wake up," sang Jacqueline.

Natasha opened her eyes. "Sh – you're not allowed to sing yet."

"I forgot." She handed Natasha a mug of water. "Your first half pint."

Natasha drank its contents without stopping. "Ugh, that was awful. Is it working yet?"

"Give it a chance. You've only been doing it for three days."

When Natasha went into the kitchen for breakfast, her mug of water was on the table. "I'm beginning to hate the sight of water."

"Think what you'll look like in eight weeks," said her father.

Natasha picked up the mug. "Seven weeks and four days, actually."

"Slurp, slurp," said Jacqueline. "You sound like an animal at a trough." She crossed off the half-pint. "Only seven more to go. This is really interesting," she said, putting the book in her school bag.

Natasha sighed dramatically. "I'll find it interesting when my spots go."

At school she religiously drank her mugs of water, but forgot to go to the toilet before she left.

"Jacqui, I've got to go back," she said when they reached the tram stop.

"No – I've got a singing lesson."

"You'll have to go on your own."

"No! It's my first one. You promised you'd come with me."

"Stop being a baby. I'll wait for you in *The Scheherazade*."

Jacqueline grabbed her arm. "No! The tram's coming."

"I'm going to wet myself," whispered Natasha as they sat down. "I'm in agony. It's all right for you, you don't have spots."

As soon as the tram reached the theatre Natasha jumped off and ran inside. She tore into the toilet with a howl of relief.

"Are you all right?" The voice came from the next cubicle.

Natasha giggled. "I am now. Is that you, Phillipa?"

"Yes. Natasha?"

"I'm waiting for Jacqui to have her singing lesson. Do you want to come to *The Scheherazade*?"

"Thanks. I'd love to."

Nicholas was reading Hugh's meticulous notes, which went back forty years. He was analyzing the number of times each opera had been performed in the last ten years when Phillipa walked into his office with a plate.

"I bought these for you and Harriet."

He looked at the two Danish pastries. "Thanks, Phillipa. Where's yours?"

She patted her stomach. "In here. I went to *The Scheherazade* with Natasha and Jacqui." Looking at his untidy desk she put the plate on top of the filing cabinet. "How can you work in this mess?"

"I don't notice it."

She untangled his telephone cord. "I can't stand chaos around me – I've got so much inside me."

He wanted to ask her if she had been put in an orphanage, but she looked embarrassed. Interested, he watched her gather up the files and put them into a tidy pile. There was an old fashioned quality about the way Phillipa dressed that puzzled him. The styles were up to date in everything except their length. Although she didn't limp, he wondered if her legs were scarred from the accident. Like other fashion conscious girls her age she wore nail polish on perfectly manicured nails and her hair was chic but natural. Her make-up and perfume were subtle. As if unaware of his scrutiny she picked up his pens, pencils and rubber and put them in their holders. Minutes later all his papers and letters were in their in, out and pending trays.

He looked at her in admiration. "I don't know how you do it."

"I don't put things down – I put them away." She handed him the plate. "Instead of leaving a letter any old how on your desk – put it away. I never have to tidy my office – it's always tidy. I never have to look for anything because I know where it is." She smiled. "Unless you've pinched it."

"If you weren't so sweet, you'd be unbearably bossy." He bit into the pastry. "Delicious."

"Good. Can I borrow your Durex?"

He gaped at her. "My what?"

"Durex. Mine's useless, it keeps tearing."

He swallowed the pastry, thankful that he hadn't choked on it.

"Nicholas, what's the matter with you? Close your mouth or a fly will decide to explore your teeth."

"I – haven't got any," he said haltingly.

She peered at him. "What are those white things in your mouth?"

"I meant – Durex. I haven't got any Durex."

44

"You had some yesterday."

"No I didn't."

"I saw it."

He shook his head. "If it's not a mad question, what do you want to do with it?"

"What do you think I want to do with it – eat it?"

He laughed. "Oh, Phillipa. This thing you want – does it have another name?"

"Sticky tape."

"Ah." He was overcome with laughter.

She looked at him in bewilderment.

"Durex is something different in England."

She looked intrigued. "You've gone red."

"Not as red as you'll be." He leant over her desk. "It's a contraceptive men use," he said softly.

Clapping her hand over her mouth to stifle her laughter, she turned scarlet. "English people are demented!"

"What on earth is going on in here?" asked Harriet. "I can hear you down the corridor. What are you doing to Phillipa?"

He put his hands up. "Nothing, Aunt Harriet. Just a slight language problem. Phillipa will explain."

"No I won't!" she said indignantly. She picked up the plate and thrust it in front of Harriet. "Have a pastry."

Chapter 5

'To the bold only
is permitted such imagination.'
La Bohème – Puccini

Harriet read the letter in dismay, wondering what the newspapers would make of it. Six months ago, when she had sacked the new director of the drama company for calling her a dried up old prude, she knew she had made enemies among the more radical actors. She had been conscious of resentment and suspected that there was a campaign to discredit her. This letter from one of the principal actors was the beginning. Underlining the salient parts of the letter, she thought how she would counter each statement.

*Harriet Shaw is so anxious not to offend the theatre's
patrons that she sacrifices creativity.*

'The singers, dancers and actors in this theatre are well paid because we have patrons. Would they rather live in poverty?'

*What do bank managers and factory owners know about
culture?*

'They wouldn't become a patron of a theatre if they were not interested in culture.'

*Why does she have to approve the scripts? Drama's
nothing to do with her.*

'I founded this theatre and am its overall head. Its reputation is my responsibility.'

*Why does she forbid strong language? If a play is about
rough blokes they don't mince about saying 'blast' and
'damn' when something makes them mad. Are playwrights
to ignore the workers and only write about the priggish
bourgeoisie?*

'Foul language will alienate the audience and the theatre will lose money. People don't come to the theatre to be regaled with bad language, they come to be entertained and enriched. The importance of healthy profits must not be underestimated. Do actors in this theatre want to earn money?'

Harriet Shaw is too old to run a theatre.

It was this line that hurt most. 'Am I?' she mused.

Nicholas was enjoying the frantic pace of the theatre. To his surprise he found opera easier to direct than straight drama. Much of the emotion in opera is relayed through the music, but actors must create emotion themselves. He was pleased how seriously the opera singers and students took their vocation. Because the school was part-time and the students worked during the day, they were down-to-earth and lacked the theatrical attitudes of the full-time drama students he had known in London. They were friendly and he had already been invited to several parties.

The standard of living in Melbourne astounded him. Phillipa rented a one-bedroom flat about a mile away from the theatre. It was on the first floor of a large Victorian house in Alma Road, which had been sensitively converted into flats. The staircase had carved oak balustrades and the front door was decorated with panels of etched glass. Phillipa's rooms were large, with good carpets and high ceilings. Her furniture was plentiful and looked expensive. Most students in the opera school, whose daytime occupations were mainly secretarial, clerical or shop assistants, shared attractive flats or houses with friends or, like Phillipa, lived alone in spacious flats. In London they would have been poorly paid. Back in England, he had known that Australia prided itself on being a classless society, but was surprised to discover how true it was.

While he considered that Harriet's refusal to stage little-known operas was commercially sound in a place as conservative as Melbourne, he wanted the productions to be new and exciting. He envisaged a contemporary version of *La Traviata* with Violetta dying from drug abuse, with the first act aria hailing the pleasures of wine changed to worshipping drugs. As he watched the music rehearsals, he considered the best way to approach Harriet with his ideas. When the rehearsal broke for lunch he went to her office.

"How long ago did you do *Traviata*?" he asked.

"Seven years," she replied promptly.

"Are we going to use the same sets and costumes?"

"Yes."

"I thought such a popular opera would have been performed more frequently."

She put the top on her fountain pen. "The Australian Opera did it three years ago."

"What were their sets and costumes like?" he asked.

"Similar to ours but more lavish. The Princess is a huge theatre. She looked at him shrewdly. "Where's this leading?"

Deciding to be candid he said, "I don't think you'll like my idea."

She closed her diary. "Tell me about it."

"You're right," she said after he had told her. "I hate it. Violetta as a drug addict would be disgusting and immoral."

"She's already a courtesan – that's hardly respectable."

Harriet frowned. "The inference is subtle. I suppose you'd want everyone strutting about in miniskirts and caftans."

"Yes."

"No, Nicholas. Opera audiences want glamour."

Accustomed to discussing the productions with his cast, Nicholas was annoyed by her refusal. "You can't just say no. We've got to talk about it."

"We don't have to talk about anything. My word is final."

"You can't run a theatre like this."

Her expression was icy. "I've been running this theatre successfully

48

for forty years. Don't you dare tell me how to run things. Until you came here you'd never directed an opera."

"Aunt Harriet, the theatre is changing and unless you change with it you'll be left behind. Theatres need new ideas to maintain standards. Violetta as a drug addict is new and exciting."

"It's sacrilege. I'd love to see your reaction if I suggested jazzing up Shakespeare."

"The best performance of *Julius Caesar* I've ever seen was updated to a modern-day – "

"How ridiculous. How can you update *Julius Caesar*?"

"It was set as a boardroom drama in America at the beginning of the depression. Julius was the chairman, and all the board voted against him, even his best friend Bruce. He was so devastated he had a fatal heart attack. The speeches of Bruce and Mark were directed at the shareholders. The language was modernized and it was one of the most riveting Shakespeare performances I've ever seen."

"It sounds ridiculous."

"Stay in the dark ages then!" he snapped.

"Traditional operas are powerful enough to stand alone without arty crackpots messing about with them."

"Some of the people in the drama company used to call me the vicar because I wouldn't try drugs." The chair scraped as he shoved it back. "Your opinion of me would amuse them."

Later that afternoon when Phillipa came into his office with letters for him to sign, she looked at him seriously. "I heard you and Harriet arguing at lunchtime. You're very alike."

Nicholas grunted. "Did Hugh and Harriet argue?"

"They believed in the same things. They were the same age," she said tactfully. "Harriet's had a bad morning." She told him about the letter Harriet had received. "She's upset because he's sent it to the papers too."

Remembering his own struggles in London with a faction in the drama company, who fought against his banning the smoking of marijuana in the theatre, he felt a rush of sympathy for Harriet. "Sometimes this sort of argument can have a good effect – it's free publicity after all. It'll probably spark off a fiery debate – I'm sure a lot of people agree with her."

Phillipa nodded. "Quite a few people in the drama company, especially the girls, are on her side. Harriet's got a good head for business, Nick. Every season the drama company do whatever plays the schools are studying so we have hundreds of guaranteed ticket sales. She's the reason the actors are decently paid. They can't have everything."

"Phillipa, I'm not asking you to take sides, but what did you think of my idea?"

"Awful."

"Okay. What about just updating it and have her dying of cancer?"

"Doing it in miniskirts is too revolutionary for Melbourne."

He sipped his tea to hide his irritation. "The streets are full of girls in miniskirts. I'm not suggesting doing it naked." He remembered what Tanya had told him. "You know *Hair* – the rock opera?"

She nodded.

"Is it banned in Melbourne?"

"Yes. If you want to see it you have to go to Sydney."

He laughed. "People travel five hundred miles just to go to the theatre?"

"Melbourne's different from London, Nick. Take things slowly, change little things, then think about being revolutionary. You've got plenty of time."

"Have I? I think Aunt Harriet would be happy if I left tomorrow."

"No. She likes you. And you like her. When you disagree, you both get upset and mooch about looking miserable."

"I expected we'd get on well. My grandmother and I had a wonderful relationship."

"Ah, but you didn't work with your grandmother, did you?"

"True. She talked about Harriet all the time and I built up an image of someone entirely different."

"What did you think she'd be like?"

"Gentle but firm. Kind, sympathetic but shrewd and clever."

"She's all those things," said Phillipa quietly. "But she has faults. You built up a picture of someone perfect."

"I didn't."

"What faults did you give your imaginary aunt?"

"None," he admitted. "You're very wise, Philly. May I call you Philly?"

She looked at her fingernails. "My parents used to call me Philly."

"Would it upset you if I did?"

"No." She looked wistful. "I'd like it."

"Were you injured in the accident?"

She ran her finger along the spiral of her shorthand pad. "Broken ribs, arm and concussion."

"Where did you live?"

"With my aunt."

He was pleased. He hated the thought of her in an orphanage. "Did she have any children?"

"She's not married. She's a doctor at the Alfred Hospital. She sent me to boarding school. It's only when I grew up that we became closer. She told me that after the accident she felt inadequate. When she came to get me from the hospital she was offhand, but it was because she was so distraught." Her voice became husky. "She told me she wanted to cuddle me, but was frightened I'd pull away. For years I thought she hadn't cared."

As she jumped up he saw her eyes glittering with tears.

Blinking them away she said with false brightness, "I've got a stack of letters to type." She looked at her watch. "I'm going away for the weekend with Jacqui and Natasha tonight – their parents have got a beach house near Sorrento."

Nicholas was pleased the friendship was developing. He had thought Phillipa was too serious. Now she laughed more often, and her conversation was spattered with, "Natasha said ... " or "Jacqui did ... "

He watched her leave his office. 'And I thought I'd suffered,' he thought. 'Compared to her I have no idea what the word even means.'

As Phillipa dressed to go to the beach and watch the sunrise, she felt happier than she had at any time since the accident. Natasha and Jacqueline's parents were welcoming without being patronizing, and she was beginning to feel she was part of the family – not a sister, but like a newly discovered cousin.

They crept out of the weatherboard house at Koonya Beach, which was set at the end of a narrow track. Jacqueline and Natasha ducked their heads and disappeared into the tea-tree bushes. Feeling like an explorer, Phillipa followed.

"We're here!" shouted Natasha.

Phillipa emerged from the scrub and suddenly the ocean was before her.

"Isn't it beautiful?" Jacqueline had to shout above the roar of the waves breaking on the rocks.

Phillipa watched Natasha lie on her stomach and slither feet first down the slope to the beach, grabbing the clumps of coarse yellow grass to slow her descent. Jacqueline went next and waited at the bottom to make sure Phillipa landed safely. They ran over to join Natasha who was dancing near the water's edge. Her hair, free from its plaits, blew away from her face like a banner, and her long, skinny legs kicked high in the air. A wave crashed on the sand, drenching their legs and spraying them with foam. Glorying in the wildness, Phillipa turned a cartwheel. Natasha grabbed her hand and they ran up the beach to the sand dunes, where they sat and waited for the sunrise.

The horizon, which had been tinged with pink when they had arrived at the beach, was now deep red. As the sun broke through, Jacqueline and Natasha cheered. They all scrambled down the slope and raced to the water. Phillipa's feet were cool on the squelchy sand. The wind blew her hair away from her face and joy sent her spirits soaring. Suddenly she wanted to be here with Nicholas. 'I love him,' she thought in surprise. Because it was against her nature to do anything without reason, she asked herself why. 'Because he's sensitive and he listens. He's irritable, impatient, stubborn, and untidy.' She smiled. 'And he's tall, divine looking and his gorgeous deep voice makes me shiver. I'd love it if he kissed me.'

"Come on, Phillipa!" yelled Natasha.

With a whoop of delight she ran down the beach after them.

By the time Phillipa returned to work on Monday, her joy had changed to trepidation as she wondered if she would be able to behave naturally in Nicholas's presence. Although she felt like avoiding him, she went into his office. "Hi, Nick," she said casually.

He looked up and smiled. "You look well. Did you have a good time?"

"Fabulous. How was your weekend?"

He grimaced. "Embarrassing. The girls in the opera school who invited me to their housewarming party asked me to bring a plate. I thought it was because they were short of plates so I turned up with just a plate."

Phillipa burst out laughing. "With nothing on it?"

"I didn't know it meant bring food. They thought it was hilarious."

Pleased she could talk to him without blushing, she indulged in the euphoria of being in love. That afternoon, instead of typing the letter Harriet had dictated, she typed on a clean sheet of paper:

Phillipa Forrester, Philly Forrester, Mrs Nicholas Forrester

"Phillipa Forrester," she said softly. "It sounds just right."

In Harriet, Natasha had found a teacher with whom she had a rapport. Used to anger or ridicule from most of her teachers at school, she always left the theatre feeling happy. She did her breathing exercises every day and she and Jacqueline spent hours discussing their singing lessons. Her complexion gradually improved and at the end of eight weeks, as Harriet had promised, not a spot marred her face. For the first time in her life she stood in front of a mirror and admired her reflection.

"I hope you're not getting vain, Natasha," said her mother.

Harriet felt a thrill of achievement as she looked at Natasha's creamy skin and delicate apricot cheeks.

"The last spots have gone – I can't believe it," said Natasha. "I'd forgotten what I looked like. I thought I'd have scars, but Mum was right. She said if I didn't squeeze them I wouldn't."

She was still too thin, but Harriet hoped that when she left school she would put on weight. "Let's see how your breathing's coming along."

She ran through the exercises and Natasha executed them faultlessly.

"Very good. Today I'm going to let you sing. You've been patient, and from now on we'll be working towards building up your repertoire. We'll start with 'Vissi d'arte'." She lifted the piano lid and put the score of *Tosca* on the stand. "Remember, never strike a note like a hammer, or the sound will be harsh. What are you going to imagine when you're singing?"

"I'm going to think of stroking the notes like I'd stroke a kitten."

"Good." She turned the pages of the score. "All the notes must be rounded, not have sharp points like an arrow. Liken the things you do with your voice to nature. For instance, when you come down from a high note, many singers have a tendency to slide to the lower note. To prevent this, think of gliding to the lower note like a bird. If you slide, you're out of control, if you glide, you're in control."

Natasha's eyes shone. "Oh, Miss Shaw, I've been looking forward to this so much."

"So have I," said Harriet.

"Love and music, these have I lived for," sang Natasha.

'She's absolutely brilliant,' thought Harriet. 'I've never heard a voice like it. She's not a new Melba – she's not a new anyone, she's unique. When I've finished with her the opera world will go crazy with excitement. I won't tell her of course – she might become conceited.' She played the last bars of music, looked up at Natasha's radiant face and swallowed the lump in her throat. "How did that feel?"

"Amazingly easy. Did it sound all right?"

Harriet almost laughed at the question. "Oh, yes. Eight weeks ago when you sang at your audition your voice was pure and beautiful. Now it has strength as well." She closed the score. "Think of your developing voice as a jeweller making a piece of jewellery. Your voice is the jewel, an uncut gem. What we've been doing for the past eight weeks is polishing and cutting it, so it has a good shape and reflects light. The last part of the procedure is to set the jewel, to enhance it, so it can be worn and admired. It's called 'technique'."

Harriet opened *The Melba Method*. "We're going to do this exercise of ascending and descending scales. The sounds are 'me' and 'ah'. Imagine that someone has handed you a gold casket and said, 'This is for you', and you say: 'Me?' Then, you open the box and inside is something you have always wanted, and you say: 'Ah!' The 'ah' must sound joyful, this will lift the voice."

Natasha nodded and did the exercise.

"Excellent. I know your imagination gets you into trouble at school, but here it's one of your biggest assets. Don't let the teachers wear you down, will you?"

"If they haven't now, they never will."

"Do you know what Einstein said about imagination?"

Natasha shook her head.

"That it was more important than knowledge."

"Really? My teachers would give me detention if I told them that."

At the end of the lesson Harriet gave Natasha back her *Melba Method*. "The exercises I've given you today are the only ones you're to practise. Keep up with the breathing exercises, I'll be testing you every week. Good-bye, Natasha."

"Bye, Miss Shaw." Natasha picked up her bag and left the studio. Seconds later she reappeared in the doorway. "Miss Shaw, I think you're wonderful." She vanished again.

Harriet felt like bursting into tears.

Chapter 6

'Her daily food is the heart.
She eats hearts!'
La Bohème – Puccini

Although Deborah had forged her mother's signature many times, her heart always thumped until she was sure she had got away with it. She took the fur coat and matching hat over to the cash register and handed over her mother's account card. The sales girl chatted as she wrapped the coat and hat in tissue paper. Taking the pen, Deborah smiled innocently and wrote Marie Ryland on the account form. This moment was the worst. The girl checked the signature, handed her the bag and Deborah walked away. Her pulse rate returned to normal as she went down the escalator to the ground floor. Resisting the temptation to buy perfume, she left Myers and stood with the crowd waiting to cross Bourke Street.

Calculating that she had time for lunch before returning to work, she went into a cafe in the Royal Arcade. After ordering toasted sandwiches and a caramel malted milk, she thought about her forthcoming audition with Harriet Shaw. While waiting for the waitress to bring her order, she took *The Age* out of her bag and turned to the letters page. As she expected, there was a continuing debate about Harriet Shaw's refusal to allow strong language in the plays performed in her theatre. To Deborah's chagrin, her letter supporting Harriet's ideology had not been printed.

As she ate her sandwich she heard two middle-aged women at the next table discussing the sudden death of a friend.

'I wish my mother would die,' she thought.

She finished her malted milk and looked at her watch. Her eyes widened in dismay. She hated the glares the other girls gave her when she came back late. They resented her because she was the managing director's girlfriend. He told her not to worry, but she longed to be

56

popular and part of their clique. She rushed back to work. As she walked through the door, she pretended to ignore the stares and whispers.

After typing three urgent letters she went home. As she walked from Elsternwick Station, she hoped her mother was out. When she turned into her street she stopped when she saw the car that was parked in the driveway. She wanted to bang the gate, slam the door and put *Medea* with Maria Callas in the title role on the stereo and turn it to full volume. Only the thought that he would defend her mother stopped her. Once she had stormed into her mother's bedroom and asked an ex-boyfriend if he liked menopausal women.

Unperturbed, her mother had laughed. "I'm a long way off that, sweetie. I was very young when you were born. You behave as if you're menopausal yourself. No wonder your boyfriends prefer me."

He had kissed her mother. "Buzz off, Deborah. You've interrupted something important."

Unable to face another boyfriend's derision, she went back into the city and had dinner in a cafe.

Deborah's feelings about life were confused. Her father had compensated for her mother's lack of affection, and when he walked out on the marriage when Deborah was ten, she missed him and felt betrayed by his failure to keep in touch with her. Although she hated her mother, perversely, she longed to be like her and envied her ability to seduce and ditch men without heartache. Deborah conquered men easily, but found the end of relationships traumatic because she never ended them; the men did. Unlike her mother, she frequently fell in love.

She had enjoyed school and had wanted to do her matriculation and go to university, but her mother told her to get out and earn her own living. So, at the age of fifteen, Deborah had joined the work force. Hating the menial clerical duties, she did a secretarial course at night school.

Two years later, she was a secretary in an insurance company. She met her father when she was walking down Collins Street in her lunch hour.

He stepped in front of her. "Deborah?"

She stared at him, then walked away.

He followed her. "I know you hate me, but let me explain – "

Deborah kept walking and refused to look at him. "You hated me," she said through gritted teeth.

He held her arm. She tried to pull away, but his grip was too strong. "I didn't. What made you think that?" he asked as they reached the traffic lights at the corner of Queen Street.

She was livid. "You leave home because you're bored with me ... "

People were staring at them, so she allowed him to guide her up the steps into the relatively private foyer of the ANZ Bank. They stood in the corner. She saw his expression of anger.

"Did your mother tell you that?"

"Yes. Don't try and deny it," she said, careful to keep her voice low.

"She lied. I left because she – had ... "

Deborah saw that he found the subject embarrassing. "Was unfaithful?"

He nodded. "Many times – not just once."

"She's still at it. Lots of boyfriends – all rich. And some of them are mine. But you should have come to see me. Why didn't you?" she asked accusingly.

"She told me you hated me. I didn't believe her, but when you didn't reply to my letters I gave up."

"Letters? I didn't get your letters – she didn't give them to me." The extent of her mother's treachery stunned her.

"Ah. I wrote to you constantly for over a year. And I sent you money and cards for your birthday. I guess she didn't give you those either."

"She didn't. I bet she opened them and took the money."

"Then she's a thief." His put his arm round her. "Come and have lunch with me."

She looked at her watch. "I can't – I've got to get back to work."

"Work? You work?" He frowned. "But I've just paid your school fees for next term."

She looked at him in bewilderment. "How long have you been paying school fees?"

"Ever since you started at Firbank."

Deborah's face hardened. "I didn't go to Firbank." She was so furious she had difficulty speaking. "I went to Elwood High School. I have never – never been to a private school."

Her father put his arm round her. "I think we've got a lot of things to discuss with your mother. You and me and my solicitor."

"You'll have to wait – she's having a holiday in America with one of her men."

For the next month Deborah's future looked wonderful. She was going to do her matriculation at Firbank when the new term began in February. Her father introduced her to opera and classical music and, when he discovered she had a beautiful singing voice, he wanted her to have singing lessons. When Marie returned from America he was going to order her to leave the house and give it to Deborah.

'I'll make friends at uni and they can come and live with me,' she thought. 'We'll have fun and parties.'

On the day her father had told her he was coming to see her mother, and bringing his solicitor with him, Deborah had waited excitedly for him to arrive, looking forward to witnessing her mother's humiliation. At six o'clock in the evening she was still waiting. Because her mother was at home, she went to the phone box down the road and rang him. There was no answer. She was disappointed, but not worried. Something must have happened at work. She rang his office first thing in the morning. The girl on the switchboard put her through to his secretary.

"I'm terribly sorry," she said. "Mr. Ryland died yesterday morning. He had a heart attack."

Although an astute businessman, her father had never altered his original will. Marie inherited everything. In revenge Deborah, knowing her mother never checked her accounts before giving them to her current man to pay, took her account cards and forged her signature whenever she wanted to buy clothes, perfume or jewellery.

After her mother had seduced her first two boyfriends, Deborah only brought boys home when Marie was away. She had been in love with an accountant who was ten years older than her. One evening while they were having dinner in a restaurant, Deborah was convinced he was going to ask her to marry him.

"Deborah, fancy you being here too!" exclaimed her mother. The man she was with looked younger than Deborah. "We must join you."

59

Gracefully, she extended her hand. "Hello, I'm Deborah's mother. You must be one of her boyfriends."

"Her mother?" he exclaimed incredulously.

Deborah's dreams disintegrated as she saw his admiration. She stormed out of the restaurant, hoping that he would follow her. He didn't, and Deborah went home contemplating getting into her mother's bed and slashing her wrists. Instead she took three sleeping tablets, so she would be unaware of their return.

Her relationships with other girls were difficult because she saw them as rivals and could not resist flirting with their boyfriends. Although living with her mother made her miserable, she stayed because the house was rightfully hers, and it satisfied her need for revenge to use her account cards.

After the death of her father, Deborah had forgotten about singing lessons. It was only when she read an article about Harriet Shaw in the paper three years later that she remembered. Deciding that having singing lessons and going to opera school would open up an exciting world, she made an appointment to have an audition.

Nicholas smelt the strong perfume and looked up from his desk. A beautiful girl dressed in a white fur coat and matching hat, which set off her flawless ivory skin, was standing in the doorway. She was holding a score of *Eugene Onegin*. Phillipa, looking extremely annoyed, was just behind her.

"Nicholas, this is Deborah Ryland," she said curtly, before turning away.

"Hello, I've got an audition with Miss Shaw."

Deborah's glamour surprised him. Her application form stated that she was twenty, but she looked more like twenty-five.

He smiled. "I'll be playing the piano for you. What are you going to sing?"

She fluttered obviously false eyelashes and smiled. Her lips, frosted with pink lipstick, parted, showing perfect teeth. "'The Letter Aria'."

"One of my favourites," he said. "Are you ready to start or would you like to sit down for a minute?"

"I'm ready. Nervous, but ready."

"Don't worry – the audition's informal," he said as he led her along the corridor to the theatrette. 'I hope she can sing – she'd make a stunning Tosca,' he thought. He opened the door and turned on the lights. "You're early – would you like to have a run through first?"

She shook her head. "I'll plunge straight in."

The door opened and Harriet walked in. "Nicholas, I … " She stopped abruptly and stared at Deborah.

To his alarm she staggered. He rushed over to her.

She shut her eyes and he took her arm. "Aunt Harriet, are you all right?"

"Shall I call a doctor?" asked Deborah.

Harriet opened her eyes. "No. I had a dizzy turn." Her face was ashen.

"I can make the audition for another time," said Deborah.

"I'm perfectly well, thank you."

The coldness of her tone puzzled Nicholas.

Harriet jerked her arm out of his supporting grasp and turned away.

He was completely thrown by her behaviour. "This is Deborah Ryland. She's going to sing 'The Letter Aria'."

Uncharacteristically, Harriet made no comment.

"Is she all right?" Deborah whispered.

He watched Harriet walk to the back of the theatrette and sit down. "I think so."

Deborah took off her coat to reveal a white dress that was six inches above her knees. He noticed that her legs were slim and shapely. With calculated grace she pulled off her hat and put it on a chair with her coat. Her dark brown hair was stiff with hair spray. Nicholas was disconcerted to see Harriet looking at her with revulsion.

He took Deborah's score and pulled out the piano stool.

Deborah looked at him, consternation in her brown eyes.

He smiled reassuringly. "Nod when you're ready to begin."

Nicholas was always delighted when someone did well at an audition. Harriet's strange behaviour made him even more pleased that Deborah had an outstanding voice. When she finished singing she looked at him.

He winked at her. "Well done," he said softly.

"Thank you for playing the piano so beautifully for me."

He closed the score and handed it back to Deborah who made sure their fingers touched.

Harriet stood up. "That was very good," she said in a tone that sounded like a reprimand. "Your higher notes are clear, and the quality of your voice is promising. I feel that it's certainly worth getting your voice trained, but – "

"Really?" said Deborah excitedly. "I'm so thrilled."

"Unfortunately, I'm fully booked at the moment, but – "

"I don't mind waiting till you've got a vacancy, Miss Shaw."

"I can't take any more pupils," Harriet said sternly. "Where do you work?"

"In town."

"Ingrid Williams is an excellent teacher who has studios in Elizabeth Street. She takes pupils I send her. You won't have to have another audition; my recommendation is all you need." She opened her bag, took out a card and handed it to Deborah. "Give her a ring and she will teach you."

"But I want to join your opera school," protested Deborah.

"You can in three years' time – if Ingrid Williams thinks you're good enough. Nicholas, show Annabel out, please."

"I'm Deborah."

"Show her out, Nicholas."

He saw Deborah prepare herself for a last effort. "Miss Shaw, I wrote to the paper telling them I thought you were right not to allow bad language ... " She trailed off as Harriet walked away.

At the door of the theatre, Deborah looked at him in bewilderment. "She didn't like me, did she?"

"She did, but she's got her quota at the moment," he lied.

"Then why did she audition me?"

"She auditions everybody, and if they're promising she sends them to Ingrid Williams."

"What if I can't get into opera school?"

"You will. You've got an outstanding voice. Don't worry, I'll see you in three years." He opened the door for her.

"Why did she call me Annabel?"

"I don't know," he said truthfully. As he watched her walk away, he felt sorry for her, and angry with Harriet for the rejection. Something was seriously wrong. Two of her senior students had just left for England and a promising beginner had dropped out when he discovered how much work was involved, but she had lied to Deborah and told her she had no vacancies. Harriet never turned away good voices.

He went straight into her office. "Why didn't you take her on? She's got a sensational voice."

Harriet continued to sign letters, but said nothing. She opened her drawer and took out a bottle of ink.

Knowing she was refusing to look at him, he felt awkward. The writing on the page in front of her shone in the light, showing the ink was still wet. Her pen did not need refilling, her movements were a distraction. "You lied to her, Aunt Harriet."

"She's dangerous."

"Dangerous?" he asked, careful to keep the disbelief out of his voice. "Why do you think she's dangerous?"

"I know the type," she said stubbornly, as she wiped the nib of her pen with a scrap of blotting paper.

He sat down. "Actually, I think that underneath the glamour and self-confidence, she looked tormented."

"Nicholas, I've lived a lot longer than you and known a lot more people. Females like her wreak havoc wherever they go. I'm not talking about physical danger," she said impatiently. "I mean ... "

"I'm listening."

She unscrewed the bottle of ink. "There are other sorts of danger. She's glamorous, and I bet she's got no female friends. She was fluttering her false eyelashes at you so much it's a wonder they didn't fall off."

"So, she's a glamorous flirt. There are quite a few of those in the opera school. Come to think of it, some of them are your students. What makes Deborah different?"

"Nicholas, have you ever seen anyone I teach who equals her for glamour?"

"Well, not quite, but – "

"There you are then."

"You're being unreasonable. And who's Annabel?" he asked.

Abruptly she looked at her watch, almost knocking over the bottle of ink. "I've got Richard Greythorn coming for his singing lesson in ten minutes."

He reached over and screwed the top on the bottle. "Aunt Harriet, you called her Annabel. Why?"

"Stop badgering me. I got her name wrong."

She was pale, and he felt concerned. Her assurance had deserted her and she appeared frail. Wondering if she had suffered a slight stroke in the theatrette, he studied her carefully. "Are you all right?"

"Yes. Stop fussing. Leave me alone," she pleaded.

He decided that her demeanour revealed grief, bursting to the surface, after being submerged. "You almost fainted. Why don't you ring the doctor and make an appointment?"

"Nicholas, please go away," she said softly.

As he left her office, he vaguely remembered seeing the name Annabel in his grandmother's journals. 'But it can't have been anything dramatic, or I would have remembered,' he thought. Worried that Harriet was about to have a heart attack, he stayed in the kitchen near her office. Just before Richard Greythorn arrived he heard Harriet walk up the corridor to the studio. Not wanting to leave her alone, he waited until he heard Richard singing, before going into Phillipa's office. "Philly, have you ever heard of anyone named Annabel?"

She put a fresh sheet of paper in her typewriter. "I knew an Annabel at school."

"I mean someone connected with the theatre."

"No. Why?"

Nicholas explained what had happened in the theatrette. "Deborah's got a superb voice, but Aunt Harriet won't teach her. She's sent her to Ingrid Williams."

"Perhaps Deborah's perfume almost gassed her," she said sourly.

"You didn't like her either?"

"No. She treated me with disdain – as if I was some dowdy secretary."

"You must have imagined it – you're not dowdy." He could see that her self-confidence had been battered. "You're very attractive."

She blushed. "Am I?"

"Yes. You're blushing."

"Shut up."

"Philly, has Harriet ever confided in you – about – a secret?"

She looked baffled. "What sort of secret?"

"I don't know. Just before I left London I discovered she'd been involved in a tragedy and that's why she came to Australia."

Phillipa looked reflective. "She might have told Hugh. It's only just struck me, but there was something about the way he used to treat her." She tapped her fingers on the desk. "I can't think of the right word. Not sympathy. Not pity. He loved her. He had from the time they first met after she'd arrived in Melbourne. Harriet was the reason he never married. Compassion – that's it. And understanding." She looked ashamed. "I'm being disloyal."

"No you're not."

She set the margins on her typewriter. "I am. It's none of our business."

"I'm her nephew."

"That doesn't give you the right to pry into her past." She turned the pages of her shorthand pad. "You won't tell her what I said about Hugh?"

"No," he said irritably.

As soon as Nicholas arrived home that night, he read the page from his grandmother's journal, pleased that his father had only torn it up, not burnt it. Only a few words were unreadable. The mystery now took on another dimension. Harriet had been engaged to a doctor, but never married him. According to her mother's writings, Harriet had left England after two tragic years. The page of writing revealed no animosity towards Harriet, and it seemed that the family had been united, not divided, by the tragedy.

If his theory was correct and Harriet was really his grandmother, who was Annabel? He made some notes to work out the chronology, realizing that his mother would have been eight at the time of Harriet's intended marriage in 1922. The engagement might have been broken because her fiancé had discovered that not only was Harriet not a virgin, she was Charlotte's mother. Had Annabel told him Harriet's secret? Annabel must have been a similar age to Deborah Ryland. For the first time, he thought about the identity of Charlotte's real father. The thought that he may have blood relations of whom he knew nothing disturbed him.

He considered other possibilities. Had the family discovered that

Harriet's fiancé was already married, and had Annabel been his wife? Harriet had obviously hated Annabel, which would make sense if the man had tried to commit bigamy. History and literature were littered with suspected and proven acts of bigamy. Had Annabel been insane, like Rochester's wife in *Jane Eyre*?

"Yes," he pondered, "that would be tragic. It would explain why Harriet left England. But why did she wait two years – and why did she give up singing?"

Chapter 7

'I don't want a fight.'

The Abduction from the Seraglio – Mozart

Harriet read the reviews of the opening night of *La Traviata,* with increasing anger. While both papers attacked her for not putting on modern opera, most of their censure, for what they called a predictable production, was directed at Nicholas. The only praise was for the singers, with whom they sympathized for having to endure an inexperienced and unimaginative director. One critic praised the costumes and the natural acting, which he felt added intensity, but this did little to alleviate Harriet's outrage.

Thinking Nicholas would use this as an excuse to get his own way and tell her he was right, she walked to his flat prepared for recriminations.

He answered the door in his dressing gown. To her surprise, he looked pleased to see her.

"Aunt Harriet, could you do me a favour and go to the milk bar on the corner and buy some cat food?"

"Do I pay you so badly you have to eat cat food?"

He laughed. "Come and see." He ushered her into the untidy bedroom and gestured towards the box lined with newspaper, in which a scrawny cat lay with four kittens. "She had them on my bed this morning. I almost had a heart attack when I felt all this movement – I thought it was a snake." He knelt by the box. "She must have sneaked in last night when I was putting out the rubbish."

As she watched him stroke a kitten with his finger, she was reminded of Charlotte as a child. The memory, and his tenderness towards a stray cat made her feel emotional. She had come prepared for a quarrel, but had found a man she suspected would not have been more excited had the critics praised him. She saw the newspaper on the chest of drawers. It was open at the page and she knew he had read the critic's judgements.

"Aunt Harriet, are you all right?"

"You reminded me of your mother." She saw his look of embarrassment. "How English you are," she said wryly. "I'd forgotten how they hate emotion. Australians are different – they hug each other and show affection," she said, picking up the paper. "Are you upset about the reviews?"

He shrugged. "Critics in London said worse things than that sometimes."

"But you had good reviews. I read all the ones you sent me."

"I only sent you the good ones; there were some bad ones too." He stood up. "As long as they're fair, bad reviews stop me becoming complacent."

"Do you blame me?" she asked.

"Partly. But even if you'd allowed me to do things my way, we still might have got bad reviews. The theatre was full, so the public are happy, which means money in the bank," he said, pulling the blood stained blanket off his bed. "It will be interesting to see what they say about *Angelica*. I'm worried the audience will miss the miracle. Perhaps she should take a step forward."

Harriet shook her head. "It's perfect as it is. Anything more would rob it of its pathos."

One of the kittens mewed and they both looked at the box.

"I'd better go and buy the cat food," said Harriet.

"Aunt Harriet, I've had a terrible thought. She might sneeze."

Puzzled, Harriet looked at the cat. "Would it matter?"

"Not her – the Virgin Mary."

She laughed. "Of course she won't."

"Or cough," he insisted.

She understood his concern, but decided to take the risk. "If she does – that'll get the critics excited. Worse things have gone wrong during an opera." She nodded. "If she sneezes it'll be a disaster or a comedy. If she doesn't you'll have a triumph."

On the opening night of *Trittico*, Richard Greythorn watched Sister

Angelica fall to her knees. "Ah! lost for ever! I have taken my life, I have taken my life! I die the deadliest of sins on my soul!" She turned to the statue of the Virgin Mary. "Madonna, save my soul, save my soul! 'twas the love of my baby!"

As the lights turned golden, the off-stage angels' chorus began singing. Having seen the opera many times, Richard expected the stage to become crowded with processions and glitter, which he thought gaudy. He was intrigued when nothing happened. Just before the end, the statue of the Virgin Mary held out her arms in a gesture of forgiveness to the dying nun. 'My God,' he thought as the curtain fell, 'I hope Nicholas is still the director when it's my turn.' When the lights came up, he went into the foyer, hoping to see the girl he had met when he auditioned. 'If I see her, I'll ask her if we can meet for coffee afterwards.' He looked over the balcony onto the mass of people, but couldn't see her. 'Trust me to go on a different night,' he thought.

After taking Harriet's advice and drinking eight pints of water a day, the acne that had distorted his features had vanished and he only had a few scars on his face. The girls at work, who had called him Spotty, flirted with him. Remembering their cruel jokes, he ignored them. Their disappointment gratified him. He had been promoted and was supervising three clerks, a typist and a stenographer. Although he was invited to their social events he declined, often rudely.

When he had begun his singing lessons, he had abandoned the idea of starting his own business. Instead, he put the money he had saved towards renting and furnishing a large flat in Brighton, near the beach. Harriet had recommended a piano teacher, and one of his first major purchases was a second-hand piano. After redecorating, he spent his evenings and weekends practising his vocal exercises and the piano, and listening to opera. If he had time, he went on Anti-Vietnam War marches.

On his way back to his seat after the interval, he saw Harriet.

"Hello, Richard. Are you enjoying it?"

"It's fantastic, Miss Shaw. *Angelica* was exquisite. It was moving without being slushy. I thought the Virgin Mary was a statue till the end."

"I hope the critics feel the same."

"They'll be insane if they don't," he said.

♪　　♪　　♪

Nicholas flung the newspaper across the kitchen. Although prepared for the attack on *Il Tabarro* and *Gianni Schicchi*, he had been confident that the critic would praise the simplicity of *Sister Angelica*. He shook the cereal packet over a bowl, swearing when most of the cornflakes fell onto the table. When the phone rang he ignored it. If it was Harriet he would be unable to control his temper.

Although the critic had blamed Harriet for the repertoire, it was him they condemned for the hackneyed productions. Becoming calmer, he read the review again, trying to be dispassionate. From their comments, he concluded that, had he been permitted to modernize *La Traviata* or *Romeo and Juliet*, the reaction to *Il Trittico* would have been more favourable.

Generally, Harriet was praised by the media. Their only complaint was her refusal to put on modern operas. Before the season had begun, *The Age* had done an article about her, affectionately calling the theatre a nursery where singers, dancers and actors could gain the training and experience to become professionals. Examples of her balance of philanthropy and financial acumen were given, especially her custom of hiring a youth orchestra, which, as well as being cheaper, provided employment for young musicians. It disheartened Nicholas that the critics had nothing but derision for him. He walked to the theatre, hoping that by the time he arrived he would be able to talk calmly to Harriet.

He found Phillipa and Harriet in her office with all the newspapers.

"They didn't even mention *Angelica*," he said from the doorway, trying to sound nonchalant.

"This one has," said Phillipa, pulling a face. "The final moments of *Sister Angelica* showed some promise. Some promise! That's all he says."

"Nicholas, I'm sorry," said Harriet. "They're being hard on you. Because you're young and English they've stereotyped you." She began cutting out the reviews. "Richard Greythorn was enthusiastic. Young people's opinions are very important."

"What are we doing in November?" he asked.

"*Bohème, Eugene Onegin, Carmen* and *André Chénier*." Harriet's expression dared him to criticize her choice.

"Have you ever thought about doing *The Consul*?" he asked. "I saw it at Covent Garden – it was haunting and dramatic."

Harriet handed the cuttings to Phillipa. "It won't make money."

"But – "

"I refuse to pander to the critics," she snapped. "Audiences like the old operas. The theatre can't afford to make a loss on any opera."

"Covent Garden had a full house. Why not try it as an experiment?"

"The population of London is ten times that of Melbourne and we compete with the Australian Opera," said Harriet tightly.

"Sadler's Wells competes with Covent Garden by being different. All their productions are done in English."

She glared at him. "Don't try to educate me about the opera scene in London – I was part of it long before you were born."

"If you're not going to allow me to have a say in things, I might as well go back to England. I don't want to be mauled by the critics because you refuse to listen to reason," he said, ignoring Phillipa's distressed expression. "They're bored with the same operas done the same old ways. They want to see something new – not necessarily a new opera, but a new production."

"I'm not going to argue with you, Nicholas, I'm too busy." Dropping the scissors on the desk, she went to the filing cabinet.

"If the critics go on like this, the theatre will close and you won't be busy at all, so stop being a dictator and listen."

Phillipa went to the door. "I'm going."

Harriet looked at Nicholas accusingly. "You've upset Phillipa now."

"We've both upset her," he said quietly, wishing he could have a cigarette.

She folded up the paper. "This is another problem," she said, picking up a letter. "The warehouse where we store the scenery is tripling its prices. Other places that charge reasonable rents are miles away, so by the time we pay transport costs the price will be the same, if not more. That's why every performance has to be a financial success," she said desperately.

He sat down. "What are we going to do? If the critics go on like this, we'll lose money. But I can't think of a compromise."

"You have thought of a compromise, but I can't come to terms with it. What might please the critics won't please me and might not please the audience."

Aware that Harriet was wavering, he said quietly, "In future, let's discuss each opera individually. When this season is over, shall we talk about how we can freshen up the four operas for November?"

She sighed. "I hate change. My ways have always worked till now."

He smiled encouragingly. "They still work, and they're an excellent foundation. All we have to do is add originality sometimes. Not to every opera, but to one in the season – two a year. Let's think in terms of improvement."

She looked annoyed. "The composers of genius don't need improving."

"But we won't be changing the music, just the time it's set. The critics think the old composers are being done to death. Imagine how bored drama audiences would get if all they were presented with was Shakespeare, Wilde and Shaw."

"Nicholas, this place doesn't run on volunteers. Everyone who takes part in the opera, ballet and drama productions has to be paid and that includes the orchestra, wardrobe mistress and musical director. Then there's Phillipa and you, the cleaner and the caretaker. And that's just the full-time staff. There are all the part-time teachers in the opera and ballet schools. If we start experimenting and the audience hate it, we're lost. And if we lose any of our major patrons ... " Despondently, she shook her head.

"Are the finances for drama, ballet and opera separate?"

"No, they're pooled. But opera productions are the most expensive to stage and they make the smallest profits. The opera school is the most costly to run because we teach German, French and Italian, as well as movement, drama and music."

"Does that cause friction?"

"No," she said, with a slight smile. "Because any money I make from interviews goes into the theatre coffers and, as I am the founder, drama and ballet have me to thank for their existence."

He nodded. "How much do *The Friends of the Theatre* raise each year?"

"They're not around to raise money – more to help with the catering at our functions."

He was amazed. "Wouldn't it be sensible to get them involved with fund raising?"

"Nicholas, they save us a great deal of money – otherwise we'd have to hire caterers," she said irritably. "Why do you have to criticize everything?"

"I'm asking questions, not criticizing. Remember, I've been here for less than four months." Deliberately keeping his voice low, he continued, "You've got this enthusiastic group of people who are dedicated to you. If you asked them to raise a million dollars in a year they probably would. When the President of the Friends speaks to you, she looks so honoured, I expect her to curtsey. Please stop accusing me."

"I'm sorry. When I started this theatre the critics raved – I could do nothing wrong." She stood up and went over to the schedule on the wall. "Now it seems I can do nothing right."

"That's not true. Remember the good things they say about you. It's just that times are changing – the young are questioning traditions. It could be exciting if you let it."

She turned and looked at him. "Am I too old?"

He saw the fear in her eyes. "No," he said firmly, touching her arm. "Definitely not. But you need to experiment. The big patrons aren't going to desert the theatre over one updated opera and neither are the audiences. They might be so enthusiastic they'll donate more money. Next season we could do something new with one opera, and weigh up the reaction.

"The old operas are timeless and so are their themes. Modern people are schemers like Iago and jealous like Othello. How many women are murdered today by jealous husbands? How many families are locked in feuds? *Romeo and Juliet* is being played out between Catholics and Protestants in Ireland every day, except their names are Bridget and Michael. Instead of sword fights, there are tarrings and featherings and bombs."

She didn't reply, but he could see that she was thinking. He decided to say no more.

Terrified Nicholas would resign, Phillipa opened her shorthand pad. She knew that neither he nor Harriet would put her in the position of choosing between them, but she felt torn. From the time of her parents' death until she met Harriet, she had never had a central position in anyone's life. It was Harriet who had helped her overcome her fear of cars by encouraging her to have driving lessons. Phillipa felt as if Harriet was her grandmother. Her feeling towards Nicholas was simple. She wanted to marry him.

She heard him walking down the corridor towards her office. Trying to hide her fear that he was coming to tell her he was returning to London, she adopted a neutral expression.

He put his head round the door. "May I come in?"

Relieved that he was smiling, she put the letter she had just finished typing in an envelope. "Only if you and Harriet have stopped arguing."

"We have."

Wanting to know what had transpired, but determined not to sound curious, she asked him about the kittens. He told her he was keeping the mother and the black one. She laughed when he told her he had named the kitten Algernon, more with delight that this showed he was staying, than amusement over the name.

"Would you like one?" he asked.

She thought about it. Deciding that a cat would be company, and give her a natural opening for conversations with Nicholas, she said she would have the grey one. "I'll call him Mozart." She put a stamp on the letter and tossed it in the out tray. "What about the other two?"

"I'll stick a notice on the board."

She opened her drawer and took out an index card. "I'll type up one of these for you," she said, flicking the ribbon to red.

Two weeks later, Phillipa was in Harriet's office taking dictation when Nicholas walked in carrying a model.

"What's that?" Harriet asked suspiciously, as he placed it on her desk.

"A solution to the warehouse problem," he said. "This is what we did in London."

"Nicholas, I'm not having abstract sets, with the audience having to imagine what the scene is supposed to represent."

Phillipa saw his expression change from satisfaction to irritation. Dreading another argument, she chewed her lip.

"Aunt Harriet, are you going to listen or shall I smash this to pieces now?"

"What is it?" Harriet asked, looking at the model doubtfully.

"Nothing much yet – just three pieces of painted cardboard hinged together with the doors and windows cut out. But – " He opened a shoe box and took out a frame which he fitted into a space for the window. "Georgian window." Removing it he replaced it with another frame. "Tudor window. I haven't had time to make anything in another period yet, but can you see what I mean? One set can be used countless times just by changing the doors and windows, mouldings, furniture and hangings. We could perform whole operas without moving any of the flats – especially ones that are all set internally."

"*Traviata's* one," said Phillipa, seeing that Harriet was looking interested. "Red brocade drapes and elaborate furniture for Violetta's salon, floral curtains and plain furniture for their country house, blue velvet for Flora's house and green for the bedroom scene."

"Yes," said Nicholas, smiling at her. "But it's not just changing the drapes and furniture. The whole set can look different by moving the position of the doors and windows. Each flat has a space for a doorway and a window, so we have the choice of three different positions. Look." He took a piece of dolls house furniture from the box. "A ballroom can be changed into a kitchen in minutes by placing a dresser in front of a door, putting up kitchen curtains, taking down a portrait and – presto, the windows are in a different position. Any window can be covered up by placing a portrait over it." He looked at Harriet. "What do you think?"

She stared at the model. "We'll only need a quarter of the storage space in the warehouse, and most of that will be for the furniture," she said thoughtfully. "It's an excellent scheme, Nicholas. And, between operas, the flats can be painted a different colour."

He grinned. "Great – you've got the idea."

That night, Nicholas and Phillipa looked out at the lashing rain and wind tearing at the trees.

"Come on, Philly, I'll drive you home." He opened the side door of the theatre and it was almost ripped from his grasp by the wind. They dashed to the car. As he turned into her street, the rain came down in torrents and they could hardly see through the windscreen. He drove carefully and pulled up outside her house.

"Do you want to come in and wait till it stops?" asked Phillipa.

"Thanks. How long do you think it'll last?"

"Hard to tell," she said, hoping it would go on for at least an hour.

As they entered her flat, Phillipa felt shy. She went into the kitchen and made coffee. When she returned to the lounge with the percolator and mugs, Nicholas was sitting on the sofa reading the book she had bought about kittens, in preparation for Mozart's arrival. As she poured the coffee, she tried to think of something interesting to say.

"Where did you get your furniture?" he asked, looking at the curtains, sofa and arm chairs that were all royal-blue velvet.

"Second-hand shops." She handed him the biscuit tin. "I found some great bargains. Some only needed polishing. Having the sofa and chairs re-upholstered cost the most."

He stirred his coffee. "I like the colour scheme, it all goes well together."

She was pleased by his compliment.

Nicholas pulled off his black jumper and threw it on a chair. "Most single young people in London either live with their parents or in freezing bedsits or crowded flats. If you were in London, you'd live in a tiny room and share a bathroom with five other people."

"How come?"

"There's no basic wage like there is here, so employers can pay what they like, and there's a shortage of housing so landlords can charge exorbitant rents."

She decided to invite him to dinner one night and cook something impressive. 'I'll ask Harriet, Jacqui and Natasha too; otherwise he might think I'm up to something – which I am,' she thought.

Chapter 8

'Oh heavens!
How distressing and how painful.'
Eugene Onegin – Tchaikovsky

Although Nicholas had been intending to move after the November productions, by August his flat, with its dreary furniture and dark woodwork, was so gloomy it was depressing him. A few days ago he had discovered the suburb of South Yarra when he went to a party given by students in the opera school. Many of the houses were Victorian terraces, with intricately patterned cast-iron verandahs, and the streets were lined with grass verges planted with trees, which Australians called nature strips.

In spite of its close proximity to the city, there was a village atmosphere. As he wandered down the streets, looking for the address the estate agent had given him, he had a sense of belonging – something he had not felt since he arrived in Melbourne. Pleased to discover the flat was in a quiet street near the Botanical Gardens, he went inside.

The large apartment with a shared garden, occupied the first floor of a corner terraced house. Because it was unfurnished, the rent was less than for his present flat. Freshly painted throughout, it was clean and light and he looked forward to furnishing it with Victorian pieces that would have been fashionable when the house was built. French windows in the lounge opened onto the front verandah, which had a lace-work balustrade. Thick stems of a wisteria vine grew up the posts supporting the roof and he envisaged the fragrant blue flowers that would trail in spring.

He went to the agent and arranged to move in the following week. Then he went to see Harriet.

"I'm very relieved," she said when he told her. "I know you've been unhappy and I thought you were thinking of returning to England." She handed him a cup of tea. "I haven't made things any easier for you."

"I haven't been exactly unhappy. I'm homesick sometimes. But I don't give up easily. I wouldn't leave you without giving it a fair chance."

"Thank you. It's more than I deserve. I've been too hard on you, but I'm not used to people disagreeing with me." She cut a slice of sponge cake and put it on his plate. "I hope there are some things you like about Melbourne."

"Yes. The innocence is refreshing. All the parties I've been to so far, I haven't seen a joint – clandestinely or otherwise."

She looked puzzled. "A joint?"

"Marijuana."

"I certainly hope not," she said primly.

He shrugged. "In London lots of people smoked joints. I was accused of being a prig. Sometimes it was hard." Memories of being taunted returned. "Especially when my fiancée found a drug-taking actor I despised more exciting than me." He knew he sounded bitter.

Harriet nodded sympathetically. "What are you going to do about furniture?"

"I thought I'd ask Phillipa to help me scout round the second-hand shops," he said, grateful for her tactful change of subject.

Phillipa was thrilled when Nicholas asked her to help him. She took him to the second-hand shop in St Kilda where she had bought most of her furniture.

Nicholas examined a Victorian bedroom suite in walnut, and looked at the price. "I wish shops would label things properly. Is that the price of the bed, the wardrobe, the chest of drawers, or what?"

The owner of the shop came over. "It's everything."

Phillipa almost laughed at Nicholas's astonished expression.

"But I can sell the items separately if you like," he continued. "The bed will be ... "

"I'll have the lot," said Nicholas. "I can't believe how cheap it is."

"People like modern stuff these days," said the owner regretfully.

"Not me," said Nicholas. "Now, I need a sofa and two armchairs, a desk and chair, and a dining table and six chairs, preferably dark wood and Victorian, but Edwardian will do. And bookcases."

The man led them to the other end of the shop. Phillipa was enjoying herself immensely and thought how blissful it would be if they were engaged and looking for furniture for their own house. By lunch time, Nicholas had found everything he wanted. He arranged for it to be delivered the following week.

"What a transformation," said Nicholas as the delivery men unloaded the sofa and armchairs.

The shabby upholstery had been replaced by green and blue William Morris chintz. As it had been Phillipa who had persuaded him to buy the suite, pointing out the quality of the woodwork, she was pleased by his approval. Armed with a tape measure, she went round making sure the items would fit in the alcoves before they were dragged across the room.

"You've got yourself a very efficient wife," said one of the delivery men.

Phillipa blushed. "I'm only his secretary."

"And my friend – my indispensable friend," said Nicholas, winking at her.

She was glad he was not embarrassed.

When the men left, Phillipa felt shy. "It looks fabulous," she said, thinking how well the furniture went with the pale yellow walls, white woodwork and honey coloured floorboards.

After arranging his books and records in the bookcases positioned either side of the marble fireplace, he took her onto the back verandah to show her the garden. Resting her hands on the balustrade, she looked at the forest of gum, wattle and jacaranda trees. Seeing dozens of birds, she said, "I hope Algernon doesn't massacre them."

"I'll get him a collar with a bell on it." He looked at his watch. "Do you have to rush off, Philly?"

"No."

"In that case, shall I throw together a meal?"

Elation surged through her. "Where are you going to throw it?"

"Probably in the bin. Cooking's not my strong point." He took out his wallet. "Can you go and get some wine?"

"Why don't I cook?"

He grinned. "I was hoping you'd say that. I'll go and buy the wine."

"I hope he kisses me tonight," she whispered as she opened the refrigerator.

After dinner they sat in front of the fire, drinking brandy, listening to Beethoven symphonies and talking about the theatre.

"Nick, you look – upset."

The Fourth Symphony had been Sally's favourite, and hearing it had brought back memories. "Yes, I was thinking … "

"About Sally?"

He nodded. "If I tell you something, will you promise not to tell Harriet?"

When he had finished, she looked horrified. "I'm sorry, Nick," she said after a long pause. "I can't think of anything comforting to say."

She looked so uncomfortable, he changed the subject, thinking how different she was from Sally. Shy where Sally was confident, and as conventional as Sally was radical. 'Philly would never have an abortion,' he thought. 'She's too sensible and moral to ever get into that situation.'

He thought how attractive she looked. Her shoulder-length hair was loose and had darkened in the winter to the gold of wet autumn leaves. She had made an impressive dinner from the limited food she had found in his kitchen. From the cheese and eggs she had made a soufflé that she served with vegetables sautéed in butter. Mashing two bananas into cream whipped with brandy she had produced a delicious dessert.

He drew on his cigarette and gazed into the fire. He was very fond of Phillipa, but if they became entangled in a love affair that did not work the consequences could be disastrous, not only for them but for Harriet as well. Their whole life was the theatre and to start a relationship with Phillipa could put everything in jeopardy.

She interrupted his thoughts. "Gosh, it's after midnight – I'd better go."

He stood up. "I'll ring for a taxi."

"Thanks, Nick. I've really enjoyed today."

She was standing close to him. When he took a step forward she didn't move.

"So have I." He put his arm round her.

"Nick, Nick," she whispered standing on tiptoe and putting her arms around his neck.

He bent over and kissed her on the lips, inhaling her perfume. Desire almost overcame his resolution. Forcing himself, he gently pulled away. "Philly, I'm sorry. I'm terribly fond of you, but when two people work together … "

"Of course, I've had too much to drink," she said breathlessly. "Sorry."

Phillipa maintained her composure until she arrived home. Holding Mozart she sat on the sofa and wept. When Nicholas had kissed her she had been ecstatic. His apology was a reminder of life's cruelty. Bitterly she remembered the last time she had experienced that type of happiness. She had been in the car with her parents, taking her mother and new baby home from hospital. She had been sitting on the back seat gazing into the bassinet where her sister lay, looking forward to wheeling the pram round to her friends as her mother had promised. It was the last thing she remembered before regaining consciousness in hospital.

The next morning Nicholas rang to find out if she had a hangover.

"No, have you?" she asked brightly.

She heard him chuckle. "Yes. Philly, about last night … "

"Nick, don't fret. It was nothing. We were both a bit drunk."

"I don't want it to affect our friendship."

"It won't," she assured him.

On Monday she returned to work and acted as if nothing had happened. She had not entirely lost hope of making him fall in love with her, but vowed that if he ever kissed her again, it would be when he was sober.

At the end of Richard's singing lesson, Harriet handed him his score of *Otello*. After praising his intelligent rendition of Iago's 'Credo', she said, "I'd like your opinion about something. Could you stay a little longer?"

"Of course, Miss Shaw."

"I know you saw all the operas in May. Did you read the reviews?"

"No. A review is only one person's opinion."

She opened a scrapbook and handed it to him. "Would you read them now and tell me what you think?"

As he read them she watched his expression, relieved that he was scowling.

"Rot," he said scornfully. "The acting in all the operas was the best I've ever seen – the characters looked natural. They didn't stand and sing, they did something. Violetta arranging flowers in Act two made her singing like a conversation. And the chorus look as if they have come into the scene for a reason. It's not just *The Chorus*. It's people who are friends and who've got occupations and families – if that doesn't add reality I don't know what does."

"Do you like modern opera?" she asked.

"Some of it." He put the scrapbook on the piano.

"What about *The Consul?*"

"Modern opera at its best," he said enthusiastically.

"Someone suggested modernizing *Traviata*, and portraying Violetta as a drug addict."

"You'd be accused of trying to please the critics," he said dismissively. "*Traviata*'s associated with superb costumes and wealth, and updating it would lose all that."

She felt pleased. Richard was young, and that he thought as she did diluted the accusations that she was too old. "Is that your instinctive reaction?" she asked.

"Yes."

"What about your logical reaction?"

"It would lose its sophistication." He thought for a moment. "*Bohème* could be successfully modernized. It's romantic, but not glamorous, and the story line is timeless."

"If you had a choice of going to a traditional or contemporary production of *Bohème*, which would you choose?" she asked.

"Contemporary. It'd be refreshing to see a new production."

"You've been very helpful, Richard."

During the week Harriet asked all her pupils similar questions. The majority agreed with Richard on *Traviata* but were divided on *Bohème*. Some were enthusiastic about a performance of *The Consul*, but others had never heard of it.

82

♪   ♪   ♪

When Nicholas went into Phillipa's office with the student reports for her to type, she gaped at him. "Nick, are you ill? Shall I call a doctor?"

"Why?"

"Your shirt's ironed." She was glad she could joke with him, and hoped it disguised her feelings.

"Very funny." He pulled out a chair and sat down.

She wrinkled her brow in pretended concentration. "Let me guess. Ah, yes," she said, as if she had just remembered. "Harriet's cleaning lady's taken you on."

"Yes. I've got ten perfectly ironed shirts hanging in the wardrobe." He smiled. "I couldn't believe it when I got home last night. The flat was immaculate. I've never lived in such pristine surroundings. Algie's cross – he used to sleep on my jumpers, but now there're all washed and folded in the chest of drawers."

Harriet came into the office. "Nicholas, how would you update *Bohème*?"

He looked startled.

"How would you deal with the technicalities? People today don't use candles, and candles must be used in the first act."

"A power failure," he said. "They have to light candles – they can't afford torches. Why?"

Harriet smiled. "*Bohème* will be done in miniskirts, Mimì can die of cancer and they'll all smoke," she announced recklessly.

He stared at her. "Are you serious?"

"Hurry and make the arrangements before I change my mind."

"Smoking?" asked Phillipa. "What if they accidentally set fire to the scenery?"

Nicholas had become used to the strict fire precautions in Australia. "Water in the ashtrays," he said. "Just a bit in the bottom so that when they stub out the cigarettes they go out properly. Smoking will make the scenes realistic and give the characters something to do with their hands."

"Pretending to smoke," said Harriet. "They can't inhale. Opera singers shouldn't smoke."

83

"For heaven's sake," said Nicholas to the girl playing Mimì. "You're in Paris. You're outside in the snow, dressed in a miniskirt and a threadbare coat. You look as if you're on Bondi Beach in a heat wave!"

"I can't act distraught and cold at the same time."

"Come here," he called. "Everyone else take a fifteen minute break."

Grabbing her hand he took her outside into the grassy area at the side of the theatre. Although it was the middle of September, a cold wind was blowing. "Take your jumper off."

"It's freezing!" she protested.

He grinned. "That's the idea. Take it off and give it to me."

She obeyed and stood shivering in a thin cotton blouse. "Can we go in now?"

"No. Tell me what you're doing."

"Freezing to death – you're trying to kill me."

"The sooner you tell me – the sooner we can go inside."

"My teeth are chattering, I'm hugging myself and rubbing my arms."

"Right. So what are you going to do when you're on stage?"

"My teeth can hardly chatter while I'm singing!"

"Act, and the audience will imagine that they are. And blow on your hands when Marcello's singing."

"You'll be sorry if I die of pneumonia," she said, snatching her jumper.

He laughed. "Your understudy won't."

'In five years, I'll be on that stage singing, and getting paid for it,' thought Richard, as he watched *La Bohème*. The transition to the modern day seemed natural.

When he came down the staircase during the interval, he saw the girl he had met at his audition. 'At last,' he thought. She was with Phillipa and another girl. Her acne, like his, had completely gone. Wondering if the girl with black hair was her twin, he squeezed his way through the crowd and said hello to Phillipa.

"Hello, Richard. This is Natasha and her sister Jacqueline."

He smiled at Natasha, pleased that he finally knew her name. "We met at our audition."

"Oh yes." She laughed. "We looked very different then. How did you recognize me?"

"Your hair."

She grimaced. "Unfortunately I can't do much about that."

"I can't think why you'd want to." Not wanting to exclude Jacqueline and Phillipa he opened his box of chocolate almonds and offered them round. "Fantastic production, isn't it?"

Natasha licked her ice cream. "I prefer it done the old way. Musetta's waltz song looks funny in a mini and high heels. And I was shocked when they started smoking."

"I'm relating more to this version," said Jacqueline. "I feel I know the characters when they're in modern dress. It makes them more real."

He noticed that her eyes, although blue, were the same size and shape as Natasha's. The only other feature they had in common was extraordinarily long black lashes. As they discussed the production, Richard thought how different they were from the girls at work whose main topic of conversation was fashion.

"What's Mimi going to die of?" Jacqueline asked Phillipa.

"Cancer."

Natasha grinned. "I've brought an extra supply of hankies."

Jacqueline nudged her. "I'll be inconsolable when you're up there dying."

"Maybe I'll be with you playing Marcello."

"And I won't be in it at all," complained Jacqueline.

"You can be Musetta," said Richard magnanimously, thinking how enjoyable it was to be talking about opera.

She shook her head. "I'm a contralto."

"You could all be in *Rigoletto*," said Phillipa.

The bell ending the interval rang.

As they went up the steps, he wanted to suggest that they all meet

85

afterwards and go somewhere for coffee, but he was worried they would refuse.

At the top of the staircase they went in the other direction.

"Bye, Richard. See you at the party on New Year's Eve," called Natasha.

'I hope I won't have to wait that long,' he thought, cursing his lack of confidence.

At the end he clapped until his palms tingled. When the final curtain came down, he saw Jacqueline, Natasha, and Phillipa on the other side of the theatre. He waved, but they didn't see him. Hoping he would meet them in the foyer, he went down the stairs, but they were nowhere to be seen. He waited in vain as the theatre emptied. 'Perhaps I'll see her at *Carmen* or *André Chénier*. I should have asked what night they were going.'

Phillipa turned the pages of *The Age*.

"Perhaps they haven't bothered to review it," Nicholas said, feeling that nothing he did would please the critics.

"Here it is." Phillipa scanned the first paragraph. "Fantastic!" She hugged him.

Harriet pulled the paper to her side of the desk. "Thank goodness for that!"

Nicholas grinned. "Does anyone mind if I read it?"

"Of course not, brilliant, young director," said Harriet.

"Is that what it says?" not daring to believe her.

Harriet smiled and gave him the paper.

Phillipa left the office and reappeared five minutes later with a bottle of champagne and three glasses. "I put it in the fridge last night. I knew the reviews would be good."

"Phillipa, you fibber," said Harriet. "You were more worried than I was."

As the audience gathered for *Eugene Onegin,* Deborah wished she had someone to go with. Everyone was in pairs or groups and she seemed to be the only person alone. She saw Phillipa with two other girls and Nicholas. She was going to join them when she saw Harriet standing nearby talking to two women and a man. Dressed in a green silk dress with a silver and pearl brooch, she looked less forbidding than she had at the audition.

"Hello, Deborah."

She looked at her singing teacher in relief. "Oh, Miss Williams."

As they chatted about Nicholas's production of *La Bohème* she felt happier.

"There's Miss Shaw." Ingrid waved. "Let's go and say hello."

Harriet abruptly left the group. Deborah saw two of them looking concerned.

"Oh, she's gone," said Ingrid. "I wanted to thank her for sending you to me."

'She went because she saw me,' thought Deborah, who had seen Harriet's expression of repugnance.

Chapter 9

'She has written.
What has she written?'
The Turn of the Screw – Britten

Articles about Harriet Shaw and her successful students, heightened Max Carveth's dissatisfaction. He stared moodily at the photo of the two baritones who had just signed contracts with the Australian Opera, noting with resentment that they were both younger than he was. Instead of signing the letters his secretary had typed, his thoughts drifted back eight years to the classes at opera school, the hours spent in the cafés afterwards, and the excitement of working on the scenes they had to prepare.

Now his social life revolved round the tennis club his father-in-law had insisted he join. None of the members were interested in opera and their conversation consisted of either dissecting every tennis match they played or discussing their children.

Jamming *The Herald* in the wastepaper basket, he went to the car park reserved for the bank's executives and got into his respectable Holden. As soon as he opened the front door of his house in Caulfield, his wife ran down the hall, crying hysterically. Terrified that something had happened to their daughter, he dropped his briefcase. Susan flung herself at him. Finally he realized what she was trying to tell him. Her father was dead.

At the time of his death, Susan's father had been on holiday in America. During the complicated arrangements to get the body flown back to Australia, Max had no time to think. As the funeral car stopped in front of St Mary's Church in Caulfield, he suddenly realized he was free. Inside the church, he opened his hymn book and thought about the letter he was going to write to Harriet Shaw. While the vicar read the eulogy, his mood swung between elation at the thought of returning to opera school, and fear as he remembered that Harriet and most of the

88

teachers had disapproved of his behaviour. Encouraged that Hugh, the most vitriolic of his detractors, had died in January, he hoped that Nicholas Forrester was more liberal. 'He's young, and from what the critics said about his production of *Bohème* he sounds radical,' Max thought.

He knew that many people envied him and Susan. Their daughter Zoe was attractive and clever. Max earned plenty of money at the bank, and they had a tennis court and swimming pool. But he detested the modern house with its chrome, glass and leather furniture, and landscaped garden. He preferred more sensual surroundings. Left to his own devices, the house would have been a monument to decadence, with antique furniture, mirrors and pictures of half-naked women on the walls, like the house he had been rented before he married.

The Edwardian terrace in Parkville had been in keeping with Max's love of hedonism, and enhanced his image as a well-off young executive, who, although not serious about the world of banking, did his job extremely well and with consummate ease. Girls came and went, and when they were not in bed they did his housework. Max bought the best clothes he could afford. A large section of the wardrobe was reserved for the formal clothes he wore to balls and dinner dances.

He had met Susan Smith at the bank. Feeling sorry for her because some of his male colleagues had made her cry with their gibes about her weight, he had taken her out to lunch. Seeing himself as Susan's rescuer, he tried to make her feel more confident by praising her two good features – glossy dark hair and beautiful hands and fingernails. She was so different from the glamorous girls he usually dated, he found her an interesting change. She lived with her parents, went to church, and wanted to stay a virgin until she got married. She asked him to meet her mother and father, but invitations from girlfriends to meet their parents made him feel hunted, as did talk about marriage. After three months, Max had still not seduced her. Threats to drop her did not work, although they distressed her.

Eventually he used the word that he considered taboo. "You don't love me."

"I do," she said ardently.

"You can't. If you did you'd want to make our relationship complete."

"Do you love me, Max?" she asked breathlessly.

"I've never talked about love with any girl before," he said, skilfully avoiding the question while priding himself on telling the truth at the same time.

"Oh, Max."

Unknown to Susan, he was also going out with two fellow students in the opera school. Exhausted by the demands of three women and alarmed by Susan's hints about getting engaged, he ended their relationship. To his relief, she took the news stoically and asked to be transferred to another branch. He was so involved with juggling his new girlfriends, he had almost forgotten about Susan when she came to his house two months later.

"Max, I have to talk to you."

He tried to remember her name.

Tears flooded her eyes. "I'm Susan."

He felt guilty. "I'm going to opera school and I can't find one of my books. Can't it wait?"

She shook her head. "I'm pregnant."

Max strode down the hall. "You said everything was all right."

He heard her gasp. "No, you told me it would be all right."

"Most girls take care of these things themselves, Susan. You've been careless."

"But I – after you told me it was all right I … "

He shook his head. "Your naivety astounds me." He looked round the untidy lounge for his German text book. "You'll have to have an abortion."

"But it's illegal." He heard the horror in her voice.

He lifted scores of music from the piano. "Not if you go to the doctor and threaten to kill yourself. Where's my bloody book?"

"I'm not having an abortion, Max, you'll have to marry me," she sobbed.

"Susan," he said, trying to sound patient. "I'm going to be an opera singer, not a dull husband tied down to a wife and child and working in the bank for the rest of my life. I'm staying single till I'm thirty. When I do marry, it'll be to a glamorous and beautiful opera singer. Stop sniffing, you sound like a pig." He knelt down and looked under the sofa. "Here it is." He pulled out the book and put it in his briefcase.

"Have an abortion. I'll give you the money."

She blew her nose. "You said you loved me. Please stand still, Max. What are we going to do? We've got to talk."

"I haven't got time." He went down the hall and took his sports jacket off the newel post.

"Are you seeing another girl?"

He tutted and rolled his eyes upward. "Of course I am, and if you've got any sense you'll have an abortion and get yourself another boyfriend."

"No. I want you to take the responsibility for your baby."

"Sue, get rid of it," he pleaded, repelled by her blotchy face.

"I'm not murdering our baby."

"It's not a baby yet – it's only a little clump of cells."

"You were a little clump of cells once, Max."

He opened the front door. "Susan, if you want to be an unmarried mother … "

"I don't – I want you to marry me."

"If you're foolish enough to have the baby, give it up for adoption. I don't want anything to do with it."

She looked devastated.

He went outside and got into his red sports car, leaving her standing on the footpath. 'She'll see sense,' he thought.

Two days later he received a summons from the chairman of the bank. Convinced that his application for a promotion to a management grade had been approved, although he was only twenty-one, he ran up the staircase to the second floor. Pleased that the chairman thought highly enough of him to tell him personally, he gave his name to the receptionist. He was ushered immediately into the luxurious office.

The chairman glared at him. "I'm Susan Smith's father."

At the end of an hour the date of the wedding had been decided, and Max went to the door hoping Susan would have a miscarriage.

Pregnancy did not suit her, she had gained more weight and looked sallow. Even dressed in the full bridal regalia, she looked plain. Happy, but plain. And fat. He had felt wretched as he took the vows at the altar. At the reception Susan's father told him he was approving a further promotion for him. Then he said, "And, Max, you'll have to give up opera school. You won't have time for that nonsense. I want you to be a proper husband and a good father to my grandchild."

For Max, his daughter Zoe, who was now eight, was the one redeeming feature in his marriage. His unselfish love for her surprised him, and everyone who knew him.

When Harriet received Max's letter, she remembered him immediately. She also remembered the girls who had arrived for their singing lessons and started crying. Max was always the reason. She began reading his file that Phillipa had retrieved from the archives. When she came to Hugh's end of term assessment, she remembered him storming into her office one Saturday after a first year drama class. It was one of the few times he had lost his temper. It was the only time she had heard him swear. She laughed at the memory, and Phillipa and Nicholas looked up from sifting through the letters that were pouring in about the production of *La Bohème*.

"I'm thinking about a most unpleasant operation that is only performed on men."

Phillipa looked at Nicholas. "What have you done now?"

"Done with a rusty saw without an anaesthetic," Harriet said with relish.

Nicholas dropped the letter he was reading. "I've got an urgent appointment."

"It's all right, Nicholas," said Harriet. "One of my ex-students wants me to have him back." She passed the file to Nicholas. "I had to deal with all the anguished girls he captivated then dropped. By the end of 1960 I felt like a social worker. Hugh wanted to have him operated on."

Nicholas shrugged. "Then don't have him back."

"There are two things to be considered. His family is rich, and while he was a student they donated a hefty sum to the theatre every year – it stopped as soon as he left."

Phillipa put the letters in a neat pile. "It's only money – is he worth all the aggravation?"

"Ah, that's the other thing. He once told me he was going to be the best tenor in the world. If he'd kept up with his singing career he would be well on the way to achieving his ambition. He was also very handsome, tall, and his physique was superb."

"He might be bald now," said Phillipa.

"He might be faithful to his wife," said Nicholas, turning the pages of Max's file.

Harriet grunted. "I doubt it."

Nicholas grimaced. "He might even be a soprano."

When Harriet's letter arrived, Max held his breath and tore the flap open.

29th November 1968

Dear Max,

Thank you for your letter.
To make sure that the quality of your voice has not changed, you will have to have an informal audition. Please ring my secretary, Miss Matthews, and she will arrange an appointment for you.

Harriet was surprised by how little Max had changed. He still had the polish, confidence and charm of the spoilt child born into a world of wealth. Intuitively she knew that his charm disguised his arrogance. From the first day she had met him, when he was seventeen, she had guessed that he was weak. Now twenty-eight, he was still extremely good looking. The light brown hair that turned blonde in the summer was as thick as it had been eight years ago, and his handsome face showed none of the signs of dissipation she had expected. His cream linen suit and burgundy striped tie looked expensive and his brown shoes and briefcase shone as only the best leather can. Gold cuff links, engraved with his initials, secured the double cuffs of his dazzlingly white shirt. His aftershave smelt of lemons.

As he sang the first note of 'The Flower Song' from *Carmen* Harriet heard that his voice also remained unchanged.

"Yes, Max, that was good, although your breath control and technique are not what they should be."

Seeing his expression of relief she realized how worried he had been.

"Thank you, Miss Shaw. So, I can start opera school in January then?"

His swift return of confidence irked her. "No."

He looked apprehensive. "Are you going to teach me?"

"Yes."

"Miss Shaw, I don't have to wait the full three years before I go to opera school, do I?"

"We might be able to cut that down to two. If you reach the required standard, you can start opera school in 1971."

"But I'm impatient to get on after wasting all those years."

"You'll be thirty-one when you join the opera school again. That's not old." She handed him his score. "Because you haven't sung for eight years your voice is still in excellent condition. Rest never harms the voice, only overworking it."

He smiled boyishly. "Is there any chance that I could start opera school after a year? I promise to do my breathing exercises – I'll start as soon as I get home."

She knew he was trying to charm her. "No, Max," she said firmly.

"But I did a whole year of opera school." His charm faded and his voice was petulant. "I can remember every lesson – I kept my notes."

"A break of eight years is too long." She looked at him sternly. "You've forgotten too much about technique and breathing and it will take you two years to catch up. If you'd done your exercises we could have got away with one year. When you start opera school you must be able to concentrate on the classes, so that when you begin your professional career your stagecraft is so ingrained it's instinctive."

She closed the lid of the piano. "You know how demanding the first year of opera school is. Most students say it's the most difficult and find the second and third years easy by comparison. Because you'll have so many things to think about, it's vital that your technique and breathing are perfect by the time you start opera school. Why did you decide to begin again after all this time?" She saw that her question unsettled him.

"My father-in-law died."

She frowned. "What has that got to do with resuming your singing career? I'm not trying to pry into your private life, but I want to be sure that you're serious. Your training costs a great deal of time and money. It's a shame when they're wasted."

He looked at her sincerely. "I am serious – very serious, Miss Shaw. But my father-in-law was also the chairman of the bank where I worked. He made me marry Susan and give up opera school."

She allowed a lengthy pause to develop, before saying, "Do you remember writing to me and telling me you were giving up singing?"

"Yes."

"Do you remember the reason you gave?"

Max looked evasive. "It was a long time ago."

She pulled his letter out from under her diary. "You told me you were getting married and your fiancée's father wanted you to become his partner in an exciting business venture. But there was more to it, wasn't there?"

Max looked embarrassed. "Well. Susan was … you know."

"I see. But how did her father make you give up singing?"

"He would have blocked my promotions."

She shook her head. "You didn't think very far ahead, did you? If you'd continued with your singing, you would have been at Covent Garden by now. I don't think I'm exaggerating when I say that your voice would be generating a great deal of excitement. It concerns me that you allowed this man to control your life for eight years. Why didn't you marry Susan and stay at opera school?"

Max looked chastened. "I don't know. At the time, I was so shocked I couldn't think of the alternatives."

"Perhaps if you had talked to me and told me the truth, instead of writing a letter, we could have worked something out."

"Miss Shaw, nothing will make me give up this time."

"Good." Although tempted, she decided not to lecture him about morality. He might have changed. She opened her diary. "Then let's set a date for your lessons."

Max left the theatre feeling elated. He got into his car and turned on the radio.

"She's got a ticket to ride," sang The Beatles.

"I've got a ticket to Covent Garden," sang Max. "In two years, I'll be surrounded by girls. Sue, you don't stand a chance!" he said loudly over the music.

Chapter 10

'Rouse again the sound of pleasure.
Drain the wine cup, tread the measure!
Joyful hours will soon be gone,
Let the night run gaily on!'
Romeo and Juliet – Gounod

"You've got to try on the trousers," said Phillipa.

Nicholas shook his head. "They'll be all right."

She looked at him in exasperation. "And if they're not?"

"I'll come back and change them."

"How much time will that waste? If you try them on now … "

He held up his hand in surrender and handed her the dinner jacket. "Okay." He turned towards the fitting rooms. "While I'm in here, choose a bow tie for me."

"What colour?"

"I don't care. And a shirt – I don't care what it's like either."

Phillipa watched him walk away. 'You asked for it, Nicholas,' she thought with a grin.

When he came out of the fitting room, she kept her expression serious as she showed him the frilly blue dinner shirt and satin bow tie she had chosen.

"I'm not wearing them," he said indignantly.

"You said you didn't care."

"I didn't think you'd choose hideous things like that. Can you see me in an electric blue tie?"

She put on a hurt expression. "I think they're nice."

He looked uncertain.

She wanted to prolong the teasing, but spluttered with laughter, and took him to the plain white shirt, dress studs and black velvet bow tie she had selected.

"Perfect," he said. "I knew I could depend on you."

Although Nicholas loathed shopping, Phillipa hoped that her presence was making it more bearable.

He looked at his watch. "Shall we have some lunch when we've bought Aunt Harriet's Christmas presents?"

"What about going to the beach? I can make sandwiches," she said, careful to sound offhand.

"Good idea, Philly."

Phillipa, delighted that she would be spending more time with him, turned away, not wanting him to see her expression. Nicholas was less impatient when they were choosing Harriet's presents, and she realized that it was buying clothes for himself that he most disliked.

At Half Moon Bay, three hours later, Phillipa tried not to gaze at his body, tanned and lean in bathing trunks.

Nicholas laughed.

"What's funny?"

He spread out his beach towel. "I've never been to the beach after Christmas shopping before. Shall we brave the sharks and go for a swim?"

"Sharks don't usually come into the bay area."

He grimaced. "But they do sometimes, and I can't help thinking that one might bite my leg off."

She sat down and undid her sandals. "Do you still feel homesick?"

He nodded. "I miss England's greenness and history."

"Are you happier?" she dared herself to ask. "Than you were when you arrived here, I mean?"

He looked contemplative. "About some things. The air's incredibly clean. And I feel healthier."

Longing for him to tell her that she was one of the reasons he was happier, she tried to look amused. "You look healthier too. Is that all?"

His expression became distant.

'He's thinking about Sally,' she thought. 'She slept with another man, aborted the baby that might have been his, but I think he still loves her. Nothing I've done or said has made any difference. I've been part of his life for almost a year, yet I've hardly left a mark.' She jumped up. "Beat you to the water!" she cried. Running down the beach, she plunged into the sea.

♪   ♪   ♪

As Harriet dressed on New Year's Eve in a ball gown of ivory lace, she hoped that the friendship between Nicholas and Phillipa would deepen into something more serious. Her desire for a match between them did not entirely stem from altruism. If Nicholas and Phillipa got married, they would stay with her as her family. Harriet's relationships with her students, were, for the most part, transient. However much affection and gratitude they felt for her, they usually left to sing with The Australian Opera or overseas. Many kept religiously in touch, but it was not the same as having a family. Even in those heady days as Covent Garden's rising young star she had wanted marriage and children. She had achieved neither. Unwillingly the image of Annabel flitted into her mind. "No," she whispered with determination. The doorbell rang and she walked down the hall and got into the taxi.

Harriet, Phillipa and Nicholas were the first to arrive at the theatre. Phillipa wore a white chiffon gown, with her hair swept up and adorned with a circle of yellow rosebuds. Round her neck she wore the pearls Harriet had given her for Christmas.

"You look like a Greek goddess, Philly," said Nicholas.

Seeing Phillipa's joyful smile and Nicholas's look of admiration, Harriet was hopeful that tonight they would become more than friends.

The studios were decorated with Christmas trees and coloured lights, and trestle-tables covered with white tablecloths were laden with food.

The President of The Friends hurried over to them. "Does it look all right, Miss Shaw?" she asked anxiously.

"Everything looks beautiful," Harriet said warmly. "I'm so grateful for all your hard work."

Later in the evening, when Harriet was filling her plate with salad from the buffet, she saw Ingrid Williams.

"Hello, Miss Shaw."

"Ingrid, how lovely to see you."

"I've been trying to get to see you for hours, but you're always surrounded by people. Congratulations on *Bohème*, it was brilliant."

The girl who had played Musetta was Ingrid's student. Harriet chuckled as she remembered the final dress rehearsal. Musetta, in a ferocious attack of nerves, had been convinced the stilettos would make her fall over and break her leg during the waltz song. Her fear had infected Mimì, who had burst into tears and said that by the time the critics had finished with her she would have no career left, but three days ago they had both signed contracts with The Australian Opera.

"Nicholas's gamble paid off. I was frightened we'd lose money, but we've got two more corporate patrons. You're doing very well, Ingrid, five of your students start opera school in February. That tenor has a lovely voice – he'll go a long way. I didn't send him to you, did I?"

"No, he found me in the phone book." Ingrid cut a slice of pavlova. "Do you remember the girl you sent me earlier in the year?"

"Which one was that?" Harriet asked, although she knew.

"Deborah Ryland – stunning looking girl."

"Oh yes. I remember. How's she doing?" asked Harriet, hoping that Ingrid would say she had left.

"Exceptionally well. She's very keen and has started having piano lessons." She hesitated. "For some reason she got the impression at her audition that you didn't like her and won't let her join the opera school. I've tried to reassure her, but she's worried, so I promised I'd speak to you."

Harriet raised her eyebrows. "How strange – I wonder why she thought that." She picked up a knife and fork. "If she wants to join the opera school in two years time I'll be more than happy to have her."

Ingrid looked apologetic. "I told her she was being oversensitive. She looks confident but she's insecure. She hasn't had much of a life – her mother treats her badly and she thinks everybody hates her. It's taken me months to get her to trust me."

Harriet speared a piece of camembert with her fork. "Oh dear."

"Anyway, I'll tell her she was wrong. She'll be delighted. I won't monopolize you, Miss Shaw, lots of people are waiting to speak to you." She kissed her cheek. "Happy New Year."

For the next hour Harriet chatted with people, but her mind was on her conversation with Ingrid. 'A lot can happen in two years,' she thought, remembering how many promising students had dropped out before they went to opera school. 'Especially women. They get

99

married, have babies and either get settled in domestic bliss or their husbands won't let them continue. I'm being ridiculous. What's the matter with me? Deborah is Deborah. She's not Annabel and I'm foolish to be thinking like this. But I can't help it,' she added bleakly.

"Is Natasha drunk?" Nicholas asked Phillipa at eleven o'clock.

"No, she's hobbling. She's never worn high heels before. Uh, ah, here comes Max."

"Hello, Nicholas, Phillipa. Terrific party."

Nicholas, who wished he could take off his bow tie, wondered how Max could look so at ease in a dinner suit.

Max smiled at Phillipa. "Would you like to dance?"

"I'd love to. Is Susan enjoying herself?"

"Um. She couldn't come."

"What a shame," said Phillipa sympathetically. "Couldn't you get a baby sitter?"

"No."

Nicholas could see Max struggling to disguise his discomfort. He grinned at Phillipa. "I'll hold your glass for you."

"Thanks," She winked at him and took Max's arm.

'Good on you, Philly,' thought Nicholas as he watched them walk away.

He saw Jacqueline going up the staircase. The wide skirt of her crimson taffeta ball gown was hitched up over her knees and she was taking two steps at a time. Giving Phillipa's glass to a passing waiter, he went over to Natasha, who was about to follow Jacqueline. Her cheeks were flushed, and her eyes glittered with excitement. She wore no make-up or jewellery and her hair hung in a shining mass of curls down her back.

"Natasha, would you like to dance?"

"I'd love to, but I can't," she said cheerfully. "I trip over my feet, and with these horrible shoes on I'll fall over. I wish I could take them off." Wincing, she lifted the hem of her yellow satin ball gown. "I've got blisters."

"Give me a look." The blister on her left heel had broken and her stocking was bloodstained. "Come with me."

She took his arm and he led her, tottering, down the corridor.

"Jacqui and I start working at Prince Henry's Hospital next week," she said excitedly.

"Congratulations. Harriet told me you had interviews."

"We found out yesterday. I'm on the outpatient reception desk and Jacqui's in admissions. We've got to wear uniforms too – it's great that we don't have to worry about clothes."

He opened the door of his office. "Leave your shoes in here."

She kicked them off and tossed them into a corner. "That's better." She looked at her feet and Nicholas admired her eyelashes which rested like thick black feathers above her cheekbones.

"Can I take my stockings off?"

He grinned indulgently. "Go on. I'll wait outside."

Emerging with a conspiratorial smile, she said, "I took my suspender belt off too."

He laughed. "If anyone goes in there tonight my reputation will be tarnished."

"Men don't have to worry about reputations." She sighed. "I wish I was a boy. They can wear comfortable clothes."

He touched the stiff front of his shirt. "This is far from comfortable, but I'd guess it's better than wearing stockings."

"I can't understand men who want to be women, can you?"

"No. We get all the exciting parts in Shakespeare."

"I went to a girls' school so I wasn't stuck with the boring female parts. I was Brutus in *Julius Caesar*. It was terrific when I had to run on my sword. 'Caesar now be still. I killed not thee with half so good a will.' That was my favourite bit."

"Bloodthirsty monster." He held out his hand. "Come on, let's dance." The strains of 'Ruby Tuesday' came from the disco in the theatrette. "Do you like The Stones?"

Natasha pulled a face. "Not much."

"Shall I teach you to waltz?"

"You can try! Do you like my dress? Philly chose it for me." She twirled round, the yards of material in the skirt swirling in her wake. Her gown was a similar style to Jacqueline's, but while Jacqueline's enhanced her voluptuous beauty, Natasha looked like a child who had dressed up in her mother's gown. Her thin arms protruded at the elbows from the puffed sleeves and her collar bones jutted aggressively above

101

the neckline.

Thinking she had the most expressive face he'd ever seen, he smiled. "It's beautiful. Come on, I'll teach you how to waltz." He took her into the largest studio where an orchestra was playing Viennese Waltzes. Natasha was an energetic but uncoordinated dancer and, as she had told him, she kept tripping over her feet. Just as she began to get into the rhythm, she was pulled from his arms and he found himself in the clutches of a girl from the drama school. "You're a handsome hunk."

"Excuse me," he said coldly, recoiling from her breath, stale from too many cigarettes. "I was dancing with someone."

"I'm prettier than her, and I can dance. She's plain and clumsy."

"You're drunk and conceited." He looked distastefully at the hand holding his arm. Her long nails were scarlet. "Let me go."

The girl scowled. "Stuck up Pom!"

"And you've got halitosis," he snapped.

"Five minutes to midnight!" announced the leader of the orchestra.

Phillipa appeared and put a glass of champagne into his hand. He looked around for Natasha, hoping she had not heard the cruel remarks, but she was not in the room.

Richard felt uncomfortable. He hardly knew anyone and was too shy to join a group and introduce himself. He had chatted briefly to Phillipa, but someone had rushed up and waltzed off with her. Knowing he looked uncomfortable made him feel foolish. Deciding to go home he walked down the corridor, turned the corner and almost collided with Nicholas.

"Richard. You're not leaving already, are you? It's only one o'clock. Stay till dawn and have a champagne breakfast – there are strawberries and mangoes too."

He was not embarrassed to admit his discomfort to Nicholas. "I don't really know anyone."

"I'll introduce you to some students who'll be starting opera school with you. Parties are awful if you don't know anyone," Nicholas said as they went into the foyer. "You did well to stay this long. Look, there's Max, Jacqueline and Natasha – they're all Miss Shaw's students."

"I've met Jacqueline and Natasha, but not Max."

Nicholas introduced Richard to Max and then turned to Natasha. "We didn't finish our dance."

"I thought you'd be relieved. How are your toes?"

He winked at her. "It's your toes we should be worrying about."

She stuck out her foot. "Nobody's trodden on them yet."

"You poor waif," said Max. "Can't you afford a pair of shoes?"

"No," said Jacqueline. "After we'd bought our dresses we could only afford one pair, so we agreed that Natasha would wear them till midnight and I'd wear them after."

Nicholas laughed. "You said that very convincingly. I'm looking forward to having you in my drama class. Now, Natasha, shall we dance?"

As they swept off, Max turned to Jacqueline. "May I have the pleasure?"

She curtsied. "Certainly. Bye, Richard, see you later. Happy nineteen sixty-nine!"

As the strains of 'The Merry Widow Waltz' came down the corridor, Richard was left alone.

Part Two

CURTAIN UP

1971

February to December

Chapter 11

'My first foolish fears
are all vanished now.'
The Turn of the Screw – Britten

On the first Saturday in February, Harriet arrived at the theatre at eight in the morning, prepared for hours of uninterrupted work, but she lacked the excitement she always felt at the start of a new year. Vocally, the first year students were the most gifted group she had ever had. Usually a class contained two voices, at the most, that could be called outstanding. This year there were seven.

In three years, Natasha's voice had developed a strength that had surpassed Harriet's expectations. Emily, a coloratura, sang the 'Bell Song' from *Lakmé* and both Queen of the Night arias, with an ease that even Harriet thought remarkable.

Max was the best tenor she had ever taught. 'I hope he won't allow anyone to stand in the way of his career, this time,' she thought.

Jacqueline's contralto was dark and expressive and she had a long range. Frank was a bass, whose voice reached astonishing depths. She had only taught one baritone as good as Richard, and that had been thirty years ago.

Then there was Deborah. For weeks Harriet had pushed aside her feeling of dread, but now she forced herself to face it. Deborah had not lost interest or got married. She was starting opera school today and Harriet would have to see her. She missed Hugh desperately. He was the only person she had told about Annabel, and she needed his support.

'She won't look like Annabel today,' she told herself. 'She dressed up for her audition, but today she'll be casual. And she won't be wearing that fur coat. I saw her three years ago and I wasn't prepared. Now I am, and I'll be able to cope with it.'

♪   ♪   ♪

Max took off his wedding ring and examined the band of paler skin that had not completely darkened despite his efforts to expose it to the sun whenever possible. Deciding it was hardly noticeable, he put it in his pocket. Susan was at the tennis club and had taken their daughter, Zoe, with her. He went into the garage and got into his car. As he drove to the theatre, he listened to a cassette of *Aida*. 'I'll be singing Radamès one day and opera lovers everywhere, will be listening to me,' he thought.

Ignoring the instruction to wear casual clothes, Deborah dressed in a Mary Quant dress. As her mother was on a skiing holiday in Switzerland, she helped herself to her jewellery and perfume. She looked at herself in the full length mirror. 'Mother, one of these days I'm going to make you cringe. I'm going to punish you for everything you've done to me. I've kept a list. I'll pay you back and mock you the way you've mocked me.'

Just after starting her singing lessons, she had bought a piano. To her fury, her mother had refused to let it in the house when it had been delivered. Because she had been unable to practise, her progress was slow and she had failed the test which would have exempted her from the music classes at opera school.

As she parked her mother's red Mercedes, her excitement evaporated. She was the only pupil of Ingrid Williams in the first year and she felt disadvantaged because she didn't know any of the other students. Apprehensively, she walked towards the theatre.

Richard, in his determination not to be late, arrived an hour early. Aware that he looked awkward standing in the deserted corridor, he sat down and took out his diary. The dates for his drama, language and movement classes were already entered, but he filled in the time by checking them. When he heard the door open, he looked up and saw an exotic, fashionably dressed girl with dark hair. He went back to his diary. She was obviously not a student.

"Hello," she said brightly. "Are you for the opera school?"

108

He stood up. "Yes."

"I'm Deborah Ryland."

Her perfume was overpowering and she reminded him of the brittle girls in the public service. "Richard Greythorn. I'm a first year."

"Oh good, so am I. I'm sure I saw you at the music test," she said flirtatiously. "Did you pass?"

He felt uncomfortable. "Yes. Did you?"

"I only just failed. Are you exempt from German or Italian?"

"No," he replied, wishing someone else would arrive.

She smiled brilliantly. "Neither am I."

Jacqueline and Natasha, wearing jeans and short sleeved shirts, burst through the door, talking excitedly. He excused himself and joined them.

Feeling rejected, Deborah stood alone. As others arrived, they greeted people they already knew and she was ignored. She followed everyone into the theatrette, and saw a girl sitting alone, biting her nails.

Deborah sat next to her. "Hello, I'm Deborah Ryland."

The girl blushed. "Hello," she mumbled.

"What's your name?"

"Emily Kuznetzov."

"How exotic. Are you Russian?"

Emily chewed the raw skin round her thumbnail. "No."

"Polish?"

Emily shook her head.

Deborah was becoming exasperated. "What are you?"

"Australian."

"How come you've got a Russian name?"

"My grandfather is."

"Can you speak Russian?"

"No."

"Are you Miss Shaw's student?"

"Yes."

Deborah tried to talk about something else, but Emily continued to answer in monosyllables. 'What a dill,' she thought. She counted the other students who were talking excitedly. Including herself there were twenty-four, of whom eleven were men. She was pleased that some of them were good looking, one extraordinarily so. She heard someone call him Max. 'It suits him,' she thought.

Nicholas was sitting at the front, marking the attendance register. When Harriet entered, silence fell. Dressed in a lilac suit with a white blouse and grey shoes, she looked elegant and authoritative.

She smiled. "Good afternoon, and welcome to the opera school. Years ago singers stood at the front of the stage and sang. I once saw a performance of *Tosca* and if I had not known the plot, I would have thought Tosca and Scarpia were lovers. These days, opera singers have to give their audience visual pleasure, otherwise they may as well stay at home and listen to their records. For the next three years, you will be learning how to be opera singers who can act, move, clearly pronounce your words in French, Italian or German, and intelligently interpret whatever role you are playing."

Deborah felt inspired. 'She's great,' she thought, nodding in agreement.

"This school is open to anyone gifted, regardless of the amount of money they or their parents have," Harriet continued. "That's why it is part-time and you're all on scholarships. Those who finish this course will automatically gain a principal place in the opera company. Then you'll be professional singers. Every year, many people audition for a place and only the best make it. We are giving you a great deal. In return, we demand your total dedication. God or nature has given you a wonderful gift. Never abuse it."

Deborah noticed that during her speech Harriet had looked at everyone but her.

During the half hour of warming up exercises, Nicholas praised Natasha's imagination, and Deborah was discouraged that he didn't praise her. After one improvisation, Max looked at her admiringly and asked if she was a model. His attention made her feel more confident.

"Drama is real life – with all the boring bits cut out," said Nicholas. "Drama is about objectives and obstacles. If you don't have objectives, you have no purpose. If there are no obstacles in the way of your objectives, there's no conflict. If there's no conflict, there's no drama."

'What a divine voice he's got,' thought Deborah.

"Objectives must be expressed in terms of 'I want' and 'I am going to'. Make them active not passive. 'I want to get the part' is passive. 'I am going to make them give me the part' is active. They must be positive not negative. 'I don't want to be poor' is negative. Who can turn it into a positive?"

"I want to be rich," said Max.

Nicholas nodded. "Good. You want to be opera singers. That's your objective. But you don't wander into Covent Garden, have an audition and get a principal role."

Deborah laughed. No one else did. She saw Harriet frowning, and lowered her head in embarrassment.

"So, your objectives have to be broken down into units," Nicholas continued. "First, you found a singing teacher and had an audition. Then you had three years of lessons before you began opera school. Now you have another three years of hard work at opera school. You all have day jobs, but even if you're tired you must come to classes, because if any are missed we'll want to know why. Miss too many classes for no good reason – and you're out. You may find the classes exhausting, but if you want to be an opera singer these are obstacles you must overcome.

"With objectives in mind, you're all going to do a series of improvisations. Deborah, Natasha, Max, Richard and Emily stay there. Jacqueline and Frank, come to the front. Everyone else, sit down and watch. This is the situation. You're waiting for a train. It's already half an hour late. You're all going somewhere important. When you've established a scene, Frank, you're going to enter, drop a bombshell, then leave. When they're reacting to the bombshell, Jacqueline, you're going to enter and end the scene. Start when you're ready."

Deborah saw that Emily was shaking with nerves. She decided to make a good impression on Harriet and Nicholas by starting the scene. "I've got to get to work. I'll be sacked if I'm late!" she said, her voice high with impending hysterics.

"What time do you start?" asked Natasha.

"Nine."

Richard looked at his watch. "Looks as if you've got the sack then."

Deborah pretended to burst into tears and was pleased when Max comforted her.

"Where are you going?" Natasha asked Emily.

She turned crimson. "Um. An interview," she mumbled.

111

"Bloody train. I've got to catch a plane to Sydney," said Richard.

Frank came into the scene and looked at them in surprise. "What are you doing here?"

"Waiting for a train, of course," said Max.

"You've missed it. They only come once a week."

"Don't be silly," said Natasha. "I use this station every day. Where's the train?"

Frank looked indignant. "I'm the station master so I know when the train comes."

Natasha put her hands on her hips. "I'm trying to get to a funeral."

Frank shrugged. "It came yesterday."

"Stop fooling around! I've got to get to Sydney today," said Richard.

Frank laughed. "What are you going to do – fly?"

"Yes, I was hoping to. What's the matter, you dimwit?"

Frank looked blank. "What?" He glared at Natasha and Emily. "Trousers! Women shouldn't wear trousers. Dressing like a man won't get you the vote." Then he turned to Deborah. "As for you – have you no decency?"

"What year do you think this is?" asked Max.

"Eighteen ninety."

Deborah screamed.

"You're crazy," said Natasha.

"I've got today's paper here – look."

Natasha mimed taking it from him. "The date! Look! Queen Victoria – "

Deborah screamed again and Frank left.

Natasha ran after him, then came back looking stunned. "He disappeared. He was there and then he … just vanished."

"What are we going to do?" asked Richard.

Deborah threw herself into Max's arms. "Help! I'm so frightened."

Jacqueline strode into the scene. "April Fools!"

Everyone laughed.

"That," said Nicholas, "was potentially a gripping scene. Frank's idea was intriguing – it gave you something to work on." He laughed. "Too intriguing actually, because it diverted you away from your objectives. Richard threw in some dry wit and his question near the end of the scene was a good attempt to get back to objectives. Natasha intelligently picked up the thread of Frank's idea. Jacqueline's ending was simple and effective."

Harriet frowned. "Unfortunately, with all the screaming, it became melodramatic."

"Deborah, you began the scene well with a strong objective," said Nicholas. "But why did you scream?"

Deborah felt confused. She thought she had added drama. "I was frightened."

Nicholas shook his head. "You overreacted. If Frank had pointed a gun at you, then it would have been natural to scream."

Deborah felt her cheeks burning, but Nicholas smiled at her. "Screaming can strain the delicate vocal cords. You have a beautiful voice, so look after it."

Towards the end of the class he told everyone to sit down. "Your homework requires a lot of thought." He picked up two boxes. "These contain pieces of paper on which is written the name of a character and the opera from which they come. Men pick a role from the blue box and girls a role from the red one. We've chosen scenes from nine operas. You won't be singing, so it doesn't matter if sopranos have contralto roles or tenors have baritone ones and vice versa. The object of the exercise is to interpret and understand your character."

Deborah, hoping she would be doing a scene with Max, was disappointed when she drew out Second Lady from *The Magic Flute*.

"This has to be ready for next week and perfected by the Saturday after," said Nicholas.

"Oh!" said Deborah before she could stop herself.

But Nicholas smiled. "Don't look so horrified. You'll be surprised by what you can achieve in a week. Dress up if you want to and use props because they are an excellent way to keep the hands occupied. Come and get the librettos, some guidelines and a summary of your first class. Then find your partners and discuss your characters."

Harriet was relieved when the class ended. Usually she mingled with the students, but she left the theatrette and went straight to her office.

Nicholas followed her. "What's wrong?"

"Deborah's given me a headache. She arrives looking ready for the catwalk, then she screams and overacts."

"There's always at least one student in every class who gets over-excited," said Nicholas. "I feel sorry for her. She reminds me of a puppy anxious for approval."

"She reminded me of a spoilt brat," Harriet snapped. She took the student's files from the top of the filing cabinet.

"What are you doing?"

"I'm going to start writing their reports."

"But we do that on Monday."

"I'm going to start them now." Upset by his attitude, she spoke harshly.

"What are you going to put on Deborah's?"

"That she disobeyed instructions to dress casually, that she's more interested in getting a man than she is in learning to be an opera singer, and that she's melodramatic and attention seeking."

"You've got be careful you don't pick on her."

"I'm not picking on her." She saw Nicholas was trying to be patient. "Did she overdress, overact and make a play for Max?"

He nodded. "But she also tried hard and was enthusiastic. If Natasha had got too excited, you'd have been gentle, maybe even amused. It's natural to have favourites, but don't show it."

Before she could argue, he left and she heard him walking down the corridor.

Dragging her mind away from Deborah, she thought about the rest of the students. She was optimistic that, with gentle coaxing, Emily would conquer her excruciating shyness. The student who had shone was Natasha. She had good ideas for the start of a scene, and during the improvisations she had befriended Emily who had hesitantly responded. Her vivid imagination, so reviled by her teachers when she was at school, was now an asset. Since beginning work she had gradually put on weight and, although still thin, she was no longer skeletal.

Harriet's thoughts returned to Deborah, who reminded her more forcefully than ever of Annabel. 'If I didn't know it was impossible, I'd believe she was Annabel's granddaughter.'

There was a knock on the door. She looked up. Jeremy Langford, a major patron of the theatre, was standing in the doorway. She had been so obsessed by Deborah she had forgotten their appointment. Normally she would have had coffee and biscuits ready for his arrival. Being recently widowed had affected his health, and he was thin but looked better than when she had last seen him.

Hoping he had not noticed her lapse of memory, she smiled. "Jeremy, how lovely to see you again."

"Hello, Miss Shaw."

She gestured towards the chair. "Would you like some coffee?"

"No thanks. It's just a quick visit." He sat down. "I'm having dinner with my daughter later."

She noticed that his dark hair was going grey at the sides. It made him look older than his forty-five years. "How are you, Jeremy?"

"Surviving. Anyway, I've heard the new opera students are exceptional this year."

"Yes. We've even got a coloratura who's as good as Lucia Popp."

"Ah, so hopefully we'll be seeing *The Magic Flute* in four years."

Harriet nodded.

"Miss Shaw, I've had an idea. What about dubbing your old recordings onto a long-playing record?"

She shook her head. "I haven't heard them for years. There won't be much profit in it."

"It'd be a limited edition. They would be sold in the foyer during the opera seasons. All your students would buy one. We could have a launch party where you would autograph the record sleeves. It will be good publicity for the theatre."

She smiled. "Jeremy, you know I'd do anything for publicity."

After he left, she went to find Nicholas. 'I'm a silly old woman. Deborah can do nothing to harm me or the theatre.'

Chapter 12

'Within me, now,
ecstasies are stirring.'
La Bohème – Puccini

"Who's Desdemona?" called Max.

Richard watched Max confidently find his partner. 'That's all I have to do,' he thought as he stood up. 'Just ask casually. Who's Mimì? I don't have to worry about making an idiot of myself – not here. I hope it's not Deborah.'

"Who's Rodolfo?"

Richard waved at Natasha. "Mimì!"

She ran across the theatrette. "This is so exciting, isn't it?"

"Yes," he said. "Let's go to *The Scheherazade*."

As they walked down Acland Street talking about the class, Richard's reticence dissolved. In the café they ordered coffee and Danish pastries and read the guidelines Nicholas had given them.

"Good," said Natasha. "We can rewrite the script to make it sound more natural."

"Remember the first time we came here?" said Richard.

She grinned. "We were both hideously spotty."

"You're beautiful now."

She looked so surprised, he felt compelled to elaborate. "Your face has character, and I've never seen such huge eyes."

Natasha flushed with pleasure. "Gosh, thanks. I'm not used to compliments. Are you still in the Public Service?"

"Yes, but now I've got opera school to look forward to I can tolerate it." He pulled the top off his fountain pen. "When I touch your hand, instead of saying 'your tiny hand is frozen, let me warm it into life', do you reckon it would sound better if I say – 'Your hands are frozen, come and warm them by the fire'?"

"Yes." Natasha sipped her cappuccino. "How are you going to

116

make 'Oh, lovely maiden, in the moonlight', sound less soppy? I'd get the giggles if a boy said that to me."

"You look lovely in the moonlight."

She nodded approvingly. "Terrific. Let's rewrite 'Your Tiny Hand is Frozen,' and then we'll work on 'They call me Mimì' and the love duet."

Three cappuccinos later they were satisfied.

Natasha put her exercise book in her bag. "We'll have to meet next week to practise. Would you like to come to dinner on Monday?"

"Yes, please," said Richard.

As she wrote down her address, he considered asking her if they could meet tomorrow and go through their lines, but decided that his real motive would be transparent.

On Monday evening, he drove straight to St Kilda from the city. The front door of the Victorian villa in Mary Street was open, and he found himself looking down a long hallway. As he rang the bell, he heard the gate bang. He turned and saw a man dressed in army uniform striding up the path.

"You must be Richard," he said, holding out his hand. "I'm Natasha and Jacqueline's father."

'Hell,' thought Richard, as he looked at the epaulettes. 'Just my luck to fall for a colonel's daughter.' He shook the proffered hand firmly and smiled.

Natasha opened the fly-screen door. "Hello, Richard. Hi, Dad."

She wore green shorts and a white blouse. Her feet were bare, and her neck and legs were the longest he had ever seen.

"Come and meet my mother."

Hoping that politics or Vietnam would not be mentioned during dinner, he followed her down the hall. 'I don't have to tell them I go on anti-Vietnam War marches. If they ask me about conscription I can honestly tell them I wasn't called up. There's no need to say I would have been a conscientious objector.' But the thought made him feel sly. 'If they want my opinion, I'll have to tell the truth – I can't ditch my principles.'

To his relief, they mostly talked about Harriet Shaw.

"Remember she's on the radio tonight," said Natasha.

After dinner Natasha and Richard went into the music room with

Jacqueline, who read their revised script.

"That's great," she said. "I wish I was doing something like this instead of the Ladies of the Night. Poor Emily's nervous, and Deborah's overpowering her." She looked at her watch. "Turn the radio on – Miss Shaw will be on in a minute."

During the interview, Harriet spoke about her memories of Melba and her own early days at Covent Garden.

"We are now going to hear a 1920 recording of Miss Shaw singing, 'Caro nome' from *Rigoletto*," said the interviewer. "In the near future her old recordings are going to be collated onto an LP."

It was the first time any of them had heard her sing.

"Why did she give it up?" said Jacqueline as the aria ended.

"Incredible," whispered Natasha. "Her top notes – "

"Sh," said Richard. "He just asked her – "

"Because I wanted to … opera singing can be … is a very selfish thing." Harriet sounded strained.

"Miss Shaw, thank you for sharing your experiences. It was wonderful to hear your voice."

"Even the interviewer sounded emotional," said Jacqueline. "I'd better go and help wash-up and let you two rehearse."

Alone with Natasha, Richard felt inept.

"I've made a list of props," she said. "Two candles – shall we use real ones or get battery ones from the prop room?"

"Battery ones," he said. "We don't want them blowing out at the wrong moment."

"I'd start laughing," she said. "Knowing me, my hair would catch fire."

He relaxed. "What else?"

"A key, paper, pen, glasses and wine, and you have to have a jug of water and a hanky. Let's have a run through and see how it feels."

In the final moments of the scene Richard walked up to Natasha. "You look lovely in the moonlight." He came closer, but instead of just gazing at her as they had planned, he kissed her on the lips. To his joy, she responded enthusiastically, and put her arms round his neck. Reluctantly, he pulled away, trying to control his excitement. Natasha buried her head in his shoulder, and he felt her heart pounding. She parted her lips and he kissed her again. "This isn't in the script," he said

118

breathlessly.

"It should be, shall we put it in?"

"Yes. But we can't kiss too long."

Natasha grinned. "Can we practise the kiss again?"

"If we do, we won't have time to practise anything else."

She wound her arms round his neck. "We must get this kiss right."

He kissed her again and when he tried to pull away she resisted.

"So it's true," he whispered, when she let him go. "I thought it was a fable."

"What?"

"That redheads are very passionate."

She giggled.

"This is the first time I've ever looked forward to Monday," he said, stroking her hair.

"Why?"

"Because I was seeing you." He took her hands and kissed them. "Come on, Mimì, let's go back to the beginning."

Deborah, looking forward to the first German lesson on Wednesday, arrived at the theatre early. The studio where the language classes were held was empty, so she sat down and studied her text book.

Ten minutes later another girl joined her. "It's Deborah, isn't it?"

"Yes. Sorry, I can't remember your name."

"Rhonda."

"That's right." Deborah closed her book. "You're from New Zealand, aren't you?"

"Yes."

As they talked, she felt the beginnings of a friendship forming. Rhonda told her she was a florist.

When everyone began to arrive, Deborah was pleased when Max sat next to her.

During the lesson, Mrs Stolze, the teacher, praised her pronunciation. Unlike her first attempt at drama, she felt confident when the class ended.

"I think I need some extra tuition," Max told her. "Shall we go to an

Italian restaurant in Fitzroy Street, and you can coach me on my vowel sounds?"

Deborah heard the others planning to go to *The Scheherazade*. "What about going with the others? I don't know anyone yet."

"You know me," he said persuasively. "Have you had any dinner?"

"No, I came straight from work."

"I'll buy you some."

She watched the crowd going out of the door. The temptation of dinner with Max overcame her desire to make friends and continue her conversation with Rhonda.

"How are the Ladies of the Night?" he asked as they walked to the restaurant.

"Boring. Emily's terrified and Jacqueline's fed up."

"Poor Emily," he said. "I felt sorry for her on Saturday. I'm glad she's not Desdemona."

"How's *Otello*?"

"Coming on well. Faye was playing it too dramatically at first, but I persuaded her to be more subtle." As Max stepped forward to open the door of the restaurant, he was vaguely aware of someone running towards them.

"Hi ya, Cobber! I thought it were you."

Shocked, Max stared at the man.

"You done well for yourself, Mate." He leered at Deborah who was looking at his tattooed arms distastefully. "Me old mate, forgot me, have ya?"

Max put on his most superior expression. "I don't know you."

"Your voice has gone all posh!" He laughed. "We lived next door to each other in Collingwood." He slapped Max on the arm. "Me mum said youse all got took off in a Rolls Royce – "

"You're mistaken," Max said coldly.

"But you're – "

"My name's Carveth. I've never seen you before, now please go away, before I – "

"Okay, okay. Sorry, Sport."

Frowning, he watched the man walk down the street, thankful he had stopped him from calling him Max. He felt his heart racing. "Fool," he muttered. "As if I'd know an uncouth bloke like him. Collingwood?"

He forced himself to laugh. "Do I look as if I come from a slum?" He was thankful that Deborah, instead of being suspicious, was looking alarmed.

"Max, I think he was up to something. Do you think we should tell the police?"

He pretended to consider it. "You might be right. He hasn't stolen your purse, has he?"

She looked in her bag. "No."

He felt his pockets as if checking for his wallet. "He hasn't taken anything. It must have been a genuine mistake."

"He sounded as if he was on drugs."

Max took her hand and squeezed it. "I would have protected you." Opening the door for her, he followed her into the restaurant.

Forcing himself to relax, Max read the menu. When he had ordered Spaghetti Bolognese for himself and ravioli for Deborah, he smiled at her. As they chatted about opera school, he tried to concentrate on what she was saying, but the memories of his father were insistent. His mother's parents had been wealthy, and when their only child had married a labourer, they disowned her. She tried to instill some culture into Max, and when he was four she had saved enough money to buy a second-hand piano.

When her husband came home from work he attacked it with an axe. "You'll turn him into a poof! I'll teach him to be a man." He dragged Max into the middle of the room and beat him. When his mother tried to stop him, he punched her so hard she fell over.

Through his pain, Max heard his baby sister crying. The neighbours called the police, and Max and his mother spent the night in hospital. His arm was broken and the long gash on his leg needed stitches.

"Max, what's the matter?" asked Deborah.

"I've got to sack someone," he said, thinking quickly. "He tries hard, and he's got a family." He shook his head. "This is the part of the job I hate." To his relief, she looked convinced.

"Have you always been interested in opera?" he asked, feeling churlish for not giving her his full attention.

"No. At school I was crazy about the Beatles, especially Paul – I hardly knew what an opera was. But when my father came back into my life – my parents divorced and I didn't see him for years ... " She swallowed hard and looked away.

He touched her hand. "My parents were divorced too," he said. "We've got a lot in common."

Forcing himself to concentrate, he listened sympathetically as she told him about her mother.

"Why did your parents divorce?" she asked.

He gestured carelessly. "They just didn't get on."

"Do you see your father?"

"He's dead." Max had no idea if this was true, but hoped it was. "Where do you live?" he asked, anxious to change the subject.

"Elsternwick."

"Alone?"

"With my mother, but she's on a skiing holiday in Switzerland. Would you like to come back and have coffee?"

Max followed Deborah's car to Elsternwick, contemplating the course his life would have taken if he and his mother had not gone into town when he was ten. 'Different day, different time, and my life wouldn't have changed. Was it fate? Even back then, I felt I was born to do something special.' His encounter with his old friend had been the only brush with his past he had ever had. For the first time, it occurred to him that he too might have been rough and common. He recalled Deborah's look of disgust. 'Girls like her, and the others in the opera school, would have looked at me like that.' The thought made him more thankful than ever that luck had changed his destiny.

His surname in 1950 had been McRae and, as he and his mother had walked through Myers on their way to the bargain basement, a smartly dressed woman stopped in front of them.

His mother tried to walk round her, but she put out her arm. "Don't rush away, please. Is this your son?"

"Yes."

"My grandson."

Max was shocked. "Dad said me grandparents was dead!"

His grandmother looked horrified. "*My* grandparents, not *me* grandparents. And it's – *were* dead, not *was* dead," she said sternly. "How can you allow him to speak like that?"

"Me dad beats me if I talk any other way," said Max sullenly.

She looked distressed. Gently, she touched the bruise on his face.

"Did he do this?"

He was aware of her beautiful coat and the smell of her leather gloves. "Yeah. And he beats me mum too."

"Max, stop it," said his mother desperately. "It's – "

"Come home," interrupted his grandmother. "I'm sorry. So is your father."

His mother started crying. Confused, he caught hold of her hand, trying to comfort her.

His grandmother put her arm around him. "Would you like to come and live in a nice big house with me? We've got a tennis court."

"Yeah!"

"The word is 'yes'." She looked at his mother. "Have you any more children?"

"There are free more of us, I got two bruvvers and a sister. I'm the oldest," Max volunteered excitedly. "Can they come too?"

She smiled. "Of course. But it's *brothers*. And '*free*' is something you get for nothing. We'll have to do something about your speech before we send you to a decent school."

Max and his brothers and sister were too awed by the Rolls Royce to speak, as they left Collingwood and drove to Beaumauris through suburbs with clean streets and trees.

His grandmother parked the car in the drive of the largest house Max had ever seen. She went onto the verandah and opened the front door. "Now, quickly, you've all got to have a shower and be nice and clean when your grandfather gets home."

Wanting to stay in the garden and climb the trees, he ran his hands over the soft grass. "We had a bath on Sunday."

"In this house," said his grandmother firmly, "you'll shower every day and wash your hair and clean your teeth."

Max followed them inside. "Me dad says it's sissy," he said, looking at the staircase, wondering what was upstairs.

His mother ruffled his hair. "Your father was wrong. He was wrong about everything." She was smiling. He had rarely seen her smile.

"What's up there?" he asked.

"Bedrooms," said his grandmother. "Come to the bathroom."

Max, expecting her to take them out into a laundry and fill a tub from the kettle, stared amazed at the black and white tiled bathroom.

He watched her turn on shining taps and saw steaming water gushing from the shower. Because he was the oldest, he went under first. The shampoo didn't sting his eyes and the Pears soap had the most wonderful smell. He didn't want to get out. While his mother supervised the others, his grandmother took him upstairs and showed him his room, which had a view of the sea.

In Collingwood he had slept on the top bunk in the room he shared with his siblings. On his first night in his grandparents' house he lay on a comfortable bed with crisp sheets and thick blankets. In spite of the cold, he opened the window and listened to the sea, frightened that in the morning he would wake to the sounds of hate.

In the morning he heard music. It was his grandmother playing the piano.

"What's that?" he asked.

"The 'Moonlight' Sonata."

"What's a sonata?"

"Let's look it up in the dictionary." She reached out to take his hand and he flinched.

"Did you think I was going to hit you?" she asked.

He was worried she thought he was a coward. "I weren't frightened."

"Look at me, Max." Slowly she extended her hand and took his. "I promise you that I will never hit you and neither will your grandfather."

"Not even when I'm bad?"

"Not even when you're naughty. Do you believe me?"

"Yeah." He smiled at her.

"What do you say?"

"Yes."

"Good boy."

After breakfast his grandparents took them all shopping. Max, accustomed to wearing trousers that were too short and tight jumpers and shirts that he had to keep till they could be passed onto his brother, revelled in the new clothes and shoes that did not have split soles. His mother reverted to her maiden name of Carveth and changed all their names by deed-poll. An elocution teacher came to the house three times a week, and as soon as they could speak grammatically they were sent to private schools.

Like the other pupils at Brighton Grammar and Firbank, they had tennis, swimming and piano lessons. For the first time in their lives they went to church. Max would rather have gone to the beach, but when he rebelled his grandfather said, "Do you want to live in this house or go back to Collingwood?"

Max stopped rebelling.

When his grandparents discovered he could sing, they began to talk about having his voice trained.

"Harriet Shaw would be best," said his grandfather.

On his fifteenth birthday they took him to see *The Force of Destiny* at the Princess Theatre in Melbourne. Max longed to be on stage singing the main part. When he was seventeen he passed his matriculation with honours. The vocational guidance personnel advised him to go to university and study mathematics. Max declined. He wanted to be an opera singer.

Deborah's car slowed down and turned into a driveway. The journey had only taken ten minutes.

He parked behind her with a growing sense of excitement. 'This is just like the old days.' Getting out of the car, he watched her lock the Mercedes. "Nice car."

"It's my mother's." She went to the front door of the cream brick house and he followed, admiring her slender legs in the short dress as she ascended the steps to the verandah.

The house was modern and, like his, was furnished in fashionable leather, glass and chrome. He wondered what her bedroom was like. She made coffee and put *Otello* on the stereo.

"I can see you as Otello," she said as she sat next to him.

"I've never strangled a woman. There are too many other interesting things to do," he said softly. Leaning forward he kissed her neck lightly. To his surprise she shied away. Immediately, he picked up his coffee. "What's your favourite role?" he asked casually.

"Tosca – she's got guts. So many opera heroines are drips."

"Do you think so?"

"Yes. Gilda should have been pleased that the duke was going to get murdered – I wouldn't have sacrificed my life to save him."

'I'd better be careful,' thought Max.

"If I'd been Violetta, I would have told Alfredo's father to jump in

125

the lake, and Butterfly should have stuck the dagger in Pinkerton, not herself. As for Micaëla – fancy trying to captivate a man by telling him to go and see his mother. No wonder he ran off with Carmen."

An hour later they walked to the door. "See you at movement class," he said indifferently. He saw with satisfaction that she was disappointed.

Emily walked to Acland Street from the dental surgery where she worked, wishing that her skin didn't erupt in red blotches whenever she was upset. With over an hour to fill in before movement class, she went into *The Scheherazade*. While waiting for her malted milk and sandwich, she daydreamed about Nicholas. She had just got to a romantic bit when Phillipa arrived.

"Hello, Emily, can I join you? I'm waiting for Jacqui and Natasha."

Emily nodded, pleased that someone as confident as Phillipa wanted her company. 'I bet she never comes out in blotches,' she thought as Phillipa ordered sandwiches and iced coffee. Wearing a smart yellow dress, which fell past her calves in the latest fashion, pearls and grey shoes, she looked sophisticated.

"That's a lovely dress."

"Thanks, Emily. I'm pleased long skirts are fashionable. I hate showing my legs."

Emily was surprised. "Why?"

"There're shapeless – just go straight up and down."

"I've never noticed."

Phillipa grinned. "That's because I hide them under long skirts. You're a dental nurse, aren't you?"

"Yes."

"That must be interesting."

"The job is, but my boss is a bully. He tells me I'm stupid in front of the patients."

"Well, in three years you can go into the opera company and tell him to go to hell."

"I don't think I'm going to make it."

Phillipa sipped her iced coffee. "Why not?"

"On Saturday I stood there like a dill. I'll probably be thrown out."

"No you won't," said Phillipa. "Harriet thinks you're a future Queen of the Night."

"I can sing I suppose, but – "

"You suppose! Oh, Emily, you're so modest."

"Singing's all I can do. Look at the others – they've all got personalities."

"So have you. You're just shy. The opera school will give you confidence. This time next year you won't know yourself."

Emily, reassured, smiled. "I only auditioned because my family nagged me for two years. I didn't audition till I was nineteen. It's amazing I passed. I was so frightened, I messed everything up. Miss Shaw was very sympathetic. She told me to practise the aria with Nicholas while she was out of the room. He was great. He told me a joke and made me laugh. When I'd stopped shaking he said, "Just have a practice. Don't worry, no one can hear you." I was praying I'd be able to sing that well for Miss Shaw, when she walked in and told me she'd been listening. I don't know how she knew I could sing, my first attempt was awful."

"Did you hear her on the radio?" asked Phillipa.

Emily nodded. "I can't wait for the LP to be released. It's incredible that she gave up such a brilliant career to come to a place like Melbourne. She could have been as famous as Melba."

"Teaching young people like you gives her a lot of satisfaction."

"Nick's wonderful." She hesitated. "What's he like to work for?"

"Smashing," said Phillipa offhandedly.

"Do you love him?"

"No." Phillipa looked embarrassed. "What gave you that idea?"

Emily, deciding she had been too inquisitive, blushed. "I guess when you're in love with someone, you think everyone else is too."

"Oh. Has he asked you out?"

Emily giggled. "No. I'm happy to worship him from a distance. Don't tell him, will you?"

"I won't tell a soul," promised Phillipa.

127

Chapter 13

'The performance is charming!
The way they're acting
exceeds my expectations!'
Così fan tutte – Mozart

Nicholas finished marking the attendance register. "Let's see the work you've prepared. We'll have Deborah, Jacqueline and Emily first with the opening scene from *The Magic Flute.*"

To his disappointment, Deborah blatantly upstaged Emily and Jacqueline. Believing Harriet would have used this as an excuse to rebuke Deborah, he was pleased she was attending the second year drama class.

When the scene was over, Emily's face and neck were suffused with red blotches. "Sorry, that was awful," she muttered.

"Don't apologize," said Nicholas. "You're here to learn. This is only your second week. It wasn't awful, but it didn't work for several reasons. Firstly, you were Jacqueline, Emily and Deborah wandering aimlessly about with spears. There was no interplay and no objectives. You must create individual characters, with different temperaments. Who's the strongest? Who's the one with the sense of humour? Think of the Seven Dwarves. Give yourselves names to suit your personalities.

"You must have definite objectives. First to kill the monster, and then to make the young man yours. The Ladies of the Night are all attracted to Tamino, and that creates the conflict, because you can't all have him."

He considered taking Deborah aside after class and talking to her about upstaging, but decided against it. She had to be taught a lesson and his telling her now would be preferable to Harriet's derision next week. "Deborah, you upstaged Emily and Jacqueline. Never do that again. Remember you're a team."

She looked so hurt he felt sorry for her. "It's all right, Deborah. I know it wasn't deliberate. Right, we'll have Richard and Natasha and their scene from *La Bohème*."

Natasha had done up her hair, and wore a long skirt and a high necked blouse. Richard began the scene by sitting at the table, writing. Nicholas was impressed to see that he had taken the trouble to get an old pen with a nib and was using an ink pot. Looking disgusted, he read through what he had written and crumpled it up.

When the knock on the door came, he called out impatiently, "Who is it?"

"I'm sorry to trouble you," Natasha answered.

Richard, looking surprised, jumped up and opened the door.

"My candle's blown out and I haven't got any matches."

He looked at her appraisingly. "Come in."

"I can't stay," replied Natasha. During her melodramatic fit of coughing she dropped her key and candlestick.

Richard led her to a chair. "Are you ill?" he asked anxiously.

They were clearly nervous. Natasha was overacting and Richard's movements were wooden, but it was obvious that they had done a great deal of work. Their moves were disciplined and they used the props effectively. Towards the end of the scene they relaxed, and Nicholas was surprised by their unrestrained kisses. When they finished, the other students clapped.

Nicholas stood up. "That was very promising. Your interplay was excellent. But in some parts, especially when you were searching for the key, there was too much movement. It's a misconception that dramatic moments are best expressed by rushing round gesticulating. Silence and stillness are more powerful. Think in terms of a significant physical action. In your everyday life, store up a bank of useful memories. Next time you're embarrassed or upset remember your physical actions. Study other people.

"When you were doing 'Your Tiny Hand is Frozen', and 'They call me Mimì', although your interpretation was good, it sounded as if you were reciting poetry. You can avoid this by breaking it up with pauses and specific movement. This scene is simple. Two people meet and fall in love. The attraction is mutual and instant. The main feelings are emotion and desire. Never try to feel emotion. It's something that happens, not something you do. You'll all remember a situation where it was important you didn't cry or laugh. Remember that the harder you tried not to – the more you cried or laughed?"

A lot of the students nodded.

"Your kisses were convincing. Stage kisses often look contrived. Frank and Rhonda, come to the front. I'm not going to embarrass you by asking you to kiss, but embrace each other as if you were about to kiss."

They did so.

"Stay like that. Can everyone see? From the waist down they look like two sides of a triangle. In a real kiss the hips and legs are close together, not miles apart."

He saw Natasha's face turning red. Richard looked pleased, but self-conscious.

"That was a very good effort. Well done."

Max felt jubilant. He and Faye had done well, and Nicholas praised his subtle characterization of *Otello*.

He pretended not to notice Deborah as she came towards him when the class ended. During the week he had avoided her. Initially bombarding a girl with attention and then backing off was a technique he had perfected before his marriage.

"You were fantastic, Max," she said.

He looked past her as if fascinated by something else. "Thanks."

"Can you help me with my acting?" she persisted.

"A private lesson?" he asked with a half smile, sure that he had conquered her.

"That's a good idea," she said brightly.

Turning away and putting his books in his briefcase, he waited for her to speak.

"When?" she asked.

"Is your mother still in Switzerland?" he whispered.

She nodded.

While the rest of the class made for the cafés in Acland and Fitzroy Street, he followed Deborah's car to Elsternwick.

Jacqueline dumped her books on the table in *The Scheherazade*.

130

"Where the hell did Deborah get to? Our scene will be dreadful next week too." Dispirited because everyone else's scene had been better, she wanted to do some serious work and figure out how they could improve.

"Do you think I'll be expelled?" asked Emily nervously.

"We'll all be expelled the way we're going."

Emily looked crushed. "At least you do well during the improvisations, but I can't do anything. Nicholas said to think of the seven dwarves – I'll be Dopey and wander round being my normal stupid self."

Jacqueline realized she had added to Emily's anxiety. "Nonsense. You're more like Bashful. And at the moment I'm Grumpy. Don't fret. I've heard about how terrific your voice is. Miss Shaw won't get rid of someone who can sing Queen of the Night." She saw other students making rehearsal arrangements with their partners or discussing their scenes.

After the waiter brought their orders, Jacqueline opened her exercise book. "We'll write the script. If Deborah doesn't like it, tough."

"It's such a hard scene," Emily said despondently. "Spears are the only props and after we've killed the monster they're redundant."

"Blood," said Jacqueline. She giggled at Emily's startled expression. "We've just killed the monster, so the spears have got blood and stuff on them. So we could occupy ourselves by cleaning them with leaves."

Emily poured her butterscotch malted milk into a glass. "And maybe they'd be blunt – we'd have to sharpen them with stones or something."

Jacqueline slapped her hand on the table, almost knocking over her coffee. "That's a marvellous idea. I would never have thought of that."

Emily smiled.

After the second performance of the scenes a week later, Nicholas was concerned about Emily's crippling shyness. The scene had improved, but she had been so nervous she dropped her spear and forgot her lines. During the tea break he spoke to Harriet, who shared his worry. At the end of the class they went into Harriet's office.

"It's just drama," said Nicholas. "I spoke to the other teachers during the week. She's all right in German and music. She puts herself in the back row during movement, but is otherwise fine. It's the performing aspect that's upsetting her. She hates being the centre of attention. It's dreadful seeing her like this."

Harriet nodded. "When she came for her singing lesson, I asked her how she felt about the classes and she admitted she found drama terrifying. And I'm sure being with Deborah is not helping matters."

Determined to avoid a diatribe about Deborah, he opened his folder. Next week I've got Emily doing Violetta with Max as Alfredo, but I don't think it's going to work. I know he's experienced, but he might be too dominating. I heard Faye complaining he was bossy."

"Put her with Natasha," said Harriet, looking at the schedule. "Deborah and Natasha are doing Susanna and The Countess. Change them round. Deborah can be with Max. When I asked Natasha about the drama class, she said it was fun. Interestingly, she's the only student who used the word fun. She's the most relaxed person in the class and I think she'll have a calming influence on Emily."

"Good idea." He picked up his pen. "So, Emily as The Countess – "

"No," said Harriet. "Emily as Susanna. Let's see what happens when you give Emily the role of helper. Besides, Susanna has to write, that means it keeps her hands occupied, and because she mostly repeats everything the countess says, she won't be worried about forgetting her lines."

Max opened his eyes and looked round Deborah's bedroom. Pink and white, it was in bewildering contrast to her appearance. 'Zoe's room's more grown-up than this,' he thought. The pink bedspread and matching curtains, patterned with koala bears, had obviously been there for years. Curious, he asked her why she had never changed them.

"This was my father's last birthday present to me before he left. I'd been at a Brownie camp for a week. When I got back it was like this – he'd bought new furniture and everything."

Max thought the white Queen Anne suite with gold embellishments was hideous, but understood how it would enchant a little girl. He took

132

her hand from under the sheet and kissed it. He wanted to sleep, but they had to work on the scene they were doing from *La Traviata.* Their partnership gave him more time. Rehearsing with Faye, courting Deborah, and lying to Susan had been a strain. Sexually, Deborah was cold. Although selfish in most respects, much of his satisfaction during lovemaking came from the fact that the girl enjoyed it as much as he did.

Deborah rearranged her pillow. "Do you think people will be surprised?"

He yawned. "What about?"

"Us going out together."

'Oh, no,' he thought. When reminiscing about his single days, he remembered the carefree sex and pleasure. He had forgotten the uncomfortable times when girls became serious about him. Closing his eyes, he tried to think.

"Max?"

"Let's keep it a secret."

"Why?"

He stroked her arm to soothe her indignation. "Secrets are exciting. They add spice."

"How?"

"Because we know something that they don't." He got out of bed and picked up his shirt. "Let's get on with the rehearsal."

Deborah giggled. "You left most of your clothes in the hall – I'll get them."

Buttoning up his shirt, he thought about how he would play Alfredo in the scene they were doing. 'He's just come back from Paris, so he'd have a coat and hat on – I can make things look natural by taking them off. I'd kiss Violetta too, but I'd – '

"Max."

He looked up.

Deborah was standing in the doorway, holding up his wedding ring. "This fell out of your pocket." She looked at the inscription inside. "Max and Susan – 1960."

Hating her devastated expression, he looked away, cursing himself for letting her get his trousers.

She threw the ring at him. "No wonder you wanted to keep it

133

secret." She hurled his trousers and shoes across the room. "Go home to your wife." She put on her black satin dressing gown and wrapped it tightly around her.

"Deborah, we've got to rehearse."

"How can we rehearse after what's just happened?" She started to cry. "Or was it just sex to you?"

"No." He crossed the room and put his hand on her arm. "Don't waste your tears on me. I'm sorry. I didn't mean to hurt you."

"What did you mean to do?" She pushed him away.

"You're so beautiful I couldn't help myself." He slid the ring onto his finger. "Susan and I aren't happy.'

Hope flashed in her eyes. "Are you getting divorced?"

"If it wasn't for our daughter we would."

She looked horrified. "You've got children?"

"A daughter. Come on, we want to do well on Saturday."

Going to the chest of drawers she took out a handkerchief. "Does your wife know about me?" She wiped her eyes, smudging her mascara and half detaching a false eyelash.

Clamping his teeth on his lip to stop the laughter that threatened to erupt, he shook his head.

"What would you do if I told her?"

His urge to laugh vanished. "She wouldn't care," he lied. "There's only one person you'd hurt and that's my daughter. You wouldn't want to hurt an innocent child, would you?"

"It's not my actions that would hurt her, Max, it's yours. And why should I care about her? She's not the only innocent person in this."

Her nastiness erased his guilt. "Telling tales isn't going to change anything. I'm not getting divorced till my daughter leaves school. Stop being spiteful." He put on his shoes. "Let's be sensible and rehearse."

"I thought you were different, but you're like all the other men – a betrayer."

Unable to bear any more, Max left.

"You were right," whispered Nicholas to Harriet as the class applauded Natasha and Emily's scene from *The Marriage of Figaro*. So

134

that Emily did not have time to get too nervous he had put them first.

Aware that the students were pleased by Emily's success, he stood up when the clapping died down. Emily, although crimson, looked less terrified.

"Good. Natasha, you showed just the right amount of anxiety and you responded to Susanna's encouragement. Emily, you managed the difficult task of helping The Countess without being patronizing or overstepping your mark as a servant. The interplay between you was good and you created a conspiratorial atmosphere."

Emily's beaming face gave him a huge sense of achievement.

The door opened and Frank came in. "Sorry, my car broke down."

"It's not good enough, Frank," said Nicholas. "Either get a new car or walk; you only live in Ripponlea. You're working with someone and it's unsettling for them and me if you're late. I was wondering if you were going to turn up and what to do about your scene if you didn't. I've got better things to do. Understand?"

Frank nodded and sat down.

"Let's have Deborah and Max next."

Nicholas thought that Max would be good for Deborah and was nonplussed by the appalling standard of their scene. At the end there was embarrassed silence.

"That was unsatisfactory," he said. "Did you rehearse this at all?"

"I was sick last week and had to cancel the rehearsals," said Max.

"You were well enough at movement and German, and you went to *The Scheherazade* afterwards."

"And you were perfectly well when you had your singing lesson," said Harriet.

Max looked sheepish. "I went to a wedding and got food poisoning."

"I expect to see a better standard next week," said Nicholas.

"It's Deborah," said Harriet later. "I don't care what excuses Max made. No one can work with her, not even Max, who's experienced and did well with Faye."

"Perhaps she wouldn't let him boss her around," suggested Nicholas. "She's got a beautiful voice, but she's taking time to sort out her problems."

"Just how many problems does she have? This week she seems to have a different problem. She wasn't trying. What problem is she going to have next week?" she snapped, angry with him for siding with Deborah.

"I think she's as nervous as Emily, but it manifests itself differently. Ingrid Williams is pleased with her."

Harriet grunted. "She's the only person who is."

Worried that Deborah would cause a scene after class, Max was pleased to see her going to her car when he left the theatre. He ran across the grass. "Deborah, we've got to arrange a rehearsal."

"Leave me alone."

"I won't be making excuses to cover up for you again. Do you want Nicholas to think you're incapable?"

She took the car keys out of her bag. "He'll think you're incapable too."

"No. I was a brilliant Otello. But nothing you've done has been good, has it?"

"I'll tell everyone you're married."

Thinking how predictable she was, he rolled his eyes. "They know already," he lied. "Miss Shaw's students mixed before we started opera school. Tell them we had an affair, and they'll think you're a slut for going to bed with a married man."

She gasped. "I didn't know – "

"But I'll tell them you did." He smiled. "You'll get the blame – the girl always does. I'll meet you here on Monday at seven. If you're not here, I'll tell Nicholas."

Without waiting for her reply, he went over to the group coming out of the theatre.

"Are you coming to *The Scheherazade,* Max?" asked Frank.

"I sure am."

Richard, Natasha and Jacqueline walked towards Acland Street together and Max and Frank fell in behind them.

"What's the matter with Deborah?"

Max tutted. "Mother trouble. Apparently she's vile. I feel sorry for her, but she goes on. I told her she should leave home, but she says … " He threw up his hand. "I don't know. Deborah's a bit obsessed. Wants

136

revenge. We tried to rehearse, but she kept crying all the time. I wasn't really sick, but I didn't want to blame her – she's got enough problems."

"Poor girl," said Frank.

"What was wrong with your car?" asked Max.

"Don't know. I managed to push it to a garage – they'll have a look at it."

"Nick's a bastard when he gets going," said Max. "It's not your fault your car broke down."

"It wasn't his fault either," said Frank. "We were told before we began that turning up late wouldn't be tolerated. I knew I'd be in trouble."

"I know, but the way he went on at you and me – like a sergeant major."

"Huh, I can tell you've never been in the army. Nick was right – I was late, and your scene with Deborah was rubbish."

Max was annoyed that his show of comradeship had been rebuffed. He looked critically at Frank's gaunt face and thick brown hair that was so wiry it looked as if it would be impossible to comb. He was slightly taller than Max, but much thinner. 'He looks starved, his clothes are three sizes too big,' he thought, aware of his own physique and expensive, well fitting clothes.

As they crowded into the café, Max sat between Jacqueline and Rhonda. "I liked your *Der Rosenkavalier*, Jacqui. You were a convincing Octavian. Does it feel weird doing a love scene with another woman?"

She shook her head. "I'm used to it."

He raised his eyebrows. "Really?"

"I went to a girls' school."

"Ah." He laughed. "We were lucky at Brighton Grammar – we teamed up with the girls from Firbank."

Frank began to talk to Jacqueline, and Max felt resentful.

"Where do you work, Frank?" she asked.

"I've got my own painting and decorating business with my sister and two mates from school. I couldn't stomach the thought of being tied to a desk all day at someone's beck and call. I had enough of that when I was conscripted. I wanted my freedom."

137

Max hid his irritation with a smirk. "So instead you're ordered about by toffee-nosed women too lazy to pick up a paint brush."

"No. Most of our work is on empty houses and flats," said Frank. "We get them ready for occupation. We do lots of stuff for estate agents. It's great, I can sing while I paint, and we take a transistor and a cassette player with us so we can listen to opera."

"I'd hate coming home every night covered in paint," said Max.

Frank grinned. "A good painter puts paint on the walls, not on himself."

Max watched Frank spreading butter on his scone. His hands were clean and uncalloused and his short fingernails were well manicured. His burgundy T-shirt looked new.

"I wish I had your job," said Richard. "I'd love to listen to opera all day."

'Shut-up, Richard, you fool,' thought Max, pouring out his tea.

Jacqueline stirred her coffee. "Did you go to Vietnam, Frank?"

"Yes. It messed up my life for a while. I'd started lessons with Miss Shaw when I was seventeen. Everything was going well, but then I was conscripted."

Max didn't get another opportunity to talk to Jacqueline because she became involved in a discussion with Frank, Rhonda and Richard about conscription. When Frank deliberately cut him out of the conversation, he was furious. He listened with contempt to Richard's passionate anti-war views. If Jacqueline hadn't appeared so interested, Max would have argued. He looked at her profile, watching the way her long eyelashes rose and fell. 'Why the hell did I waste time with Deborah?' he thought.

He studied Frank, assessing his potential as a rival. 'He's so thin he's almost ugly.' Then he saw that Frank's eyes were a vivid and unusual colour. 'Not brown, not green – hazel I suppose.' He was smiling at Jacqueline.

Max's confidence faltered. 'He's only a painter,' he tried to reassure himself. 'A manual labourer – he's not good enough for her. She needs someone refined. He probably doesn't even own a suit.'

He tried to think of a way to capture Jacqueline's attention, but to use the clichéd lines he had used on girls before seemed wrong.

Chapter 14

'When there comes back to me
that dreadful vision
My mind is over clouded
And the words that I speak
are often foolish.'

Il Trovatore – Verdi

Harriet felt strained. After her radio interview in February, her students had bombarded her with questions. It had been over forty years since she had heard herself singing and she had forgotten how she sounded. Unprepared for the interviewer's question as to why she had given up her career, she had badly stumbled over her reply.

Yesterday a journalist from *The Australian Women's Weekly* had rung and arranged to interview her after Easter. To avoid questions about her reasons for leaving London, she offered to talk about her memories of Dame Nellie Melba and the future plans for the theatre. The journalist also requested photographs of her when she was young. When she'd left England, she hadn't wanted any photographs to remind her of the past, but gradually her mother had sent them. As soon as they arrived, Harriet had put them in a trunk in her spare room.

She knew looking through them would unleash painful memories. 'It's good publicity for the theatre,' she thought as she lifted the lid of the trunk.

The first thing she saw was her Queen of the Night coronet. Her mother had sent that too. Just looking at the rhinestones flashing in the evening sunlight made her throat tighten. She remembered her last performance in *The Magic Flute*. It had been a night of triumph. A night of curtain calls and encores. Her fans cheering and asking for her autograph at the stage door.

Pushing the coronet aside, she pulled out the first two photos she saw. 'They'll do.' She shut the lid of the trunk. 'I'm not torturing myself any more.'

On the day of the interview Harriet got up later than usual. Wanting to have as little time as possible to worry, she had set the alarm for eight instead of seven. After showering she dressed in a mulberry wool suit. 'This time I'll be prepared,' she thought, pinning a cameo brooch on the high neck of her pink silk blouse. 'Perhaps she won't ask any awkward questions.'

At the theatre her spirits were lifted by Phillipa and Nicholas, who told her she looked lovely.

When the journalist arrived, Phillipa showed her into Harriet's office. Vivien Anderson was an attractive young woman with a confident manner. Her English accent had an Australian inflection. Straight, sun streaked hair reached her waist. She regarded Nicholas admiringly when Harriet introduced them.

Vivien took a cassette recorder out of her briefcase. "Do you mind if I tape the interview? It saves me taking notes and I can be accurate when I'm writing the piece."

Harriet knew that to refuse would seem strange. While preparing, she had imagined Vivien with a notebook. With the tape recorder, her full attention would be on Harriet. She made herself smile. "Not at all."

Nicholas and Phillipa left, and Vivien switched on the tape. Pretending to assume that *The Australian Women's Weekly* was mostly interested in Melba, she told a few stories and was pleased that Vivien laughed. She was about to begin another when Vivien interrupted her.

"Miss Shaw, I heard you on the radio a few months ago. When they played one of your songs, your voice, to me, sounded better than Melba's. But you gave up singing. Why?"

"Remember, Melba was in her sixties while I was in my twenties. I only sounded better, because recording technology had improved."

"You're very modest."

"Just honest."

"Why did you give up your singing career?"

Harriet smiled the contemplative smile she had practised in front of the mirror. "I'd been thinking about starting my own theatre. I wanted to improve the quality of opera performances. For a long time it was a dream, but then I came to Australia for a holiday and, here it was. A new country, the home of Melba, crying out for its identity in the artistic world. England didn't need me, but Australia did." She tried to read Vivien's expression. "Even today, singers have to go overseas to make a name for themselves," she continued. "I wish I'd been able to do something about that."

"Was that the only reason?"

"Yes."

Vivien looked perplexed. "But, surely you would have been more successful than Melba?"

"I wouldn't have been able to cope with the fame Melba had. She was very good at publicity; I was beginning to dislike it."

To her relief, Vivien moved on and asked how they decided which operas were suitable for updating.

As the interview was drawing to a close, Vivien reached over to the recorder. "Do you miss England, Miss Shaw?"

The question threw Harriet. "No. Well ... sometimes."

Vivien's hand hovered over the off button. "Do you have any family there?"

"My sister – Nicholas's mother."

Vivien looked puzzled.

"She was born when I was twenty."

"Oh, really? Have you been back to see her?"

"No." Acutely aware of the tape, Harriet knew an explanation was expected. "I've been ... well ... too busy here."

Vivien turned off the recorder. "Have you got your pictures?"

Harriet gave them to her. "The top one is when I was Queen of the Night and the other is Musetta. The dates are on the back."

"Gosh. You were stunning." Vivien put them in her briefcase. "I'll bring them back as soon as we've finished with them."

Harriet stood up. "Let's go and find Phillipa and Nicholas, and we'll show you round."

As Vivien took photos and wrote notes, Harriet noticed her interest in Nicholas. When she spoke to him her smile was brighter and her voice warmer.

"How long have you been in Australia, Vivien?" he asked.

"Seven years." She checked her watch. "I must go. Thank you for your time, Miss Shaw. If you want to contact me about anything just

141

ring me. This is my card."

She also gave one to Nicholas.

Three nights later, Nicholas took Vivien to a restaurant in Collins Street. The neckline of her red crepe de Chine dress was just low enough to give him a tantalizing glimpse of cleavage. They decided to have steak, and Nicholas chose a bottle of Australian Burgundy.

"Does your aunt know you're taking me out tonight?" she asked after they ordered.

"She guessed." He grinned. "She and Phillipa almost fainted when they saw me wearing a suit."

Vivien took a blue enamel cigarette case out of her handbag. "Your aunt disliked talking about her reason for giving up her singing career."

'She's intuitive,' he thought. He found his lighter and lit their cigarettes. "What makes you think that?"

"When I changed the subject and asked about her plans for the theatre, she relaxed."

"How?"

"Her shoulders were stiff. They relaxed as soon as we began talking about something else. At the end of the interview I brought up the subject of the past again and she was rattled."

He was disturbed by her observations. Although he wanted to discover what had happened to Harriet, he didn't want the media speculating about her past. The wine waiter came to their table. Pretending to be absorbed in watching him open the bottle, Nicholas considered what to say.

When the waiter left, he regarded Vivien with an expression of amused scepticism. "Do you think she murdered someone?"

She picked up her glass. "Nothing like that. You think I'm imagining it, don't you?"

"Yes." He sipped his wine. "Very good. I can't get over how little an excellent bottle of wine costs here."

"Nicholas, I've interviewed lots of people. I know when they like talking about something and when they don't. Your aunt enjoyed talking about Melba and the theatre. She hated talking about her reasons for giving up her career. I'm pretty sure she's hiding something."

'Bloody hell,' he thought. Realizing nothing would deflect her, he shrugged. "We've all got something to hide. How many things are there that you wouldn't tell me about – or anyone else for that matter?"

"A few," she admitted.

"Let's take that further." He put his cigarette in the ashtray and leant back in his chair. "You become famous. Someone who's jealous tells the newspapers things about your past. Would it make headline news? Would it shock people?"

She smiled. "I suppose not."

"Exactly." He picked up his cigarette. "Maybe there is another reason she gave up her career, but if you knew about it you probably wouldn't even be interested." Witnessing Vivien's tenacity he was careful not to change the subject abruptly. When the waiter came over with their dinner, a new topic of conversation seemed natural.

"This smells delicious," said Vivien, looking at her T-bone steak. She cut a piece. "Just the way I like it – pink in the middle."

He picked up his knife and fork. "Why did you come to Australia?"

"I came with my fiancé, but he hated it. He went back home and I stayed."

"Were you upset?"

She smiled. "Not for long. There's so much here that I could never have in London. I can afford to rent a beautiful flat in Albert Park, I've got a good job, and no money worries. I grew up in a council house in Hammersmith. My parents were always short of money. I'm twenty-nine and I've a better standard of living than they'll ever have. It was here that I got into the habit of speaking properly – saying 'I did', instead of 'I done'. 'What were you doing?' instead of 'What was you doing?' I seldom hear Australians speaking ungrammatically. When I do hear someone using bad grammar I notice it.

"Trouble is – there's always a catch." Vivien pulled a face. "I'm not all that keen on Australian men. Most of them are obsessed by football and cricket. The nice ones bore me and the others are bossy and try to run my life. You don't miss England, do you?"

"Yes," he said. "I loathe the heat, flies and mosquitoes."

"And I don't suppose you ever had to worry about money."

"Why do you suppose that?"

"Your accent. Funny how I'd forgotten about English class divides.

Here no one worries about accents." She shook her head. "You would never have asked me out in London."

"I'm not a snob," he said indignantly. "I would have been attracted to your personality, intelligence and your lack of pretensions." He smiled. "You're also very attractive."

She laughed. "In London my hair was mousy. The sun's turned it to ravishing tones of blonde and everyone's always asking what hairdresser I go to. And I look healthy, instead of pale."

Her frankness impressed him. He finished his steak and offered her a cigarette. As she leant towards his lighter, her hair fell across her face. He saved it from falling in the remains of the sauce on her plate. She brushed it back and their hands touched. She left hers where it was, and he held it.

"Thanks for bringing me here, Nicholas. I'm having a lovely evening."

"So am I." He squeezed her hand lightly and she returned the pressure. "Would you like dessert, coffee and a liqueur?"

"I'd like anything that will prolong the evening," she said softly.

They were the last people to leave. When Nicholas drove her to her flat, it was after midnight.

"Are you free on Saturday night, Vivien?"

"Yes."

"Would you like to go to the pictures?"

"I'd love to."

He saw her to her door. "See you Saturday. I'll ring you about the arrangements."

She took her keys out of her handbag. "Would it be possible for me to watch a class? I could write an article about it."

"Good idea. I'll ask Aunt Harriet tomorrow."

As soon as Nicholas arrived at the theatre next morning, Phillipa noticed a difference in him. He looked happier. Harriet raised her eyebrows in indulgent enquiry. His only response was an almost boyish smile. He didn't say anything. He didn't have to. Phillipa had sensed his interest in Vivien the day of the interview. Vivien's attraction to him had been obvious.

Yesterday, when he had arrived at the theatre wearing a suit, she

144

had been astonished. Later in the day he had shown her three ties and asked which one she thought went best with his navy suit and white shirt.

She had forced herself to laugh and say lightly, "Really, Nick, you never worry about clothes – you must be keen." She looked at the silk ties, remembering that she had bought him the burgundy and navy striped one last Christmas. "The green, I think."

Harriet was enthusiastic about Vivien watching a class and writing another article. "More good publicity," she said. "Do you think a first-year drama class would be the most interesting?"

Nicholas nodded.

Hiding her misery under a cloak of efficiency, Phillipa gave him the schedule for the next four weeks.

"Thanks."

Normally he would have been impressed that she had typed it up so far in advance, but he studied the pages in silence.

"In three weeks they're doing the first run through of scenes from *Rigoletto, Figaro, Butterfly, Lucia di Lammermoor* and *Lohengrin*." He handed the list to Harriet. "Lots of variety."

Harriet nodded. "Plenty of drama and interest too."

"Shall I tell them in advance she's coming?" he asked.

"No," said Harriet. "It might unsettle them. She can sit quietly at the back. If she wants photos she can take them after the class."

Phillipa went to her office to type the letters Harriet had given her. 'I've lost him,' she thought. 'I knew he'd ask her out when she gave him her card.' She was angry with herself. 'I lost him before I even had him. As soon as Vivien saw him she let him know she was interested. Why can't I be like that?'

The next week was agonizing. Nicholas took Vivien out twice. At night Phillipa lay in bed, unable to sleep as she imagined them talking and kissing. Vivien's influence extended to Harriet, who was delighted by the double page spread in *The Australian Women's Weekly*. The day after the magazine went on sale they were inundated with phone calls from people wanting to join *The Friends of the Theatre*. By the end of the week they had two new corporate patrons. Phillipa felt that her own usefulness was being eclipsed by Vivien's.

♪   ♪   ♪

"Blasted critics!" said Harriet. "They're never satisfied."

Nicholas picked up the paper from her desk and read the article that complained about the repertoire for next season. "What about putting on *The Consul*?"

"No. Let them complain." She was vexed with herself for giving him the excuse to support the case for modern opera. "They're happy with the updating. They loved *Così Fan Tutte*."

"It might be a useful experiment to include a scene from *The Consul* in the third year students graduation production."

"You never give up, do you? I said no and I mean no."

He threw the paper on the desk. "I can't understand your prejudice against modern opera!"

"Losing your temper's not going to make me change my mind, Nicholas. As soon as you don't get your own way you have a tantrum."

"It's trying to reason with you. You refuse to discuss anything. Don't moan to me about the critics again. Anyway, some of the singers would like to do *The Consul*."

She glared at him. "Are you trying to turn them against me?"

"So you doubt my loyalty now? A few years ago you asked all your students if they'd like to do *The Consul* and you told me that many would. Sack me if you think I'm disloyal!" He slammed the door as he left her office.

Harriet looked at her watch. She had ten minutes to calm down before Frank arrived for his singing lesson.

Harriet went into Nicholas's office, as he put the phone down. She hadn't seen him since their argument.

"Nicholas, I'm sorry about yesterday."

"Are you sorry you doubted my loyalty?"

She didn't reply.

"Obviously you're not," he said coldly.

"I find it difficult to trust people," she admitted.

He leant back in the chair and folded his arms. "Thanks for lumping me together with people in general. I thought you trusted Phillipa."

146

"I do."

"Ah, so she's the exception."

She sat down. "Nicholas, stop it. I'm not used to change. I've allowed you to update some operas, but I'm frightened of doing modern opera."

"Why not ask some of the patrons for their opinion about *The Consul*? That's all I want to do. One modern opera. Please compromise and let the third year students do one act for their graduation. It would be a good way to test the reaction."

She sighed. "All right."

"Thanks, Aunt Harriet."

"I know I haven't heard the end of this. If the scene from *The Consul's* successful you'll argue that we should do the whole thing. You won't be happy until we're doing a modern opera every season. Now, how's Vivien?"

"Fine."

"How non-committal."

"Do you like her?" he asked.

"She's very ambitious, isn't she?"

"What's wrong with that?"

She stood up. "You're so touchy. I wasn't critizing her," she replied irritably.

Harriet returned to her office. Vivien worried her. She felt that loyalty would never stand in the way of her ambition. She knew Vivien was interested in why she gave up singing. Nicholas's mother had already warned her that he had found an incriminating page from one of their mother's journals. She hoped he had not told Vivien. Nicholas did not perturb her so much. If he had known where to look he would have done so by now. Vivien's journalistic experience could be dangerous. 'All she has to do is find out from the archives at Covent Garden when I sang my last performance, and the newspapers three days later would give her the reason,' she thought.

Chapter 15

'She whose purity, whose modesty
have, I feel,
called me to a virtuous life!'
Rigoletto – Verdi

Max was excited to find he was playing the Duke to Jacqueline's Maddalena. The casting of Frank as the assassin Sparafucile troubled him. 'I know he's keen on her,' he thought. He glanced at Frank's profile. 'Has he got what some women would call an interesting face? No, she'd have to be out of her mind to prefer him to me. What am I worried about? That she might be attracted to his smile?'

After announcing the parts, Nicholas held up two daggers. "Those of you doing *Rigoletto*, listen carefully. These daggers look the same, but this one has a red mark on the handle." He plunged it into the table in front of him. To a few gasps, he thrust the other into his chest. "This has the green mark. Look, no blood. The blade's retractable." Pulling the dagger out of the table, he said, "This is the one used at the beginning by Sparafucile. The other is the dagger he stabs Gilda with. It's easy to make the switch, but you must concentrate."

At the end of the class, Max went up to Jacqueline. Before he had a chance to say anything, Frank joined them and said to her, "It'll be fun working together."

Natasha, who was playing Gilda, ran up to them. "Fantastic! The last act of *Rigoletto*'s so dramatic."

"I'm looking forward to working with you, Natasha. You've got a good imagination," Max said, thinking it would be smart to make a friend of Jacqueline's sister. "Let's go to *The Scheherazade* and get the script written."

Natasha shook her head. "We can't tonight – we're going out to dinner; it's our mother's birthday."

"We'd better meet tomorrow," said Richard.

"Finding a spare studio's impossible on a Sunday," said Max. "The second-years prepare their workshops and the third-years rehearse their graduation scenes."

"What about coming to my flat?" asked Richard.

"Good idea," said Max. "How about two o'clock – I sleep late on Sundays." He wanted to spend the morning with Zoe, and Susan always insisted on a proper Sunday lunch.

As Max drove to Brighton, he realized that, with Jacqueline living with her parents, seducing her would be difficult. He was the first to arrive at Richard's. As he looked round the spacious first floor flat where every window overlooked the communal gardens, he envied his freedom. Preferring opulence to simplicity, he hated the atmosphere Richard had created. 'I'd never paint walls white,' he thought. 'Makes it look monastic.' He looked at the black-framed photos on the walls. 'Even these are black and white – if it wasn't for his clothes I'd think he'd got a colour phobia,' he thought looking at Richard's casual navy trousers and pale blue shirt.'

"I took those," said Richard.

"Really?" Max was surprised by the professional quality.

"I take my camera everywhere and when the light's right I snap. The best ones I get blown up and framed."

'Why waste time photographing trees and water, when you could be taking pictures of beautiful girls?' thought Max. 'I'd get rid of these and have mirrors. This flat could be something.' He visualized red brocade curtains and upholstery replacing the grey velvet Richard had chosen. "Is the furniture yours?" he asked.

"Yes," said Richard. "It took me about a year to save up and buy everything I wanted. Furnished flats I looked at weren't that much more expensive, some with one bedroom were cheaper, but I wanted my own things. I turned the second bedroom into a music room."

'Could I rent a small flat without Susan finding out?' Max wondered. He tried to calculate the costs, but Richard's talking interfered with his concentration.

"I decorated it myself," he was saying. "When I saw how good the black picture frames looked on the white walls, I decided to paint the woodwork black too. I think it adds drama."

149

The only thing Max liked was the scarlet painted mantelpiece in the music room. It was, he thought, an adventurous experiment that worked. The books filling the shelves on both sides of the open fireplace in the lounge made the room less austere.

When the others arrived, Richard made coffee and put a tin of biscuits on the table.

Max, wanting to impress Jacqueline, took control of the discussion. "Right," he said. "Let's work out our objectives and obstacles. Natasha, what are Gilda's?"

"To save the duke, but the only way is with her life."

"Why?" asked Max. "Could you warn him?"

"No. Because Maddalena and Sparafucile will see me entering the inn."

"Good. Jacqui?" asked Max.

"The same as Gilda."

"And mine," said Frank, helping himself to a biscuit, "are to stop my fool of a sister getting emotional over a man and losing us the money."

"Mine are the most basic. To seduce Maddalena," said Max.

Richard doodled on his notepad. "I want to show Gilda what the duke is really like and get him killed. My motive is love, my objective is revenge."

"What about emotions?" asked Natasha. "The emotional memory exercise isn't going to work because we've never experienced anything like this." She grinned. "Well, I haven't."

"I have," said Frank.

Richard nodded. "A professional assassin," he said slowly.

"What?" said Natasha.

"In Vietnam," said Frank.

Jacqueline put down her mug. "You weren't an assassin."

"What was I?"

"A soldier," said Max, annoyed because everyone's attention was on Frank.

"What's a soldier other than a professional assassin?" Frank asked bitterly.

Max saw Jacqueline looking at Frank in concern. "It's different," she said.

150

"No, Jacqui, I killed people."

"Rot," said Max. "Let's get on. Save your guilty outpourings for a psychiatrist."

Richard broke the uncomfortable silence. "The rest of us have to use our imaginations."

Frank, looking embarrassed, flicked through his folder. "Here we are. 'The more images we can find, the more we can respond to'," he read. "'Relax. Don't try too much'."

"Ha," said Natasha. "My teachers were always complaining I didn't try hard enough at school."

"Let's do a run through and see if we can get the feel of it," said Jacqueline.

At the end of the evening, as they got ready to leave, Max consoled himself with the thought that they would all be meeting tomorrow after work to work out the dagger switch and stabbing with Nicholas. Wanting Jacqueline to think that his outburst against Frank had been caused by his impatience to get on, he asked him if he wanted a lift home.

"No thanks, Max, my car's fixed."

To his relief, Frank sounded amiable.

Max, who had noticed Richard and Natasha's interest in each other, watched as Natasha and Jacqueline ran down the steps. "Don't get tied down to one girl – enjoy your freedom," he said softly.

Richard looked at him strangely and Max knew he had said the wrong thing. "I'm practising being the Duke," he joked.

"Ah, very good – I thought you were serious for a minute."

'You foolish bloke,' thought Max.

"Normally," said Nicholas, "you'd have scenery, which makes changing the daggers easier. The safe dagger is on a shelf which is hidden when the door opens. Sparafucile picks up the real dagger, stands behind the door when Maddalena opens it, and does the swap. How are you going to divide the stage?"

"With chairs," said Frank.

"Good."

'It was my bloody idea, not yours,' thought Max, jealous that

Jacqueline was looking at Frank.

Nicholas looked at the table on which they had put wine flagons and goblets. "Any thoughts as to how you're going to swap the daggers?"

"Well, I thought – "

Nicholas held up his hand. "Wait, Max. I want the ideas to come from Frank."

"If I put the safe dagger on the table behind the flagons at the start of the scene, then stand with my back to the audience before Jacqui opens the door, I could swap them then."

"Good. Set up the stage and try it."

'That was my idea too, you bastard,' thought Max.

"I suppose Jacqui could switch them," suggested Richard.

"No," said Nicholas. "it's safer if Frank does it. "Let's see how it works."

Frank went to the table. "I turn my back on Jacqui when she's pleading with me," he said as he slid the real dagger through a gap in the flagons, and pulled out the safe one. "Will that work?"

Nicholas nodded. "You'll need to practise – it was obvious you were doing something, but good idea, well thought through, Frank."

"It was all of us really," said Frank.

"Just one more thing," said Nicholas. "When you pick up the safe dagger, press it to make sure it retracts. It's a precaution – things can easily go wrong."

It was only when Nicholas left the theatrette, that Jacqueline looked at him. "Let's take it from the beginning," she said.

When Max and Richard finished, they sat down to watch. Aroused by the scene he had just done with Jacqueline, Max tried to think how he could manage to see her alone.

Jacqueline grabbed Frank's arm. "When the hunchback comes, take the rest of the money and kill him instead."

He stopped sharpening the dagger. "Murder the hunchback? What do you think I am, a liar and a cheat?"

"I'll warn him!"

He stuck the dagger in the table. "What about the money?"

She threw herself at his feet. "We must save him. I love him."

Frank pulled the dagger out of the table and inspected the blade. "If someone comes before midnight they can die in his place, then we can still get the money."

Jacqueline put her head in her hands. "It's late and the night's too stormy."

Looking exasperated, Frank turned his back on Jacqueline. Max watched to see if he could see Frank switch the daggers. His mind on the success of the scene, he was pleased he could detect nothing.

There was a knock and Jacqueline jumped. "Was that someone knocking?"

Frank shook his head. "It was the wind."

"I'm sure it was someone knocking."

He looked at her indulgently, and then stiffened as he heard a louder knock. Jacqueline stood frozen with expectation. "Who's there?" she asked breathlessly.

"I'm lost. Please give me shelter for the night," said Natasha.

Jacqueline turned to Frank in excitement. "A long night it'll be for him!"

"Open the door."

Jacqueline mimed opening a door. Natasha, dressed in jeans and a plumed hat, came through the gap in the chairs. As Frank grabbed her, her hat fell off and her hair tumbled down her back. He stabbed her and she went limp in his arms.

Max wondered if Jacqueline would think he was being nasty if he told Frank he was overacting.

"Did either of you see me swap the daggers?" asked Frank.

"No," said Richard. "But I wasn't looking out for it."

"I was," said Max, deciding to praise Frank. "And I didn't see a thing. Well done."

Jacqueline didn't seem to have heard. "I think I should stab Gilda," she said.

"What?" said Natasha and Frank in astonishment.

"The idea came to me when her hat fell off," explained Jacqueline. "If her sex is revealed, it'd be a twist."

"Sparafucile's killed lots of people. Would he care what sex they were?" asked Natasha.

Jacqueline stroked the ostrich plumes in the hat. "Perhaps he's never killed a girl."

"It's an interesting thought," said Richard.

Frank waved his dagger at Jacqueline in mock anger. "I want to kill Gilda! Don't rob me of my big moment."

Natasha shook her head. "But seriously, it deviates too far from tradition. Miss Shaw will have a fit."

Although Max didn't like Jacqueline's idea, he decided to be her champion. "It's worth a try," he said. "Do it and I'll watch."

Richard and Max went to the front of the studio and sat down. Max, wanting to support Jacqueline, hoped he would like her idea.

At the end Richard clapped. "Chilling. Jacqui, you genius!"

Max went over to Jacqueline and put his arm lightly round her waist. "Well done, Jacqui. Shall we do another run through? Frank, would you like to watch the whole scene, see how effective it is? I'll do your part."

Frank nodded. "Okay." He went to the front and sat down.

"Well, what do you think?" Max asked when they finished.

"Jacqui's right," said Frank, looking at Natasha regretfully. "I was looking forward to killing you."

Natasha gave him a push. "Maniac. Let's go to *The Scheherazade*."

On Saturday afternoon, Nicholas and Harriet sat in the front row of the theatrette watching the *Rigoletto* scene. Nicholas, acutely aware of Vivien's presence at the back, hoped the students would do well. They were all in costume. Jacqueline's feet were bare and she wore a red gypsy dress with a low bodice. She looked self-conscious, and Nicholas attributed this to the low cut of the dress. At the beginning of the act Natasha wore a long cloak, which hid her boy's costume of breeches and riding boots.

As the scene drew to its conclusion, Nicholas winced in sympathy when Natasha's hat fell off. The tableau froze. Nicholas thought the scene was ruined. Wondering what Vivien would be thinking of the debacle, he watched Frank lower his dagger and turn away. 'Improvise!' he thought. 'What the hell's wrong with you, Frank?'

Jacqueline snatched the dagger from him and stabbed Natasha in the chest. They left the stage to enthusiastic applause.

Nicholas stood up. "Remarkable use of imagination. The ending was brilliant. It was more powerful because it reveals certain traits in the characters of Maddalena and Sparafucile. It shows that though he is a professional assassin, he can't kill a woman. And Maddalena is so unhinged by her feelings for the Duke, that she can stab a defenceless girl to save his life. The irony about *Rigoletto* is that the Duke sings 'Women are Fickle' just before a girl dies for him. Your version doubles the irony, because a woman also kills for him."

"It was Jacqui's idea," said Frank. "We thought she was mad at first. We thought you'd have a fit."

"Never be afraid to use your imagination," said Harriet. "If your ideas are too wild we can tone them down. One reason these classes are held is to develop your imaginative powers. Nicholas may be your teacher and have years of experience, but he doesn't arrogantly assume that he is the only person with good ideas. Jacqueline, are you embarrassed by the low cut of the dress?"

She blushed and nodded.

"It showed," said Harriet. "Maddalena's a role you'll be playing a great deal in your career, and it requires you to be sexy. At one stage you covered your cleavage with your hand. That would have worked if Max had been looking at you and you were pretending to be coy, but he wasn't. Being sexy isn't about flaunting various exposed parts of the body. Sensuality is inbuilt. You could play Maddalena in a high necked, long white dress or flannelette pyjamas, and still ooze with sex appeal."

"Frank, considering you couldn't stab Gilda, your expressions were too evil and verged on the melodramatic," said Nicholas. "Sparafucile lives in an age when life was cheap. Ask yourself why you became an assassin. Was it because you were poor, uneducated and had to make money? How do you feel before and after a killing?

"Natasha, good on the whole, but you need to think more deeply about what you're doing, and why. How did you feel towards your father when you realized he was right about the Duke?"

"I don't know, I didn't think about it," she confessed.

"In some parts, your performance was too one-dimensional," he said. "You didn't interplay with Richard enough. Allow him to comfort you, or push him away if you prefer, but communicate with him. Richard, when you told Gilda to dress as a boy, you might well have turned to the audience and said, 'I don't know why I'm telling her this, but it's in the script.' After you've shown Gilda what a swine he is, what are your plans? Will you ever let her marry? Are you trying to protect her, or are you protecting yourself from a lonely old age?"

"A bit of both, I think."

"Remember – objectives, obstacles and your character's inner life," said Nicholas. "In this scene the Duke is the only person unaware that anything's going on. All he thinks about is how he's going to seduce Maddalena. But, Max, are you really shallow? Is your motto 'Love them and leave them,' with the secret postscript, 'Before they leave me?' You must come across as sincere. Maddalena must think that you feel as passionately about her as she does about you."

"Maddalena," said Harriet. "you've lured lots of men to their deaths. During the week think about why the Duke is different."

"Let's have the *Figaro* group," said Nicholas.

Just before the class ended, Nicholas stood up. "Could the *Rigoletto* cast stay behind, please. Everyone else can go."

"This is Vivien Anderson, from *The Australian Women's Weekly*," said Harriet. "She's writing an article on the opera school and she'd like to take some photos."

"Shall we see if we can find a spare studio and rehearse alone?" Max asked Jacqueline after the photo session.

During their rehearsal he had to steel himself not to open his mouth when he kissed her. Instinctively knowing she was a virgin, he used subtle tactics, gently stroking her arm and gazing into her eyes as he said, "Maddalena, I'm a slave to your beauty."

Triumph surged through him when he felt her shudder. As soon as they finished, he physically distanced himself. "Right," he said cheerfully, "let's find the others."

They walked to *The Scheherazade*. It was empty. Max looked at his watch and was surprised to see how late it was. "Are you doing anything tonight?" he asked.

She shook her head. "Richard and Natasha are going to see *Romeo and Juliet* – the Zeffirelli film. They asked me to go with them, but I think they'd rather be alone," she said with a conspiratorial smile.

"Shall we go somewhere for dinner?" he asked.

"That'd be great."

Max was astonished by his happiness.

After class, Nicholas and Vivien went to his favourite pizza restaurant in Elsternwick, where the pizzas were made by cheerful Italians in view of the customers. It was licensed for people to bring their own wine, and Nicholas brought a bottle of Chianti.

When the waiter had taken their order, Vivien said, "If I hadn't been interested in opera, after today I would be. I was impressed – by the students and you."

"Thanks." Feeling pleased, he picked up his glass. "Have you always been interested in opera?"

"Not till I came to Australia. A girl in the office was an opera fanatic. She took me to see *La Bohème*, but she educated me first. She told me the story and played me the highlights and said that in the last act you can see all the white hankies appearing because most of the audience are bawling their eyes out. I was scornful, but during the performance I started crying during 'Your tiny hand is frozen', and didn't stop till the end of the act. When Mimì was dying I was a weeping wreck." She watched one of the cooks throw a circle of dough in the air and expertly catch it. "Why does Rigoletto tell Gilda to dress as a boy?"

"Because she's travelling alone, and it will be safer."

"Why didn't you tell Richard that?"

"He's got to work it out for himself."

"Oh look," she said. "Max and Jacqui have just come in. Are they going out together?"

"I hope not." Nicholas, who had his back to the room, frowned. "Max is married."

Vivien looked shocked. "Blimey. Is he? They haven't seen us. Are you going to tell her?"

He grimaced. "I'd rather not."

Vivien nodded. "It might be an innocent friendship."

Nicholas, remembering what Harriet had told him, doubted it.

"He's incredibly good looking and charming," said Vivien.

Unexpectedly, Nicholas felt a spurt of jealousy.

She grinned. "But not as handsome as you. I prefer men with dark hair – they look mysterious. And you're – careless and thrown together."

He sipped his wine. "Is that supposed to be a compliment?"

"Definitely. I bet Max preens in front of the mirror for ages and blow-dries his hair, whereas you probably tumble out of bed, stagger into the shower and dress in the first things you pull out of the wardrobe."

"I do comb my hair," he said, surprised by her accurate description of his mornings.

"Yes, but I bet you let it dry naturally."

He nodded.

"Max would have his hair cut regularly – I'd say you leave yours till it starts annoying you."

"Right again."

"You're both handsome – Max exploits his looks, you don't. I bet he shops for ages, looking for things that match perfectly. Now you – I bet you hate shopping."

"I don't have to do it often, thank goodness. Phillipa and Aunt Harriet buy my shirts, ties and jumpers at Christmas and birthdays."

She touched the sleeve of his shirt. "Actually, I'm surprised you iron anything."

"I don't – my cleaning lady does."

She looked aghast. "A cleaning lady? That's a hangover from the awful English class system."

"This is Australia, Vivien. Hard work's rewarded. My cleaning lady drives a newer car than I do." He grinned unashamedly. "I'm lazy, disorganized and untidy. But honest. I could have let you think I ironed my shirt specially because I was going out with you."

Vivien raised her eyebrows. "Max would have."

He refilled their glasses. "He wouldn't admit his wife did them."

158

Chapter 16

'She loves me it is clear.
Oh, how troubled is my path.'

Fidelio – Beethoven

Max spent a sleepless Saturday night agonizing about how to tell Jacqueline he was married. 'I've got to tell her before Phillipa or Deborah do,' he thought, imagining Phillipa's reaction when she discovered he was taking Jacqueline out. He woke on Sunday with a headache. Susan had invited a dozen people from the tennis club for a barbecue. He spent the day wishing he could escape from the conversations about work and children.

On Monday night when they met at the theatre to rehearse, Jacqueline looked delighted to see him. Guilt diluted his pleasure. The rehearsal went so well that Richard suggested that they go to *The Pancake Parlour* in the city and treat themselves.

Max had promised to play chess with Zoe before she went to bed. He was about to say he had work to do at home, when he saw the way Frank was looking at Jacqueline. 'If I don't go he'll give her a lift. I can't give him the chance to ask her out. I'll make it up to Zoe at the weekend,' he thought. "Jacqui, would you like to come in my car?"

When they arrived, Frank sat next to Jacqueline, and Max was forced to sit at the end of the table.

'She's mine, Frank,' he thought, picking up the menu to disguise his anger. 'Compared to me, you're nothing. The only advantage you've got is that you're single.'

"I'm having brandied apricots," he heard Richard say.

Max had never been in *The Pancake Parlour* before and its rustic furnishings and friendly staff made him feel carefree. The self-congratulatory mood of the others was infectious. His pancakes, when they arrived, were piled high with cinnamon dusted apples and whipped cream. The iced chocolate came in a tall glass topped with a scoop of ice cream. Wanting to avoid irritating talk about the Vietnam War, Max was pleased when Natasha started talking about the classes. As they finished their pancakes, Jacqueline caught his eye and smiled. Her expression was unmistakably one of attraction. His jealousy evaporated.

When he arrived home after midnight, he saw Susan waiting on the verandah.

"Where have you been? I was worried," she asked as soon as he got out of the car.

He looked at his watch. "Sorry, I didn't realize how late it was."

"I thought you'd had an accident. I nearly rang the police."

He held the door open for her and they went inside. "Go to bed, I'll lock up."

"You were supposed to play chess with Zoe. She hardly sees you now. She went to bed in tears."

He put the security chain on. "Sue, if you handled things better she'd understand. It's bad for her to see you panicking."

On Saturday, their second performance of the *Rigoletto* scene earned enthusiastic applause from the students, and Nicholas congratulated them on the development of their characters. After class, Max was about to ask Jacqueline out, when he saw Deborah standing nearby. He moved away and was pleased when Jacqueline followed him.

"Gosh, I'm still reeling from Nick's praise," she said.

"Are you doing anything later, Jacqui?"

She shook her head.

"Would you like to come to the pictures?"

"I'd love to. What about *Romeo and Juliet?* Richard and Natasha said it was fantastic."

Before the picture, he took her to a Chinese restaurant in Little Bourke Street. Several times, before their dinner arrived, Max nearly told her about his marriage. By the time they were eating, he decided against it. 'I can't tell her in public, she might start crying,' he thought.

After the picture, as he drove Jacqueline home, he tried not to think about Susan and Zoe.

"Richard's still here," Jacqueline said, pointing to his car. "Come in for coffee and we can all rave about *Romeo and Juliet*."

160

"Sorry, Jacqui, but we're frantic at the bank. I've had to take work home. I'd better not have too many late nights." He walked her to the front door. It was open and he could hear the strains of Mozart and the murmur of voices. He was tempted to join Richard and Natasha, but knew that if he was too late Susan would be upset and infect Zoe with her misery.

"I enjoyed tonight, Max, thank you," said Jacqueline softly.

He stroked her hand. "There'll be more, I promise."

"Good," she whispered.

He kissed her lips. She leant against the wall and put one arm round his neck as she returned his kisses. The image of Susan and Zoe faded. A mosquito buzzing round their heads broke the atmosphere. Max swatted the mosquito with his hand, leaving a smear of blood on the cream stucco wall. He went back to his car without touching Jacqueline again.

During the week Max saw Jacqueline only during classes. Feeling he must make an effort to spend more time with Zoe, he went home instead of joining the others for coffee afterwards. On Saturday he reluctantly decided not to go to *The Scheherazade*. "I'm sorry I haven't seen much of you this week," he said to Jacqueline. "I've been so busy. We've had lots of people away sick and I've had to take work home every night."

She looked disappointed, but said sympathetically, "It happens all the time at the hospital."

"Think of me slaving away over columns of figures, while you're having coffee and cake."

At *The Scheherazade*, Jacqueline sat at the table with the others. Lost in her thoughts about Max, she hardly heard the conversation.

"Where's Max?" asked Rhonda. "We've hardly seen him this week."

Natasha nudged her. "Wake up, Jacqui. Where's Max?"

"Probably with his wife," said Deborah.

There was shocked silence.

"What?" said Richard. "He's not married."

"He's not, is he, Jacqui?" asked Natasha.

"No," said Jacqueline. "He would have told me."

"I only found out accidentally," said Deborah indignantly. "He took me out to dinner and when he was paying the bill his wedding ring fell out of his pocket. I wouldn't go out with him after that. Ask him if you don't believe me."

Harriet shut the lid of the piano. "What's wrong, Jacqueline?"

"Nothing."

"Then why have you spent the whole lesson looking and sounding as if you're about to cry?"

Jacqueline felt her face growing hot. "Is Max married?" she blurted out.

"Yes," said Harriet coldly. "He's also got a daughter."

Jacqueline burst into tears.

Harriet handed her a tissue. "I should have known it was Max," she said angrily. "Has he taken you out?"

"A few times." Jacqueline wiped her eyes. "I didn't know he was married."

"I'm angry with Max, not you," she said more gently. "Forgive me for asking such a personal question, but, are you – expecting a baby?"

Jacqueline shook her head. "We didn't do anything like that."

"Good. I'm very relieved." She went to the door, opened it and looked out. "I'll be with you in a minute," Jacqueline heard her say.

"I'm sorry, my next pupil's arrived. Go into Phillipa's office, she'll make you a cup of coffee." She put her hand on Jacqueline's shoulder. "You'll get over him. You haven't done anything silly and your life's not ruined, thank goodness. I know it's hard, but it's better to find out now."

Max was dismayed when Jacqueline ignored him before movement class. Deborah, looking stunning in a black leotard and tights, smiled spitefully at him and he guessed she had told Jacqueline he was married. When the class began he stood at the back trying to work out what to do.

The music stopped and the exasperated voice of Miss Jones, the movement teacher, cut into his thoughts. "Natasha, what are you doing? Are you trying to kill your classmates?"

Natasha was in the front row and Max could not see her face, but he saw Deborah smirk, and he wished that she was the one being shouted at.

Miss Jones turned the tape back on. "Let's try again."

The music started and stopped a minute later when Natasha crashed into Emily.

"For God's sake, Natasha!" exploded Miss Jones. "You've got the grace and co-ordination of an elephant with three legs. Go to the back and get out of everyone's way. Stand behind Max and don't kick him. Try and take this class seriously, Natasha. Movement's important. I can see you falling into the orchestra pit during a performance."

Max was ready to give Natasha a sympathetic smile, but when she turned around he saw she was about to burst out laughing. Admiring her pluck, he winked at her, but she scowled at him.

After class he cornered Jacqueline. "Why are you ignoring me?"

"You're married, you bastard. And you've got a daughter."

"I married her because she was pregnant, Jacqui."

Her expression became guarded. "Was the baby yours?"

"Yes, but – "

She tried to push him away.

"She trapped me!" he said, grabbing her arm.

Jacqueline broke free and ran down the corridor into the changing rooms.

"Are you coming to *The Scheherazade*, Max?" Deborah's voice came from behind him. "Or are you going home to Susan?"

"Stop sneaking about, you snake!" As he walked down the corridor he heard her giggle.

At *The Scheherazade* Deborah watched Jacqueline miserably sitting between Natasha and Emily.

"Jacqui, did you ask Max if he was married?" she asked innocently.

All conversation stopped.

"No. I don't care if he's married or not."

"Really? I wouldn't go out with a married man."

Jacqueline glared at her. "I'm not going out with him."

"Let's go, Jacqui," said Natasha. "We've got a busy day tomorrow."

"That was a nasty thing to do, Deborah," said Frank as the door closed after Jacqueline.

"Me? What about Max − "

"There are ways of doing things," he said coldly. "Public announcements intended to humiliate − "

"If his wedding ring hadn't fallen out of his pocket, I'd still be going out with him. I'd want someone to tell me the truth."

"In public?" said Faye.

No one spoke to Deborah for the rest of the night. 'Why am I getting the blame?' she thought bitterly.

On the way to the tram stop the next morning, Natasha's attempts to cheer Jacqueline up were unsuccessful. Usually they talked excitedly about opera school, but Jacqueline looked depressed.

Natasha looked at her in concern. "Is it Max?"

"What else would it be?" Jacqueline began to cry.

"Oh, Jacqui," Natasha said sympathetically as they reached the tram stop. "He's a swine. Do you want to talk about it?"

"Not on a tram full of people, you idiot!" Jacqueline whispered savagely.

"Sorry."

When they arrived at the hospital they went into the canteen for breakfast. Natasha picked up a bowl of stewed prunes and turned to Jacqueline, who was gazing into space. "You're holding up the queue. Are you having scrambled eggs?"

Jacqueline shook her head. "I'm not having anything."

"You've got to have something."

"I'm not having anything!" snapped Jacqueline.

"Well go and sit down then, and get out of everyone's way."

Jacqueline banged down her tray and stomped out of the canteen.

At lunchtime, they took their sandwiches and fruit over to the Shrine of Remembrance and sat on the grass.

Natasha's attempts to start a conversation were in vain. "Jacqui, stop this," she said, annoyed by her refusal to behave normally. "You haven't been going out with him for long."

"His wife trapped him by deliberately getting pregnant."

"Who told you that?"

"He did."

Natasha stared at her in disbelief. "And you believe him? You naive idiot."

Jacqueline threw the remains of her sandwiches at Natasha. "Thanks for being so understanding!" She jumped up and ran down the slope.

Stunned, Natasha picked the bits of beetroot and cheese off her white uniform and scattered their half-eaten sandwiches on the grass for the birds.

Feeling ashamed of herself for her behaviour at lunch time, Jacqueline went over to the outpatients counter. "Natasha?"

Natasha turned round from the filing drawer. "What?"

"It's German tonight."

"Look at the mess you've made of my uniform."

"I'm sorry. I'm so confused."

"Why the confusion? He's married. Don't go out with him any more." She picked up another pile of index cards. "There are plenty of single blokes at opera school. Forget Max."

"How can I forget him when I'll have to see him all the time? You make it sound easy."

"Sorry."

Jacqueline went back to the admissions office, distressed to find she was dreading opera school instead of looking forward to it.

Max knew that Miss Shaw had heard about his interest in Jacqueline the moment she opened the door to her studio. Her face was rigid with disapproval. She didn't smile and ask him how he was as she usually did, she simply sat at the piano and began the lesson. At the end she glared at him. "Up to your old tricks again, Max?"

"My marriage is unhappy," he said cautiously.

"Whose fault is that?"

He didn't reply.

"Well?" she insisted.

"Mine."

She pulled his score off the stand and snapped it shut. "When you were at opera school last time, I had a succession of unhappy students who were the victims of your immoral behaviour. Exercise restraint. I don't want Jacqueline's career ruined by you – as it would be if she became pregnant." She handed him the score. "I'll see you next week. Think about what I said."

Depressed by her denunciation, he wanted to convince her of his sincerity. "Miss Shaw, I feel deeply for Jacqueline."

"You're not in a position to feel deeply about anyone apart from your wife." She stood up. "If your feeling for Jacqueline is genuine, which I doubt, think about her reputation and her future and leave her alone. Years ago you had deep feelings for at least eight girls in your class. Your feelings didn't last long. Unfortunately, theirs did."

"Miss Shaw – "

"You're used to getting what you want, aren't you, Max?"

"Miss Shaw, I've changed – "

"Yes, you're married now and you have a child. Start behaving like a husband and father, instead of a bachelor." She went to the door and opened it. "Good-bye."

Humiliated by her lecture, he went along the corridor to the studio where the German lessons were held. Miss Shaw's opinion was important to him. She was one of the few women unimpressed by his looks and charm, but he hadn't expected her to be so unmoved. 'She should have listened to my side of things,' he thought.

When he entered the studio, Jacqueline was sitting next to Frank. They ignored him so he sat between Faye and Emily and chatted to them in spite of their coolness. When the class began, he tried to concentrate, but his thoughts strayed to Jacqueline and the best way to convince her he was genuine. He considered telling her the truth about his childhood. 'Would she be scathing or sympathetic?' he wondered.

He was startled to hear his name. "Max, would you come to the front and read your chosen song to us, please?" asked Mrs Stolze. "What have you prepared?"

He stood up and dropped his score of *Fidelio*. "Um – Florestan's recitative and aria."

"Would you like to do it in English first or German?"

"English," said Max.

"What's Florestan's overriding emotion?"

166

"Despair."

"Do his feelings change as the aria progresses?"

"Yes. He starts off despairing, then tries to be uncomplaining, but bitterness gets the better of him. But he feels proud that he has done what is right, and then he feels hopeful."

"Well thought through, Max. Read your interpretation in English and then go straight into the German."

"Oh, God. How dark it is! How terrible this silence!" He paused and looked at Jacqueline who immediately lowered her head.

"Quite good, Max," said Mrs Stolze when he had finished. "Your English interpretation was faultless. Your German faltered in places and your emotions got a bit lost in the middle, but that's to be expected in the beginning."

During the break, Jacqueline avoided him and when Richard glared at him he felt furious. 'Smug git,' he thought.

He went over to join another group and began to flirt with Faye, hoping to make Jacqueline jealous.

"How's your wife, Max?" Faye asked.

"Jealous and not as attractive as you."

She blushed, but said with composure, "I don't have affairs with married men."

"I wasn't asking you to," he said with a cruel smile.

When class resumed, Max took malicious satisfaction in Richard's appalling effort with the German version of Papageno's aria. He stammered and became so embarrassed his rendition was delivered in a monotone.

"Languages aren't my strong point," Richard apologized.

"Don't worry," said Mrs Stolze sympathetically. "I can hear an improvement since last week. You obviously work hard."

After class Max went over to Jacqueline. "Jacqui, I must talk to you."

She turned her back on him and joined Frank. He felt devastatingly jealous as he watched them go outside together. Expecting Frank to give him a triumphant look, he interpreted his refusal to do so as a sign of confidence. 'You think I'm not worth bothering about, Frank? You're wrong.'

Max took two days' annual leave. After calculating what rent he

167

could afford, he narrowed his search to furnished flats within walking distance of the theatre. St Kilda was a strange mix of seedy and respectable areas. Dingy streets were just yards away from tree lined avenues and gracious Victorian villas with beautiful front gardens and elaborate iron railings. He soon found a flat he liked in Park Street. The fact that it was a few minutes' walk from Mary Street where Jacqueline lived was another advantage. After he had signed the lease and paid the bond and two weeks' rent, the estate agent gave him the key.

'I'll move in next week,' he thought. 'I'll get it all sorted out first – there're lots of things I have to buy.'

Stimulated by visions of his new life, he drove to town and went into Myers. He had never bought domestic items. When he was eighteen and had moved out of home, his mother and grandparents had given him all the necessities. Faced with a bewildering choice of saucepans, gadgets, glasses and cutlery, he looked about helplessly. Bored, he was about to go and buy bed linen first, when he saw a display labelled *Starter Set – Everything a Beginner Needs for the Kitchen! Free Delivery.* Max bought one.

As he was choosing sheets and pillowcases he wondered if Frank had asked Jacqueline out. 'What if she accepted?' The thought panicked him.

That night when Susan was having a shower he looked in her diary and saw that the women's guild of the church were having their monthly committee meeting the following afternoon. He spent the morning in his flat. The starter set was delivered, and as he put it away in the kitchen a sensation of freedom enveloped him. 'I can invite people round after opera school. I can have parties,' he thought as he put the cutlery in the drawers. In the bedroom, as he made the bed, he imagined making love to Jacqueline and wondered what she looked like naked.

Then he went home and began to pack. As he put his records in a box, he composed the letter he was going to leave for Susan. Not wanting to upset her too much, he decided not to mention divorce. 'A trial separation,' he thought, taking his boxed set of *Der Rosenkavalier* off the shelf. 'That will get her used to the idea.'

"Max, what are you doing?"

He froze. He heard her walking towards him.

"What are you doing?" She sounded as if she had something caught in her throat.

Slowly he turned round, wondering why she had come home early. He saw from her distraught expression that she had seen the half-packed suitcases on the bed. "Sue, I've got something to tell you. Sit down."

"No. Tell me." Her breathing was jagged.

"I want a trial separation."

Her face was so white he thought she was going to faint.

"Why?"

"I need my freedom."

"You were going to leave without telling me." She began to cry. "How could you?"

"No – I was going to write you a letter."

"If I hadn't come back now you'd have just gone." She sank into an armchair, making high pitched squeaks that reminded him of the sounds his mother had made when his father had beaten her.

"I wanted to avoid a scene like this," he said softly. "I don't like hurting you." He saw her make an effort to control herself.

"No, Max, you wanted to avoid witnessing this. You're like a hit and run driver who can't face up to the devastation he's caused."

"What sort of man would want to witness this?"

She looked straight at him. "What sort of man would cause this?"

Unable to hold her gaze, he stared at the cover of *Der Rosenkavalier*. "I'll pay the mortgage and Zoe's school fees, the bills, and you can keep your car."

Mucus dribbled from her nose. "This isn't about money. Is that all you think I care about?"

"Don't cry." He gave her his handkerchief. "It's only a trial separation."

"Where are you going?"

"I've found a flat near the theatre."

"How long have you been planning this?"

"I might be back sooner than you think – that's if you'll have me, you might find you're better off without me." He touched her shoulder. "I know I'm not much of a husband – you deserve better."

"Is there another woman?"

"No, no."

"Then why?" She wiped her eyes. "You come and go as you please. It's another woman. It must be."

"No." He loosened his tie. "I just hate our life and all your friends comparing their children and trying to outdo each other. I hate mixing with boring accountants and businessmen."

"You're a banker."

"Eventually I'm going to be an opera singer. I'm not made for this life, Sue. The other students are young and carefree."

"What about Zoe? I know you never cared for me, but I thought you loved her."

"I do."

She threw his handkerchief at him. "You can't, Max, otherwise you wouldn't leave her."

"I'll take her out on Sundays."

She left the lounge and he heard her weeping in the bathroom. Feeling guilty, he went into the bedroom to finish packing. When Zoe arrived home, Susan made him tell her he was leaving.

"Don't go, Daddy," she begged.

He almost gave in when she stood on the verandah, crying, as he backed the car out of the drive, but the thought of Jacqueline was too strong. Thinking that unpacking would recapture his earlier feelings of independence, he hung his suits and shirts in the wardrobe, but all he could think about was Zoe. Arranging his records did not lighten his mood. Nor did the realization that he had no towels and had forgotten to pack his toiletries.

The next morning, unable to have a shower, clean his teeth and shave, he rang work and told them he was ill. After buying new toiletries and towels he had a shower. Then he wrote to Jacqueline. As he dropped it into the letterbox, he felt more positive.

Max and Susan had a joint savings account that contained twenty thousand dollars. He planned to withdraw ten thousand and open his own account, but when he went back to work the next day, he discovered the account was closed. He rang Susan and demanded his share of the money.

"If you keep this up, Max, I won't let you see Zoe on Sunday."

170

Then she hung up.

Her revenge shocked him. 'I should have drawn out my half before I left.' After recalculating his expenses, he abandoned his plans to buy a piano, stereo and a washing machine. He threw down his pen. 'Until pay day I can't even afford an iron.'

At the end of April, Harriet had a meeting with all the teachers in the opera school to discuss the progress of each student. To her disappointment the movement teacher and German teacher found Natasha a source of exasperation.

"She disrupts the class," said Miss Jones. "She doesn't take movement seriously. When she does something wrong – she thinks it's funny. If I say go left she goes right, if I say three kicks she does four, or two, or none at all. I wish I could ban her."

Mrs Stolze complained that Natasha didn't concentrate. "She's hopeless. She just drifts off into a dream."

When the meeting was over, Harriet tried to think of the best way to deal with Natasha. She valued Miss Jones who had, over the years, turned many clumsy or overweight students into charismatic performers. To her chagrin Deborah's reports had been excellent.

By the time Natasha arrived for her singing lesson the following afternoon, Harriet had worked out what she hoped would be the solution.

At the end of the lesson, she praised Natasha's progress and then said, "You take your singing lessons with me very seriously, don't you, Natasha?"

"Oh yes, Miss Shaw," she replied earnestly.

"And you take your drama classes seriously too?"

"Yes."

"Do you take your movement classes seriously?"

Natasha blushed. "I'm not very good at movement."

"That's not what I asked."

"Um … I … I don't know."

"Miss Jones says you disrupt the class."

Natasha looked guilty. "I don't mean to – but when she tells me off

171

for doing something wrong – she makes me laugh. She says I'm like an elephant with three legs. If she just said I was clumsy I wouldn't laugh, but an elephant with three legs – it's funny – well I think it is."

Harriet managed to keep her expression serious. "Movement's important, Natasha. You've got excellent posture and a well-proportioned body. You're still a bit thin, but when you stand still you look good, so your lack of co-ordination must have come as a shock to Miss Jones. You've got to get it right now. The stage is hard and unforgiving. Joan Sutherland was lucky – Franco Zeffirelli befriended her. You might not be so lucky. What about German classes?"

"They're all right," said Natasha warily.

"Really?"

"Yes. I don't laugh in those."

"Do you concentrate – or do you drift into dreams?"

"I drift," she admitted.

"What do you dream about?"

"Usually being a famous opera singer."

Harriet took her hand. "Next time you find yourself dreaming, remember if you don't concentrate you'll never be an opera singer, and all it will ever be is a dream. You have a beautiful voice, but in the international world that's not enough. Imagine this. You audition at Covent Garden for a leading role and sing brilliantly, but you stomp clumsily onto the stage and your German pronunciation's impossible to understand. The girl after you has just as good a voice, her German is faultless and she's graceful. Who are they going to choose?"

"Not me. I'm sorry, Miss Shaw. I didn't mean to let you down."

"You haven't let me down, but you'll disappoint me if you don't improve."

Chapter 17

'Merry marriage bells are wiser,
Good advice they bring:
Bar the door like any miser,
Till upon thy hand is a wedding ring!'

Faust – Gounod

"Philly, would you like to move into a flat with Natasha and me?" asked Jacqueline.

Phillipa felt a sensation of belonging. "I'd love to." Since Natasha and Jacqueline had begun to talk about moving out of home, she had hoped to be included, but was afraid of mentioning it in case they didn't want her. She liked her flat, but was lonely with only a cat for company. The prospect of sharing her life and belongings with Jacqueline and Natasha excited her. 'This is how I felt when my sister was born,' she thought.

"Do you think you'll be able to put up with Natasha's mess?" asked Jacqueline.

"I'll reform her." Seeing Jacqueline's sceptical expression she grinned. "I will."

When the May opera season ended, they took a day off work and went to an estate agent.

"I have just the thing for you girls," he said. "A house in Gardenvale."

Phillipa shook her head. "We want to live in St Kilda."

"Gardenvale's not far away," he said forcefully. "From Balaclava Station it's only three stops. This house has four double bedrooms. Unfortunately, the man who owns it rented it to yobbos who left it in a mess. He said that if I let it to some civilized girls, they can have six weeks' free rent, on condition that they clean and redecorate. Come on, I'll drive you there."

From outside, the cream weatherboard house, with its red

corrugated iron roof and white picket fence, looked attractive. A bougainvillea climbed over the pergola across the driveway and in the front garden were two wattle trees, a jacaranda and a hibiscus bush.

"This will look colourful in the spring," said Natasha.

Picturing the mix of purple, yellow, blue and red flowers contrasting with the assorted greens of the leaves, Phillipa was unprepared for the stench of stale beer, cigarette smoke, mould and urine that hit them when they went inside. Stains and cigarette burns obscured the colour of the carpet. She saw Natasha's expression change from anticipation to horror.

"This place stinks!" said Phillipa angrily to the agent.

"Wait," he said. "It's worse because it's been shut up for a while." He unlocked the back door. "Go into the garden while I open all the windows."

Too taken aback to speak, they stood in the garden, which was full of trees tinged with autumnal red and gold.

"Beautiful, isn't it?" said the agent when he joined them. "You won't get this in a flat."

"We can't live in a garden," snapped Natasha.

"The house won't take long to clean."

"You clean it then," said Jacqueline.

He looked at her condescendingly. "Six weeks' free rent is a lot to turn your nose up at."

Natasha grunted. "We'll have to spend more than that on disinfectant."

Inside, the agent showed them round. He had not exaggerated when he said the rooms were large. The layout, with a central hall, reminded Phillipa of her parents' house. She found the similarity comforting. A cold wind gusted through the windows, diminishing the smell. Phillipa looked at the open fireplace in the lounge, visualizing the three of them sitting in front of a fire on winter nights, talking and drinking cocoa. The dining room adjoining the kitchen was large enough for a table that could seat eight. "This place could be fabulous," she said.

Jacqueline nodded. "The extra room's a bonus. We could use it as a music room."

"It's going to take ages to clean," complained Natasha. "And it's too far away from the theatre."

"Let's buy a car," said Jacqueline. "We can afford a good second-hand one – it'll only cost us a third each."

"Yes," said Phillipa, thinking how good her furniture would look in the lounge. "Shall we draw lots for bedrooms?"

"Hang on," protested Natasha. "We haven't decided anything yet. We haven't got time to clean and paint it."

"Yes we have. It's nearly the end of term, so there's no opera school for three weeks," said Jacqueline enthusiastically. And we can book some annual leave. Come on, Natasha, use your imagination and think what we can do."

"I know what we can do, but we haven't got time," Natasha said irritably.

Phillipa sighed, disappointed by Natasha's lack of interest. "Let's go home and think about it."

The next day Natasha asked Richard for his opinion.

"I see what you mean about the stink," he said going over to the back window. "Beautiful garden – it's like a woodland." He put his arm round her. "If you live here, you'll be closer to me."

Her expression brightened. "I didn't think of that. I wanted to live in St Kilda. I'm terrified of being late for class. What if our train's late or there's a traffic jam? Nicholas shouts at people when they're late."

"I've never been late, and I live further away than this. Till you buy a car, I'll call for you and Jacqui on Saturdays. You're not going to find anything as big as this for the money. I'll help with the cleaning and painting. What about asking Frank if he'd help?" Richard looked conspiratorial. "I reckon he'd be good for Jacqui – she's fretting over Max."

Richard was pleased Max no longer came to *The Scheherazade* after opera school. Noticing how tense Jacqueline was when he was around, it meant that Frank had the chance to talk to her without her being distracted. As soon as they told Frank about the house he offered to help.

"It's filthy," warned Jacqueline.

"That's okay. I'm used to cleaning up messes left by tenants."

"Are you sure you want to spend your spare time doing what you do

175

all day?" asked Phillipa.

He nodded. "It's fulfilling going into a house or flat that's been neglected or decorated in hideous taste, and transforming it into something beautiful. Give me the address and I'll meet you on Saturday morning. I'll lend you brushes and ladders. And don't buy any paint – I can get it cheap. I've got some colour charts in the car."

After they had opened all the windows and doors, Frank took claw hammers out of his station wagon. "We'll pull the carpets up first."

Richard was impressed by the way Frank took charge without being bossy. He had looked around the house, making a list and working out the order in which jobs had to be done. Soon the carpets were piled in the back garden ready to be made into a bonfire.

"It looks better already," said Phillipa, putting bottles of bleach and disinfectant on the sink and handing out rubber gloves.

"We'll wash the floors now," said Frank. "I suggest we do one room each." He picked up two buckets. "Take your mops and disinfectant to a room and Richard and I will be your water carriers."

Natasha put the back of her hand to her forehead. "I've been sent to my room!"

Frank looked at Jacqueline. "Is your sister prone to these strange turns?"

"Only when she has to do housework," she replied with a grin.

After filling two buckets with hot water, Richard carried them into the front bedroom, where Natasha was waiting. "One for you," he said, putting it on the floor.

She leant over the steaming bucket and kissed him. "I love you," she said, plunging her mop into the water.

Richard was astonished. He laughed softly. "Natasha."

Before looking at him she began to mop the floor, splashing their feet in the process. "Oops, sorry."

"I love you too."

She dropped her mop and threw her arms round his neck. "Good."

He kissed her. "I was waiting for the right time to tell you. I was thinking of a picnic in the forest or – "

"Where's my bucket?" asked Jacqueline, with an edge to her voice.

176

"Come on, you two. Now's the time for work."

Frank had brought his cassette recorder. When he put on *Orpheus and Eurydice* Jacqueline moved into the lounge with him. Richard, scrubbing the skirting boards in the hall, heard her say, "I haven't finished the back bedroom, but Kathleen Ferrier makes me go all shivery."

"People will say that about your voice one day."

'Good response, Frank,' thought Richard.

At the end of the day the house smelt of disinfectant and bleach.

Frank pulled off his rubber gloves. "That's got rid of the pong."

"We're all going out for dinner. Frank, would you like to come?" asked Natasha.

"I'd love to, thanks."

Richard, not wanting to alert them to his strategy, ignored Natasha's smile of intrigue.

"Tomorrow we can start painting," said Frank. "It won't take long with the five of us. I'll do the woodwork and the ceilings – they're the most difficult bits."

Jacqueline began to rinse the sponges. "When do you think it'll all be finished?"

"A couple of weeks – you'll be moved in before the new term starts. Do you have to buy any furniture?"

"No," said Phillipa. "I've got a lounge suite and a dining table and six chairs. Jacqui and Natasha are bringing all their bedroom furniture and a piano."

"What are you going to do with the floors? The boards are in good condition. They'd look wonderful polished."

"I'll hire a machine, if you like," said Richard. "That's how I did mine."

Natasha hugged him. "What would we do without you?"

"We'd manage very well!" snapped Jacqueline. "Could we stop all this revolting, soppy rot!" She stomped outside.

Richard was astounded. "What's the matter with her?"

"She's pining for Max, I think," said Phillipa.

Natasha, looking furious, went towards the back door. Wanting to avoid a row that would embarrass Frank even more, Richard stopped her. "I'll talk to her," he said, deflated that his ploy to manoeuvre them

177

into a liaison had failed.

Jacqueline was sitting on the back verandah with her elbows on her knees.

Torn between lecturing her about her ungrateful behaviour and being sympathetic, he crouched next to her. "Max, I suppose?"

She nodded. "It's awful seeing him three times a week. He keeps looking at me. I dread the time when we'll have to do another scene together."

He understood how she felt and thought about suggesting that she talk to Miss Shaw.

"His wife trapped him into marriage by getting pregnant."

Exasperation mingled with Richard's pity. "And Max was the victim?" he said, making no effort to hide his cynicism. "Did she get pregnant by herself? Why should men have fun with girls, then leave them with the responsibility? Imagine how you'd feel."

"She should have had it adopted."

"You're being callous." He stepped off the verandah and pulled up a few weeds growing near the hydrangeas. "I know Max is handsome, but go beyond the superficial and think about his character. He deceived you. That's not very laudable, is it?"

"I suppose not," she said ungraciously.

"No suppose about it, Jacqui." He saw a tear hovering on her eyelashes. Deciding that part of her anguish was jealousy over Natasha's happy relationship with him, he spoke more gently. "Do you really expect anyone who cares for you to be happy about your involvement with a married man?"

She shook her head.

He put his hand on her shoulder. "Soon you'll be sharing a great house and experiencing independence – look forward to it. Don't let Max make you sour. Go back to being the happy girl you were a few months ago."

"It's hard, Richard."

"But not impossible," he said gently.

She smiled slightly. "No."

Three weeks later the house was transformed. The day after they moved in, Frank arrived with champagne and flowers. "To christen your new

178

home," he said, holding up the champagne.

Natasha thought that his diffident manner meant that he had also wanted to see Jacqueline. "Gosh, thanks, Frank."

"Nice car," he said pointing to the Rover 90 parked in the driveway.

"Yes," she said proudly. "Richard helped us choose it. We only own a third each, but it's still exciting," she said, leading him into the kitchen.

"Hello, Frank," said Jacqueline. "We were just talking about you. We're taking you out to dinner one night to thank you for your help. And Philly and I were saying how right you are about decorating being satisfying."

He pulled the foil off the champagne. "Does this mean I've got three recruits?"

"No! I hated it," said Natasha, delighted by Jacqueline's manner. "I would rather have spent the break going to the beach house and having picnics."

"Natasha's a hedonist," said Phillipa, filling a vase with water.

Jacqueline unwrapped the yellow roses. "Shall we have a house warming party?"

"Yes," said Natasha, taking four glasses out of the cupboard. "Who shall we invite?"

"Everyone in the opera school," said Phillipa.

"Except Max," said Jacqueline firmly. "I have to see him at the theatre, but I don't have to see him here."

Natasha winked at her. "Good on you, Jacqui." She saw Frank smile. 'Everything's going to be all right,' she thought.

"I don't want to invite Deborah either," said Jacqueline.

Phillipa put the vase in the middle of the dining table. "I don't like her much either, but it would be mean to leave her out."

Jacqueline grimaced. "She enjoyed telling me about Max."

"She was pleased because she was hampering his plans," said Natasha. "I don't think her spite was directed at you."

Jacqueline shrugged. "Okay. We'll invite her too."

Max was swamped with money problems. Zoe's school fees went up and Susan enrolled her in private swimming, tennis and piano lessons. He sold his car and had the phone in his flat disconnected. He had no intention of depriving Zoe, or of letting Susan know she was causing him hardship. Cutting back on expensive toiletries and clothes was painful. He hated not being able to play the piano and listen to music. He loathed going to the laundromat and constantly ran out of clean clothes. Because he never hung anything up, his suits were rumpled. Frequently forgetting to set the alarm he would go to work with an empty stomach, longing for the orange juice and bacon and eggs that Susan had always made for him. If he did have time for breakfast he would discover that he had no milk for his cereal and tea or butter for toast.

Taking Zoe out on Sundays was traumatic. He couldn't afford to take her to the pictures or out to lunch, and without a car picnics in the country were impossible. So he took her to the Botanical Gardens or the beach, and when it rained they went to the museum or played cards, chess and scrabble at his flat. Zoe tried to persuade him to come back home and cried when they parted. Instead of enjoying his freedom he was wracked with guilt and worry.

He had not heard from Jacqueline. He had been sure that as soon as she got his letter she would capitulate. 'I should have got this flat, and stayed at home till I knew how she'd react to the news I'd left my wife,' he thought, angry with himself for not being more devious. 'I might as well go back to Susan.' Only the thought that it was what she had plotted when she had taken the money from their account stopped him. 'I'll give it another month,' he thought, unable to bear the humiliation of letting her know that she had won.

One day the letter he had sent Jacqueline was in his box. At first he thought she had returned it, then he saw the post office stamp informing him that the house number did not exist. When he checked her address in the phone book he realized he had reversed the numbers. 'Fool, fool, fool,' he sang happily, putting his letter in a new envelope.

On Monday morning, Jacqueline received Max's letter that her parents had redirected. She rushed into the bathroom. "Max has left his wife!"

Natasha spun round. "What difference does that make?" she asked

180

with a mouthful of toothpaste.

"It means he's serious about me," she said ecstatically.

"What about his daughter?"

Jacqueline fixed her gaze on the toothpaste dribbling down Natasha's chin. "What about her?"

"She's his daughter!" spluttered Natasha spraying toothpaste. She spat into the basin as if she was spitting out poison. "I'm sure Mum and Dad will be very proud of you, Jacqui. How are you going to tell them?"

"If you keep screaming I won't have to tell them, they can probably hear you from here."

"What's Miss Shaw going to think? What's everyone going to say when you're named as the other woman in a divorce case?"

"I don't care. I didn't know he was married in the beginning."

"But you know now!" said Natasha, pouring mouthwash into a glass.

Jacqueline looked in dismay at her disgusted expression. "When we were at school," she said quietly, "I stuck up for you – it didn't matter if you were right or wrong. You were always in trouble and I always defended you." She saw Natasha's anger fading. "So why can't you help me?"

Natasha dropped her toothbrush in the holder. "Because, you're – too wrong," she said slowly. "Nothing's prepared me for you being in this predicament. I'm sorry, Jacqui. I thought when we started opera school everything would be perfect."

"So did I."

"Can't you get interested in someone else?"

Jacqueline shook her head. "Could you? If you discovered Richard was married?"

"I don't know," she said, turning on the tap and diluting the mouthwash. "Oh, Jacqui, please don't go out with him. You weren't his first choice – Deborah was."

Jacqueline looked away. She saw Phillipa walking down the hall, tying the cord of her dressing gown.

"What's going on?" she asked.

"Max's left his wife."

"No. Oh, hell. What are you going to do?"

"I love him."

Natasha came out of the bathroom. "That's your answer, Philly," she said gravely.

Jacqueline looked from Phillipa to Natasha. Trepidation was etched in their faces. "Don't turn against me. I need your support."

Phillipa closed her eyes. "You need a psychiatrist."

Natasha sighed. "Come on, Jacqui, or we'll be late for work."

Max's triumph that he was once again Jacqueline's boyfriend was dulled by Natasha's cool attitude towards him.

"My parents are upset," Jacqueline admitted. "But they said I could invite you to the beach house for the weekend."

He tried to think how he could get out of it, but had already told Jacqueline that he couldn't see Zoe on Sunday because she was on a camping holiday.

"Don't worry," she said. "Richard and Philly are coming too."

"Jacqui, I haven't got a car."

"You can come in the Rover with me. We were all going in Richard's car anyway."

By the curt way Jacqueline's parents treated him when they arrived at Koonya Beach, Max judged they would be difficult to charm. Her father refused to shake his hand. Her mother simply informed him that he and Richard would be sharing a bedroom.

Too angry to begin unpacking, he watched Richard put his aftershave and deodorant on the bedside table. "They think I'm not good enough for their precious daughter."

"Don't spoil the weekend by being cynical," said Richard quietly. "It's not their fault you're married."

"They greeted you like a favourite son – even though you're a pacifist. Have you told Colonel Howard how you got out of conscription?"

"I wasn't called up."

Max sneered. "Would you have gone if you had been?"

"No. I don't want to learn how to kill." Richard put his jumpers in the chest of drawers. "We spend our childhood being told life is sacred, but as soon as we're old enough the unlucky ones are sent off to learn how to slaughter people who have a different ideology – all in the name of patriotism."

"You would rather have gone to jail?"

"No. I would have changed my name and moved to another state. I'd no intention of being a sacrifice for a bunch of fascists."

"What does the *Colonel* say to your philosophy?"

Richard remained silent and Max smiled slyly. "He doesn't know, does he? What would he think of you – especially when he finds out that you would have been too cowardly to face the penalty for breaking the law."

"I'm used to being taunted by shallow fools who blindly follow the pack," said Richard quietly. "If the subject comes up I'll tell Colonel Howard how I feel. Or would you prefer to tell him first?"

"I'm sure he'll appreciate being told he's a shallow fool who follows the pack."

Richard looked at him steadily. "You're a wasteland of shallow thoughts and materialistic values, Max. All your life you've had every privilege your doubtless snobby parents could give you. They gave you everything except a decent example."

Imagining what Richard would say if he knew about the squalid house where he had spent his childhood, Max smiled.

Richard walked to the door. "You're rotten. I hope Jacqui realizes before it's too late – she's too good for you."

"Your parents hate me," said Max, when he and Jacqueline were alone in his flat after the weekend. "They hardly spoke to me. I might as well go back to Sue. At least I'd have my daughter." Seeing Jacqueline's distress, he put his arm round her. "You can't help having an awful family."

"They aren't awful, Max. Just concerned because you're married."

"Is being married a crime? I'm getting a divorce. Is that a crime too? Natasha and Richard hate me. They'll turn you against me."

"No one can do that."

He kissed her hard on the lips and neck. Roused by her passionate response, he pulled her shirt out of her jeans. While he stroked her spine he brought one hand round and unbuttoned her shirt. Slowly unzipping her jeans, he pushed them down.

183

She fell to her knees and covered her face with her hands. "I can't! What if I get pregnant?"

"I'd never get you pregnant. Trust me."

"Accidents happen. That's why you got married."

"Sue wanted to get pregnant. I'll take care of things," he whispered.

"No!" She scrambled to her feet and pulled up her jeans.

Shaking with frustration, he said, "I left my wife and daughter for you and my reward is a few kisses."

"You didn't do anything for me, Max. It was your choice. I had nothing to do with it."

"You had everything to do with it. Don't pretend you're innocent."

She buttoned up her shirt. "Did I ask you to leave home? No. Did you tell me you were married? No. This is your fault, Max. Because if you'd worn your wedding ring and interspersed your conversation with references to your wife and daughter, I would never have become interested in you."

Infuriated because he had no defence against her argument, he went into the hall and opened the front door. "Go home to the virginal cloister. Surrender your virginity on your wedding night to a man your father chooses."

"I'll choose my own man. I'm not going to get pregnant and be forced into marriage like you were. But I couldn't get married because you're married already."

As soon as she went outside he slammed the door. "That's it," he muttered despairingly, knowing that he had never been unkind to a girl genuinely worried about becoming pregnant. He slumped against the wall. Tomorrow he would go back to Susan.

A few minutes later the doorbell rang. It was Jacqueline. "I left my keys," she said coldly, ignoring his smile. "Please find them for me, I'll wait out here."

"Jacqui, I'm sorry." Fearful of seeing continuing coldness in her expression and knowing he deserved it, he looked away. "I've never behaved like that before. I've never wanted anyone so much. You've done something to me that I can't fathom. I lost my temper because I feel helpless. There are so many things against us. Your family hate me – perhaps they're right ... I'll get your keys." He went into the lounge, conscious of the irony. Years ago girls had believed his false

184

endearments, but the only girl who meant more to him than just a sexual plaything, doubted his sincerity. Her keys were on the floor near the sofa. As he picked them up he heard her behind him. He held them out to her.

"Max," she whispered, making no attempt to take them.

"Jacqui."

The key ring dangled between them.

"There's never been anyone I would have left Zoe for." He jiggled the keys. "Take them."

She shook her head.

"Jacqui, if we do ever make love, I don't want it to be because we're quarrelling."

"But, we're not quarrelling," she said.

Richard had been withdrawn all week.

'I'm losing him,' Natasha thought in a panic as they sat in *The Pancake Parlour*. 'What did I do?' She dredged her memory for clues as to what had gone wrong.

Richard poured wine into her glass. "What are you having?"

She looked at the menu, and tried to sound cheerful. "These buckwheat pancakes sound yummy."

"Yes."

'He's bored with me,' she thought. She took a sip of wine. "Richard, what's wrong?"

He stared at her.

"Something's wrong, isn't it?"

"Yes."

'He's fallen in love with someone else,' she thought. 'Who?'

"Natasha, I've done something stupid."

Her heart thudded. "What?" Visions of him with another girl at opera school almost made her cry. She swallowed and lifted her head. 'I'll pretend I don't care,' she thought. 'I'll say I was going off him anyway.' Hoping that wine would dull the pain she took a large mouthful.

"Does your father – does he know I'm a pacifist?"

She put her glass down. "What?"

"Does your father know I'm a pacifist?"

She was exasperated. "I don't know. What's all this about?"

"Did you tell him – or your mother?"

"No."

He put his finger in a drop of wine that had spilled on the table and drew a circle with it. "Your father's in the army."

"Is he? Gosh, I didn't know."

"Natasha, this is serious. What's his opinion of people who go on anti-Vietnam War marches?"

"Richard, are you telling me that you've been off with me all week – worrying me to death, because my Dad doesn't know you're a pacifist?"

"Yes."

She laughed.

"What's funny?"

"I thought you wanted to break it off with me."

"Your father will probably want you to. I think it's significant that you haven't told him."

"What's brought all this up now?"

Richard told her about his argument with Max.

"My parents won't take any notice of anything he said."

"He'd only tell them the truth. I can't see a colonel being happy about my attitude."

"Dad only joined the army because of the war. He really wanted to be a teacher. But does it matter what he thinks?"

"Yes."

"Why? You're carrying on as if Queen Victoria's on the throne."

"I like your parents and I want to think that they like me."

"They do, Richard. Isn't it obvious?"

"Yes. But would they respect me if I told them what I told Max? Or even worse – if Max told them?"

"Who cares?"

"I do."

"When you went on anti-Vietnam war marches did you break the law?"

"No."

186

"You never hit a policeman?"

He looked indignant. "Of course not."

"Smash up windows or property?"

"No."

"Well, what are you worried about, you idiot?"

"I would have broken the law if I'd been called up."

"But you weren't called up so you didn't break the law. Look, if you'd been in jail, my parents would go mad, but you've done nothing wrong. Don't fret about Max – he wouldn't have the guts to tell my parents anything."

"Natasha, I'd feel better if I had a word with your father about this."

She leaned over the table. "And I'd feel better if you gave me a kiss," she whispered.

Chapter 18

'All day for love I languish'
The Marriage of Figaro – Mozart

Before opera school resumed after the break, Deborah had her first term assessment with Nicholas. After telling her that the reports from movement, German and music were excellent, he moved onto drama. "You're trying too hard, Deborah. During the improvisations, you give the impression that you want to be better than everyone else. It's not a contest. Even when you have a small part you have a tendency to upstage the principals. I have the feeling you're desperate for approval."

In spite of his compassionate expression, she blushed. She had the urge to tell him about her mother.

"Don't be embarrassed," he said before she had a chance to speak. "There's nothing wrong that we can't put right. Sometimes you're overpowering. Pull back. When someone speaks to you during a scene, give them your attention. Remember the sinking ship improvisation?"

She nodded.

"Emily suddenly came out of herself. She went to you, doing a very good impression of a frantic mother, and asked you if you'd seen her little girl. You ignored her. She gave up, thinking she'd made a fool of herself. As you were the first person she approached, you had the opportunity to develop her scene. Stop thinking of the impression you're making and concentrate on the scene." After giving her a copy of the report, he opened the door for her. "See you next week."

She wondered what he had said to the others. She had no one to compare assessments with and was as unpopular with her fellow students as she was with the girls at work. 'Everyone's got friends except me,' she thought, seeing a group swapping their reports. Her tentative friendship with Rhonda had ended acrimoniously when Deborah had gone out with a second-year student, not realizing Rhonda

188

was keen on him. Faye and Rhonda had moved into a flat near the theatre, and if they invited people back for coffee they excluded her.

To her surprise she received an invitation to Phillipa, Natasha and Jacqueline's house warming party. "I'll apologize to Jacqui for telling her about Max in front of everyone," she thought, imagining the friendship that would result.

Deciding that buying an expensive present would make them like her, she went into Myers. She had heard Rhonda saying she was going to buy a cheese-board, and knew Emily was giving them a casserole dish. Rejecting practical things like mugs or towels, she settled for a set of crystal wine glasses. Because she was paying with her mother's account card she chose the most expensive.

Wearing a long black dress with a low neckline, Deborah got out of the taxi and went up the winding path. The front door was open. 'How can they afford to live here?' she wondered as she looked down the long hallway. 'It must cost a fortune.' She was dismayed when Jacqueline, dressed in trousers and a white polo neck jumper, opened the fly-screen door.

"Gosh, sorry, am I early?" Deborah said. "Shall I go for a walk and come back when you're ready?"

"We are ready," said Jacqueline coolly. "Come in."

Cursing herself for her mistake, she followed Jacqueline into the kitchen, wondering how she could dress so casually for a party. Natasha was also wearing trousers. Phillipa, who was filling a pavlova case with whipped cream, wore a brown velvet suit and a cream silk blouse.

'I hope the others dress up,' she thought, handing the present to Natasha.

"Thanks, Deborah. We didn't expect presents." She tore off the wrapping paper and lifted the lid. Instead of being delighted by the six crystal glasses lying in nests of crimson satin, Natasha appeared embarrassed.

"What's wrong?" Deborah asked, thinking some were broken.

"They're gorgeous." Natasha looked more uncomfortable. "But you shouldn't have – spent so much."

Deborah saw the price label on the inside of the box. She could think of nothing to say. Jacqueline's expression, as she carried a plate of sandwiches to the table in the dining room, told her that she could not buy their friendship.

The silence was broken by the arrival of Frank. The fruit bowl he had bought them was proclaimed beautiful and Phillipa immediately filled it with oranges and apples.

The doorbell rang again and Jacqueline went to answer it.

"Can I do anything to help?" Deborah asked.

"Hello, Harriet," said Phillipa.

'Oh no,' thought Deborah. She turned around and smiled, trying to look confident. "Hello, Miss Shaw."

Harriet ignored her and handed Phillipa a present.

Deborah's face burned when she saw the six mugs, a milk jug and sugar bowl. She had seen the set in Myers and knew it had cost a quarter of what she had spent on the glasses.

As the evening progressed, her depression intensified. Not only had she bought an expensive and unsuitable present, she was overdressed. Most of the other girls were wearing trouser suits or caftans. Vivien, along with three others, wore hot-pants.

Deborah drifted over to the group Nicholas was with. To her amazement Emily was looking confident.

"No, no, let someone else play," said Nicholas.

"Oh go on, you're so good," said Jacqueline.

"Please, Nick," pleaded Emily.

He grinned at her. "Only if you sing."

She laughed. "Okay. Any requests?"

He looked exasperated. "I thought you'd refuse!"

"Well, I didn't, so you can't back out now."

"Emily, how much have you had to drink?" he asked.

She giggled. "Three glasses of punch."

"No wonder you're willing to sing." He flung his arm round her waist and dragged her into the music room. "You can't get out of this now." He went to the bookcase, pulled out a score of *The Barber of Seville* and sat at the piano.

Deborah stood beside him and turned the pages. Emily ended the aria with a curtsy and everyone cheered.

"Richard, Max, will you sing the duet?" asked Phillipa, handing them the score of *The Pearl Fishers*.

190

Max bowed. "Certainly, Philly."

When they had finished and the clapping died down, Nicholas turned to them. "You'll be doing that together in Covent Garden one day. Right, now I want to hear Natasha and Jacqui sing the 'Nocturne' from *Béatrice and Bénédict*."

Deborah was so absorbed in the beauty of the duet and the way Natasha's voice floated over Jacqueline's rich low notes, she almost forgot to turn the page. She saw them smile at each other. 'I wish I had a sister,' she thought.

"Sublime," said Nicholas, as the duet ended.

Everyone begged everyone else to sing, and Deborah longed for it to be her turn. But it never was. Miserably she watched Nicholas close the lid.

"Thanks for turning the pages, Deborah," he said.

Before she had time to respond Vivien put her arms round him.

'It's not fair,' she thought. 'Max should be ostracized, not me. And Jacqueline's broken up a marriage, but she's as popular as ever.'

The morning after the party, Nicholas took his cigarettes off the bedside table. He removed two, lit them and passed one to Vivien.

"Did you notice Phillipa and Frank last night?" she asked.

"No, I was too busy noticing your legs."

"They were kissing."

"Really? I wonder if she was drunk."

She laughed. "You sound like a disapproving father."

"I'm pleased, just surprised. I know this sounds mean, but sometimes Philly's a bit dull. She's so tidy and efficient."

"I'm tidy and efficient," she said indignantly.

He put his arm round her. "But you're sexy with it. Philly would never wear hot-pants."

Vivien put her cigarette in the ashtray. "The girl who was turning the pages for you – Deborah – she's not popular. Miss Shaw doesn't like her either, does she?"

"She doesn't know her. Ingrid Williams is Deborah's teacher." To stop her probing any further, he stubbed out his cigarette and kissed her.

Frank and Phillipa sat in a restaurant in South Yarra.

"You look pensive," said Frank as he refilled their glasses.

Remembering how pleased Nicholas and Harriet had been when she told them Frank had asked her out, she smiled wryly. "We've talked about Jacqui all night."

He looked evasive. "She's a friend of yours. Isn't it natural that we'd talk about her?"

She slid her spoon into her crème caramel. "You wish she wasn't going out with Max, don't you?"

"Yes," he admitted.

"Did you ever ask her out?"

"No, I knew she was upset about Max and I was waiting for her to recover. I didn't want to rush her. Sorry. I didn't mean to lead you on."

"You haven't. I'm not madly passionate about you either."

"I got that feeling." He ate a piece of apple pie. "I wasn't sure if it was because you were shy, or because you didn't want to be with me."

"I wouldn't have come if I hadn't wanted to be with you, Frank. I like you, but more as a friend really. I know we kissed at the party, but I was ... "

Frank grinned. "Drunk?"

She nodded. "A bit." 'And I was trying to make Nick jealous, but it didn't work,' she thought. "Were you kissing me to make Jacqui jealous?"

He looked horrified. "No. What sort of a bloke do you think I am? You're attractive, I like you and I enjoyed kissing you."

Phillipa picked up her glass. "Now we've been honest I feel better. I've enjoyed tonight," she said truthfully. "There's no reason why we can't do this again, is there?"

He winked at her. "None that I can think of."

Determined to be useful, Deborah helped Frank and Emily fill the portable barbecue with screwed up newspaper and nuggets of coal. The beach at Half Moon Bay in Black Rock was almost deserted. In winter the only visitors were dog walkers and illicit lovers.

"Who else is coming?" she asked, careful not to say anything that would offend anyone.

Frank lit a piece of kindling. "Nearly everyone, I think."

"Good. It should keep fine. It'll be fun, won't it?" She knew she was sounding trite.

"Should be," said Frank.

Overcoming the urge to say anything else in case she babbled, she concentrated on helping him get the fire going. As people arrived she handed out paper plates and filled glasses with wine or lemonade. Her satisfaction was demolished when Rhonda arrived and scowled at her, then whispered something to Faye. They looked at her and giggled. Not wanting them to see her blushing she turned away. Her humiliation was curtailed when Max and Richard started arguing about Vietnam.

"Only traitors go on peace marches," Max said.

"Peace isn't treachery, but sending conscripts to Vietnam is – the government are sucking up to America," said Richard.

Although he spoke calmly Deborah saw the anger in his eyes.

"So you want Australia to be taken over by communists? Very patriotic."

Frank turned away from the fire. "If the Japanese couldn't invade during the war I hardly think we're in peril now."

Max tutted. "Just because doing your National Service interrupted your singing career for a few years."

"We all know what interrupted your singing career, Max," said Natasha.

'I should have said that,' thought Deborah as people laughed. Politics bored her, but she wanted to snipe at Max. She tried to think of something clever to say.

Max laughed. "Natasha, how does your father feel about you going out with a coward – oh, sorry – pacifist? Or hasn't Richard had the guts to tell him?"

Richard raised his fist, but Frank grabbed his arm.

"Don't, Richard, don't let him provoke you!" begged Natasha.

Deborah wished Richard had broken Max's nose.

193

"A smashed jaw would shut you up for a few months!" shouted Richard.

Max stepped backwards. "Go on, peace lover, hit me!"

"Quit it, Max, or I'll bloody well let him thump you," said Frank, struggling to hold Richard.

Natasha stepped between them. "And what are you a lover of, Max? Getting girls into trouble and being unfaithful to your wife, that's what!"

Frank and Natasha calmed Richard, but the atmosphere had become strained. Jacqueline and Max stood apart, and it was clear that she was agitated. When the first lot of sausages and chops were cooked, Max went over to Richard and held out his hand. "No hard feelings?"

"Yes, a lot of hard feelings, Max. You can't just say what you like and think I'll forgive you because you put on the charm. And I know you're only doing this because of Jacqui."

Max looked so uncertain, Deborah smiled. She hoped he'd put himself even more in the wrong by insulting Richard again, but he nodded. "Okay, I apologize for calling you a coward, I was wrong."

"Thank you, Max," said Richard formally. But he did not shake his hand.

Deborah sat with Emily. She tried to encourage her to talk, but Emily was upset by the row and the conversation was one-sided.

After lunch they all cleared up the rubbish and put it in a box.

"Let's go for a jog along the beach," said Frank.

Natasha kicked off her shoes. "I'll race you!"

"Wait for me," said Phillipa pulling off her shoes and socks.

Frank and Natasha tore off, and Phillipa ran down to the water's edge. When Jacqueline joined her, they pursued Natasha and Frank. They had gone about twenty yards when Phillipa shrieked and hopped about holding her foot. Richard raced up to her and Deborah followed. Blood was pouring through Phillipa's fingers.

Jacqueline picked up a piece of glass. "She trod on this."

Deborah felt sick. Richard carried Phillipa back to their belongings, leaving a trail of blood in the sand. The others crowded round.

He put her on the rug. "Lie down, Philly. I'll hold your leg up to try and stem the bleeding, but I reckon you're going to need stitches."

Jacqueline picked up a bottle of wine. "Philly, I'm going to pour some of this into the cut to clean it."

Phillipa shut her eyes and winced. Max held her hand.

'Creep,' thought Deborah, looking in dismay at the blood soaking the sand. "She'll bleed to death," she whimpered.

"Shut up, you fool," snapped Jacqueline. "Don't worry, Philly, you haven't severed an artery, it's just a very deep cut."

"If you're going to have hysterics, Deborah, have them somewhere else," said Max.

"Hold her leg for me, Jacqui," said Richard. He pulled off his jumper, unbuttoned his shirt and wrapped it round Phillipa's foot. "Let's get you to hospital." He helped her stand. "Put your arm round my neck."

Deborah watched him carry her to the top of the cliff. Impressed by the way he had taken control, she felt that it would be worth the pain Phillipa had suffered, to be the object of his chivalry. At that moment she realized she was in love with him.

Every year the *Friends of the Theatre* organized a party to celebrate Harriet's birthday at the end of August. This year her LP was being launched at the same time. Invitations were sent to anyone who had anything to do with the theatre. As an opera student Deborah was automatically invited. Obeying the instruction on the invitation not to bring a present, she was dismayed to see Emily, who had arrived at the same time, carrying a brightly wrapped parcel.

"I thought we weren't supposed to bring anything," said Deborah.

"Oh, everyone ignores that."

"I didn't know – I didn't bring one."

"Don't worry about it."

'I didn't even buy her a card,' she thought, following Emily into the theatrette. A table piled with gifts and presided over by the president of *The Friends*, was the first thing she saw. 'Why can't I get anything right?' she thought. While she hovered near the door Emily went over to the table.

"Excuse me, Deborah," said Richard.

"Sorry." She stepped aside to let him and Natasha pass. Feeling like an outcast she watched them put their presents on the table. In his grey pinstriped suit, pink shirt and burgundy paisley tie, Richard looked urbane. 'He's more handsome than Max,' she realized. 'He's sincere – Max is affected.'

All over the theatre, groups of people talked and laughed. Aware that she was not wanted in any of them she wandered down the corridor, trying to look as if she had a purpose. Nicholas and Vivien strolled around holding hands, Jacqueline and Max were dancing and Richard had his arm round Natasha.

At ten o'clock the president of *The Friends* handed Harriet an enormous bouquet of flowers. "Every year, we comply with Miss Shaw's request to put 'No Presents' on the invitations, but the pile of gifts gets bigger. This shows how much we appreciate what she has done for her students, staff and the theatre." She turned to Harriet. "You have given us so much – these are tokens of our gratitude."

Deborah expected Harriet to make a long speech, but she smiled and said, "Thank you for coming to my birthday party, and for your presents. I hope you all enjoy the evening."

Vivien took photos, and Jeremy Langford said, "As you all know, some of Miss Shaw's old recordings have been made into an LP. It has just been released and is on sale in the foyer tonight. Miss Shaw will be happy to autograph the covers."

As the crowd in the theatrette dispersed, Deborah went into the foyer and stood in the queue waiting to buy the record. Bewildered by Harriet's attitude towards her, she had not been going to buy one, but when she had heard 'Caro nome', on the radio, she had been overwhelmed by the richness of her voice.

She went back to the theatrette to get the cover signed. Harriet was surrounded by people waiting for her autograph. Between taking photos, Vivien, who was covering the release for *The Australian Women's Weekly*, was talking to people who had bought the record. When Deborah's turn came, Harriet's smile stayed in place, but all the warmth left her eyes.

"Miss Shaw, I cried when I heard you on the radio," she gushed, hoping she could rectify whatever she had done to warrant Harriet's loathing. "Why did you give up?"

She recoiled as Harriet's mouth hardened and her eyes filled with hatred. The flash on Vivien's camera went off. Feeling under attack, Deborah went into the kitchen. She looked at the cover. On all the others Miss Shaw had written, kind regards, or love and always the name of the person. On hers was simply her signature.

"Deborah!"

She jumped, almost dropping the record.

"Sorry, I didn't mean to startle you," said Vivien. "I'm asking people about the record and why they bought it."

Deborah forced herself to look composed. "Miss Shaw's not my teacher."

"Have you ever been Miss Shaw's student?"

"No."

Vivien smiled. "So you don't know her?"

"No. Well, only through the theatre."

"Good." Vivien opened her notepad. "That means your opinion will be unbiased." She looked at Deborah expectantly.

"I've never liked 'Caro Nome' much," said Deborah. "It's an interesting aria technically, but when I heard Harriet Shaw's record on the radio – it moved me. Her voice was exquisite. Lots of singers have exquisite voices, but hers was passionate – that's the only word I can use to describe it, but it was more … it was – yes, I could see a young girl in love."

Vivien finished scribbling in her shorthand pad. "Thanks, Deborah, that's great. This will be in *The Australian Women's Weekly* in two weeks' time. I think I'll use the photo of you getting Miss Shaw's autograph."

'You won't when you see it,' thought Deborah.

Vivien studied the photo of Harriet and Deborah. At Natasha's, Jacqueline's and Phillipa's house warming party she had seen Harriet looking at Deborah with dislike. When Nicholas had told her that Harriet didn't know Deborah, she decided she must have imagined it. Then she had seen Deborah asking Harriet to sign her record cover. "If Harriet doesn't know Deborah, why does she hate her?" she murmured.

Harriet epitomized the type of woman Vivien admired and wanted

197

to emulate. In varying degrees she was treated with devotion, awe, respect, love and loyalty. She hadn't needed marriage or children to stave off loneliness, the theatre was her life and her students and staff were her family. Vivien never thought of Harriet as old. Unlike many elderly people who were obsessed with illness and the past, she never mentioned her health and only talked about the past when she was asked.

Well dressed and elegant, Harriet's clothes, appearance and house were obviously important to her. In her youth, Vivien had associated old age with stale smells. Her grandparents had hardly ever washed. Their house, that was without a bathroom or hot water, smelt worse than they did. But Harriet smelt of soap and Chanel perfume. Her house was filled with the fragrances of coffee, fresh air, furniture polish, and flowers. Since the release of her record she had become an enigma, and Vivien wondered how many people accepted her reasons for giving up her singing career.

When Nicholas arrived to take her out to dinner, she showed him the photo.

He shrugged. "Perhaps she had a pain."

"Come on, Nick, that expression is loathing. See poor Deborah's face. Look at the other photos. She's smiling at Natasha and Jacqui, kissing Phillipa, shaking hands with Jeremy Langford and laughing with Frank. In every other photo she's happy."

"It's just an unfortunate shot."

"I don't think so. And neither do you."

"Vivien, if there had been any scandal involving her, I would have known about it years ago."

"You're a hopeless liar, Nicholas."

"And you're a journalist with an inventive imagination. If we don't hurry up, the restaurant will be full."

Nicholas didn't get home until three that morning. After dinner, he had gone back to Vivien's where they had talked and made love. He had forgotten his concerns about Harriet but, alone in his flat, they resurfaced and he was unable to sleep. His relationship with Vivien was fulfilling. She was intelligent, uninhibited, and interested in people, but her curiosity about Harriet's past disturbed him.

He wanted to warn Harriet to disguise her dislike of Deborah, but

198

he would have to explain why. Rather than risk causing Harriet to distrust Vivien, but determined to let her know the seriousness of the situation, he decided to lie.

"Too many late nights?" said Harriet when he arrived at the theatre.

"No. Too many worries," he replied irritably. "About you. Vivien showed me the photos she took of you signing the record covers. The one of you and Deborah is horrendous. Vivien thinks it's an unfortunate shot, but I know better. Deborah looks as if you've spat at her. You've got to hide your feelings."

Harriet looked defensive. "Thank you for telling me."

Chapter 19

'Within my heart a flame is raging,
A flame that ne'er can find assuaging;'
Il Trovatore – Verdi

Not wanting Nicholas to be suspicious of her motives, Vivien let a week pass without mentioning Harriet. When the editor approved of her proposal to do a series of articles about the theatre, she wrote to Harriet.

5th September 1971

Dear Miss Shaw,

My editor has asked me to approach you regarding a series of articles they would like to run about the National Theatre and its history. The first would deal with its foundation. Of particular interest would be any opposition you encountered when you were planning it and, in contrast, people who were helpful and believed in your mission. The second article will concentrate on its early days, while the others will focus on the successful singers you have taught and inspired. The length of the series will depend on you, but it could go on for at least a month.

To her delight, Harriet rang her as soon as she received the letter. Wanting to do some research first, she arranged to do the first interview a week later.

In the newspaper archives, Vivien discovered that she was not the only person who had been puzzled by Harriet. In 1941, Harriet had been invited to sing at a fund raising concert for the war effort. Her refusal had been criticized and she was branded as unpatriotic. The newspaper attacks only abated when it was revealed that rehearsals for a concert given by her students, in aid of the Red Cross, were already under way. Held in the Town Hall, the concert raised a lot of money, but even then a reporter challenged Harriet's refusal to be one of the singers. Her explanation that she was the organizer and thus could not sing, did not convince him.

'It doesn't convince me either,' thought Vivien.

While she was reading the review of the concert, she recognized the name of one of the young singers. Ingrid Williams.

'Deborah's teacher,' she thought excitedly.

As soon as she got back to her office, she rang Ingrid and arranged to take her out to lunch.

Ingrid was disappointingly enthusiastic about Harriet. During their main course, Vivien raised the subject of the 1941 concert and asked Ingrid if she could understand why Harriet had refused to sing.

Squeezing lemon over her trout, Ingrid smiled. "It wasn't obvious then, we were all too young and puffed up with our own importance, but yes, I know why now."

Vivien hoped her expression did not betray her eagerness.

"You've heard her record?" asked Ingrid.

"Yes."

"What did you think?"

"Amazing – I'm not a singer, but – "

Ingrid waved her knife in the air. "That's just it. I wanted to be a singer, but I wasn't good enough to make it to the top. I could have sung in the chorus, but I didn't want to – that's why I teach. I wanted to be famous like Harriet – most of us did, but out of all of us in that year only one made it professionally – and you know something?"

"No," Vivien almost whispered.

"He sang in the chorus of the Australian Opera. He auditioned for Covent Garden and Sadler's Wells, and didn't make it. If Miss Shaw had sung, she would have made us all sound insignificant. She said it was our night, and she meant it. I remember her telling a reporter, 'Write about the future not the past. I am the past, these young men and women are the future. Help their careers by concentrating on them.' What she didn't say was that she was not going to steal our glory. And

201

she would have. No reporter would have bothered with us if she'd sung." Ingrid laughed. "We would have deserved it though, we were a conceited lot." She looked contemplative. "I'm sorry I never heard her sing. My parents did – they saw her at Covent Garden once. My father said it was the sound you'd only expect to hear if you went to heaven. He thought she was better than Melba. Technically, Melba's voice was perfect and pure but cold – Miss Shaw's had passion. They were so excited when I passed my audition with her."

It was when Vivien was paying the bill that she realized that there was something wrong with what Ingrid had said. 'Why hasn't she ever heard Harriet sing?' she thought. "Ingrid, this whole singing lesson thing intrigues me," she said innocently. "Would it be intrusive if I sat in on one of your lessons?"

"I don't think so. I'll let you know. Does the type of voice matter?"

"No. I'm just interested in how you do it."

Through Nicholas, Vivien asked if she could observe one of Harriet's lessons.

Because Harriet had been Ingrid's teacher, Vivien had expected their teaching methods to be similar, and they were. But apart from the fact that Harriet was more inspiring, there was one striking difference.

Ingrid used her singing voice to demonstrate how various techniques improved the tone.

During the lesson with a young soprano, Harriet did not sing one note.

Vivien went home and sat at her desk.

WHY? she wrote in her notebook. *Because she can't?*

"No, that doesn't make sense," she murmured. "But, she used to have a brilliant voice and no one has heard her sing for years. Why not? The only thing I can think of is because she can't." She sharpened her pencil. *Did she lose her voice? If so, how? Is that the reason she gave up her operatic career?* she wrote. Leaning back in her chair, she tossed the pencil on the desk. "Blimey."

"I'll catch you!" shouted Richard.

Natasha ran down the beach and plunged into the ocean. He stopped

202

in the shallows and watched her dive into a breaker. When she surfaced he saw her looking for him. Long strands of hair lay across her face like seaweed. He stepped out of her line of vision.

He and Natasha had been dating for eight months, but this was one of the few times they had been alone. Her parents were on a cruise and relations between Natasha and Jacqueline were strained so Jacqueline had stayed in Melbourne with Phillipa instead of coming to the beach house.

Natasha turned and saw him standing at the water's edge. Catching the next breaker, she body surfed to the shore and the wave dumped her on the sand at his feet.

"You beast!" she gasped. "I thought you'd been caught in a rip or attacked by a shark."

He knelt beside her and slipped the straps of her swimming costume off her shoulders.

Natasha put her arms round his neck and kissed him. "Richard, make love to me."

He smiled. "Are you sure?"

"Yes."

"Is everything … is it safe?"

"Yes, yes," she said impatiently.

He jumped to his feet and held out his hand.

"No, here. I can't wait any longer," she said, wriggling out of her costume.

"You've waited eight months and you can't wait another minute?" he said, lying next to her.

She laughed. "No. Not another second."

A wave engulfed them and they leapt to their feet, coughing and laughing.

"That's cooled us down," said Natasha.

Richard picked her up. "Not for long," he said, carrying her over the hill into the sand dunes.

"As this is your last term, we've set you some tough challenges," said Nicholas. "We've never given this to first-year students before, but we know you can do it. Your talent, imagination and dedication are remarkable, and we're looking forward to seeing what you do with the scenes we set you for the rest of the term."

Max had not realized how serious Nicholas had been until he handed out their homework. Sounds of alarm reverberated round the theatrette.

"Help!" squawked Jacqueline.

"Sorry, Max," said Emily. "I'm your Brünnhilde."

"Don't panic," he said, happy he had not been put with Deborah. Passionate about Wagner, he was looking forward to acting Siegfried, even if he wasn't singing it. He looked down the list and saw that Richard was Wotan. Since the argument on the beach Richard and Frank had avoided him and he wanted to redeem himself. Knowing they were both Wagner fans he went over to them. "This is going to be exciting."

"Exciting?" said Emily. "I'm terrified."

He looked at her encouragingly. "I'm looking forward to it. Come on, I think we all need some strong coffee."

"How could Nick be so cruel?" said Rhonda as they went into *The Scheherazade*.

After they ordered, Natasha giggled. "Frank, how are you going to be a dwarf?"

"With the same degree of difficulty you're going to have pretending you're swimming at the bottom of the Rhine," he replied.

Jacqueline picked up a knife. "We could cut off your legs."

"No need. I worked it out," Frank said quickly. "Alberich is going to be a dwarf in character not stature. He renounces love so he can get the gold and anyone who does that must … "

"Be a sport, Frank," said Max. "Jacqui's dying to cut your legs off. Don't spoil her fun."

"Why couldn't Wagner have written normal operas?" moaned Faye. "Why did he have to write about gods doing impossible things in impossible places?"

Emily flicked through the copy of the *Götterdämmerung* libretto. "I don't think I can do this," she said nervously.

"Of course you can," said Max. "At least we're on dry land."

Richard looked at the list. "The Rhinemaidens have got the most difficult scene," said Richard.

Jacqueline grimaced. "The logistics will take us a week."

"Think, think," urged Natasha. "Let's take one scene at a time. Nick's bound to do them in sequence so he'll take ours first. Could we locate the Rhinemaidens anywhere else?"

"Down a coal-mine," said Frank.

"Let's do it in the dark and then no one can see us," said Jacqueline. "Nick did encourage us to be original."

Natasha's eyes widened. "Or a gold-mine."

They looked at her.

"How do you do it?" asked Emily in admiration.

"It just popped into my head. Word association, I suppose," she said.

"I was joking," said Frank.

"Joke some more," Rhonda begged him.

"Don't get carried away, it might be too complicated," said Natasha. "We could be sitting on the river bank sunning ourselves."

Faye shook her head. "What about the gold?"

Natasha checked her libretto. "Flosshilde warns Woglinde and Wellgunde that Alberich might have designs on it, but then they realize he's interested in them. So we're sure it's safe. And we've got to be careless, because he steals it."

"Hang on," said Max. "My flat's near here. Would you like to come back and we can discuss our scenes and maybe even work out some moves."

"Yes," said Rhonda.

"Frank, do you want to phone Phillipa?" asked Max. "Let's make a bit of a party out of it."

He nodded. "Thanks, Max."

"She can be our audience," said Jacqueline.

Max stood up. "I'll go and get a cake or something. Give me about half an hour."

In the milk bar, he bought a fruit cake and a packet of chocolate biscuits. When he got to the till he was embarrassed to find he was three cents short. He was going to put the biscuits back, but the girl smiled. "Don't worry. Pay me next time."

"That's very kind of you – I'm not usually so forgetful." Her smitten expression did nothing to quell his fury with Susan for making him destitute.

In his flat they worked till midnight.

"Thanks, Max, that was fun," said Rhonda as they prepared to leave. "And we got a lot done."

Jacqueline wanted to spend a bit of time with Max before she went home. "Philly, do you mind leaving the car and going with Richard and Natasha, I'll be along soon, but I need to ask Max something."

Phillipa looked at Richard. "Is that all right?"

"Sure," he said. "Thanks, Max, that helped a lot."

Phillipa gave Jacqueline the car keys.

"I won't be long," Jacqueline said as they went to the door.

As soon as they left, Max pulled her into his arms and kissed her. "I've been wanting to do that all night," he said as they went into the bedroom.

An hour later Jacqueline sat up. "I wish I didn't have to go."

He kissed her shoulder. "Then don't."

"I have to else Natasha will worry."

"Get dressed and we'll go to the phone box."

"Have you got any change? I got rid of all mine in *The Scheherazade*," she said.

"Hell," said Max. "I've got no change either."

She sighed. "Oh well."

"Jacqui, I want to spend the night with you and wake up in the morning curled up together."

"Max, I can't. They'll worry."

"No, they'll be asleep. Look, I'll put the alarm on for six. You'll be home before they wake up." He pulled the quilt over her. "And anyway," he said, putting his arms around her, "They'll know where you are – and what you're doing."

They were woken by the door bell.

"I forgot to put the alarm on!" said Max.

"What time is it?"

"Sorry, Jacqui, it's nine o'clock." Max pulled on his dressing gown and went into the hall.

Before she had time to get out of bed and grab her shirt, Natasha,

Richard and Phillipa were in the bedroom.

Natasha's face was red with fury. "We've been frantic! Why didn't you ring?"

She pulled the quilt up to her chin. "Max hasn't got a phone."

Richard glared at her. "There's a phone box down the road, you inconsiderate little cow." His disgust made her feel exposed.

"Don't speak to her like that," said Max. "It's none of your business where she spent the night."

"You slimy creep!" shouted Natasha. "Why don't you go back to your wife?"

"Natasha's been ringing hospitals, Jacqui," said Phillipa. "I wanted to come here first, but she insisted you'd never deliberately worry us."

"She didn't," said Max. "I forgot to set the alarm. Now stop all this melodrama."

"And you had the car, Jacqui, so Natasha had to phone Richard and get him out of bed."

"Well, now you know she's not lying in the morgue, go home," said Max.

Jacqueline saw Richard looking at their clothes strewn around the room. Last night she had felt daring. Now she felt sordid.

Nicholas was going to joke about Phillipa's glum expression, but stopped, thinking it might be the anniversary of her mother's or father's birthday. "What's wrong, Philly?" he asked gently.

With her chin in her hands she sat at his desk and told him about Jacqueline staying with Max and the resulting quarrel. "Natasha and Jacqui haven't spoken to each other for two days. It's awful."

"I can imagine. You must wish you lived alone again."

"No. In spite of everything I like belonging and sharing things. If it wasn't for Max … " She sighed. "Jacqui won't admit she was wrong."

"I'll talk to her," said Nicholas.

"No. She'll accuse me of being a blabber mouth."

"I'll be discreet. She needs to talk to someone impartial."

That evening he found Jacqueline in *The Scheherazade* filling in time between her singing lesson and the German class. "Hello, Jacqui, mind if I join you? I'm not interrupting your homework, am I?"

"No. I was just revising." She shut her German book.

"What time are you meeting Natasha?" he asked after their coffee and toasted sandwiches arrived.

"Didn't Phillipa tell you about our fight?"

"Fight?"

She told him what had happened. "I would have apologized, but they all barged in and Richard and Natasha hurled abuse at us." She put sugar in her coffee. "Everyone's against Max. My parents don't like him either, but they think Richard's perfect. He could have gone to jail. At least adultery's legal."

"That's spiteful and not worthy of you, Jacqui."

"Even you're against me." She banged her cup in the saucer.

"No I'm not. Neither is everyone else. They're concerned."

"He can get divorced in three years," she said wiping butter from her fingers with a paper serviette. "Anyway, they're trying to change the divorce laws to one year's separation."

"If you get pregnant he's not free to marry you."

Her expression was defiant. "I'm on the pill."

"Not always a hundred percent reliable, Jacqui. Apologize to Natasha. Your relationship with Max is difficult enough without alienating your family."

She glared at him in frustration. "Max did the right thing."

"Did he? Jacqui, he didn't love Susan, but he made her pregnant."

"He married her. What would you have done?"

"I would never have got myself into that position."

"Oh, aren't you just too bloody good to be true!"

"Perhaps if Max had been more like me, you wouldn't be in the mess you're in now," he said quietly. "You're the one who's suffering. Stop lashing out at the people who care about you."

"I'm not in a mess – he loves me."

"Does he? He didn't love his wife, and I doubt he had anything other than superficial feelings for all the other girls he seduced." He lit a cigarette. "How's *Das Rheingold*?"

She grunted. "Ask Natasha."

"I'm asking you. Is it affecting your scene?"

She nodded.

"You've got to have the framework of a scene by Saturday. If you haven't I'll be hurling abuse. Not just at you and Natasha – Faye will get it too."

"That not fair."

"I know it's not. It'll be hard on Faye because she was excited about working with you and Natasha. I demand professionalism, Jacqueline. This is not a kindergarten. You're training for a difficult and cruel profession. If you can't even get through a scene at opera school because you've had a row with your sister, how are you going to manage at The Australian Opera or Covent Garden? What are you going to do if you have a fight with your leading man? Refuse to work with him?

"The audience don't care about your emotions off the stage. One day you'll be an opera singer and whatever turmoil there is in your private life the audience deserve the best you can give." He stubbed out his cigarette. "Remember, Jacqueline, I expect a good performance of the Rhinemaidens on Saturday." He put some money on the table and left.

Phillipa was so horrified when he told her what he had said, he began to worry that he had made things worse. He was relieved when she bounded into his office the following morning.

"Jacqui apologized, Natasha apologized and then they both cried."

"So everything's all right till next time," he said.

She put her head in her hands. "Don't. I couldn't stand it."

Desperate to solve his financial problems Max applied for a highly paid position with The Commonwealth Bank. He could no longer afford to go to the laundromat and had to wash his clothes in the bath. His flat was untidy and dirty. Unlike the girlfriends he'd had before his marriage, Jacqueline never did his housework. The day before the interview he asked her if she would iron his shirts.

"Why can't you iron them?"

"I've never done any ironing before. I can't do it … I've scorched so many shirts … "

"Never? What about before you got married?"

"My girlfriends did it."

"What fools."

"They were loving and generous."

"They were fools. Women have changed. And some men are changing too. I bet Richard doesn't ask Natasha to do his ironing. He's capable of looking after himself."

"Jacqui, please, just this once. I hate ironing."

"So do I, but I iron my own clothes and I've no intention of doing yours as well."

He threw the shirts across the room. "You are the most selfish person I've ever met."

"I'm going home." She went to the door. "And pick up your shirts or they'll be even more difficult to iron."

"I'm sorry, Jacqui, I'm being a bastard."

She sighed and leant in the doorway.

"Forgive me," he said putting his arms around her.

"We argue too much," she said quietly.

He held her tightly. "I get preoccupied about Zoe and I'm worried about money."

"It's more than that. I only see you on Sundays when Zoe's away. Sometimes I feel like your dirty secret."

"If Susan found out about you, I hate to think what she'd do. Everything would be all right if it wasn't for her. If I get this new job, things will be different. I won't tell her about the extra money." He held her face in his hands. "Everything will be all right, I promise."

His first interview went well and he was invited to attend a second. Gloom filtered away as he worked out what he would do with the extra money. After the second interview on Monday he was sure the job was his. On Thursday he received a rejection letter.

Chapter 20

'Oh, heavens, what a humiliation I suffer!
Oh, cruel husband, to reduce me to this!'
The Marriage of Figaro – Mozart

"We don't have to spend lots of money to have fun," said Jacqueline jiggling a bag in front of Max on Saturday after opera school.

"What's in there?"

"Sandwiches and fruit for a moonlight picnic on the beach. Come on, we'll drive to Brighton."

The full moon had risen and was shimmering on the water by the time they finished their sandwiches. The beauty and peace did not soothe Max's irritability and frustration.

Jacqueline put her head on his shoulder. "Beautiful, isn't it?"

He heard the determination to be cheerful in her tone. He could have pretended, but he was feeling bitter. "What are Richard and Natasha doing tonight?" he asked.

"Going to see *The Graduate* with Philly and Frank."

Max wished he could have gone with them, but last week he had received two accounts he was unable to pay. "I hate not being able to afford to go anywhere. Richard's six years younger than me, and he and Natasha are always going out to dinner and the pictures."

"I've told you that I'll pay."

"No. It hurts my pride. Richard lives in a big flat and owns a car. He's got a piano and everything. He's a menial public servant and I'm a manager in charge of dozens of people. And Frank's little better than a labourer."

"Don't spoil things, Max, we're enjoying ourselves."

"I'm not. We're here because I can't afford to go anywhere else." As soon as he said it he realized how callous he sounded. He put his arm round her. "I hate being poor. I'm not free, Jacqui. I was trapped

211

by marriage and now I'm trapped by poverty. I have to check before I go to *The Scheherazade* to make sure I've got enough money for a cup of coffee. It will never end. When we get divorced she'll find some other way to get at me. That's what's making me miserable. And the injustice. Susan's father left her everything. She doesn't need my money. I could take her to court, but that would distress Zoe."

"I'm sorry, Max, I wish I could help."

Suddenly he had an idea. He was about to blurt it out, but thought it would be better to work out a strategy. "Let's go for a walk," he said taking off his shoes.

They strolled in the shallows. Deciding it was warm enough for a swim they left their clothes in a pile and went into the water. They kissed and he felt his depression lifting.

"Have you ever made love in the sea?" she asked wrapping her legs around him.

He had, but decided it would be wiser to let her think it was a unique experience for him as well.

When they left the water Jacqueline laughed. "I didn't bring any towels."

It was cold in the breeze and he shivered. He watched Jacqueline as she rubbed her hands over her hair making the water run in rivulets down her back and shoulders. "You're as beautiful as a statue," he said.

She smiled and looked shy. "I'm too fat."

"No. You're voluptuous – statuesque."

She laughed. "My only resemblance to a statue at the moment is that I'm cold." She began putting on her clothes.

As he watched her he had an idea. When they had dressed they went back to the rug.

He cuddled her. "You're certainly liberated," he said approvingly. "Stripping naked on a suburban beach. Weren't you frightened someone would come?"

"I was thinking of something else," she said dreamily.

"I've decided I like women's lib." He hesitated, wondering if she guessed where he was taking the conversation. "Are you liberated enough to consider living with me?"

She jerked away from him. "You said that if Susan – "

"I've got two bedrooms and I can say you're my lodger. We could do so much. I could afford to take you out."

"No, Max. My parents would have a fit."

Curbing his aggravation, he stroked her hair. "You've got to stop them controlling your life, you're a grown woman."

"They don't control my life, but they'd be upset if – "

"Please, Darling. What's more important to you, them or me?"

"Don't, Max. What about Susan? I don't want to be involved in a divorce case."

"She wouldn't know."

"I've got commitments to Philly and Natasha. We signed a lease for a year, I can't leave them with extra rent to pay."

"They can find someone else. Please, Jacqui, it's our only chance."

"No. I don't believe in living together."

"Oh, very liberated. You're a hypocrite, Jacqui. You preach liberation when you don't want to iron my shirts, but now you've slunk back to the Victorian age because you haven't got the guts to come and live with me." He stood up. "If you loved me you'd want to live with me," he said striding to the water.

She caught up with him. "Be patient. When you're divorced we can get married."

"Marriage, marriage, marriage! You're just like all the other bloody girls!" Ignoring her shocked cry he continued, "Why should I buy a book when I can join a library? If you cared about me you'd want to live with me. If you don't, we're finished. I need a woman now."

"Well go and find one!" She ran back to their picnic and threw the sandwich box in her bag. "Find some subservient drip who'll do your ironing because you're too lazy to do it yourself."

He knelt on the rug. "Jacqui, I'm sorry."

Moonlight caught the tears streaking her face. "Get her to buy you a washing machine, car, a piano and stereo!" She tugged at the rug trying to pull it from under him. "You want me to live with you because you can't look after yourself and you're short of money. Get off!"

He stood up and held out his arms placatingly. "Jacqui – "

She yanked the rug up, scattering apple cores and orange peel over the sand. "As to your library book analogy, you'll find that when you want a particular book from the library, someone else has got it." She flung the rug over her shoulder and stalked up the beach.

He followed her to her car park.

"I'm not giving you a lift," she said unlocking the driver's side.

"How am I going to get home?"

"Walk!" She slammed her door and started the engine.

He knocked on the window. "Jacqui!"

She drove off.

It took him over an hour to walk home.

Natasha was surprised to see the Rover parked in the drive when she and Phillipa returned home after *The Graduate*. She heard the shower running in the bathroom.

"Jacqui?" she called.

"What?"

Natasha went into the bathroom. "You're home early."

"So?" asked Jacqueline turning off the water and pulling her towel off the rail. "What's it got to do with you?" Violently she pulled the shower curtain aside and stepped out.

"Have you and Max had a row?"

"We've broken up. Go on – gloat."

"No. I hate it when you're unhappy. What happened?"

She put on her dressing gown. "He asked me to live with him."

Resisting the urge to condemn him, Natasha followed her down the hall into her bedroom. "I'd miss you. So would Philly, but ... perhaps you should live with him," she said slowly.

"Are you mad? What about Mum and Dad?"

Natasha sat on the bed. "Keep it secret. I wouldn't tell anyone. If it didn't work out, no one would know. But if you get married after he's divorced and it goes wrong, you'll have the stigma of being a divorcée to contend with. It's not called a trial marriage for nothing."

Jacqueline shook her head. "I don't want to live with him. It's marriage or nothing." She sat at the dressing table. "Do you think he loves me?"

Natasha wished she could say no, but she had seen Max's expression when he looked at Jacqueline.

"You don't, do you?"

"Actually, I do," Natasha said reluctantly. "And that's the problem. Yours and his."

Max was overwrought when Jacqueline made a point of sitting as far away from him as possible at Saturday's drama class. He tried to suppress his panic and concentrate on what Nicholas was saying.

"We're coming to the end of your first year, and it's time to put all the work you've done on the opera scenes into a musical performance," said Nicholas. "Miss Shaw and I have selected six scenes for you to work on from now until the end of term. They'll be performed in the theatrette accompanied by a pianist. Your audience will be the second and third-year opera students.

"Until now your scenes have been based on your own interpretation and timing. Now you'll have the discipline of the music and you'll have to tighten up everything. Next year you'll be doing this regularly so it will be a valuable preliminary exercise. As an additional challenge all the scenes will be new to you, although perhaps not the characters."

Max had been hoping that he would play The Duke to Jacqueline's Maddalena, and Nicholas's words depressed him. There were not many operas involving love scenes between tenors and contraltos.

"We've chosen scenes from *Aida, Eugene Onegin, Madame Butterfly, The Flying Dutchman, Così fan tutte* and *Norma*," said Nicholas. "The production will be principals only, any scenes involving the chorus will be reorganized."

Max was excited to discover that he was playing Lensky to Jacqueline's Olga in *Eugene Onegin*. Even Deborah's inclusion as Tatiana did not upset him. After class he walked over to her. "Hello, Olga," he said softly, disregarding her scowl. "I did a lot of thinking when I was walking home from Brighton."

She looked at him haughtily. "I'm not going to apologize."

"I don't expect you to. I'm saying I'm sorry." He saw her pupils dilate. "It's hell without you. Please forgive me."

Her eyes glittered with tears, and he knew he had won.

Taking her hand he kissed it. "My heart is ruled by one emotion, one constant yearning for devotion, for you are my goddess and my muse."

"You know your lines already, Max. So do I."

He saw her struggling to keep her expression cold, but her flushed cheeks and the amusement in her eyes exposed her.

"This is a more appropriate quote. How like a man to fly into a passion. They're foolish, impulsive; they argue and quarrel, but never a moment consider what fighting may lead to."

He smiled. "Wrong act, but I get the point. Nick and Miss Shaw couldn't have picked a better scene for us."

A chance encounter with an old school friend who had just returned from a trip round the world and was looking for somewhere to live, solved Max's problems. Reasoning that he would be providing cutlery and china, Max charged him two thirds of the rent. With the deposit he was able to pay his outstanding accounts. To his surprise Jacqueline had helped him clean and tidy the flat before the man came to view it.

Able to think clearly, now he was no longer plagued by debt, he neutralized Deborah's hostility by meeting her before the others arrived for their first rehearsal.

"I'm sorry I treated you badly. But I think you got your own back." He made it sound as if he admired her for outwitting him. Encouraged by her softening expression he continued, "We have to work together, and we've got the same aim. Let's stun the second and third-year students with our brilliance."

To his relief she agreed. Tension during the rehearsals was masked by politeness and their genuine attempts to treat each other with respect.

Going to restaurants and the pictures with Frank and Phillipa and Natasha and Richard was fun. However much she had pretended otherwise, he knew Jacqueline had missed being with them. Anxious to achieve a reconciliation he was at his most charming. He was grateful that Frank and Richard, apparently as determined as he was to avoid antagonism, never discussed Vietnam in his presence. Because Max still had to be careful with money they interspersed visits to the cinema, theatre and restaurants with picnics and barbecues.

Inspired by Jacqueline's idea of moonlit picnics, Phillipa roasted a chicken, made a potato salad and chocolate cake, and they all went to Half Moon Bay after opera school one night. As they sat on the sand listening to the sea and talking about their scenes, Max felt optimistic enough to think he might be able to buy a car in six months' time.

♪   ♪   ♪

Susan's heart thumped as she walked into Prince Henry's Hospital.
Hoping that Jacqueline Howard would agree to see her during her lunch
hour, she had her speech prepared. If necessary, she would cry and beg.
The sign for the admissions office seemed to jump out mockingly, she
didn't even have to look for it. The area was crowded and she was able
to stand unobtrusively and observe the staff at the counter.

A girl with black hair was preparing a folder for a patient. Susan
moved closer to look at her badge. The quality of the photographs taken
by the private detective had been poor and she had been unable to
distinguish the girl's features. This was her rival. An attractive young
woman, not slender, not fat either, but well proportioned. Jacqueline's
hair gleamed in the lights and Susan enviously noted her clear skin and
alluring eyes outlined with long lashes. A white uniform enhanced her
innocent appearance as she smiled kindly at the old man in front of her.

Susan felt ugly and obese. 'As soon as she sees me, she'll know
why Max prefers her,' she thought. 'If she's nice she'll pity me, if she's
nasty she'll be contemptuous.' Unable to face either expression, she left
the hospital, feeling pulverized with jealousy.

When Zoe was doing her homework that night, Susan sat in the
darkening garden. 'I knew I'd lose him when he went back to opera
school. I'm plain and fat. I've got no weapons.' She shivered as a cool
wind gusted across the garden.

"Mummy, what's wrong?"

"Nothing, precious ... " She trailed off and stared at Zoe.

On Sunday, when Max arrived to take Zoe out, Susan opened the door.
"I want to talk to you," she said crisply.

"What's going on? Where's Zoe?"

She walked into the lounge.

He followed. "Well? Where's Zoe?"

"You told me there was no one else. You lied. There is. Jacqueline
Howard."

"You've made a mistake," he said failing to hide his shock.

"Liar. I hired a private detective."

217

"I don't live in poverty so you can hire people to spy on me!"

"Give her up and come home, or you'll never see Zoe again."

He tried to look astonished. "Jacqueline's just a friend."

"Stop lying, Max. You don't kiss friends passionately on the doorstep. If you want to see Zoe again come home."

"No. I'll fight you in the courts for access."

She smiled. "You don't know where she is. If you don't come back by six o'clock I'll go and join her. My cases are packed and in the car. Australia's a big place. I'll change our surname and you'll never see her again."

"I'm not stupid, Sue. You can't just vanish. What about the house?"

She gestured carelessly. "Move back when I've gone. I've rented somewhere – a long way from here. You won't find us because I've used a different name." She laughed. "Do you think I won't do it? I'm not the gullible girl I was when we met, Max. You've hardened me."

"I'll tell the police you've kidnapped my daughter. I might not be able to find you, but they will." He picked up a recent photo of Zoe and Susan from the desk. "Especially when I give them this." He saw doubt flicker across her face. "You'll be hunted. Think about how having her mother branded a kidnapper will affect Zoe. Don't subject her to that."

"You've subjected her to enough," she said bitterly. "She's suffering because she's the only girl in her class who comes from a broken home. She wants you back more than I do. She needs you to help with her homework and projects like other fathers help their children. Her school work's falling behind and the teachers are concerned."

"All right, I'll make time to see more of her."

"No, that's not good enough. You're not the one who sees her excitement turn to unhappiness when you don't turn up on Sundays or are hours late."

"It's your fault I couldn't come, Susan, because I didn't have any money for the train fare."

"You're not the one who has to comfort her when she cries in bed at night because she's lost her father. You're not the one who has to assure her that her father didn't leave home because he disliked her. That's what she thinks, Max."

"I'll come home."

"And Miss Howard?"

"I love her." To his satisfaction he saw a spasm of pain cross her face.

"You have to choose between them. If you don't I'll take the risk and go. The police won't be interested if I tell them Zoe's not yours. She is of course, but they won't know that."

"You wouldn't put her through that?"

"Not unless you force me to, Max."

"Oh, God. You win," he said, wondering how he was going to tell Jacqueline.

She folded her arms. "And give up opera school."

"Why?"

"Because you'll still see Jacqueline. I know your deceitful ways. You'll keep your flat and won't tell her you've come home."

He realized that his desire to hurt Susan had provoked her. "I'll go to the estate agents and give up the flat. You can come with me, but don't make me give up opera school too," he said wishing he'd let her think that Jacqueline meant little to him.

"You shouldn't have been unfaithful."

Memories of the last time she had wrecked his singing career made him cautious. "I'll have nothing more to do with Jacqueline, I promise."

"Your promises are worthless. Give up opera school – or give up your daughter."

"Sue, please," he said frantically. "If I become an opera singer, you, me and Zoe will be rich. We'll be famous. We can travel everywhere and stay in fabulous hotels. We can buy houses all over the world – "

"Max, I don't want to be famous. I want us to be a family again. Now listen carefully. If you come home and I find out you're being unfaithful, I'll take Zoe away. Next time there won't be any warning." She glanced at her watch. "You're wasting valuable time."

"I hate you so much, Susan, I hope you die."

"The deadline is six o'clock," she said quietly.

Harriet went into Nicholas's office and dropped a letter on his desk. "From Max. He's giving up opera."

"Doesn't sound as if he had much choice," said Nicholas when he

219

finished reading it.

"Of course he had a choice. He's always let others dominate his life. If he'd gone home and promised to give up Jacqueline, his wife would have come to terms with it. For a Don Juan, Max knows very little about women." She put his letter back in the envelope. "We've lost our best tenor."

Nicholas's thoughts shot to the scene at the end of term. "We've got to find another Lensky. A student from the second-year will have to do it."

"Even the best one's nowhere near as good as Max," she said. "It's just like last time. He wrote me a letter then too. I had a broken-hearted girl weeping all over me when she came for her singing lesson and now I'll have another. Although I have less sympathy for Jacqueline – she knew he was married." She sighed. "What a waste of a beautiful voice. He should have made the most of his marriage and concentrated on his singing. At least he would have had something. Now he's got nothing."

"Except his daughter," said Nicholas. "She must mean a lot to him."

"Yes, she's the one person Max loves more than himself."

When Phillipa arrived she told them that Jacqueline had also received a letter from Max that morning.

"Another letter," said Harriet scathingly. "How is she?"

"Howling her eyes out. Natasha's taken the day off work."

Later that afternoon, Nicholas and Harriet were in his office when Phillipa burst in. "Natasha's on the phone. Jacqui's saying she wants to die!"

Harriet looked worried. "You'd better go home and see what you can do."

Nicholas stood up. "I'll come with you and talk some sense into the little idiot."

"Nicholas, be careful," Harriet said. "If she's feeling suicidal ... "

"She's not feeling suicidal – she's saying she wants to die – there's a difference. She's got movement class tonight."

"She won't make it tonight," Harriet said.

He grinned. "Do you want to bet?"

Harriet frowned. "It's not funny. The girl's distraught."

He took his car keys off the desk. "The girl's wallowing in self-pity. Come on, Philly."

Natasha met them in the hall. Her fraught expression reminded him of how she looked on the day of her audition.

"Where is she?" Nicholas asked.

"In bed. She hasn't had anything to eat or drink all day."

"Has she said she wants to die or that she wants to kill herself?" he asked quietly.

"Wants to die."

"She hasn't tried to take any pills or looked for razor blades?"

Natasha shook her head.

"Good. You and Philly go and get her something to eat and drink. Then get yourself ready for movement class."

"I can't leave her!"

He shook his head. "You won't – she'll be with you."

Natasha made an incredulous noise. He put his hands on her shoulders, turned her round and gave her a gentle push towards the kitchen. "Oh, wait," he said. "I presume she's wearing a nightdress?"

"Pyjamas."

Although he knew Jacqueline had been crying nearly all day, her face was so red and swollen he was shocked. Her bedroom was stuffy and smelt of sweat. He opened the window. "Jacqui, stop it. You're being indulgent, hysterical and selfish. All this melodrama about wanting to die is upsetting Natasha. You knew Max was married." He sat on her bed. "Did you ever think about how his wife felt when he left her?"

She turned her back to him and buried her face in the pillow.

"Did you?" he insisted. "If you're feeling like this now and you've been his girlfriend for less than a year – think about how she must have felt."

"Go away."

"No. Get up. You have to go to movement class tonight."

She looked at him in horror.

"Yes. Only death or serious illness excuse you from attending. Are you dead?"

"I wish I was."

"But you're not. Get up."

She scrambled out of bed and grabbed her dressing gown from the back of the door. "You don't know how it feels."

221

"Don't I? And what makes you think that?"

"Well, you don't, do you?"

"I do actually," he said coldly. "I was engaged once."

Her mutinous expression faded. "Oh."

Grabbing her arm he marched her into the kitchen and made her drink a glass of water before she had the soup and toast Phillipa had prepared. Natasha looked at him in amazement. He winked at her. She smiled and winked back.

"Good," he said to Jacqueline when she had finished. "Go and have a shower."

"Can't I have just one night off?"

"No. Joan Sutherland sang a performance the night her mother died."

In the bathroom, Jacqueline cleaned her teeth and stepped under the shower. When she finished washing her hair she turned off the hot tap, gasping as the cold water hit her. Only when she was shivering violently did she get out of the shower and wrap herself in a towel. With her finger she wrote MAX on the misted mirror and put crosses through his name until it was obliterated. "I'll never do it again, never," she vowed.

She went into her bedroom and sprayed herself with the *Miss Dior* perfume Phillipa had bought her for her birthday. Dressing in jeans and a new white shirt she went into the kitchen. They stopped talking and looked at her.

She smiled. "Crying might be good for the soul – but it's hell for the face."

Nicholas waited for Jacqueline after movement class. "Do you still want to die?"

"No."

"Good. I'll take you out for coffee." He saw Deborah looking curiously at them. "Not with the others. We'll go to a café in Fitzroy Street."

They chose a table by the window and Nicholas ordered two cappuccinos.

"Well, everyone was right," she said despairingly.

"You had to find it out for yourself, Jacqui. That's why I want to

222

talk to you. You're free and attractive and have a great future. Max could have been a famous tenor. Instead he only has the knowledge of what might have been." He lit a cigarette. "You're lucky his wife made him leave; imagine the ordeal of having to see him three times a week. The theatre is a vocation – and that can be difficult. At the moment your working and social lives are separate, but when you join the opera company they'll be the same. That's how it was with me. I mixed exclusively with people from the theatre. When my fiancée broke our engagement I resigned because I couldn't bear to work with her every day."

She looked contrite. "I'm sorry I said what I did – about you not knowing how it feels."

"That's okay. The pain will fade. The first month is the worst. There seem to be happy couples everywhere."

"That's because there are happy couples everywhere," she said in exasperation.

"No, it's because you only notice the happy couples. You're conscious of lovers and what they've got that you've lost. Be aware of the suffering souls too."

"Yes," she said thoughtfully. "I'll see plenty of them at work tomorrow." She grimaced. "I've been incredibly selfish."

"Everyone does inconsiderate things, but learn from your mistakes and don't repeat them."

"Nicholas, if a married man ever asks me out I'll slap his face. But I didn't know Max was married in the beginning – does that exonerate me a bit?"

"A lot."

"Thanks. I'm glad you made me go to class."

At the weekend, Jacqueline and Natasha went to the beach house alone. Suspecting that Jacqueline wanted to heal the rift between them, Natasha didn't want to flaunt her relationship with Richard. They bought fillets of flounder at the fishmonger's and went to the sand dunes. They lit a fire and when the flames died down they placed the rack over the coals. Soon the aroma of barbecuing fish mingled deliciously with the ocean breeze.

Natasha took the bottle of Chardonnay out of the ice box. Although she wanted to talk about emotions, she was frightened Jacqueline might erupt. "How are you getting on with Max's replacement?" she asked, judging it to be a safe subject.

"Okay. Max had a much better voice, but he was bossy." She took the glass of wine Natasha handed her. "I wish Deborah wasn't Tatiana. She keeps looking at me with a smug expression. It's great working with music though."

"I find it restricting. We've been used to doing things in our own time," said Natasha cutting a lemon in half. "I'm going to miss having Nick as our teacher next year."

Jacqueline carefully took the fish off the barbecue with tongs and put them onto the plates. "Me too. Natasha, I want to talk to you," she said solemnly.

"Are you pregnant?" she asked in alarm.

"No."

"Phew!"

Jacqueline laughed. "Stop being careful with me. You're worried how I'll react, aren't you?"

Natasha nodded. "You've had an awful time."

"It was my own fault. This year was supposed to be wonderful for us. Because of me it's been rotten. I just want to say I'm sorry."

"Jacqui, next year is going to be fabulous. Soon there'll be six of us sitting here picnicking. Philly and Frank, Richard and me and you – with a great boyfriend."

Jacqueline raised her glass. "Here's to him, whoever he is."

It was a perfect, early summer's day and Phillipa and Frank spent Sunday afternoon at Half Moon Bay. They had a swim and then strolled over the sand to their Lilos.

"There're going to be a lot of sore people tomorrow," said Frank looking at the array of sunburnt flesh.

Phillipa picked up her towel and began drying herself. "Now that Max's back with his wife you've got a chance with Jacqui."

"I'm not interested," he said rummaging through his beach bag.

"Why not?"

He squeezed suntan lotion into the palm of his hand. "Why do you think? Turn round."

She knelt down and he rubbed the lotion over her back.

"I disapprove of Jacqui's behaviour. When she knew Max was married she should have had nothing to do with him. She was overwhelmed by his good looks. He wasn't a very pleasant bloke. Anyway, I'm happy with the ways things are. I thought you were too."

"I am," she said, pleased by his reaction.

"Then why do you want me to go rushing off with Jacqui?"

She turned round and faced him. "I don't. I just thought you'd want to. I didn't want to stand in your way."

"Stoical little thing, aren't you?" He kissed her nose. "Let's leave things as they are."

"No. Let's not." She pulled the plugs out of the Lilos.

"What are you doing?"

"This beach is too crowded."

He looked puzzled.

"Your sister's away. Your flat's empty."

He sat on his heels and stared at her. "You mean – you want to … "

"Change our relationship. Yes."

Grinning, he picked up their towels and Lilos, grabbed her hand and hurried to the car.

Nicholas and Harriet had almost finished the end-of-year assessments. The first and second-term assessments had been with Nicholas only, but they did the final one together. They had left Deborah till last.

Nicholas opened her file and looked at Harriet. "Ready?"

Harriet nodded. She had promised him she would treat Deborah fairly. Already she was tense. Deborah looked nervous. Harriet knew she was the reason. Unlike most of the other students, Deborah had dressed up for her assessment and looked elegant in the white linen dress that revealed six inches of her slim thighs. The square neckline was discreet and she wore a polished coral necklace with matching earrings. Harriet had never liked coral. Annabel had loved it. Deborah's perfume was, as usual, overpowering.

225

Trying to concentrate on the differences between Deborah and Annabel, Harriet made herself smile. "Good afternoon, Deborah."

"Good afternoon, Miss Shaw."

It was Annabel's voice. A different accent but the same timbre. Harriet's face ached from her false smile. 'She's not Annabel,' she thought. 'She's Deborah. Annabel never wore too much perfume or false lashes. Her hair was soft – not stuck in place with hair spray.'

Nicholas smiled encouragingly at Deborah. "This is a chance for us to discuss any problems and talk about your strengths and weaknesses," he began. He looked at her file. "We'll start with German. Mrs Stolze has given you an excellent report. Your preparation is thorough and your pronunciation and interpretation are very good."

Deborah smiled.

'Annabel's smile,' thought Harriet. 'Annabel's perfect teeth.'

"Mrs Stolze makes everything interesting and gets us involved," Deborah said earnestly. "Keeping the focus on opera's helpful too. I know most of your professional productions are in English, but this course will help me when I go overseas, or get into the Australian Opera." She looked apprehensively at Harriet.

Trying to look approving, Harriet nodded.

"Good," said Nicholas. "According to Miss Jones, you're naturally graceful and coordinated. Your music report is also excellent," he said. "We think it would waste your time to attend any more. You only just failed your exemption test last year, so the piano lessons are all you need. Now we come to drama. This is more difficult because I'm your teacher – but don't be afraid of telling me what you think. It's for my good as well as yours."

"I think you're really good."

Harriet saw that Deborah, who had begun to relax with all the praise, became nervous again.

"What do you think has been your greatest area of improvement?" Nicholas asked.

Deborah hesitated. "Well, I had some problems in the beginning, but I think I've – well – sort of – almost overcome them now."

"Could you be more specific?" asked Harriet.

"Well … I overacted."

"And you think you've overcome this?" she asked, hearing the coldness of her voice. Sure that Nicholas was glaring at her, she avoided looking at him.

Deborah looked wary. "I'm trying," she said.

"You're progressing, Deborah," said Nicholas. "I noticed an improvement after the first term, but sometimes you forget and slip back. You still get too excited, especially during a dramatic scene – you need to be more in control. This term some of your acting has been sensitive and subtle." He paused. "Am I right in thinking that you have a problem with personal relationships within the opera school?"

Deborah blushed and looked down at her beautiful nails that were painted pearly pink. "Yes," she said finally.

"It's making things difficult for the people who work with you," said Harriet. "Even in the performance of *Eugene Onegin*, I could see there was a great deal of tension between you and Jacqueline."

"She hates me because I told her Max was married."

"It's not just Jacqueline," said Harriet. "Casting you is hard because the others don't want to work with you. Have you made any friends in the opera school?"

Looking totally humiliated, Deborah shook her head.

"Deborah, we're trying to help," Nicholas said. "I know this must be miserable for you, but let's see if we can work something out. I have a suggestion. Would you like to repeat the first year?"

Deborah looked shocked. "No."

"It is not a punishment. Look on it as a fresh start," said Harriet trying and failing to make her voice sound sympathetic. "You can learn from the mistakes you made this year and begin again. You'll have the advantage of experience and you can help the new students."

Deborah shook her head and Harriet knew she was fighting to hold back her tears. "No, I couldn't."

"We're not going to force you," said Nicholas soothingly. "I don't know if we can repair past damage, but I think part of the problem is that you intimidate people. You're always thinking of the impression *you* are making. Next year when you do the workshops try to visualize the impression the *scene* is making."

Harriet struggled to be fair. "Your performance as Tatiana was very good and you worked well within the discipline of the music. You have an excellent voice and Ingrid Williams is pleased with you."

Deborah looked at her in surprise, but the beginnings of a grateful smile faded. Harriet knew she looked grim.

Nicholas opened the door. "Happy Christmas, Deborah."

Harriet waited till the sound of Deborah's footsteps receded, before looking at Nicholas. He said nothing, simply looked at her and slowly shook his head.

He made her feel like a child caught in the act. "I praised her."

Nicholas gathered up all the files. "It was the way you looked at her and your tone of voice."

"I didn't say anything that wasn't true. She has difficulty making friends – even you admit that. I'm not alone in my dislike, Nicholas."

He shrugged and left the office. Harriet felt ashamed. Her sense deserted her whenever she saw Deborah and she knew that it always would. "Oh, Annabel, you knew what you were doing, didn't you?" she whispered. "You really knew what you were doing."

Part Three

INTERMEZZO

1973

January to December

Chapter 21

'I never meant to do this.'

The Consul – Menotti

"Happy New Year, Nick!" said Vivien.

He pulled her into his arms and took her into the middle of the studio. "Watch out," he said, steering her out of the way to avoid a collision with Richard and Natasha. He grinned. "Only Natasha could turn a waltz into a polka." The skirt of her amethyst coloured ballgown brushed his legs as she and Richard spun by.

The past year had been frustrating for Nicholas. The new first-year students were mediocre. Most lacked imagination, and teaching the drama classes had been tedious. Not wanting Vivien to be bored by them he had advised her to follow the progress of the second-year students. Even the most sarcastic critic had enthused about the amazing talent they had witnessed at their workshop productions.

The second-year drama teacher had consulted him about the final scene from *Faust*, which they were going to perform. "That carry-on in the prison is so slushy," she said. "I want to make the audience feel horrified."

Nicholas nodded. "Instead of Marguerite collapsing after the trio, she could be escorted from the cell to her execution by two warders."

"Brilliant – "

"Wait. What about … the flats sliding away to reveal a silk screen," he said slowly. "The audience see her silhouette mounting the steps to an unseen scaffold. A dummy, with a rope round its neck, drops into view and swings out of time with the music."

"Yes!"

Nicholas was gratified that Deborah, cast as Marguerite, had excelled herself.

The scene from *The Consul*, done by some of the third-year students for their graduation performance, had been praised by the critics. In spite of this, Harriet still refused to do the whole opera. None of the operas planned for the next season were suitable for updating. Worried that the theatre would be lambasted by the critics for its old-fashioned approach, he decided to talk to Harriet again.

He invited her to his flat for lunch in early January when the theatre was closed. Borrowing some of Phillipa's recipe books, he prepared chilled cucumber soup, grilled salmon with salad, and strawberries in orange juice to finish. The subject of *The Consul* came up naturally, but when he tried to persuade her to take the risk of doing the whole opera he was met by her obstinate refusal.

He forgot his resolution to be rational. "You've deliberately chosen things that can't be updated," he accused.

"I've chosen operas that suit the voices we have. What do you suggest? That we do *The Magic Flute* so you can have fun updating it? We don't have anyone who can sing the Queen of the Night, but shall we turn it into a mezzo role – just for you?" She smiled. "You remind me of your mother. When she wanted something badly and couldn't have it – "

"Never mind my mother. Let's do *The Turn of the Screw* then."

"Are you mad? That's even worse. I'd rather do *The Consul*."

"Then let's do it. You're just frightened it won't make money. It will. It's compelling and haunting. Lots of Jews and Eastern Europeans live around St Kilda. They'll identify with it."

"No."

Needing to get away before he lost his temper, he collected their plates and took them into the kitchen. He returned with the strawberries and a jug of cream. Putting them on the table, he said, "I'm your nephew, but you treat me as though I mean nothing to you. We've been working together for five years, but if I went back home tomorrow you wouldn't miss me. You don't trust me and sometimes I think you don't even like me," he said quietly.

She looked upset. "Oh, Nicholas, you can't really feel like that."

"I do. You shut me out. I know something terrible happened a long time ago, but exactly what, is a mystery. You don't confide in me. You could at least tell me why Deborah upsets you."

He saw her flush as she poured cream over her strawberries. "I don't confide in anyone."

"But I'm not just anyone."

She passed him the jug. "Family traits, Nicholas. You don't confide in me either. When I ask you about Vivien, you close up. You've been going out for almost two years, but I don't know how you feel about her. I know when you take her out only because you come to the theatre wearing a suit. You're obviously very fond of her, but I have no idea how deep your feelings go or if you want to marry her."

"She doesn't believe in marriage. She doesn't even believe in living together. She values her independence too much."

"Does that upset you?"

He shrugged.

"There you go again – you accuse me of shutting you out. You're secretive and so am I. It's a genetic thing."

"It must be. My mother refused to tell me about your tragedy, and, close as I was to Grandma, she didn't tell me either. They told me you left London because you wanted to start your own theatre – but that's not true, is it?"

"No it's not – you're right. It might look like a theatre, but it's actually a farm. How clever of you to work it out."

In spite of her attempt to joke he saw that she looked wary.

"Are you my grandmother?" he asked recklessly.

Instead of being angry, she laughed. "No. Although I often wished Charlotte was my daughter. When I took her for walks, I enjoyed it when strangers thought she was mine."

Her reaction made him know that she was telling the truth. He felt disappointed. "That would have been too easy, I suppose," he said.

"What?"

"I thought Annabel … " Seeing her expression he stopped.

She looked out of the window. "The garden's very colourful."

"Yes. Would you like some coffee?"

Vivien sat on the smooth rock and dangled her legs in the clear water of the stream. The realization that she wanted to marry Nicholas shocked her. She kicked her leg and an arc of water flew through the air. 'What's happened to me? I've always been rabidly anti-marriage.' She recalled her outburst a year ago, when she and Nicholas had gone to the wedding of a woman in the opera company. "I bet she gives up her singing career. Marriage and motherhood makes women boring and turns them into drudges," she said as they drove to the reception. "I'm not spending the best years of my life pushing out pups. I've seen it happen so often. Girls have a baby and their personality gets subjugated by demanding kids."

She tried to work out the best way to tell him that she had changed her mind about marriage, but not children. The fact that he wanted children worried her. 'He might not want to marry me,' she thought as she watched him swimming towards her. 'But it'd be a shame to let his genes go to waste.' She gazed at his sun bronzed body. 'Maybe for him I could have one baby. Just one. He wouldn't make me stay at home and look after it. I could still have a career. We'd be well off. We could afford a nanny. When it got older we'd send it to boarding school.' She grinned. 'I never thought I'd feel like this about anyone.'

It had amazed her how much she missed him on the nights they didn't see each other. 'He's so different. He doesn't dominate me and he approves of career orientated women. The girls at work are right. I'm lucky to have such a liberated and handsome boyfriend.'

It was the middle of January and she and Nicholas were on a week's camping holiday near Mount Buffalo. When he had suggested they go camping, she had been dismayed. She remembered the crowded campsites of her childhood holidays.

"They were full of screaming brats and irritable parents," she protested.

"This will be different," he promised.

As soon as they had driven into the deserted clearing in the forest, she had been enraptured. It had rained heavily the day before, scenting the air with wet leaves and earth. After erecting a tent and pumping up their Lilo they built a fire and barbecued sausages and chops. They spent their days swimming in the stream, talking and making love. The only time they saw anyone was when they went into the nearby town of Bright to buy food.

For the first time, he had confided in her about his arguments with Harriet over *The Consul*. Feeling that this marked a turning point in their relationship she wanted to help him.

234

Nicholas climbed onto the bank. "You look incredibly sexy with your hair up." He rubbed suntan oil onto her back. "We haven't done much sight-seeing."

She laughed. "We haven't done any."

He untied the halter of her bikini and kissed the back of her neck. "Shall we do some now?" he murmured.

She lay down on the bank and pulled him on top of her. "No."

After their holiday Vivien rang Seamus O'Flynn, a friend of hers who was a journalist on *The Age*. She arranged to meet him the following day for lunch.

She explained that Harriet was worried that doing a modern opera would reduce their audience and patronage.

"It probably would," said Seamus, dunking a roll into his minestrone soup. "Melbourne people are so conservative."

"Could you do an article praising modern opera?"

"Sure, if you think it'll help. Which one does she want to do?"

"She doesn't, but Nick wants to do *The Consul*."

"Friction, is there?" he asked casually.

"No," she said quickly. "Miss Shaw's frightened of losing money, but Nick thinks *The Consul's* so good it's worth taking the risk."

"He's right. I wish there were more people like him in Melbourne," said Seamus. "Okay, I'll see what I can do."

Not wanting Nicholas to think she had been interfering, Vivien didn't tell him. Seamus rang her a few days later and told her the article would be in *The Age* the next day. She opened the paper. Above a photo of the theatre was the heading:

Dispute Over Modern Opera

Halfway through the piece she dialled Seamus's number. "You swine," she said as soon as he answered. "I didn't tell you they had bitter disputes about *The Consul*!"

"I guessed. You gave yourself away when you denied there was friction. Harriet Shaw doesn't have mild disagreements – she has violent ones. She once sacked the drama director because he wanted to do a play that had four letter words in it."

Vivien slammed the phone down.

Harriet walked into Nicholas's office and placed *The Age* in front of him. He looked up and saw her accusing eyes. When he finished reading the article that praised him and condemned her, he handed the paper back. Matching her cold expression with his own, he said nothing.

"Well?" she demanded.

"You think I had something to do with this?"

"I think you had everything to do with it."

"Thank you."

She looked less certain. "Then who – "

"People must know about our disagreements. Phillipa – "

"Phillipa would never do this."

He stood up. "But I would?"

After he left she stayed in his office regretting her haste. When his phone rang, she picked it up.

"Oh, Miss Shaw, it's Vivien." She sounded distraught.

"What's wrong?"

"Have you seen that awful article?"

"Yes."

"I'm sorry – it's my fault."

Harriet kept the anger out of her voice. "Oh. Why?"

"Nick told me he wanted to do *The Consul* and you didn't, so I spoke to Seamus O'Flynn – he's a friend of mine – "

Harriet put the phone down.

Nicholas found Harriet sitting in his chair when he returned to his office half an hour later.

"You told Vivien about our arguments over *The Consul*."

"Yes. So what?"

"She told Seamus O'Flynn."

"She wouldn't do that."

"She did. I've spoken to her. Now you've succeeded in giving the theatre bad publicity, perhaps you'd like to do as O'Flynn suggests and start your own opera company. As he says, you are too modern, subtle and clever to work with me. I don't deserve you. Without you I would be nothing."

He saw the hurt in her eyes, but felt unable to do anything about it. "Are you sacking me?"

"If it wasn't for your mother, I would, Nicholas."

Vivien answered the door immediately. "Nick, I've been frantic. That hideous article. Come in."

He remained in the doorway. "Did you speak to Seamus O'Flynn?"

"Come inside."

"Did you speak to Seamus O'Flynn?" he repeated slowly.

"Yes, but – "

He had been hoping she would say no. "Did you tell him that Harriet and I argued about *The Consul*?"

"It's not that simple – let me explain."

"Did you?" he shouted.

"Yes, but – "

He turned away and she grabbed his arm. "I was trying to help you."

Violently, he pulled away and she almost fell. He ran down the stairs. The sounds of her crying echoed down the stairwell. He wrenched open the door and ran to his car.

Harriet and Nicholas didn't speak to each other for three days. Then she had to ask him something. She questioned him coldly and he replied with equal coldness. Apart from necessary dialogue, they avoided each other for the rest of the week.

The following Tuesday, Nicholas was on his way to the first rehearsal of *The Force of Destiny*. Suddenly he remembered the photo Vivien had taken of Deborah getting Harriet's autograph. In the light of her revelations to Seamus O'Flynn, the photo took on an alarming significance. Hoping she had not decided to use it already, he rushed back to his office and dialled her number at work. As soon as she answered he hung up. He was supposed to be discussing how he saw the production being staged with the cast, the musical director and Harriet. Grabbing a sheet of paper he wrote,

Vivien,

I'm returning your key. Don't bother to return mine. I've changed the lock.

He shoved it in an envelope, but did not seal it. On his way out he saw Phillipa.

"Nick, where are you going? You've got – "

"I've got to go out."

"Don't make things any worse! What about – "

"I'll explain later." He opened the door and ran to his car.

Feeling like a trespasser he went into Vivien's flat. The room she used as an office was extremely tidy. A typewriter was the only thing on her desk. He went to the filing cabinet. 'Please don't let it be locked.' To his relief it slid open. Everything was labelled with tabs and he opened the suspension file marked *photos*. The ones of Harriet's party had been taken over a year ago, but Vivien kept the files in date order.

He remembered her lectures about his untidiness. "Being organized makes life easier, Nick," she was always saying. 'It makes life easier for a thief too,' he thought when he found the photo of Harriet and Deborah. Finding the negative was more difficult. He cursed as he held each one up to the light. It was almost the last one. Careful to put the folder back in the right place and close the cabinet properly, he left. Outside he searched the row of letter-boxes for her flat number. He put her key in the envelope with his note and pushed it through the flap.

When he returned to the theatre Harriet was in the studio with the cast.

"Ah, you're back, Nicholas," she said neutrally.

"Yes. Sorry, everyone. I had to rush home – there was an emergency."

At the end of the session she walked towards him. "Come and see me now," she said quietly. Only her eyes betrayed her fury.

He followed her into her office and shut the door. "Aunt Harriet, before – "

"How dare you walk out and leave the rehearsal in the lurch! It's clear that you're intent on ruining me. I regret that you're my nephew.

When this season is over go back to England. You've betrayed me, and I'll never forgive you. You're loyal only to yourself and your monstrous ego."

"Are you going to ask me what I was doing?"

"I don't care."

"And you accuse me of having a monstrous ego." He put his hand on the desk and leaned towards her. "Firstly, I've broken up with Vivien because of that article," he said softly. "Secondly, I went to her flat this morning because I remembered she had something. I stole it. I was worried she might use it against you. It would make an excellent story. Imagine the headline. *Why does Harriet Shaw hate Deborah Ryland?* He placed the negative and photo in front of her. "The journalists would have had fun speculating about this. And how long would it take them to find out about Annabel?" Without waiting for her reaction he left.

As he walked down the corridor Phillipa ran after him.

"Nick! Is everything all right?"

"Don't be ridiculous," he snapped. "If anyone wants me, I've gone home."

An hour later his doorbell rang. It was Harriet.

"Yes?" he said formally, not opening the fly screen door.

"May I come in?"

"You want to enter the home of a traitor?"

"Stop being melodramatic. I've come to apologize."

He opened the door and she followed him into the lounge. He lifted Algernon off the sofa and she sat down.

"I'm sorry I accused you, Nicholas. By way of reparation you can do *The Consul* next year."

Her voice was husky. He was surprised to see that she was close to tears.

He lit a cigarette. "I was naive to tell Vivien, but I had to talk to someone. You and I couldn't discuss it without arguing. I felt alienated."

Algernon jumped onto her lap, and she stroked him. "I've had a vile week."

"So have I."

"I know Vivien didn't believe in marriage, but did you want to marry her?"

He was about to shrug when he remembered their mutual accusations of secrecy. "She didn't want children. Even if she had it wouldn't have worked. She's too fussy and didn't like Algie being allowed to sleep on the furniture. After dinner I'd want to linger over coffee, but she wanted to do the washing up. She would have nagged. But I'm sorry it's ended like this."

"Did you love her?"

"Not as much as I loved Sally. With Vivien something was missing. I'm not sure what. She was … a bit hard."

"If *The Consul's* a success we'll do whatever you like the year after."

Her willingness to go against her principles, made him realize how sorry she was.

While Phillipa opened the morning mail, she wondered what to do about Frank. The thought of hurting him upset her, but this time she was going to do everything she could to get Nicholas. Her spirits had soared when he and Vivien had split up. Two days ago, Vivien had rung him while he was dictating a letter, and Phillipa had answered the phone. She covered the mouthpiece and told him who it was.

"Tell her I'm not in."

"I think you should speak to her."

"Shut up, Phillipa, it's none of your bloody business."

She told Vivien he was out and hung up. On one of the rare occasions in her life, she lost her temper. "Don't tell me to shut up! It's not my fault your love life's in tatters," she said, throwing her shorthand pad and pencil on the desk.

He had looked at her in astonishment. "Phillipa, I'm – "

"You bloody shut up, Nicholas!" She marched out of his office and slammed the door.

That night he had arrived at the house with a bunch of flowers. "I'm sorry, Philly. My rudeness was inexcusable."

She decided to be aloof. With a slight smile she took the flowers. "Thank you, Nicholas. I'll see you tomorrow." She closed the door,

240

hoping she had aroused his interest. From the window she watched him return to his car. With a feeling a triumph she saw him look toward the house with a puzzled expression.

Since then, his attitude towards her had changed. He was regarding her as a person again, whereas he had begun to treat her like an efficient machine.

The phone rang and she answered it. While listening to the caller, who was a member of the public expressing his views on modern opera, she began reading a letter. It was from Seamus O'Flynn. Unless it was marked personal, she opened all the opera mail.

Dear Nicholas,

Vivien told me you refuse to see her because you think she broke a confidence. She didn't. She asked me to do an article supporting modern opera. I drew my own conclusions. Years ago Miss Shaw sacked a drama director because he wanted to put on a play she disapproved of. It made a good story, but I'm sorry it's caused trouble between you.

"It's tuneless rubbish. Tell Harriet Shaw I agree with her." The man finished his tirade against modern opera.

Phillipa thanked him and took his name and address for the mailing list. She put the letter from Seamus in her handbag. 'Letters get lost in the post,' she thought. 'Damn my conscience. I don't believe him. Vivien probably asked him to write it because she's desperate to get Nick back. Well, she's too late – it's my turn now.'

Chapter 22

'Emotions that I comprehend not,
and longings never guessed before!'
Tannhäuser – Wagner

Natasha peered into her pan. "I'm hardly finding any."

"You're too impatient," said Richard. "Watch me."

She stretched out on the riverbank and stared up into the gum trees.

'I'll take her out to dinner tomorrow,' he thought as he swirled the pan. 'I'll ask her then.' He breathed in the scent of the eucalyptus trees.

A kookaburra laughed. "Imagine what the early settlers thought when they first heard that," she said. "They probably thought an escaped convict was hiding behind a tree with an axe."

"You're not watching," said Richard. "I can see some already."

She sat up and peered into the pan. "Look at that bit – it's the size of a pea!"

Richard picked out the pieces of gold and put them in a jar with the others.

"What are we going to do with all this gold?" she asked.

'Perfect opening,' he thought with a smile. "We could have it made into a wedding ring."

She stared at him in delight. "For me?"

"Who else?"

She dropped her pan in the creek.

He pulled her to her feet and swung her round.

She kissed him. "When?"

"When we've finished opera school. Let's forgo the first season and go to England for a six-month honeymoon."

Her eyes shone with excitement. "Yes!"

"We'll go and choose an engagement ring next week."

"I don't want one."

"You're having an engagemnt ring." He pulled her shirt out of her jeans. "I've been saving up for ages."

"All right," she said, kissing his neck. She began to undo the buckle of his belt. Teasingly she stopped. "What about all the gold?"

"We've got enough for a wedding ring. Let's practise being married."

Artistically, Deborah's second year of opera school had been an outstanding success. Her performance of Marguerite had received a standing ovation. Nicholas, Ingrid Williams and the second-year drama teacher had been generous in their congratulations, but she waited in vain for Harriet's praise. At the party afterwards, strangers sought her out and enthused about her voice and her interpretation of Marguerite's character. Vivien had interviewed her for *The AustralianWomen's Weekly*. The article, which had photos of her in costume and evening dress, hailed her as the future Australian star of the opera world. It praised her voice, glamour, beauty and dedication.

But since February, when Natasha and Richard had announced their engagement, she had been depressed. Natasha glowed with happiness, and she envied her. For years Deborah had been gazing in jewellers' windows at engagement rings and reading brochures about diamonds. Natasha's one carat, square cut diamond flanked by emeralds, was something she would have chosen herself. The fact that she was three years older than Natasha added to her sense of failure.

'I'm twenty-five, I should have been married years ago. I should have a baby by now,' she thought.

Attempting to take her mind off her unhappiness she threw herself into her work at opera school. Every night she seriously studied her subjects, and turned down her boss when he asked her out.

She put the needle on the beginning of *Don Giovanni,* and sat down with the score listening to the pronunciation. When side one finished she heard a man's furious voice. She went to the door and listened.

"If he leaves my daughter I'll kill you!"

Regretting she had no make-up on, but finding the temptation to witness her mother's quarrel irresistible, she went into the hall. "If you do carry out your threat, I promise I didn't hear you say that."

"Who are you?" he asked rudely.

Deborah tried to remember where she had seen him before. "Her daughter – unfortunately."

He laughed contemptuously. "You're pathetically transparent, Marie. You're waiting for me to reel over with shock. I suppose you think you look thirty, but there's no stopping the downward pull of gravity. You're ageing, Marie, and it's showing."

Deborah laughed. "I suppose he adores you too, Mother."

Two days later Deborah was in a music shop in Collins Street, waiting to pay for the complete *Tristan and Isolde.*

"Good afternoon."

She jumped.

"I didn't mean to startle you. Do you remember me?"

She smiled. "The downward pull of gravity."

"I don't always behave like a thug. Are you rushing home?" he asked.

"I never rush home – except when my mother's away."

"Have you got time for a cup of coffee?"

She looked at her watch. "Yes, I'm filling in time before opera school."

"Opera school? The National Theatre?"

"Yes."

"You must be good."

He took her to the Regent Café near the town hall. When he had ordered he looked at her thoughtfully. "Are you Deborah Ryland?"

"How did you know?"

"I knew I'd seen you somewhere." The waitress bought their coffee. "You were Leonora in *The Force of Destiny* in the workshops last year, weren't you?"

She put sugar in her cappuccino. "Yes."

"And Marguerite?"

She smiled. "Gosh, you've got a good memory."

"You've got a good voice. That scene from *Faust* was particularly memorable."

"In what way?" she asked, wanting to hear more praise.

"It was chilling. At the end you expect Marguerite to fall down dead, but you were taken off by guards, and the audience saw you

244

mounting the scaffold. I thought that was the end and I thought it was an excellent variation. Then when your – well not your body of course – dropped into view, it was a shock. The audience gasped. Sorry, I haven't introduced myself, I'm Jeremy Langford."

She snapped her fingers. "I thought I recognized you. You're a patron of The National Theatre, aren't you?"

"That's right."

"Do you go to all the workshops?"

"Yes. Harriet Shaw's nurturing of young talent is something I admire. She's an inspirational woman."

Not wanting to hear him complimenting Harriet, she smiled seductively.

He shook his head. "Stop flirting. It makes you look like your mother."

She blushed. "Why don't you like her? You're the only man I know that doesn't."

"She's cruel and self-obsessed. I met her at the tennis club and despised the men who made fools of themselves over her and pitied the women whose lives she disrupted. Now my son-in-law's infatuated with her."

"Has he left your daughter?"

"No, but he's unhappy and confused, and so is my daughter. Marie does something to otherwise normal, decent men."

"But never you?"

"No."

"Why not?"

"I hate women like her – and men too. They're destroyers. And I knew what she was from the moment I met her."

"Did she try you out?"

He nodded.

Deborah giggled. "She must have been piqued. What about your wife?"

"I'm a widower," he said abruptly.

"Oh, I'm sorry."

He looked at his watch. "Come on, I'll drive you to opera school."

Neither of them had finished their coffee and she knew that the mention of his wife had upset him. 'I always wreck things,' she

245

thought.

She settled down in his Jaguar. "This is a nice car."

"It's reliable, comfortable and it gets me where I want to go. That's all I demand of a car. It's a mode of transport, not a status symbol." His slight smile took the reprimand out of his words.

"My mother won't go out with a man unless he's got a posh car."

"I have no desire to discuss your mother."

"Neither have I. But I'm used to men wanting to talk about her. Most of my boyfriends end up dropping me for her." She tried not to sound sour.

"That must be … " He shook his head. "I can't think how it must be for you."

She looked out of the window, seeing the image of her mother, mocking her. Uncomfortable with silence, she wanted to resume the conversation, but judged that talking about herself would bore him. Suddenly she remembered something. Five years ago, she had had a boyfriend who was a stockbroker. All he had ever talked about was the stock market. "Are you the Langford in *Langford Lighting*?"

"Yes. My grandfather started it and my brother and I went to work there as soon as we left school."

She decided to impress him with her knowledge. "Why did you go public?" she asked, intending to tell him she read the financial section of the paper.

"It was the right time." He didn't ask her how she knew, or seem surprised.

Deborah realized he was used to talking business with women. "Your policy of catering for everyone, whatever their financial situation, ensures you'll always have a strong market, whatever the economy's like," she said, repeating her ex-boyfriend's words. "Attractive but affordable light fittings for young couples, through the spectrum to magnificent chandeliers." Thinking she sounded false, she stopped.

"Do you have any investments?" he asked.

"No, but I'm thinking about it."

"Harriet Shaw's one of our shareholders."

'She would be,' thought Deborah.

When he pulled up outside the theatre, he got out of the car and opened the door for her.

"Thank you, Jeremy."

"It was a pleasure."

Deborah stood on the pavement and watched as he drove away. His dislike of her mother and his attitude towards her, dispelled some of her depression. When he rang her three days later and invited her out to dinner, she accepted.

They had dinner in a French restaurant in Collins Street and talked mostly about opera. Afterwards Jeremy drove her to his large house in Camberwell. From what she could see in the dark, all the front gardens were substantial and the houses were mostly hidden from view by high hedges and trees. Just before Jeremy turned into his drive she counted four Rolls Royces parked in the street.

In the lounge he put on a record of opera overtures. "Would you like coffee and a liqueur?"

"Cointreau and coffee, please."

The room was full of books and family photos. She looked wistfully at him when he returned with white coffee cups with gold rims, and a percolator on a silver tray. "This is a nice house, it feels cheerful."

He put the tray on the coffee table. "It was once. I'm going to sell it and buy something smaller now the children have left. I'm not happy here since my wife died, the place is lonely."

"How many children have you got?"

He poured out the coffee. "Three. Two boys and a girl."

"They were lucky to have come from a happy home."

"Why do you live with your mother, Deborah?"

"She lives with me, I don't live with her. It's my house."

He sat in the armchair opposite her. "Your house?"

"My father meant to leave it to me, but he died before he changed his will."

"So, it's your mother's house?"

"Morally, it's mine."

Jeremy shook his head. "Legally it's your mother's. Why don't you share a flat with a girl from the opera school?"

'No girl at the opera school would want to share a flat with me,' she thought. "I've got my reasons. My mother's careless. I use her account cards."

"Does that make you happy?"

"Yes."

"For how long?"

"Quite a while. I do it all the time."

"Very risky. You're stealing."

"I'm reclaiming what's rightfully mine."

"Deborah, is it worth it? While you live with your mother you'll be unhappy; she'll see to that. Forget what belongs to you and leave. You'll only lose eventually."

She finished her coffee. "No. I'm careful. I only put things on her account that she'd buy – cosmetics, perfume and clothes. I pay for opera records and scores myself."

"There's a proverb. It goes something like this. Those who seek revenge should dig two graves. I have a modification. Depending upon your opponent dig only one – for yourself. Rigoletto is a good example. The Duke got away scot-free. When you think about revenge, put your mother in the role of the Duke." He stood up. "Think about it. I'll drive you home."

Deborah hid her relief. When he had invited her to his place she had thought he would want to sleep with her.

While Jeremy walked up the beach looking for a rubbish bin, Deborah rinsed the plastic plates and cups in the sea and put them back in the picnic basket. Since their first meeting four weeks ago he had taken her regularly to the pictures, the theatre and dinner, but had made no move to seduce or even kiss her. She found his attitude relaxing and intriguing. Today he had driven her to Seaford, a beach resort with miles of natural foreshore reserve. The town had a mix of holiday homes and permanent residents.

When Jeremy came back she stretched. "I'm going for a swim."

"You shouldn't swim on a full stomach, you'll get cramp," he said as he straightened his towel and sat down.

"I'll go for a little paddle then." She started towards the water with her hips swinging.

"Deborah, be natural."

She turned round. "Natural?"

"Sit down. I want to talk to you."

248

Curious, she sat on the towel beside him.

"You're trying to be like your mother," he said gently. "You're obsessed with her. Why?"

An urge to pour out all her confusion and pain to someone interested in her feelings overcame her. "She used to tell me I was ugly. My father ... " She buried her face in her hands.

He put his arm round her. "It's all right, cry, don't worry. You poor little thing. Your bloody mother."

When she stopped crying, she wiped her eyes and jumped up. "I'm going for a swim."

He ran after her and dragged her away from the water's edge. "Why? So I won't see your red eyes and runny mascara?" He pulled her hands away from her face. "Who cares, Deborah, who cares what your face looks like?" Gripping her chin in his hand he studied her face. "Yes, your eyes are red, what else can you expect when you've been bawling for five minutes? Do you think that because I've seen you like this I'll never want to see you again?"

Tears ran down her cheeks. "I don't know."

"What's your mother done to you?" He took her hand and propelled her back to their towels. "Deborah, stop trying to copy her. She has what is to some people a sexy walk, but you, in trying to copy her, have exaggerated it so much it's comical. It's a caricature not a true copy. You wear the same perfume, but you use so much that instead of subtly smelling of perfume you reek of it. Everything you do smacks of desperation. Next time we come to the beach I don't want to see a scrap of make-up – you wear too much anyway. It's supposed to enhance your face not hide it."

"Do you really want to see me again?"

"Of course. Do you want to see me?"

"Yes." She was stunned that she wanted him to kiss her.

Deborah thought about Jeremy all week. A warm, relaxing feeling, so different from her normal highly strung nervousness, crept over her. She found a new job and was determined to be popular with the other girls. Tentatively at first, she began to wear less make-up. One day she abandoned her hair spray, and felt badly groomed on her way to work. When she arrived, the receptionist stared at her. "Golly, your hair looks great."

When Jeremy came to take her out that evening he nodded approvingly. "Much better." He stroked her hair. "Mmm, nice and soft, not stiff with glue."

"It feels untidy."

"It looks real, it used to look like a wig," he retorted.

Jeremy stood behind Deborah with his hands on her shoulders, looking into the mirror. "Now, what's wrong with that?" he asked. "You look natural. Your skin's smooth, so why cover it with make-up?"

"My eyelashes are short, can't I put some mascara on?"

"No. We're going for a drive to Sherbrooke Forest, not to a ball. You probably pull most of your eyelashes out when you remove those false things."

They drove up the mountain to Sherbrooke Forest, stopping on the way to have scones for morning tea. In the forest they strolled along the narrow tracks, dwarfed by the towering eucalyptus trees and tree ferns. Suddenly Jeremy stopped and put his finger to his lips. "Lyre birds," he whispered. Just ahead was a small clearing where two lyre birds were engaged in a courting ritual. Deborah and Jeremy stood in awed silence and watched their graceful and intricate dance. When the birds ran off into the forest Deborah said, "I wish I'd brought my camera."

"Wasn't it lovely?" he said.

Deborah nodded. "I've never been here before."

"We used to come here often when the children were young. We had some great picnics and barbecues."

She had visions of his happy family with the children playing hide-and-seek in the forest while he and his wife cooked the sausages. "My mother never took me anywhere."

He put his arm round her and she rested her head on his shoulder. Jeremy turned his head and gently kissed her cheek and then her mouth. Her stomach fluttered and she returned his kiss without the revulsion she usually felt. She put her arms round him. He stopped kissing her and ran his hand through her hair.

"I thought you were never going to kiss me," she murmured.

"I want to know someone first. I can't understand all this talk about free love and living together instead of getting married, and women

250

burning their bras, hippies and all the other crazy things that go on these days. I'm thankful my children more or less see things my way. Does the age difference between us worry you?"

"No," she replied truthfully. "You've treated me better than any man I've ever known." She looked up into the trees and saw two blue and red Rosellas. "Does my age worry you?"

"Yes," he confessed. "You're younger than my daughter, not much, but still younger. I haven't been out with anyone since my wife died. A lot of our friends tried to match me up with spare women, but I hate that. Let's go and have some lunch."

Deborah hoped Jeremy would drive her to his house and make love to her, but he took her home and, after seeing her to the door, kissed her cheek and left.

As she watched Richard read the passage in Italian, Deborah wondered if it was possible to love two men. Away from opera school her thoughts were occupied by Jeremy. She used to have daydreams about Richard that lasted all day. Now she thought about Jeremy, but not with the intensity with which she had thought about Richard. She had hoped that she had lost interest in him, but as soon as she saw him at opera school she blushed.

"That was good," said the Italian teacher. "Does it feel easier now?"

Richard smiled. "Suddenly everything's fallen into place."

"It happens like that. A lot of people become disheartened and give up, instead of being patient. Everyone has their own pace. You worked hard and I knew you'd get there in the end." She picked up another book and opened it. "Deborah, let's see how you get on with this passage from *Madam Butterfly*."

"Excellent," she said when Deborah had finished. "You have a natural ear for languages, you're very lucky."

"Thank you," said Deborah.

If Richard would only come over after class and tell her how good she was and ask her to help him. But he didn't. No one talked to her after class.

'If they knew I was going out with Jeremy Langford they'd treat me with respect,' she thought.

"Deborah, wake up, it's late – I have to get you home," whispered Jeremy.

She snuggled deeper into the bedclothes. "Will I see you again?" she asked shyly.

He stroked her cheek. "Yes, you will."

Deborah felt happy. 'I wonder if you can become addicted to sex?' she thought in his car on the way home.

Frank parked his car outside Phillipa's house and switched off the engine. "You're losing interest in me, aren't you Philly?"

For weeks Phillipa had felt guilty about Frank. She wanted to end their relationship, but had not known how. She was relieved that he had brought up the subject.

"Have I done something to upset you?" he asked.

"No, Frank. I like you a lot, but I think we've come to the end." She hated his look of hurt. "I'm sorry."

"I thought we had something special. We don't fight, we get on well. We laugh together."

"It's not enough. We're not exactly passionate about each other, are we?"

"We like each other and that's a solid basis for a relationship, Philly. Passion burns itself out. I thought you were sensible. Two people have to live together, share a house and a bed, and tolerance is more enduring than passion and romance. You're throwing away substance for a shadow."

"Yes. I want passion and romance, what's wrong with that?" she asked hotly, frustration at his lack of understanding dulling her guilt. "You sound cool and practical like my aunt. She packed me off to boarding school when I was ten. I missed a lot of affection when I was growing up and that's what I want now."

"I show you a lot of affection," he protested.

"I want more – I don't know what. But I'll know it when I find it."

"If you don't know what it is how will you find it?" he said flatly. "I know I'm not the most exciting bloke in the world. Max was exciting and look what he did to Jacqui. Do you think I'm dull because I want to

252

stay in Australia and don't want to sing at Covent Garden?"

"No. I'm surrounded by people who can't wait to get to Covent Garden and I find your loyalty to Australia touching. I'm very fond of you, but I want more."

He hit the steering wheel. "Why did you start going out with me?"

His anger startled her.

"Why, Philly?" he demanded.

"You just happened to be there, I suppose."

"Thanks very much. I just happened to be there! God, what an insult." He got out of the car and slammed the door.

Before he could get to Phillipa's side to open her door she scrambled out. "Frank, I didn't ... "

He opened the front gate for her. "Goodbye, Phillipa," he said formally.

"Frank, we can still be friends."

He shook his head.

"Yes. We'll still see each other at the theatre."

"I won't be seeking you out, Phillipa. It's not just you I'll miss – I'll miss Jacqui, Natasha and Richard too."

It was then she realized that his feelings for her were stronger than she had thought. "You can still go round with them."

"Not when you're with them."

She watched him walk to his car and wondered if she was being unrealistic.

"Phillipa, I don't understand," said Harriet. "I feel terribly upset. You and Frank get on so well together, what more do you want?"

Phillipa shook her head and wondered what Harriet's reaction would be, if she were to reply, 'Nicholas. I want Nicholas.' She wished she could tell Harriet how she felt.

"Don't throw away happiness for something you don't know exists, Phillipa."

'That's like what Frank said,' Phillipa thought wearily.

Things were not going as she had hoped. Expecting understanding she had been upset when Jacqueline told her she was mad, and Natasha and Richard had urged her to change her mind. Nicholas told her she was deranged. She had hoped their mutual circumstances would provide a bond between them, but he tried to persuade her to go back to Frank. Miserably, she realized that her destruction of Seamus's letter had been in vain. Nicholas would be back with Vivien now, and she would still be with Frank. That she was responsible for Nicholas's continuing unhappiness made her feel guilty.

Harriet, certain that Phillipa and Frank would be getting engaged soon, had been looking forward to the wedding. Over the years many students had asked her to be their guest of honour and make a speech at the reception. She had always been delighted to accept. The weddings she enjoyed most were the ones where she knew both bride and groom. Many speeches introducing her were prefixed by, 'If it had not been for Harriet Shaw we would never have met.'

Natasha and Richard had asked her to be their guest of honour and she had already drafted her speech.

Unsure of what to say to Frank she felt uncomfortable about his next singing lesson. As she waited for him to arrive she decided to let him bring up the subject and say nothing if he did not. She noticed his controlled misery as soon as he walked into the studio.

'He probably doesn't know if Phillipa's told me,' she thought.

Guessing that her failure to ask, as she normally did, how he was, would indicate her knowledge, she took his *Melba Method* and ran through the exercises with him. Immediately she knew how deeply Phillipa had wounded him. His voice was tight. Pain affected his throat. She remembered the change in his voice when he had come back from Vietnam. His horror of the war and his experiences were more marked in his voice than on his face. It had taken a year of patient coaching to get him back to where he had been before he left.

In the middle of an exercise he shook his head. "Sorry, I can't go on."

She remembered how often his lessons had ended like that after Vietnam. He would sit down and she would listen while he told her about his guilt that he was responsible for the death of other humans. To her relief her responses to his agonized questions had usually been right.

"Sit down, Frank."

254

"I suppose you know about Phillipa?"

"Yes. I think she's made the wrong decision and one she'll regret."

"You know, Miss Shaw, it's not that there was someone else. If she'd fallen in love with another bloke – sure I'd be hurt, but I could accept it. It's that there's no one else and still I'm not good enough. I don't know why – that's the thing. I can't understand it."

"Neither can I."

"I was going to ask her to marry me. I was trying to work out how to go about it, but she started to cool off ... become distant and ... I don't know. I'm glad I didn't ask her." He rubbed his eyes. "When I got back from Vietnam I thought I'd never suffer like that again. I was wrong."

Harriet did not know what to say. For the first time ever, she felt angry with Phillipa.

Chapter 23

'Ah, their rejoicing seems to taunt and deride me!'
Puritani – Bellini

Nicholas and Harriet sat in her office going through the records of the third-year students that had been kept since they began opera school. Out of the twenty-four students who had started, nineteen were left. Choosing the four acts from four operas for the graduation production was always difficult because every student and their type of voice had to be taken into consideration. They cast Jacqueline as Maddalena in *Rigoletto*, Frank as Sarastro in *The Magic Flute* and Emily as Queen of the Night.

"Natasha and Richard for Scarpia and Tosca?" said Harriet.

Nicholas nodded. "Provided Natasha can act as if she hates Richard."

"Do you foresee any problem?"

"I was joking. I heard Natasha say to Richard a few weeks ago that it would be wonderful if they could do Tosca and Scarpia one day."

Harriet smiled. "This will make them happy."

"What about Deborah?" asked Nicholas picking up her file. "Marzelline? Pamina?"

"First Boy."

He looked at her in disbelief. "First Boy? What about a principal role?"

"Pamina or Marzelline would go to her head," she said.

Nicholas felt uneasy. Up to that moment he had been enjoying the creativity of casting. "If she's capable of a major role she must be given one – not a minor one like First Boy. She'd be an excellent Marzelline."

"No. I'm happy with her as First Boy."

"Who do you think should be Marzelline?"

"Rhonda."

"Rhonda? She's not as good as Deborah."

"Are you questioning my ability to judge who can sing a role and who can't?"

Nicholas was aware that to persuade her to change her mind he would have to be subtle. "No. Rhonda would be good, but Deborah would be brilliant. You've got to be fair. Have you given Natasha a leading role because she's one of your favourites?"

"Of course not!" she snapped.

"Then you can't give Deborah a small part because you don't like her. It will cause problems. Ingrid Williams won't be happy about it. The theatre's reputation will suffer and so will yours. Who are the other two boys?"

"Judy and Faye."

"Why have you given them minor roles?"

"Judy's been plagued with throat and chest infections for eighteen months, and since Faye started going out with that uncouth lout who hates opera, she lacks dedication."

He nodded. "I agree. However, Deborah is dedicated and healthy. In the workshop scenes last year she had major roles that she sang and performed superbly and would lead people to assume she'd be given a principal part in the graduation production."

Harriet was stubbornly silent.

"Why did you give her those roles last year?"

"I wanted to give her a chance, but they proved too much for her – as I suspected they would."

"Rubbish. She was sensational. Her Marguerite was astounding."

"No, Nicholas, it was the production that was astounding. Deborah could have done better. Her interpretation was self-centered."

"She was sensational, and you bloody well know it!"

She glared at him. "Please don't swear. I know some young people today use all sorts of vile words, but when I was young no gentleman used bad language in front of a lady. I don't know where you get your temper from."

He was determined not to allow her to digress. "You've got to give her a proper role! Aunt Harriet, you've got five major soprano parts and three brilliant sopranos. You've given Emily and Natasha two roles and you've got to give Deborah another, because if you don't you'll be wasting her incredible talent."

She closed Deborah's file. "I'm going to leave her as First Boy."
He was furious with himself for mismanaging the argument. "When she complains you can deal with her. Tell her that you hate her so much you're determined to hamper her singing career."

"That's unfair. I don't hate her."

"You want her to leave, don't you? You can't expel her so you want her to leave and this is your method. You do want her to leave, don't you?"

Harriet looked away.

"You want her to leave, don't you?" he insisted. "Because you've always hated her because she reminds you of Annabel – whoever she is." He ruthlessly ignored her expression. "She's not Annabel and it's unfair to treat her as if she is. For God's sake, who is Annabel? What did she do to you?"

Harriet shut her eyes. Nicholas saw with alarm that she was pale. "Sorry," he said. "Shall I get you some water?"

She put her head in her hands. Worried that she was about to have a heart attack he went into the kitchen, filled a glass with water and returned, relieved that she had not collapsed. He gave her the water. "I'll say no more. Deborah is First Boy."

"I suppose you think I'm emotionally blackmailing you?" she said.

"No. Lots of things can be feigned, but no one can act going as pale as you just did. But I wish you'd confide in me. I might be able to help."

"Can you change the past, Nicholas?"

"No."

"Then you can't help."

Phillipa and Richard finished clearing up the remains of the sandwiches they had eaten while they waited for the Beethoven Night at the Myer Music Bowl to begin. Natasha sat on the rug peeling an orange. She looked serene, and Phillipa envied her.

"I really feel sorry for all those people who aren't us," Richard said.

"So do I," said Natasha.

'Well, you two would,' Phillipa thought resentfully. 'Life's been easy for you. You've got brilliant futures to look forward to.' She looked at the evening sun glinting on Natasha's curls. 'Marriage, long honeymoon in England, main roles in Harriet's theatre for a few years, then you'll be off to Covent Garden. You'll be wealthy and famous and have no worries. Even Natasha's untidiness and hopeless cooking won't be a problem for long – you'll have cleaners, cooks and troops of people looking after you.'

Jacqueline took an apple from the picnic basket and nudged Richard with her foot. "How would you feel when the parts for *Famous Scenes from Favourite Operas* are announced and you'd only got a minor part?"

Natasha put the orange peel in a bag. "Don't talk about it. I'm a nervous wreck."

'Huh, you don't look like a nervous wreck,' thought Phillipa. 'You know you'll get a main part – you all do.' She was confused to find herself wishing that Frank was with them. Usually it was Nicholas she wanted. Worried by her emotions she only half listened while Richard, Jacqueline and Natasha discussed what roles they wanted and who they thought would get what. She was depressed that Nicholas had not asked her out. At the theatre Frank avoided her, but when he had to speak to her he was cool, calling her Phillipa not Philly.

Jacqueline laughed and Phillipa realized that although Natasha and Jacqueline were her close friends she could never tell them how she felt about Nicholas. Last year Jacqueline, hurt by Natasha's impatience over her inability to get over Max, had frequently confided in Phillipa, sometimes crying and telling her how much she missed him. 'So why can't I tell her about Nicholas?' she asked herself. 'Is it me, or is it them? Would they laugh at me or be sympathetic? Why do I think they'd laugh? They're my best friends. What's the matter with me? Why don't I try it? Why don't I just say to them now – look help me – I'm in love with Nicholas.'

The orchestra began to tune up.

"Lucky Emily, at least she knows she's getting Queen of The Night because no one else can sing top F's," said Jacqueline.

Richard refilled their glass with wine. "Frank will get Sparafucile or Sarastro. Though I suppose he's more likely to get Sarastro. Miss Shaw wants to build up his repertoire."

259

'Oh, Frank,' thought Phillipa. 'Stop it, I don't want Frank I want Nick.'

"All this supposing is giving me the horrors," said Natasha. "Let's talk about something else."

'Yes, let's,' thought Phillipa.

"How's poor Nicholas, Philly?" Jacqueline asked.

Phillipa grimaced. "Grumpy."

"I was amazed about him and Vivien breaking up," said Richard.

"She shouldn't have gone blabbing to the newspapers," said Natasha.

'She didn't,' thought Phillipa. 'I'm being punished for destroying the letter from Seamus O'Flynn, instead of giving it to Nicholas. Four people are unhappy … we used to be happy … and it's all my fault.'

The conductor arrived and, when the clapping died down, the orchestra launched into Beethoven's Third Symphony. In the fading light Phillipa listened, remembering how Frank had enjoyed making love to music. "Lights down, curtains closed, Beethoven on and clothes off!" he would say. In winter, when his sister was away, he would light a fire and after a candlelit dinner with wine they would make love.

Tears ran down her cheeks.

"If you would like to discuss your role, make an appointment with Phillipa to see either Miss Shaw or myself," said Nicholas.

Deborah watched Richard hug Natasha. The studio was alive with excitement with almost everyone happy with the role they had been given. Rhonda looked at her and smirked.

"Have a twenty-minute break," Nicholas called above the noise.

Instead of going to the kitchen with the others, Deborah went to the toilets, where she shut herself in a cubicle and cried. For weeks she had been learning the part of Tosca, imagining herself sweeping elegantly across the stage in a white dress that would show off her dark hair and eyes. She had imagined the rehearsals and the intimate contact she would have with Richard who was certain to be cast as Scarpia, and his eventual realization that he loved her. In her daydreams Jeremy was valiant, vowing he would always love her and if she ever needed him he would be there.

She had only worried that she might not get Tosca, she hadn't thought it possible that she would get such a small role. Judy and Faye, the girls who had been cast as the second and third boy were close friends. She'd had an altercation with Judy during the New Year's Eve party last year when Judy had caught her kissing her boyfriend. Judy had never forgiven her and Faye had taken her side against Deborah.

She knew that many girls in the class would be happy to witness her humiliation and she wasn't going to give them the satisfaction. Gritting her teeth, she let herself out of the cubicle, bathed her eyes in cold water and repaired her make-up. Satisfied there were no traces of tears she marched down the corridor and went into the kitchen.

Two days later she was sitting in Nicholas's office. She had made the appointment to see Nicholas and was dismayed to see that Miss Shaw was with him.

She looked at Deborah coldly. "The invitation was for you to discuss the role you had been given, not complain because you don't think it's big enough."

"I'm not – I don't think the role of First Boy suits me."

"Why not? Is it within your vocal range or not?" asked Harriet.

"Well, it is, but – "

"What's the problem then?" she asked impatiently.

"I don't think the role is me."

"What role do you think is you?"

"Tosca," she said, spurred on by Nicholas's sympathetic look.

"Are you suggesting I call Natasha in here and tell her I'm giving the role to you?" asked Harriet.

She had not planned to say anything about Jeremy, but the realization that nothing else would change Harriet's mind, made her desperate. "Jeremy Langford is my boyfriend," she said. "It would be a shame if you lost his patronage."

Nicholas stood up.

Deborah was taken aback by his livid expression.

"Natasha is Tosca and you are First Boy. If you want to leave the school over this, let me know by tomorrow so you can be replaced. And don't you ever dare blackmail Miss Shaw again." He held open the door for her.

She began to cry.

He shook his head. "Tears don't work on me."

Jeremy opened the door. "Deborah, what's the matter, what's happened?" He guided her inside and shut the door. "Is it your mother? Darling, please stop crying – tell me what's happened."

She threw her handbag on the sofa. "Miss Shaw has given me the part of First Boy."

"Why?"

"I don't know. You've got to do something."

He stared at her and took his hand from her arm. "What do you expect me to do?"

"Go and see Harriet Shaw. Tell her that you'll withdraw your patronage unless she gives me a major role. I want Tosca."

He walked over to the window. "Presumably Tosca's been given to someone else?"

"Natasha Howard."

"She's got an outstanding voice. She'd be a fine Tosca."

"I'll be better – she's too plain."

He turned away from the window. "Plain? You think she's plain? She's got the most beautiful eyes I've ever seen." His face hardened. "I respect Harriet Shaw, and have no intention of interfering in her decisions."

Deborah felt like screaming with jealousy. "I won't go to bed with you ever again if you don't go and see Miss Shaw."

"You have overestimated your power – and mine," he said coldly. "Nobody tells Harriet Shaw what to do, and no one tells me what to do either. You're just like your mother – I thought you were different, but you just wanted to use me for my position."

Deborah realized the enormity of her demands. "I'm sorry, I didn't mean it, I was just upset. Miss Shaw hates me – I don't know why."

He went to the sofa and picked up her handbag. "She can see the real you – unlike me. I saw you as an innocent girl who had been shockingly treated by a vile mother. I was wrong. You're as corrupt as she is. I was mad to think otherwise."

She was appalled. "No. Jeremy, I'm sorry," she whispered hoarsely.

"Everyone makes mistakes, please forgive me."

"Deborah, your first mistake was to think that I had power over Harriet Shaw. Your second was to presume that I would use it if I had. You only see life from your point of view, you never look at it from anyone else's angle. You have to be the star. But you're in the back row of the chorus of life, and that's where you'll stay."

She began to tremble. "Jeremy, I'm sorry." She flung her arms around his neck and sobbed. He stood still for a moment and she longed to feel his arms round her.

"It's over, Deborah." He pushed her away. "Out."

She walked slowly to the front door. He followed her, opened it and the fly screen, but refused to look at her. She stepped outside and he shut the doors.

"Nicholas, I'm going to give you more independence," said Harriet. "Shall we begin with the third year's *Famous Scenes from Favourite Operas*? How do you feel about a totally free rein in the production?"

He looked at her in surprise. "It'd be exciting – I'd probably realize how much I rely on you," he said tactfully.

"I'll get involved in some productions, I can't bow out entirely."

"I'd never expect you to. You have to choose the cast. Thanks for this. I feel excited and honoured," he said sincerely.

"Ingrid Williams rang me and asked why Deborah had been given a minor role. I told her that we had so much talent this year that the choices were very difficult."

"As soon as she sees the production she'll know that Deborah should have got a principal role," said Nicholas.

"I know. This isn't going to be the end of things as far as Deborah's concerned."

That night when Nicholas arrived home there was a letter from Tanya in his letterbox.

1st May 1973

Dear Nick,

*I'm getting married! I've never felt like this before. He's
very liberal and wants me to continue with my acting
career. You'd like him. He owns a house in Kensington, so
unfortunately this means I'll be moving out of your house
at the end of November. I've told your parents and they
said they could put it in the hands of an agent, but to tell
you first.
I'm enclosing a wedding invitation – I know it's a long
way to come, but if you're planning a holiday or decide
you're sick of the sun ...*

After reading the rest of her letter he was going to write to his
parents telling them to put the house in the hands of an estate agent,
when he suddenly thought of something. He rang Harriet.
"That's a wonderful idea," she said.

Nicholas sat in the theatrette with Natasha, Richard and Guido Callati,
who was playing the part of Mario, Tosca's lover. His voice was good,
but he was two inches shorter than Natasha, and although only twenty-
five he was overweight. He had emigrated from Italy with his parents
when he was twelve. Being fluent in seven languages he worked as an
interpreter.

Nicholas handed Richard a knife with a retractable blade. "The
stereo's set up with the Maria Callas and Tito Gobbi record, so have a
run through. Don't sing, just act it."

When they had set up the stage with a table, chairs, desk and chaise
longue, Nicholas put the needle on the record and sat in the front row
with his notebook. Natasha, wearing jeans and a green jumper over a
white shirt, made an unlikely looking Tosca, but she reflected such

264

believable emotion without being melodramatic, that Nicholas was surprised. Richard looked too young and sensitive to be a totally convincing Scarpia, but Nicholas saw a detestable character in the making. Although he sometimes overacted, his movements were good and some of his expressions were cold blooded. Guido also overacted, but Nicholas understood and had expected this.

Physically Guido and Natasha were ill-matched, and Nicholas was pleased that Guido spent most of the scene on the floor covered in blood. 'A painter's smock will hide his paunch,' he thought. 'How am I going to make Richard look sexually unappealing?'

When they finished, he put the record back in its sleeve. "How did that feel?"

"We've got a long way to go," said Natasha, sitting on the table and swinging her legs.

Richard nodded. "I overacted a bit."

"I overacted a lot, I think," said Guido.

Nicholas was pleased by their constructive self-criticism. "There are a few thoughts I want to throw your way," he said, looking at his notes. "Scarpia, you're so overcome with lust for Tosca, that you nearly rape her. Then you hear the drums and you taunt her with the fact that Mario has only another hour to live. Instead of continuing to chase her, you allow her to pray. Why? At that point you were Richard watching Natasha sing 'Vissi d'arte'. You must be Scarpia plotting his next move.

"Why are you allowing her to pray? Do you believe in God? If you do, that will affect your expression. Do you just pay lip service to God and the Church? You go to church, but do you fear God, love God or not believe in him at all?"

Richard nodded. "I'm playing with her – I know I'm going to win, but I'm mentally tormenting her."

"Does the sight of Tosca praying excite you? On the other hand you might feel scornful."

Richard thought for a moment. "If I believe in God, I'd feel apprehensive. After all, what if God answers her prayer?"

"Which he does," said Natasha.

"Natasha, why do you pray?" asked Nicholas. "Do you think God is listening? Consider the words of 'Vissi d'arte'. 'Oh God, why have you in this my darkest hour repaid me like this?' Do you really, really hope he'll answer your prayer?"

She nodded. "I'm not playing for time or anything. I believe in God."

"Do you have any scruples about killing Scarpia?" asked Nicholas.

"No. When I see the knife I know God wants me to kill him."

Nicholas smiled. "Good, Natasha. Your emotional moments were outstanding. You didn't overact, which was something I'd expected because the action's so full of drama."

She grimaced. "I imagined I was in a Nazi occupied town in France, and Richard was Mario – it brought it closer and made it more real."

Nicholas stared at her. He looked at Richard imagining him dressed in a Nazi uniform.

"What's wrong?" asked Natasha.

"I'm thinking."

"I think I know what you're thinking," said Guido.

"Dare we?" asked Nicholas slowly.

Natasha's eyes widened. "Update it to the war?"

Nicholas nodded. "Scarpia an officer in the Gestapo, and Angelotti and Mario members of the Resistance. Change Bonaparte into Montgomery and Melas into Rommel. Substitute Rome … for where?"

"Some vague city in Europe?" said Guido. "Yes! It would work. But the decision should rest with Natasha and Richard. It's their scene."

"No," said Natasha. "We're all important. The whole scene revolves round you, Guido. You're the poor bloke who gets tortured."

"How about torturing him on stage, in front of Tosca," said Richard.

Nicholas laughed. "Am I to take it that you like the idea?"

"Yes," replied Guido and Richard.

"Natasha?"

She frowned. "Will I have to wear a short dress and high heels?"

"No, still a long evening dress. Remember, Tosca's been singing at a classical concert, not in a cocktail bar."

She smiled. "Great. Yes, let's do it."

"If we have any Nazi uniforms in wardrobe, could we do a run through with me in costume, see how it looks?" asked Richard.

"Yes," said Nicholas. "I'll see if I can get some for your next rehearsal."

"Do you think Miss Shaw will approve?" asked Guido.

"I hope so," he replied.

"When are you going to tell her?" asked Richard.

"I'm not."

"Ooh," said Natasha. "What if she hates it?"

"We'll have to think again," said Nicholas.

Natasha looked at Richard and shuddered. "Funny what a uniform can do. I won't even have to act frightened now."

Richard buttoned up the jacket of the Gestapo uniform. "I feel sinister." He stood in front of the mirror looking at his reflection. The second pair of knee high boots he had tried on fitted.

Nicholas grimaced. "You're going to have to have your hair cut very short."

"Okay – if you wanted me bald, I'd have my head shaved."

Nicholas looked at him thoughtfully. "Would you?"

"Yes."

"No!" shrieked Natasha. "Don't you dare."

Nicholas laughed. "Don't panic – it was only an idea."

They went into the theatrette and Nicholas put the record on.

Although Richard was the only person in costume, the uniform made the scene more tense. The high boots changed the way he walked and even with his longer than period hair he looked arrogant. He did not overact, he let his menace come from the fact he was in Nazi uniform.

At the end of the scene Richard jumped up. "How was it?"

"Frightening," said Nicholas. "It's going to work." He turned the stereo off. "The first music rehearsal's next week, but during production rehearsals you'll do as little singing as possible. We don't want to strain your voices. On Friday night we'll do a run through without music. We have five months to work on this. But it has to be ready to perform for Miss Shaw twelve weeks from now."

After the rehearsal Richard and Natasha went back to his flat and did another run through to the record.

"Nicholas is brilliant," said Richard. "I feel much more Scarpia-like. And we haven't started singing it yet."

"I almost started crying during 'Vissi d'arte', I felt so alone, frightened and desperate. It's a bit scary." She put her hand on her chest. "It all comes from inside. I feel drained."

"Too drained to make love?" he murmured in her ear.

She pulled him into the bedroom. "I'm never too tired for that."

Vivien was miserable. Missing Nicholas and distressed by his refusal to speak to her she tried to plan how to get him back. She wrote to him, but received no reply. When she rang him he hung up as soon as she spoke. She had gone out with several men, but none of them interested her.

She had planned to do a preliminary review of *Famous Scenes from Favourite Operas* for *The Australian Women's Weekly*. When she had discussed it with Harriet before she and Nicholas had broken up she said that she intended to tantalize the readers. Nervous about seeing Nicholas and Harriet again and worried that they would humiliate her by asking her to leave the theatre, she considered asking a colleague to cover it for her.

Immediately she decided against it. 'I'll write a letter – a business letter,' she thought, putting the magazine's headed paper in her typewriter.

20ᵗʰ July 1973

Dear Miss Shaw,

As you may remember, I was booked to write an article on **Famous Scenes from Favourite Operas.** *If you no longer wish me to do it, please let me know.*

Yours sincerely,

Vivien Anderson

She sent it to Harriet's house not the theatre.

Harriet never wanted to see Vivien again, but from experience she knew that people like her would not give up easily. 'If I tell her to stay away she might get suspicious, and start digging into my past,' she thought.

She took the letter to work and gave it to Nicholas. "What are we going to do?"

He shrugged.

"Don't stand there shrugging, Nicholas."

"What do you want to do?" he asked.

"I don't want her here."

He dropped the letter on her desk. "Then write and tell her."

"What reason do I have?"

"The article Seamus O'Flynn wrote. She gave him the information."

"Is that a good enough reason? She's been sensitive enough to write. I feel I should let her come and take photos and do the article. It might seem petty not to. And it's good publicity."

He pulled out a chair and sat opposite her. "I didn't tell you before, but she's interested in your past ... has been since she first met you. She asked me lots of questions. I said I knew nothing, but she didn't believe me."

What he said confirmed her suspicions. She had lived with the worry of having her secret exposed for so long she wondered why the thought of discovery still terrified her. "Trust you to get involved with a journalist, Nicholas."

"It's not my fault you've got a dark secret."

"It's hardly a dark secret."

"Then what sort of secret is it?"

She took her glasses off and rubbed her eyes. "I don't know."

He smiled. "You must – it's your secret. Listen," he said carefully. "I don't want to know what it is – "

"Yes, you do."

"Okay, I do – but not at this moment. I'm trying to get a few things clear and see if I can assess how dangerous Vivien is. This thing that happened – did you ... this will sound awful, but ... "

"Get on with it, Nicholas."

"Did you do anything criminal?"

"No."

269

"Well that's all right then, isn't it?"

"No." She bit her lip. "A crime was involved."

He groaned. "I give up. You're talking in riddles."

She opened her glasses case and took out the cleaning cloth. "Of course if Vivien did find out what happened, your curiosity would be sated."

He pushed back his chair. "Thanks. I don't know why I care about you – as you seem to dislike me so much."

She shut her eyes. "I'm sorry. I find talking about this painful and I say stupid things and think stupid, hurtful thoughts. The experience has made me bitter – very bitter." She sighed. "As you can see." She heard him come back to the desk and sit down. Opening her eyes she looked at him. "And selfish. How do you feel about seeing Vivien again?"

"Not very happy. I'm not one of these people who can remain on good terms with old girlfriends. But it's good publicity for the students and the theatre."

"Shall I write and tell her to come?"

He nodded.

Dear Vivien,

Thank you for your letter. Of course it's all right for you to cover the preview of Famous Scenes in October. The performance begins at 1 p.m. You may interview the students afterwards and take photos, but as they will be nervous please don't go backstage till after the performance.

Yours sincerely,

Harriet Shaw

270

Chapter 24

'Come then, Here on the stage
you shall behold us in human fashion,
and see the sad fruits of love and passion.'
Pagliacci – Leoncavallo

The hairdresser combed Richard's wet hair and picked up the scissors. "Ready?"

Nicholas looked at Natasha standing in the doorway of the dressing room. "Are you sure you want to watch?"

"I'm here to make sure you don't shave him." She groaned as the hairdresser cut off the first lock and dropped it on the floor.

Ten minutes later Richard's hair was very short.

Natasha pulled a face. "You look awful."

The hairdresser picked up a broom. "Well, that's nice – your fiancée thinks you look awful."

Richard grinned. "That's okay – she's supposed to hate me."

"I still think he should be bald," said Nicholas.

The hairdresser nodded. "He's too handsome. The audience won't understand why you're revolted by him."

"Wouldn't you be revolted by a Nazi?" asked Natasha.

"Well ... yes," she said.

Nicholas picked up a box. "Natasha, can you give this to Emily?"

"What is it?"

"A surprise for her."

"What?" asked Natasha.

Nicholas smiled secretively. "You'll see."

On the way back to her dressing room Natasha had the first pangs of nervousness. It was eight weeks before the opening night, and they were preparing to perform *Famous Scenes from Favourite Operas* in front of Harriet. Natasha felt that performing for her alone was more nerve racking than having a packed auditorium, complete with critics.

In the dressing room Emily was pacing the floor. "I'm terrified. I don't think I can do this."

"Look, you've got a present." Natasha gave her the box. "Nick said it was a surprise."

Emily took the lid off and lifted out a glittering crescent moon and star coronet. "Gosh. It's beautiful." She opened the envelope and took out the card.

Dear Emily,

This was made for me when I was Queen of the Night at Covent Garden. It is yours when you sing the role at this theatre.

Harriet Shaw

"Oh, Emily, what an honour!"

"My lucky charm," said Emily softly.

Natasha pulled off her jeans and shirt and put on the long satin petticoat. As she waited for the hairdresser she worried that she would forget everything and trip over her skirt. She was about to give in to a fit of panic, but decided that this would unnerve Emily even more.

The hairdresser arrived and Natasha looked at her accusingly. "I hope Richard isn't bald."

She plugged in the curling tongs. "The way you're going on anyone would think I wanted to cut off his head not his hair."

As the other students began to arrive the atmosphere became increasingly excited. The hairdresser did Emily's hair in a Grecian style and placed the coronet on her head. "It looks terrific," she said as she secured it with hairpins. "Natasha, I'll do you next." She ran her hand through Natasha's curls and unplugged the tongs. "No need for these."

Natasha looked absently at her reflection as the hairdresser wound the curls round her finger and piled them high on her head.

"No hair spray because Nicholas wants you dishevelled at the end," she said as she pinned up the last curl. Picking up the pearl tiara she slid it into place. "Great. Break a leg and all that."

The make-up artist finished with Emily and sat in the chair opposite

Natasha. She opened her make-up case and set to work. When she finished she stood back and looked at Natasha in approval. "Wow. What a difference."

"Oh, Natasha!" exclaimed Emily. "You look … so beautiful."

Natasha temporarily forgot her nerves and gazed at her reflection in amazement. "Golly. Maybe I should start wearing make-up." The other girls in the dressing-room crowded round her in excitement.

Nicholas put his head round the door. "How's it going? Oh, Natasha. Has Richard seen you yet?"

She giggled. "I want to put my dress on first."

He went to the rack and took her costume off the hanger. It was an empire line dress in emerald-green velvet with a full skirt and a deeply cut neckline. She stepped into it and he buttoned up the back for her. Emily handed him the pearl necklace and he put it round her neck.

Nicholas took her arm. "Come on, princess, let's go and find your prince."

Richard looked at her in such astonishment that Nicholas laughed. "Isn't she gorgeous?"

Richard hugged her. "Darling, you look beautiful."

"Careful of her hair and don't smudge her lipstick," warned Nicholas. "Remember, Natasha, you're supposed to hate him."

Phillipa and Nicholas stood on the stage as the set was changed from *Fidelio* to *Tosca*. A dresser, made of papier mâché, was removed to reveal a panelled door, and the red check kitchen curtains were replaced by royal blue velvet drapes. A large fireplace made to look like marble was carried on and a Nazi flag unfurled and hung on one wall. During the other three acts, Nicholas had been aware of Vivien sitting near the back of the theatre. So far he had avoided talking to her, but suspected that she would try and see him afterwards when she came backstage to take photos.

"Where do you want Hitler, Mate?" asked a stage hand.

"Over the fireplace."

Heavy table and chairs, a desk, and a sofa were put in place.

The new stage manager went up to Nicholas. "Your sets are great. I've never seen such fast and quiet scene changes. The picture of Adolf and the flag give it a miasma of evil. Miss Shaw seems enthusiastic."

Nicholas frowned. "So far – this one's the real test."

Phillipa nudged him. "Cheer up. You're such a pessimist."

Harriet sat in the darkened auditorium waiting for the curtain to rise on the second act of *Tosca*. Normally she went backstage to see how things were progressing, but because this was Nicholas's production alone, she had behaved exactly like a member of the audience. She had been delighted by *Fidelio, Rigoletto* and *The Magic Flute*. The singing was superb and the productions had been polished with touches of originality. She suspected that Nicholas had done something different with *Tosca*, and she was intrigued. The curtain rose and her eyes widened with shock.

"Richard sounds fantastic," said Phillipa.

With shaking hands Natasha picked up the glass of water and sipped it. "I'm so scared. I'm frightened that everyone will be successful except me. That's the trouble with going on last."

"You'll be fine once you get on stage," said Emily. "I was terrified, but as soon as I started singing I was okay. If I can do it, you certainly can."

"You were fabulous, Emily. Congratulations. I'm so nervous I forgot to say anything before. Your costume really suits you – you should wear black more often."

Emily swirled around. The chiffon, sewn intermittently with tiny rhinestones, floated round her. "I don't want to take it off."

"I wish we were doing the cantata, it would get me into the swing of things," said Natasha.

Phillipa took Natasha's cloak off the rail. "Put this on. They'll be calling you in a second."

"I want to go to the toilet."

Jacqueline squeezed her hand. "You don't."

Richard's voice could be heard over the intercom. "God created beauty and wines of various merit. I want to taste all I can of the heavenly produce!"

Natasha shuddered. "I hope Miss Shaw likes it. Doing it in this period makes it so real."

"When I see Richard in that awful uniform I feel queer," said

Phillipa.

Emily laughed. "As long as he doesn't."

The intercom crackled and the stage manager called for Tosca.

Natasha stood up. "Pray for me."

"We'll keep everything crossed," promised Jacqueline.

"Champagne's in the fridge," said Phillipa cheerfully.

Natasha walked to the door at the back of the stage and waited for her cue.

"Break a leg," whispered the stage hand as he opened the door.

Natasha stepped onto the stage. The conductor smiled encouragingly at her. She saw Harriet's outline in the middle of the theatre and during the scene with Mario she resisted the unexpected urge to look into the auditorium. She felt hopelessly unlike Tosca. She was just herself standing on stage in a strange dress. Almost in a daze she watched Guido being taken off.

Richard put his hand on her arm. "Now, let us have a friendly talk together. There is nothing to alarm you."

He pulled out a chair and she sat down. Suddenly, her nervousness disappeared. Her wits sharpened, and she was Floria Tosca in war torn Europe.

From the back row of the auditorium Nicholas was torn between elation and uncertainty. Richard's very short hair and Nazi uniform made him look sinister in spite of, or perhaps because of, his youth. Nicholas could not decide which. Natasha's entrance had been perfect. She had looked bewildered, wary and apprehensive. Richard, Natasha and Guido had studied books about Hitler's occupation of Europe and if Harriet hated this production they would be disappointed. He could see her outline in the middle of the theatre and wished he knew what she was thinking. He had sat as far away from Vivien as possible, but out of the corner of his eye he saw her at the other side of the theatre.

He watched Richard striding to the door of the room where Cavaradossi was being tortured. "Tosca was never more tragic on the stage! Bring him in here, let her see him screaming!"

Guido, his face and clothes covered in blood, was dragged on.

Nicholas worried that Harriet would be revolted by the torture.

Richard grabbed Natasha's hair and pulled her head back. "Tell me where Angelotti is!"

"No, no!" She pulled herself free and ran to the door.

Richard barred her way and dragged her into the middle of the room. She covered her face and he pulled her hands away. When she closed her eyes he smacked her across the face. Nicholas winced. 'It's too violent,' he thought distractedly.

Guido yelled in agony and passed out.

Natasha looked at Richard. "The well in the garden!"

Richard smiled. "Angelotti is there?"

"Yes!"

"Stop the torture now!" Richard ordered.

Natasha knelt beside Guido and cradled his head in her arms.

"Floria," he said weakly.

"Darling! How you have suffered, my beloved. But that brutal tyrant shall suffer too!"

"Floria, did you talk?"

Natasha stroked his hair. "No, my love, no."

Richard roared with laughter. "Spoletta, go and look in the well in the garden."

Guido pushed her away. "You have betrayed me! Damn you!"

Sciarrone burst in. "Dreadful, dreadful news!"

"What has happened, tell me quickly!" snapped Richard.

"Our troops have been defeated!"

Richard walked towards him. "Defeated? How? When? Where?"

"At El Alamein!"

"Damn and blast!"

"Montgomery is the victor!"

"Rommel?"

"No, Rommel has retreated!"

Nicholas was relieved that the new lines came out clearly.

"Jacqui, stop prowling around," said Phillipa. "You're giving me the willies."

"I'm more nervous about Natasha than I was about myself. I'm terrified she'll fall over or miss her cue."

"No she won't," Phillipa said soothingly.

"She sounds better than Maria Callas," said Emily.

"There you are. See?"

"What if Miss Shaw hates it?"

"Then they do the traditional version," said Phillipa.

Richard laughed, and as Nicholas listened to his rich, expressive voice he almost forgot Harriet.

"Oh yes, I'm said to be mercenary. But I don't sell myself to a beautiful woman for money. No, no. If I must betray what I have sworn, I will have a different payment. How I've waited for this moment!" Slowly he undid the buttons on his jacket. "Goddess of song, you have scorned me and defied me. It was your beauty that made me love you, it is your hatred that has enslaved me." He took off his jacket and hung it neatly on the back of a chair.

During rehearsals they had all debated how to do the scene, and had tried Scarpia pulling off his jacket in a frenzy and throwing it on the floor. Richard and Guido had preferred that version, but Natasha and Nicholas had felt that calculated actions were the cold blooded signs of a man in absolute control.

Richard took off his tie.

"How despicable you are!" She ran to the door.

"I will not use violence, you are free – go ahead. Your hopes are vain. The Mayor will only grant pardon to a corpse." He pushed his braces off his shoulders. "How you hate me."

"Oh God!" She picked up the glass of wine and flung its contents in his face.

"But this is how I want you." He picked up a table napkin and wiped his face.

She backed away. "Don't touch me, I hate you, hate you! You are vile and depraved!"

"What does it matter? Aching with hate or aching with love." He undid the top button of his shirt.

'It's too sexual,' thought Nicholas. 'Aunt Harriet will sack me. How did I ever think she'd approve of this? The critics will annihilate me if this goes on. What if his trousers fall down?'

At the sound of drums Richard strolled to the window and looked down. "Can you hear? It's the drums. They are leading the condemned men to their last journey. Time is passing! Do you know what gloomy business is being carried out down there?" He beckoned to her. "A scaffold is being raised."

Natasha fell to her knees and crossed herself. Richard looked at her scornfully, his shoulders shaking with silent laughter. He took a cigarette from a box and lit it. Leaning on the table, he watched her with an expression of amusement as she sang 'Vissi d'arte'.

'Will I resign or wait till she sacks me?' pondered Nicholas. 'Shall I apologize? There's eight weeks to sort out a traditional performance.'

'It's almost over and nothing's gone wrong yet,' though Natasha with relief. She went to the table, poured a glass of wine and drank it quickly. She poured another. In the act of putting the bottle down, she froze, her eyes riveted by the knife on the table. Richard was busy writing. She saw him surreptitiously put the blood capsule into his mouth. 'I hope he doesn't choke on it.' Still looking at him, she picked up the knife and concealed it in the folds of her dress.

He finished writing the safe conduct pass and stood up. As he walked towards her, she saw the small mark on his shirt where she had to stab him. The pressure of her thrust would be enough to break the membrane of the blood bag.

"Tosca, you are mine at last!"

She stabbed him in the chest and a bloodstain appeared.

"Curse you!" he yelled.

"This is the kiss of Tosca!"

Richard staggered. "Oh, help me, I'm dying! Oh, help me I'm dying!"

"Are you choking on your own blood, you tortured me too much!"

The bloodstain spread as he clutched his chest. "I'm dying. Help!"

"And killed by a woman!"

"Help! I'm dying!" Blood ran from his mouth.

"What mercy did you ever show me?"

He fell to his knees and crawled towards the door. "Help me – dying!"

"Can you still hear me? Look at me! It's Tosca. Oh, Scarpia!"

He reached the door and tried to open it. "Help, help!"

Natasha lifted her skirt and kicked his hand away. "Are you choking on your own blood?"

"I'm dying!"

"Die in damnation. Die! Die! Die!"

Richard collapsed.

Jacqueline and Phillipa hugged each other.

"That was fantastic!" said Emily. "Natasha sounded wild."

"Richard really sounded as if he was choking," said Frank. "I hope no one replaced the knife with a real one."

"God, don't say things like that!" said Jacqueline.

"It's okay, the curtain's hit the floor. Richard's just spoken. Calm down, Jacqui, you're so jumpy," said Phillipa.

Frank grinned. "I just heard him ask for an ambulance."

"Shut up, Frank," said Phillipa.

He glared at her. "Don't tell me to shut up, Phillipa."

"Sh, Miss Shaw will be giving her verdict in a sec," said Emily.

The theatre was silent. Nicholas was engulfed by failure. After the others, Harriet had applauded. When the lights went up he walked down the aisle, and stood at the end of her row.

She looked at him. "I'm shocked to the core."

The curtain rose and the cast stood nervously in a group.

Harriet walked into the aisle. "That was the most horrifying, violent, marvellous performance of *Tosca* I have ever seen. You were all absolutely incredible. There is nothing I can criticize – not the tiniest thing. Congratulations."

Richard and Guido kissed Natasha and clapped each other on the back.

Nicholas looked at Harriet in amusement. "You enjoyed teasing me, didn't you? I really thought you didn't like it."

"At first I was furious. But ten minutes into the act, I realized that I'd never watched *Tosca* and felt frightened and revolted. I've seen *Tosca* so many times it lost its power to shock me – till today. You've surpassed yourself. It's a long time since my hair's stood on end – it stood on end twice during that act. It was very disturbing, as it should be. It should shock people."

He saw Vivien going backstage. "I thought you'd sack me for making it too sexual."

"Nicholas, he's trying to rape her, rape is sexual."

"What about the critics?"

"If an old maid like me approves, the critics will go into raptures. Next time we'll do the complete *Tosca* that way."

"Hang on. It's hard enough to lift one act out of time and place but I doubt if I'd be able to do it with the whole opera."

"You did it with *Bohème*."

"That has no historical foundation."

"*Don Carlos* is historically wrong. I've only one suggestion. Change the order and do *Rigoletto* last, because it's the only final act in the group, and it'll be a more fitting finale than *Tosca*."

"I'm so happy you like it, I'll do them in any order you want."

"You're teaching me, Nicholas. If you had suggested doing this, I would have said no, and we would have argued about it. But seeing it made me realize how powerful it was. I'll try and be more adventurous. You've been right so many times."

He put his arm round her. "Come on, Philly's got champagne backstage."

Deborah felt so unhappy she was tempted to go home instead of staying for the celebration party. Judy and Faye had ignored her before and after their performance. Emily was the only person who had spoken to her. After *The Magic Flute* Miss Shaw had been ecstatic about Frank and Emily's performance and had skillfully managed to praise Faye and Judy without including Deborah.

She watched Vivien taking photos of Richard and Natasha. 'Last year it was me she was fussing over, now it's someone else,' she thought. 'She's probably forgotten who I am.'

Jealously, she had seen Natasha's startling transformation. Not only did she have the man and the part Deborah wanted, she looked stunning as well. Throughout *Tosca* she willed Natasha to trip over or crack on her top notes. Instead, people were crowding round her and telling her she was better than Maria Callas. 'Anyone would think she was the only one who'd been on stage today,' she thought as Miss Shaw put her arms round Richard and Natasha.

Richard handed Natasha a glass of champagne. "To Floria," he said, raising his glass.

The others clapped, and Natasha, her eyes shinning with happiness, raised her glass. "To Scarpia, Nicholas, Miss Shaw, and to all of us for doing well today."

Deborah smiled stiffly and joined in the clapping. Seeing Rhonda looking slyly at her she wandered over to Emily. "You were great, Emily."

"Thanks, Deborah. I hope I can do it again for the performances."

"You're the real star today," she said softly. "Lots of us could do Tosca, but you're the only one who can sing Queen of the Night."

"Tosca's much more difficult," said Emily generously. "All I had to do was stand and sing. Natasha's got to act. She was riveting. Look at her. She's so happy, confident and in love," she said wistfully. "With make-up on she's stunning. She's got everything. I wish I was like her."

'I wish I was her,' thought Deborah.

When she left the theatre she was surprised to find Vivien waiting for her.

"Hello, Deborah. Are you doing anything later?"

"No."

"Can I take you out to dinner?"

Deborah was delighted Vivien had remembered her. "Oh, gosh. Thanks. I'd love that."

"Right. How about *Fanny's* in Lonsdale Street at eight?"

Deborah smiled. "That'd be lovely."

Convinced that she was on the trail of a story, Vivien searched through her wardrobe. Wanting Deborah to see her as concerned and guileless she chose a cream suit in fine wool and a pink silk blouse with a lace collar. She did her hair in a chignon and looked in the mirror. 'A picture of innocence,' she thought.

As soon as she had realized that Deborah had a small part and not even a solo, she postponed her plans to get Nicholas back. He could wait. Knowing he was avoiding her she had stayed out of his way. Her interest in Deborah was not only because of Harriet's dislike. Beautiful and glamorous with a stunning voice, Deborah was definitely on track to being a famous opera star and Vivien felt that it would help her journalistic career to befriend her. She imagined travelling all over the world as Deborah's publicity officer. And she knew Deborah needed friends. Ostracized by her fellow students she was obviously unhappy. Vivien wondered what it was about her that antagonized both males and females.

She caught a tram to the city and arrived at *Fanny's* early. When Deborah was ushered over there was a bottle of champagne in an ice bucket by their table.

"Don't worry about the prices," she said as a waiter handed them menus. "This is on expenses. The editor wants to know how your career's progressing."

Deborah looked despondent. "Not very well – as you saw."

Vivien sipped her champagne. "Have you been ill?"

"No."

"Tell me about it later," said Vivien casually, hoping that by the time they were having dessert, Deborah, relaxed by the champagne, would tell her everything.

During the soup she kept to generalities. When their main courses arrived she told Deborah funny stories about her job and asked her about her past and her plans for the future. She waited until Deborah had almost finished her duckling before saying, "I was surprised you haven't got a big role – the girl who sang Marzelline, her voice wasn't nearly as good as yours. Pamina and Gilda weren't as good as you either. Why did they get major parts and not you?"

"I don't know."

"Were you upset?"

Deborah put her knife and fork together. "Very."

"Have you any idea why you've not been given a major part?"

She looked cautious. "No."

Vivien guessed she was worried that what she said might end up in the magazine. The waiter removed their plates and gave them the dessert menu. Vivien let the conversation lapse while they decided what to have.

"Is Miss Shaw biased against you because you're not her student?"

"No, I went to her first. She sent me to Ingrid Williams because she had too many students and couldn't take on any more."

'Interesting,' thought Vivien as the waiter put her strawberry mousse in front of her.

"But I think it was because she didn't like me for some reason."

282

Vivien picked up her spoon. "Have you any idea why?"

Deborah shook her head. Vivien felt she was keeping something back. 'It can wait,' she thought. 'I've made a connection with her, I'll keep it up.' She smiled. "Would you like a liqueur and coffee?"

"Benedictine and coffee with cream, please."

Before they left the restaurant Vivien gave Deborah her telephone number at work.

In the taxi on the way home Deborah wondered if she should have told Vivien about Harriet calling her Annabel. She had been tempted, but the thought of what Harriet would do if Vivien wrote an article about it had stopped her. 'She'd fail me in the graduation and not let me join the professional company next year.'

Chapter 25

'Will some disaster come to me?
Ah, no, this is folly!'
Rigoletto – Verdi

'Opals are unlucky.'

Richard was troubled by the statement about the opal pendant he had bought Natasha for her twenty-third birthday. Deep green and blue, in a gold setting, it was suspended on a fine gold chain. But since he had bought it, three people had told him opals were unlucky. Natasha had been thrilled and had worn it to Harriet's eightieth birthday party where it had been much admired.

He tried to shake off his unease. "It's because there's no opera school tonight and I'm on my own." It was no good. His pessimism grew. "They're sensible drivers, but suppose a drunk crashes into them?" He shook his head. "What's wrong with me?" He put on *The Marriage of Figaro*. "Life's great. Natasha and I are getting married in three months, we've glittering futures. Nothing will go wrong. Nothing can go wrong."

Two nights later, Nicholas had Natasha, Richard, Jacqueline, Phillipa and Harriet to dinner. Although Phillipa was pleased Nicholas had accepted her offer to do the cooking, part of her felt resentful. She had spent all afternoon shopping and preparing pâté with fresh herbs, beef casserole in red wine and lemon cheesecake. Nicholas was grateful and told her how marvellous she was, but she felt as if she was always helping everyone. 'Maybe that's the only reason people want me around. Not for me, but for what I can do,' she thought.

Concerned she was in danger of becoming embittered, she tried not to envy Natasha who sat opposite her. Since the preview run of *Tosca*, Natasha, now aware how good she could look, had bought make-up and new clothes. Phillipa had taken her shopping and they arrived home with trouser suits, silk and cotton blouses, boots and shoes and six pairs of stylish trousers. Frustratingly, Natasha had resisted Phillipa's efforts to persuade her to buy dresses or skirts. "The only dresses I want to wear are ball gowns," she had said. "And I don't want to wear them much."

Richard took a mouthful of casserole. "This is delicious, Nick."

"Don't thank me. Philly did it. She did everything."

Natasha smiled. "I hope I get lots of recipe books for wedding presents, otherwise Richard will starve."

"What about women's liberation?" asked Harriet.

Phillipa looked at the diamond in Natasha's engagement ring flashing in the light. Her cream silk blouse set off the opal pendant perfectly. 'Tokens of love,' she thought, aware that Frank could have been with her tonight. She wondered where he was and what he was doing. The thought of him alone upset her. The thought of him with a new girlfriend did not comfort her. 'It should,' she thought.

After dessert Nicholas picked up an envelope from the sideboard and handed it to Richard. "Your wedding present."

Richard opened the envelope and took out a photo of a house and a key. "Very intriguing."

"It's the key to my house in England. A friend of mine was looking after it, but she's getting married soon. Would you like to stay there when you go over for your honeymoon?"

"What a brilliant present!" exclaimed Richard.

Natasha jumped up and kissed him. "Thanks, Nick. Thanks."

Vivien's piece about the preview of *Famous Scenes from Favourite Operas* in *The Australian Women's Weekly* was, Nicholas thought, a perfect piece of journalism. The photos of all the main performers were good and her opinions of the performance were enticing while giving nothing away. The captions under the photos were sure to encourage audiences to come.

Natasha Howard *and* **Richard Greythorn** *star in a sensational production of* **Tosca.**
Emily Kuznetzov's *brilliant coloratura voice will set the opera world aflame.*
Frank Pearce's *voice is so deep and resonant the theatre almost shook.*
Jacqueline Howard's *Maddalena in* **Rigoletto** *was beautifully sung, sensual and emotional.*

"I suppose we should write and thank her," said Harriet.

Nicholas nodded and put the magazine aside for Phillipa. "Although it is her job."

"Which she does extremely well. It's due to her that we've got a lot of new patrons."

"I'll have to find another girlfriend who's a journalist."

Deborah posted the anonymous letters to all the men she had found in her mother's address book, informing them Marie had a dangerous, shameful and infectious social disease that could cause insanity and blindness. In the following weeks she slyly watched her mother. Flowers stopped being delivered, the phone calls ceased and she would wait in vain for a boyfriend to call and take her out as arranged. At first she had been furious, now she was desperate.

One night Marie waited anxiously.

Deborah smiled. "Where have all Marie's men gone?" she sang. "They've come to me actually, Mother," she said sweetly. "I've got youth. Men aren't interested in menopausal hags. They tell me how old you're looking. It must be something to do with – how did Jeremy Langford describe it? That's right, the downward pull of gravity." She looked closely at Marie's face. "Yes, it's really setting in. You'd better have plastic surgery."

Marie looked at the clock. "You have one hour to pack your things and get out of this house, Deborah."

"You can't make me leave. This is my house."

"On the contrary," Marie replied coolly, "it is mine."

286

"It's mine. Dad meant to leave it to me."

"But he didn't, he left it to me. You have lodged here long enough."

"You can't force me to leave!" shouted Deborah.

Marie looked bored. "The police could take you to the police station, and question you about your fraudulent use of my account cards."

Deborah felt sick. "You knew."

Marie looked in the mirror and ran her fingers through her dark hair. "I've known for ages. I was saving the information for the right moment."

Deborah began to tremble. "I haven't got any money."

"Tough. Leave your car. I'll sell it and get back some of the money you stole."

"Let me stay till I find somewhere to live," Deborah pleaded.

Marie sprayed herself with perfume. "No. If you are still here in an hour I'm calling the police – you could go to jail. Count yourself lucky that I'm allowing you to take your clothes – as you paid for most of them with my money, technically they're mine."

"You never paid the accounts – your boyfriends did!"

"Deborah, if you are not out of here in an hour – I'm calling the police."

Stumbling down the street with two cases wrenching her arms, she remembered Jeremy's proverb about revenge. 'He was right,' she thought wishing she had heeded his warning. Remembering that she had the key to the office in her bag, she caught a tram to the city and let herself in, grateful that she knew how to turn off the burglar alarms. She spent the night on the couch in the board room. Everyone was amazed when they arrived and found her already at her desk, instead of being an hour late.

She spent the next day trying to find a flat, only to discover that she needed two weeks' advance rent and a hundred dollars for the bond. She finally booked into the YWCA hostel.

On Wednesday afternoon, she was told to go into the partners' office. They were standing together. Her stomach churned.

"We've just had lunch together," said one. "We had an interesting discussion about you. You're sleeping with both of us."

"You're sacked," said the other.

287

Deborah sat in the waiting room praying. Her name was called and, hardly daring to breathe, she went into the surgery.

The doctor looked at her sympathetically. "I'm sorry. The pregnancy test was positive."

She felt cold. "I can't keep it," she stammered.

"It can be adopted. There are a lot of childless couples desperate to adopt. I can arrange – "

She was frightened she was going to faint. "I want an abortion."

His expression changed. "Abortion is illegal."

"But under certain circumstances – "

"Your case is not covered by those circumstances. What about the father of the child?"

"I don't know who he is."

"Change your sexual habits, Miss Ryland, or you will be in even more trouble," he said sternly.

Deborah only vaguely heard what he was saying about adoption and homes for unmarried mothers. She left the clinic and walked down Collins Street crying. At the tram stop she knew that people were looking at her, but was too distraught to care. When the tram arrived she sat down and stared out of the window. 'If only I had someone who could help me.' She thought about telling Ingrid Williams when she had her next singing lesson, but decided that she would be more shocked than sympathetic.

When the tram stopped outside Prince Henry's Hospital, Natasha boarded and sat next to her. "Gosh, what's wrong, Deborah?"

She wiped her eyes. "My mother's always stealing my boyfriends and now she's thrown me out of the house. I've just lost my job because I wouldn't go to bed with the boss."

"How terrible," said Natasha, her eyes widening in sympathy.

"I'll kill myself."

Natasha looked alarmed. "Things will get better. It won't take you long to find a new job – and flats are really easy to find."

Resisting Natasha's efforts to comfort her, Deborah sobbed until the tram reached the end of the line at St Kilda Beach. They alighted and walked towards Acland Street.

"I'm going to *The Scheherazade* to wait for Jacqui, Philly and Richard. Would you like to come?"

288

"I'm going to kill myself."

"No!"

Deborah was pleased with the effect she was having. "Look, I've got nowhere to live and no job. I'd be better off dead." She turned and walked towards the beach.

Natasha ran after her. "You can stay with us till you find a new job."

"Oh, Natasha, thanks. You've saved my life."

"What the hell did you ask her to stay here for?" shouted Jacqueline as soon as they arrived home. "You had no right to do it without asking Philly and me."

"She was going to kill herself."

Phillipa tutted. "Of course she wasn't."

"She's had a terrible time," insisted Natasha. "She lost her job because she won't sleep with her boss – "

"Rot," said Richard, irritated by Natasha's perception of Deborah. "I bet it was because she never did any work."

Jacqueline pulled her score out of her bag and dropped it on the sofa. "The only night I have to work overtime and you go and invite that slut to stay here. Where's she going to sleep?"

"We can pump up a Lilo and put it in the music room."

"Oh, terrific." She threw up her hands. "How are we going to practise? Tell her you've changed your mind."

"I can't. It's only till she finds a new job. As soon as she gets some money she'll find herself a flat."

"Why hasn't she got any money now?" asked Richard.

"I didn't interrogate her," snapped Natasha.

"She's a private secretary so she earns a lot more than you do – and she's three years older," said Richard. "So why can you afford to live in a house and own a car and she can't?"

"The rent's divided three ways. Deborah would have to live alone in a flat – "

"I could afford to live alone years ago," said Phillipa.

"Exactly," Jacqueline said. "She hasn't got one friend at the opera school – doesn't that tell you something? You're so dumb, Natasha. Come on, Philly, let's go and make the cocoa."

289

Scowling, Natasha went over to the sofa and sat down.

Richard sat beside her and put his arm round her. "I'm sorry. The thought of her living here upsets me."

"What do you think she's going to do – corrupt us?"

"No ... spoil things."

"Richard, she won't be here long enough to spoil anything."

"Natasha, can I speak to you for a minute?" asked Nicholas. He took her into his office and shut the door. "Sit down. Look, I hope you know that I'm only thinking of you."

Natasha sighed. "Is this about Deborah?"

"Yes."

"I suppose you think I'm a fool too."

"No, I think you're kind, but a bit naive."

Natasha planted her elbows aggressively on his desk. "Everyone hates Deborah, but they refuse to understand her. My mother would never throw me out on the street, no matter what I'd done. Just because a million people think one way and one person opposes them, the weight of numbers doesn't make that person wrong and the million people right!" she declared passionately. "What about the hordes who followed Hitler?"

He was startled by her outburst. "Sorry. I didn't mean to preach at you. But I think Deborah will cause you harm."

"I want to give her a chance. Jacqui and I had a happy childhood, but Deborah didn't. She's unhappy."

"Natasha, she's caused a lot of her own unhappiness. I used to feel sorry for her too. Then she started going out with Jeremy Langford – his company donates a great deal of money every year to this theatre. When she didn't get a major part she asked him to tell Miss Shaw he would withdraw his patronage unless she gave her the part of Tosca."

"Oh." She twisted her engagement ring.

He noticed that her nails, that she had once kept short, were longer and painted with clear nail polish.

Natasha looked at him. "She was wrong – but I can understand how disgruntled she was. I thought she was my greatest rival for Tosca. Why didn't she get a major role?"

Nicholas, not wanting to betray Harriet, remained silent.

"Miss Shaw doesn't like her, does she?"

"What makes you think that?"

She fiddled with the cuff of her yellow angora jumper. "I can tell. Not many people like her – but she should have got a major part. It was wrong of her to try and bribe Miss Shaw – "

"Blackmail – bribery is too soft a word – it was blackmail."

"Okay. But it was wrong of Miss Shaw not to give her a major role. I suppose she was desperate."

"That's no excuse for blackmail."

She shook her head. "I know. I'm not condoning it, but – "

"I'm trying to protect you, Natasha. I've been watching Deborah recently, and the way she watches you alarms me. She hates you."

"Nick, I don't need protecting," she said impatiently. "I know you're older and wiser than I am, but I've got to learn by experience. Parents can't keep protecting their children, and the older and wiser can't keep protecting the younger and sillier. If I'm wrong, then ... " She shrugged. "I'll have to learn the hard way."

Suddenly, he longed to take her in his arms. She was so innocent, brave and passionate. A strong wave of emotion swept over him. "You have a lot of courage, Natasha. I hope the price you have to pay for your ideals isn't too high."

She stood up. "No price is too high, if at the end you still have your integrity," she said solemnly.

His throat tightened as she walked out of his office.

Deborah tried to make friends with Phillipa and Jacqueline. Phillipa's dislike was veiled, but Jacqueline was openly hostile. She loved the casual and social atmosphere of their house. The phone rang constantly and people were always calling in. Natasha, Jacqueline and Phillipa had a camaraderie she had never experienced in a friendship.

She envied Natasha and Jacqueline their parents, who often visited bringing cakes or gifts for them and Phillipa. Most of the furniture in Jacqueline's and Natasha's bedrooms belonged to their parents who had allowed them to borrow it. The only source of conflict was Natasha's untidiness, which annoyed Phillipa who was always tidying up after her. Deborah thought that Natasha used Phillipa. Once when Phillipa was searching for mugs, she found three in Natasha's bedroom. She took them into the kitchen and washed them irritably.

"What a mess Natasha would be in if she didn't have you to tidy up after her, Phillipa. Does she ever thank you?"

"It's nothing to do with you," said Phillipa.

On the public holiday in November they had all woken late, dressed and gone into the kitchen to have breakfast. A skirmish broke out between Phillipa and Natasha. Phillipa shrieked and tore out of the kitchen knocking a chair over, and Natasha ran after her with a dripping wet sponge. Jacqueline stood in the doorway laughing. "Run, Philly, run!" she shouted.

Natasha caught her and tried to thrust the sponge down Phillipa's front. Phillipa screamed and broke free.

"I'll catch you, Phillipa Matthews!" yelled Natasha.

"Our poor neighbours," Deborah said.

Jacqueline spun round. "*Our* poor neighbours?"

Deborah tried to feel superior. "Isn't it time you all grew up? You behave like overgrown girl guides."

"You behave like a prostitute. When you're forty, you'll be pathetic. The only men you'll be able to attract will be gigolos."

Deborah tittered, determined not to let Jacqueline know how her words hurt. "At least I don't have affairs with married men. Max was heartbroken when I refused to go out with him any more. You're jealous. When you're forty, you'll be fat – you're plump now." She smiled. "You couldn't keep Max. He's back with his wife and has forgotten all about you."

Jacqueline's face turned red. "Max won't forget me. Because of me he had to give up opera school and his singing career. But men sleep with you and then forget you."

Further argument was curtailed by Phillipa and Natasha's boisterous return to the kitchen. When Richard came over they spent the day working in the garden. Deborah's offer to rake up the newly mown grass was rejected.

When everyone returned to work the next day, Deborah vacuumed, washed the kitchen floor and did the ironing. 'That should please them,' she thought as she folded up the ironing board. Then she took Joan

Sutherland's biography out of the bookcase. On the flyleaf was written,

To Natasha,

You're going to have as many curtain calls as Joan Sutherland.

With all my love,

Richard.

His handwriting was strong and he had used a fountain pen with a thick nib and black ink. Feeling jealous she took it outside and sat in the sun. She read the first chapter trying to push aside her anxiety about being pregnant and what she would do when it began to become obvious. She had an interview that afternoon. Closing the book she went inside to get ready. The sun had made her sleepy and she lay down on the sofa and fell asleep. When she woke it was six o'clock. She had missed the interview. She had a rehearsal at seven. She ran all the way to the station and just missed the train.

When she arrived at the theatre Nicholas glared at her. "Why are you late, Deborah?"

"I'm sorry. I had an interview."

"Get on stage!" he shouted. "If you're late again you're out!"

Deborah rushed on to the stage and joined Judy and Faye. They were both so nasty that she broke down.

Nicholas stopped the rehearsal. He told the cast to go and have an early coffee break, and took Deborah into his office. His exasperated expression made her feel worse. She needed sympathy. She wanted someone to love her. She thought of Jeremy, knowing that if she had been sensible she would not be in this situation.

"I had an interview," she sobbed. "They were running late and I couldn't walk out in the middle – I'm desperate for a job! Jacqui's being horrible to me and I've got to find a flat."

Nicholas passed her a handful of tissues. When he spoke his voice was neutral. "I know things are difficult at the moment, Deborah, but you must be on time. Opening night's five weeks away. The three boys can't function if one is missing. Remember that if you do well in this performance you'll have a place in the opera company. Why not look for temporary work till then?"

"I was so shocked about everything … I hadn't thought of that. Thanks, Nicholas."

"You'll only have a place if you do well in the performance," he reminded her. "We'll start again in fifteen minutes."

As soon as Deborah walked into the kitchen all conversation stopped. She knew they had been talking about her. Determined not to let anyone know she cared, she put a spoonful of coffee in a mug. Gradually the hum of conversation began. She went over to Emily who was alone. "Sorry I was late. I'm trying to … "

In dismay Deborah saw Faye coming towards her. "Did you sob in Nicholas's arms?"

Deborah felt her eyes filling with tears.

"Don't cry," Emily said helplessly as Faye stalked off.

"Why does everyone hate me?"

"You flirt with their boyfriends," said Emily.

"What can I do if a man comes over and talks to me?"

"Talk to him normally. Imagine you're talking to a woman."

"You don't hate me, do you?"

Emily smiled wryly. "No. But I don't have a boyfriend."

Because weekends were the only time Phillipa, Natasha and Jacqueline were together in the mornings, they made breakfasts on Saturday and Sunday special. Deborah entered the kitchen as Natasha was setting the table.

"Can I do anything to help?" she asked.

Jacqueline carried the grapefruit halves to the table. "Yes, get a job and start paying rent. Better still – find somewhere else to live."

"Jacqui, don't," said Natasha, looking apologetically at Deborah. "Sit down."

Phillipa whisked four eggs in a bowl and cut the tomatoes in half. Deborah sat at the table feeling uncomfortable. When Phillipa came to the table they started eating their grapefruit. As soon as they finished,

Jacqueline poured the cereal into the bowls Natasha had put on the table. She looked at the fourth bowl and turned to Deborah. "You haven't paid us any rent."

"I did all your ironing and I vacuumed. You never even thanked me," Deborah said defensively.

"Sorry, Deborah," said Natasha. "I thought Phillipa did it. We take it in turns. Thanks."

"She should do something to earn her keep," said Jacqueline.

Natasha grabbed the packet of cereal from Jacqueline and gave it to Deborah. "Jacqui, stop it."

During breakfast they talked about the arrangements for their trip to the beach house next weekend. Deborah wished she was going with them.

Jacqueline put slices of bread under the grill. "It'll be the first restful weekend we've had for ages – we won't have another one till after the show."

Richard arrived just as they finished their eggs and tomatoes.

"Hello, Richard," she said brightly.

He ignored her. Phillipa poured him a cup of coffee. "Thanks, Philly. What are the arrangements for next weekend?"

Jacqueline smiled at him as she carried a fresh stack of toast to the table. It was the first time she had smiled all morning.

"Richard, could I have a lift to opera school?" asked Deborah when there was a pause in the conversation.

Jacqueline spread Vegemite on her toast. "Anything else you want? Free board, free food and now you expect a free taxi service. Catch a train."

"No," Natasha said. "Nick will go mad if she's late. There are hardly any trains on Sunday."

Richard scowled. "Just this once – I'm not giving you a lift back."

Deborah suddenly remembered that a man her mother had set out to catch a few years ago had been cold towards her. She had taunted her mother with her failure.

"He pretends he's indifferent," Marie had replied. "He has a wife, four children and a conscience, but soon he'll forget them and come crawling to me."

She was right. Although Deborah remembered the episode with

295

revulsion, it gave her hope. She looked at Richard's profile and imagined him kissing her.

That night when they arrived back at Gardenvale, Richard could smell the heavy perfume Deborah used. It penetrated every room and had eradicated the subtle scents of soap, furniture polish, the fresh tang of Natasha's cologne, Phillipa's French perfume and Jacqueline's lavender water. He hated her being in the house he regarded as his second home.

Phillipa opened the fridge. "Are we going out or having dinner here?"

"Let's go out. Deborah will be back soon," said Jacqueline. "But let's have coffee first."

Richard sat at the kitchen table. "How much longer is she staying? She gives me the creeps."

Natasha spooned coffee beans in the grinder. "And the way you and Jacqui go on gives me the creeps. I don't know why everyone dislikes her."

Natasha's innocence troubled him. "That fact alone should alert you. We can't all be wrong."

"Look, while she's here, can't you be polite to her?" said Natasha.

He shook his head. "I'm not a hypocrite."

Jacqueline filled the percolator with water and lit the gas. "Deborah hates you, Natasha – you're Tosca, and she's crazy about Richard. You should see the way she looks at you."

"I don't believe you," Natasha said obstinately.

Chapter 26

'Day now is breaking
The weary world awaking
lending new sorrow
and sadness to the morrow'
Tosca – Puccini

On Friday evening, Deborah watched as Natasha, Jacqueline and
Phillipa came home from work and rushed around preparing for the
weekend at the beach house. Far from making friends and finally
belonging somewhere, she felt more lonely. Since yesterday, there had
been a change in Natasha's attitude towards her. Now, she was
offhanded. "Shall I feed Mozart while you're away?" she asked
Natasha.

"No, we've asked our neighbours."

"Can I do anything to help?" she asked, trying to make Natasha feel
guilty.

"No thanks," said Natasha as she put her bag in the hall next to
Jacqueline's.

Deborah followed her into the kitchen where Jacqueline was
grinding coffee beans. She stared at Natasha, hating her. Suddenly she
realized Jacqueline was looking at her. Defiantly she held her gaze.
Jacqueline stared at her so long, and with such penetration, that
Deborah felt her mind was being invaded.

Jacqueline walked slowly over to the table and leant over her.
"You're evil," she said menacingly. "You hate Natasha, and I know
why. You're interested in Richard, as much as a self-obsessed creature
like you can be interested in anyone. Now, get out and keep away from
us until we have gone."

Deborah felt her face flushing. Jacqueline continued to stare at her.
Feeling that everything was happening in slow motion, she stood up.
Shaking with embarrassment she went into the music room and shut the

door. She heard Richard arrive, and at eight o'clock she heard them all go outside. Going into the lounge she looked out of the window. Natasha and Richard got into his car and Phillipa and Jacqueline were in the Rover.

'At least I'll have two days' respite from talk about the bloody wedding,' she thought.

She had endured endless chatter about the dresses, bouquets, vintage cars, and had seen the green and silver invitations. Jacqueline had made it clear that she would not be receiving one. Deborah was the only person in the opera school not invited. So many people were involved it was impossible to go anywhere in the theatre without hearing someone talking about the wedding. Jacqueline and Phillipa were the bridesmaids, Nicholas was a groomsman and Frank and Emily were going to sing. Judy, who worked in the shoe department of Myers, had helped Natasha, Jacqueline and Phillipa choose their shoes. Faye was making the wedding cake and Rhonda was doing the bouquets. Knowing Deborah was not invited, the three of them took delight in talking about it whenever she was nearby.

Aimlessly she wandered into Natasha's bedroom. It was in its normal chaotic state. The bed was unmade, a wardrobe door hung open, her bedside table was strewn with books, a tin of talcum power and a bottle of eau-de-cologne. Two drawers in her chest of drawers were open and a pile of dirty clothes lay in the middle of the floor. Deborah had only seen Natasha's room tidy once and she had been struck by the unusual and strangely sensuous decor. Lilac walls were enhanced by a dark green and purple floral quilt cover, matching curtains and pine furniture.

She relieved her feeling by kicking the pile of dirty clothes round the room. 'She won't notice.'

She went into Phillipa's extremely tidy and clean bedroom. Her broderie anglaise quilt cover and the lace doilies on the dressing table and chest of drawers were snowy white. The books in her bookcase were neatly arranged. Unlike Natasha and Jacqueline's room, Phillipa's had an air of permanence.

'This is Phillipa's home, but Jacqui and Natasha just live here,' she thought, looking at the framed prints on the Wedgwood blue walls. The single bed was brass and the rest of the dark furniture looked antique

298

and glowed with recently applied furniture polish. Photos in silver frames stood on the dressing table, mantelpiece and chest of drawers. Deborah picked up one of a man and woman with a child she recognized as Phillipa. It was posed but relaxed. Phillipa looked happy and without the sadness that now shadowed her eyes. The couple were obviously her parents and Deborah studied them. They were holding her hands but looking at each other with affection. She felt a stab of pity for Phillipa who had lost so much. She looked closely at the woman. 'She looks kind – like a proper mother. I wish I'd had a mother like that. Why couldn't my mother have been killed instead of Phillipa's?'

Richard pushed the cassette into the tape deck on the dashboard, and the car was filled with the 'Moonlight' Sonata. For some inexplicable reason, Natasha felt uneasy. At first she put it down to the music, but when it had finished and a more lively piece started she felt the same.

"Are you okay?" asked Richard.

"It's the thing with Deborah, I think. Yesterday I saw her staring at me as if she hated me. I've been an idiot. All of you were right. I'm sorry."

Richard shook his head. "Don't worry. Now you know what she's like she can't do you any harm. Hopefully she'll be gone soon."

When Richard walked into their bedroom the next morning Natasha and Jacqueline were standing by the window. Natasha's hair, hanging down her back almost to her waist, caught the rays of the sun and glowed fiery red. The contrast with Jacqueline's black wavy hair was picturesque.

'If I was an artist I'd want to paint them,' he thought. "Here's your tea," he said.

"Oh, Richard," said Jacqueline. "You're spoiling us. Thanks."

Natasha stretched and looked towards the third bed. "Where's Philly?"

He grinned. "Dressed and getting stuff ready for the picnic."

When they had drunk their tea, they dressed in bathers, shorts and shirts and went into the kitchen.

Phillipa put a pile of sandwiches in a Tupperware box and gave it to Jacqueline. "Stick that in the Esky for me."

Natasha went to the linen cupboard in the bathroom and took out towels, rugs and beach bags. She tossed suntan cream in the bags and went back to the kitchen.

Richard picked up the Esky. "Are you two going to put sandals on?"

"Of course not," said Natasha.

"Remember Philly's accident," he warned.

"This is Koonya Beach not Brighton," said Jacqueline.

As they walked down the tea-tree lined track in single file the invigorating air blew in from the ocean. They found a sheltered valley in the dunes and stripped to their bathers and pumped up the Lilos.

"Shall we swim first and work up an appetite?" asked Phillipa.

"Race you to the water!" said Natasha. "Last one in is a dill!"

They all ran over the top of the sand dunes, slid to the bottom and raced down the beach.

"I won!" shouted Natasha as she plunged into the ocean.

"It's freezing!" shrieked Phillipa before a wave knocked her off her feet.

"Keep away from the rocks, Philly," called Jacqueline.

"There's a strong undertow," said Richard. "Be careful we don't go too far out."

Phillipa pushed her hair away from her face. "Are there any sharks round here?"

"Probably," said Natasha.

"Here comes one now!" screamed Jacqueline.

Phillipa looked behind her in terror and Jacqueline laughed.

"Philly, your face," gasped Natasha doubling over with uncontrollable laughter.

"That was a terrible thing to do!" said Phillipa indignantly.

Richard laughed. "It was worth it just to see your face."

Phillipa grinned and beat the water violently in Jacqueline's face and she ducked and swam behind Richard. "Save me, save me!"

He picked her up and threw her in Phillipa's direction. "That will teach you! Come on, let's go and eat."

Back in the sand dunes they dried themselves and applied suntan lotion. They ate their picnic and drank wine in contented silence. Before sunset they put on their shorts and shirts and walked along the beach exploring the rock pools.

"Gosh, the tide's coming in fast!" exclaimed Phillipa.

Jacqueline looked at the sky. "A storm's brewing. Look at those black clouds. It's deceptive because the sun's still shining."

"'Strewth, they are black," said Richard. "They're moving fast too. The sea's getting rough, we'd better go back. Look at that enormous swell."

Natasha, with her back to them, squatted down to examine a rock pool.

"Natasha, come off the rocks!" called Richard.

"Look at that huge wave coming – Natasha!" shouted Jacqueline in alarm. "She can't hear us!"

As they ran towards Natasha, the wave exploded on the rocks, engulfing Richard, Phillipa and Jacqueline and knocking them over. Natasha was swept into the sea. Frantically they scrambled to their feet and looked at the water. Realizing Jacqueline was going to jump in, Richard grabbed her. "No!" he yelled, "Wait till we see her!"

"There she is!" shouted Phillipa.

Jacqueline tore off her shirt. "We need a line. Quick! Take off your shirts!"

As Richard pulled off his shirt he saw that his arm was cut and bleeding badly. He tied their shirts together and gave one end to Phillipa and Jacqueline. Holding the other end, he jumped into the water, wincing as the salt water stung his cut. He saw another gigantic wave coming. 'Please don't let it sweep Jacqui and Philly off the rocks,' he prayed diving under it. He struggled against the rip towards Natasha. The line was too short and he had to let go. Forcing himself to stay calm, he remembered to swim across the rip not against it. When he surfaced she was gone. Frantically he looked round and saw she had been swept nearer to Jacqueline and Phillipa. Being battered against the rocks was the main danger and he wanted to swim round them and go ashore in one of the bays but, frightened that Natasha might be bleeding from being cut, he rejected the idea.

'Better to get onto the rocks before sharks are attracted by the scent of our blood,' he thought.

Going with the tide was easy and seconds later he reached her. Grabbing her hair he hauled her over to Jacqueline and Phillipa who pulled them out of the water. They all carried Natasha to the sand, only seconds before a gigantic wave hit the rocks. Richard collapsed on the sand panting and coughing.

Jacqueline shook him. "Look!"

He stared at the gash across Natasha's forehead in horror. Her cheek was horribly swollen and already turning purple.

"She's unconscious," said Jacqueline.

Phillipa knelt over Natasha checking her breathing and heartbeat. "She's breathing, and her airways are clear, but she might have a fractured skull."

Jacqueline grabbed Richard. "Go and get help. Philly and I will stay with her. The house at the end has a phone. If there's no one home, break a window and phone for an ambulance."

"It'd be better to carry her to the car and drive to hospital," he said.

"I don't know," said Jacqueline helplessly. "What if she stops breathing? At least we can do mouth to mouth here, we can't if you're carrying her."

"Let's get her further up the beach – the tide's coming in too fast. Go and get the rug, she's got to be kept warm."

Richard carried her back to the sand dunes and laid her on the rug. A clap of thunder made them jump. Natasha's eyelids flickered.

"Is that a good sign?" asked Jacqueline.

"I think so. We must get her to hospital. Philly, keep your fingers on her pulse while I carry her. We'll check her breathing as we go along. Where's the nearest hospital?"

"Frankston, but that's miles away," said Jacqueline.

"It's not that far if we drive." He put his ear on Natasha's chest and felt a surge of relief when her heartbeat was normal. He picked her up in his arms and carried her to the car.

Jacqueline, Phillipa and Richard sat in the hospital waiting room. Richard squeezed Jacqueline's hand. "Shall I get you some water?"

She bit her lip and shook her head.

"You're terribly pale."

"You should see someone about your arm," said Jacqueline.

Although she was part of the drama and desperately hoping that Natasha's injuries were not serious, Phillipa felt like an outsider. She was only a friend and although Jacqueline and Natasha told her she was almost family, she had only known them for five years. Richard was soon going to be Jacqueline's brother-in-law and both he and Jacqueline had far more to lose than she had. She knew that if she told Jacqueline how she felt she would hug her and tell her not to be silly, but nevertheless she felt on the periphery.

Suddenly she felt lonely. She had no family except an aunt she saw once a week. An aunt who had been too dedicated to her medical career to spend time caring for her orphaned niece. Harriet was eighty and Phillipa worried about her because, realistically, she could die at any time. Natasha and Richard's forthcoming wedding had unsettled her. Their happiness and plans for the future made her realize how much she was going to lose. In five years they would all be singing at Covent Garden and she would be alone. The thought of living by herself again depressed her.

To shake off the feeling, she allowed herself to imagine Nicholas falling in love with her at Natasha's and Richard's wedding. She imagined twirling round the ballroom, dressed in the green silk bridesmaid dress, with Nicholas who would suddenly realize how much she meant to him.

A doctor came into the waiting room smiling. "No fractures, just concussion, bruising and shock. The gash on her head looks a lot worse than it is. She needs to spend a few days here for observation, and she's not to return to work for two weeks. Now, young man, I'll get a nurse to do something about your arm."

They all hugged each other, and a nurse dressed Richard's arm. They then went in one by one to see Natasha. She looked dazed and her face was a swollen mass of cuts and bruises.

Overwhelmed with relief, Richard gazed at her. "Oh, Natasha, I was so terrified you were going to drown."

She smiled weakly. "I bashed my head. I was terrified of being pounded to death on the rocks. I was trying to swim round them and get to the sand but I couldn't work out where I was. Then – I can't remember ... "

He took her hand and kissed it. "Your face is going to be all the

303

colours of the rainbow tomorrow, I'm glad we're not getting married next week."

After they had all seen her, Jacqueline rang her parents.

"Mum and Dad are coming down tomorrow," said Jacqueline. "They'll stay till Natasha gets out of hospital. I haven't got a rehearsal till Friday so I'll stay till then."

Disconsolately, Deborah answered the phone on Saturday night. The countless calls were never for her. "Could I please speak to Miss Matthews?"

"I'm sorry, she's away for the weekend."

"It's the Alfred Hospital here. I need to contact her urgently."

"I don't know the address."

"When will she be back?"

"Late Sunday night, I think – or it might be Monday morning. I'm her friend, can I take a message?"

"Could you tell her that her aunt has had a heart attack?"

When she put the phone down she realized that Natasha's and Jacqueline's parents would be able to contact Phillipa. She opened the phone book and found the number. 'If I ring their parents and sound upset they'll think how nice I am, and Jacqui might stop hating me,' she thought as she picked up the receiver. To her disappointment, no one answered the phone.

When Deborah heard the front door open on Monday morning, she rushed into the hall. "Phillipa! I'm so sorry – your aunt's had a heart attack. I rang the hospital this morning, and her condition is stable but very serious." She looked outside expecting to see Natasha, Richard and Jacqueline. "Where are the others?"

Phillipa was pale and looked dazed. "Natasha had an accident."

"Oh, no. What happened?"

Phillipa explained.

"How awful," said Deborah. 'Pity she didn't drown,' she thought.

"Natasha has to stay in hospital for a few days – her parents are down there. Jacqui's staying … " She started crying.

Feeling pleased because someone needed her and she could do

something useful Deborah put her arm round her. "Can I do anything – ring anyone?"

"Could you phone Nick or Harriet for me?"

"Okay." When she put down the phone she turned to Phillipa. "Nick said he'll meet you at the hospital. Come on, I'll drive you." She grabbed a handful of tissues and hurried to the car.

On the way to the hospital Phillipa opened her handbag and pulled out her diary. "Could you do me another favour, Deborah?"

"Of course."

"Richard's staying at the beach house till tomorrow – could you ring his office and tell them? I was going to do it ... "

"Yes, write down the number for me – I'll do it as soon as I get back." Deborah carefully stopped at a school crossing. Used to her Mini and her mother's Mercedes, the heavy Rover 90 was unlike any car she had ever driven.

"Thanks."

"What about Richard – do you want me to give him a message? If you write him a note I'll drop it round tonight if you give me his address."

"That's kind of you, Deborah, thanks." Phillipa tore a page from the back of her diary and wrote Richard a short note.

Nicholas was waiting in the foyer of the Alfred Hospital. He hugged Phillipa.

"Shall I wait?" asked Deborah.

"No. I'll bring her home," said Nicholas.

Deborah drove back to Gardenvale feeling elated. Nicholas had smiled at her and Phillipa had called her kind. 'With Phillipa on my side, surely Jacqui will thaw,' she thought.

Late in the afternoon Phillipa arrived home with Nicholas.

"How is she?" asked Deborah.

"Still unconscious," Nicholas said softly. "Phillipa's going to stay at her aunt's flat. It's near the hospital so she'll be able to visit her more easily."

As soon as they left, Deborah looked at the address Phillipa had written on the envelope. She found a street directory. Calculating that it was about a mile and a quarter away, she walked. His flat was near

Firbank, the exclusive school she should have attended. Making a detour she looked through the gates at the girls in green uniforms gathered in the playground. She felt a pang of bitterness and turned away.

Five minutes later she was standing in front of an attractive block of flats set back from the street and surrounded by bushes set amid well tended lawns. 'So this is where he lives,' she thought. She went up the steps to his flat and pushed Phillipa's note under the door.

'Maybe now they'll start liking me,' she thought. 'They might even invite me to the wedding. I'll have to give up on Richard, but he must have some friends he can introduce me to.'

Envisioning handsome men surrounding her and asking her to dance at the reception, she wandered back to Gardenvale. Then reality set in. She was pregnant.

Chapter 27

'Guard yourself from women's tricks'
The Magic Flute – Mozart

Thinking that the sunlight sparkling on the water was affecting his vision, Richard blinked. The strange flickering lines were still there. Worried, he slowed the car and shook his head. The lines stayed. Checking his rear mirror, he pulled into the car park belonging to the Beaumaris Life Saving Club. He switched off the engine and shut his eyes, but he could see the flashing lines. 'I'm going blind,' he thought. He tried to be calm. 'No. I wouldn't be able to see anything if I was going blind.' The lines enlarged and he could see their coloured edges. He opened his eyes and turned on the engine. 'It's getting worse – I've got to get home.'

Most of the traffic was going in the opposite direction and his way was clear. He found it difficult to read signs, but he knew the road and made it home, thankful he had not had an accident. The lines were no longer in the centre of his vision, they had widened and he could see more clearly. Walking carefully up the steps he had difficulty unlocking the door to his flat. He went into the bedroom and lay down. Ten minutes later his vision was normal. On his way to the kitchen to make a cup of coffee he saw Phillipa's letter lying in the hall. As soon as he read it, he picked up his car keys, but concerned that he might have a recurrence of the strange lines, he decided to walk to Gardenvale.

He was halfway there when he experienced small black holes in his vision. His tongue felt enlarged and his mouth flooded with saliva. His head throbbed. Five minutes later he felt so ill he wanted to collapse on the nature strip. Determinedly he made himself keep on. He reached the house in Gardenvale, staggered up to the front door and rang the bell.

Deborah had just experienced her first bout of sickness and wondered when she would start to put on weight. The thought of everyone's

307

reaction, and the taunts she would get, filled her with misery. When Richard rang the doorbell, she burst into tears and opened the door. He stared at her and she saw his pallor.

"Is Phillipa here?" he asked less curtly than usual.

"Come in," she said, wiping her eyes and thinking quickly. "Did you get her note?"

He nodded.

"She's at the hospital now. What a terrible weekend. How's Natasha?"

"Okay."

"Good. Sit down. Phillipa will be back soon," she lied.

Richard went into the living room and sat on the sofa with his head in his hands.

"What's the matter, Richard?"

"I can't see properly. Bits of things are missing. I've had zigzag flashing lines in my eyes."

Deborah knew immediately what was wrong. "Have you got a headache?"

"Yes."

"It's a migraine. My father used to get them."

He looked relieved. "Oh. I've never had one before. I thought I was going blind or something."

"I'll get you a drink," she said sympathetically. She went into the kitchen and poured brandy into a glass. She opened a new bottle of vodka, slopped some in and tasted it. Satisfied that she could only taste brandy she took it into him. "Brandy's good for migraines. My father said it really helped when he had his. Your blood vessels are dilated and that's what causes the hallucinations. Brandy gets them back to normal."

He took the glass. "Thanks." As she had hoped, he drank it quickly.

"Look, why don't you go and lie down – I'll wake you when Phillipa gets home."

"Thanks," he said gruffly. He went into Natasha's bedroom.

Pleased that he had believed her lies, she went into the kitchen and made coffee to which she added vodka. He was lying on the bed fully clothed, but had taken off his shoes. She wondered how difficult it would be to undress him.

Keeping her manner detached she made room for the mug on the bedside table. "You need to keep warm, Richard. Get under the quilt." She picked up his empty glass and left the room. In the kitchen she filled his glass with the same measure of brandy and more vodka than before. She took the biscuits and glass into Natasha's bedroom. He was under the quilt and she smiled when she saw his trousers and shirt on the floor.

He took the glass. "When's Phillipa getting back?" His speech was already slurred.

She looked at her watch. "Soon." She went back to the kitchen and stayed there for ten minutes. When she returned, the glass was empty, and Richard was asleep. After undressing, she splashed Natasha's eau-de-cologne on her neck and drew the curtains. She pulled back the quilt, took off his underpants and got into bed beside him. 'When he wakes in the morning and finds us naked in each other's arms, he'll think we've made love. He'll have to be responsible for the baby I'll tell him he had conceived.' Smiling, she imagined Natasha's reaction. 'I'll tell him the baby was premature and hope he believes me.'

Phillipa hardly heard the consultant's words of sympathy. Desperate to get out of the hospital, she refused the offers to get her a taxi. She walked across the park to her aunt's flat. Now she knew her aunt was never coming back, the flat looked more impersonal than ever. It was so tidy and free of clutter it could have been furnished for short term rent. Her aunt had never accumulated anything. As soon as something ceased to be useful she had thrown it away. The bleak feelings of loneliness grew in intensity. Now, she had no one. Not one single living relative.

With a clarity she had never experienced, she saw her future with a perception free of fantasies. Nicholas would never be anything other than a friend. He would not fall in love with her at Natasha's and Richard's wedding or at any other time. She was just a secretary with no talents. She was not like Harriet who inspired passionate devotion and respect. There would be no one like Hugh loving her for years while receiving little in return. When Jacqueline, Natasha and Richard went to sing in Covent Garden she would still be a secretary. A lonely, prosaic secretary with no friends. She had never found it easy to make friends and her immediate affinity with Jacqueline was something she had never previously felt for any of her contemporaries.

As darkness fell, she sat in her aunt's flat wishing their relationship had been something she had valued more. She remembered her coming to collect her from the hospital bringing her here. Every night for weeks she had cried herself to sleep in the dismal bedroom with its cream walls and basic dark furniture. They had been so awkward with each other and Phillipa had been pleased when it was time to go to boarding school.

On her first day she had been the first to arrive and her aunt had told her sternly that she expected good marks and reports. Years later she had confessed to Phillipa that she had cried all the way home. The other boarders consisted mainly of girls whose parents lived in the country or overseas and they had been homesick and tearful when term began. Phillipa had wished that she too had someone to cry over.

When she phoned Nicholas and Harriet there was no reply. Loneliness engulfed her. She went to bed and slept until five the next morning. Unable to bear spending any more time alone, she had a shower, packed, and rang for a taxi to take her to Gardenvale.

'I hope Deborah's still there,' she thought. 'Even she's better than no one.'

When she arrived at seven and opened the front door the house was in darkness. Thinking Deborah was still asleep, she turned on the hall light and quietly opened the door of the music room. The bed was empty, but her suitcases were there. Puzzled she went into the lounge. "Deborah?" she called. She went back into the hall. Natasha's bedroom door was open and she could see someone in the bed. She went into the room and turned on the light.

Shocked, she stood in the doorway staring at the bed. "Oh, God," she whispered. She walked over to the bed and pulled back the quilt. They were both naked. Richard was on his back and Deborah lay on her side with her bent leg resting over Richard and one arm over his chest.

She shook Deborah awake. "What are you doing?"

"What do you think?" said Deborah softly.

Rage replaced Phillipa's shock. She pulled Deborah off the bed onto the floor, grabbed hold of her hair and slapped her face. Deborah screamed. Richard woke up, struggled into a sitting position and vomited. He looked at Phillipa and Deborah, then fell back on the bed groaning and holding his head.

Phillipa grabbed Deborah's wrist and dragged her into the hall. Deborah bit her hand. Phillipa felt her teeth breaking the skin and released her grip. Deborah jumped to her feet and raked her nails down Phillipa's face. With a yelp of pain, Phillipa yanked open the front door, pushed her outside onto the verandah. Deborah tried to run back inside, but Phillipa slammed the door.

The smell of vomit assailed her when she went back into Natasha's bedroom. She pulled the quilt off the bed. "Get up, Richard!"

He groaned.

She grabbed the pillows and threw them on the floor. "Get out of that bed! I want the sheet."

He opened his eyes. "I'm going to be sick."

She went into the kitchen and returned with a bucket. "Be sick in that – now get off the bed!"

He rolled onto the floor and heaved. Phillipa grabbed the bucket and shoved it under his mouth just in time. "Oh, my head," he groaned.

She slapped his back. "You bastard."

He sat with his head in his hands and began to shake. "What's happening?" he asked.

"Stop it, Richard. I'm not innocent or stupid."

She took the sheet off the bed, took it into the laundry and shoved it in the washing machine and switched it on. When she went back to the kitchen she saw that the new bottle of vodka was half empty. A bang on the window made her jump. She turned to see Deborah gesturing wildly. Phillipa undid the catch and pushed up the window. "Get out of here, slut!"

"Phillipa, please! I need my clothes, let me come in."

"No. Go and live in a brothel – you won't need any clothes there."

She banged the window shut on Deborah's fingers. She howled in agony. Phillipa opened the window and as soon as Deborah pulled her hand away she slammed it shut. She watched as Deborah turned on the outside tap and held her injured fingers under the cold water. Pain contorted her face. Turning off the tap she looked up at the window. "Please let me come in, Phillipa!"

311

Phillipa shook her head and watched Deborah go round the side of the house. She went into the lounge and looked out of the front window. Deborah ran across the road and spoke to a man who was about to get into his car. He gaped at her in astonishment. She said something and the man looked horrified. Then he put his arm protectively round her and took her into a house diagonally opposite.

"You've found another man already," she muttered. "That didn't take long." She took a sheet out of the linen cupboard in the bathroom and carried it and a glass of water into Natasha's bedroom. Richard was kneeling on the floor with his head in his hands. Roughly, she held the glass to his lips. "Drink this." He took a few sips, but as soon as the water hit his stomach he was sick again. She put the sheet on the chest of drawers and went to the phone and dialled Nicholas's number.

He sounded sleepy and she guessed she had woken him. "Nick, it's Philly."

"How's your aunt?"

Her throat constricted and she had difficulty speaking. "She died."

"Oh, Philly. I'll come over … where are you?"

She wanted to tell him about Richard and Deborah, but to her dismay she began to laugh hysterically.

"Philly, where are you?"

Her attempt to reply came out as a squeak.

"Are you at your aunt's flat?" he asked slowly.

"No," she managed to gasp.

"Are you at Gardenvale?"

"Yes."

"I'm on my way."

When Phillipa opened the door Nicholas stared at her swollen eyes and scratched face. "Oh, Philly, I'm so sorry about your aunt."

She started to cry. He put his arms round her and held her till she stopped.

"What's happened to your face?"

She told him about Richard and Deborah.

"Oh hell," he said. "Let's get something on those scratches."

They went into the bathroom. He bathed them in warm water and applied antiseptic cream. "There. Now you look as if you need some coffee." In the kitchen he ground the coffee beans and spooned them into the percolator basket. "Harriet and I will help you with the funeral arrangements. Would you like a notice to go in the paper?"

Revelling in the luxury of being fussed over by Nicholas, she nodded.

He filled the percolator with water and put it on the gas. "Just tell me what you want and I'll do it for you."

"I hope I don't end up in jail," she said suddenly as a thought occurred to her.

"Why on earth should you?"

"Deborah came round the back and begged to be let in to get her clothes. I opened the window and told her to live in a brothel. Then I banged it shut on her fingers. It was an accident, but I'm not sorry. I bet she'll go to the police and say I attacked her."

He took the gold lighter Harriet had given him for his thirty-first birthday out of his pocket. "How could you have attacked her? We've only just arrived here. We've been at your aunt's and I've just brought you home. We haven't seen Deborah, have we?"

"Oh, Nick, we can't lie to the police."

"I can and I will. If it came to it, I'd tell the same lie in court."

She put an ashtray on the table. "That's a serious offence."

He lit a cigarette. "Yes, perjury actually. I'd gladly perjure myself for you."

She felt happy. She felt like putting her arms round him and kissing him. She wondered what would happen if she did. 'Would he kiss me back?' Her stomach clenched in anticipation of the fantasy becoming reality. 'My aunt's just died and I'm feeling happy,' she thought. 'God, what am I? Selfish? Shallow?'

"Where's Richard?" he asked, breaking the atmosphere of intimacy.

"Still in Natasha's bed. He's ill. We had a new bottle of vodka and now it's half-empty. They must have drunk it."

They went into Natasha's bedroom and looked at Richard. Nicholas gave him a rough shake but he covered his ashen face with his hands like a sick child. He turned to Phillipa. "He'll just have to sleep it off. Come on." In the doorway he turned. "Did you take the sheet off the bed?"

She nodded. "Why?"

313

"Where is it?"

"In the washing machine. Richard was sick all over it. Pity he wasn't sick all over Deborah. Why?"

"Nothing."

They went back to the kitchen.

"Sit down, Philly. Do you want something to eat?"

She shook her head. "I'll just have coffee. Help yourself to breakfast – cereal's in that cupboard. Shall I squeeze some oranges for you?"

He waved her back to the chair. "Sit down. Hopeless as I am, I can make orange juice." He took four oranges out of the fruit bowl. "I'm going to make you some too – and you're going to eat." He cut the oranges in half. "You've had a terrible morning and starving yourself isn't going to help." He squeezed the oranges, filled bowls with sultana bran and poured their coffee.

"Thanks, Nick. What are we going to do about Richard?"

"Did he say anything?" He carried everything over to the table.

Phillipa shook her head and put a teaspoon of sugar in her coffee. "He asked what was happening. As if he didn't know."

Nicholas blew out a plume of smoke. "All this is out of character. If he asked you what was happening I'm inclined to believe he doesn't know."

"Ah, come on, Nick. All this is very in character for Deborah."

"Yes. But not for Richard." He flicked his ash into the ashtray. "You say he was throwing up – given that there's half a bottle of vodka gone I'd say he's got a gigantic hangover – she must have got him drunk."

"Don't give me that – he's not a schoolboy – he's twenty seven! What were they doing in Natasha's bed? I saw them. They were naked."

Nicholas stubbed out his cigarette. "If you saw a man standing over a dead woman with a knife, you could come to the conclusion that he stabbed her, when in reality he found her dead, saw the knife and picked it up."

"But this is different. He got into Natasha's bed willingly. I hardly think Deborah had the strength to carry him. There are no other conclusions to be drawn."

"Aren't there?" He poured milk over his cereal.

"Can you think of any?"

He nodded. "Several. Pity you washed the sheet."

She blushed. "Oh. Is that why you wanted it?"

"Yes."

"I've destroyed the evidence." She chewed her lip.

He frowned. "Or lack of it. I can't imagine Richard being unfaithful to Natasha."

Richard woke and lay in bed, hoping that he had had a nightmare. He sat up and looked round Natasha's bedroom. His fears increased. Memories of Phillipa's fury and Deborah screaming returned. 'It was a dream. It must have been … it can't have happened.' Struggling against nausea he got dressed and walked unsteadily into the kitchen. Nicholas looked at him speculatively. Phillipa glared at him.

"Feeling better?" Nicholas asked calmly.

"No. I feel awful."

"You look awful," Nicholas agreed. "You've got a lot of explaining to do. What happened?"

With a sense of dread Richard realized that he had not been dreaming. "I don't know."

Phillipa made an exclamation of contempt and pushed back her chair. She strode towards him and he stood aside to let her pass. The sudden movement made him feel ill and he clung to the back of a chair for support.

"Philly, don't go. I need a witness," said Nicholas.

She came back to the table, yanked out a chair and sat next to Nicholas.

Richard sat down opposite them. "I don't understand."

"Phillipa came home this morning and found you and Deborah in Natasha's bed. You were both naked. As I said, you have a lot of explaining to do. Tell me what happened."

"I don't know. I can't remember."

"You must remember something," said Nicholas impatiently. "Why did you come here?"

"I got Phillipa's note about her aunt. I thought she'd be here. I felt sick … I couldn't see properly. Deborah said I had a migraine … her

315

father used to get them. That's all I remember."

Nicholas took a sip of coffee. "What happened next? Did you go home?"

"No."

"What did you do? And if you tell me you can't remember, I'll bang your head against the wall till you do."

Richard groaned. "I came inside."

"Why? Phillipa wasn't here. She was staying at her aunt's."

"Deborah told me she'd be home soon. I'm going to be sick." He stumbled to the sink and dry retched.

Nicholas found some aspirins and filled a glass with water. "Sip the water slowly, then take these."

He almost gagged on the first aspirin. Nicholas looked at his watch. "Hurry up. I can't sit here till eternity. I've got a rehearsal to go to. You've only got a hangover."

Richard shut his eyes and swallowed the second aspirin, trying to remember what had happened next. "She got me a drink ... brandy. I drank it."

Nicholas frowned. "Why?"

"She said it was good for migraines."

"And you believed her?"

"Yes."

Phillipa shook her head. "You idiot."

Richard closed his eyes. "My head felt as if someone was hitting it with a hammer – if she'd given me arsenic I would have taken it."

"What about the vodka?" asked Nicholas.

"Vodka? I didn't have any vodka."

Phillipa tutted. "You did. You had half a bottle."

Richard shook his head and the room spun. He slumped forward onto the table and lay his head on his arms.

"When did you first kiss her?" he heard Nicholas ask.

"I didn't."

"You must have." He felt Nicholas put his hand on his arm. "Come on, Richard. It's quite clear what happened. You were missing Natasha. You'd had a nasty shock – Deborah was sympathetic and you kissed her and couldn't stop. Perhaps you thought she was Natasha," he said reasonably.

316

Richard was so incensed he sat up despite his dizziness and throbbing head. "No. I could never confuse them! I hate Deborah I'd never kiss her – never!" He closed his eyes and fought against the nausea.

"You did more than kiss her."

"No. No."

"Tell me the truth and I can help you," Nicholas said persuasively.

"I am telling the truth."

"If you lie I can't help you."

"I'm not lying."

Nicholas stood up suddenly. "Tell me what happened and I can help you. We can think up some story to tell Natasha. If you don't tell me the truth you and Natasha are finished."

"It is the truth."

"Deborah's beautiful … perhaps you couldn't resist her?"

Richard was appalled. "I hate her. I've always hated her!" he shouted.

Nicholas smiled grimly. "Don't shout – you'll wreck your vocal cords." He picked up his cigarettes. "I'll drive you home. Drink plenty of water and go to bed."

"Are you sure you've finished your interrogation?"

Nicholas took his cup to the sink. "Yes. And I believe you."

Richard was relieved, but, angry with the way Nicholas had questioned him, he was determined not to show it. "I don't care if you believe me or not."

"I'd start caring if I were you. I may be the only ally you have."

"No. You've got me too," said Phillipa.

"Am I supposed to be grateful, Phillipa? If I'd found you in a compromising position I would have judged you more kindly than you've judged me. Obviously, I have a higher opinion of you than you have of me." He looked at Nicholas. "Than both of you have of me."

"Sorry I condemned you, Richard," said Phillipa softly. "Nicholas believed you – don't blame him." She left the kitchen.

"Don't be too hard on Philly. Her aunt died last night."

"Oh no."

"I'll drive you home."

"How am I going to tell Natasha?"

Nicholas shook his head. "Sorry. I can't help you there."

"I think I'm going to be sick again."

Although Harriet was upset by what Nicholas was telling her, she knew that she finally had an excuse to expel Deborah. Ashamed, she knew that her main feelings should have been distress for Natasha and Richard. She let Nicholas finish and closed the diary on her desk. "I tried to warn you about Deborah. But no – you thought I was unfair. I knew something like this would happen, but you ignored me."

"So is this my fault?" said Nicholas. "If I'd agreed with you what could we have done about it? Nothing. You had to have her in the opera school – that was nothing to do with me."

"You always defended Deborah and made me feel vindictive."

"I didn't defend her after she tried to blackmail you. Anyway, let's see if we can sort out this mess or neither Richard nor Natasha will be capable of doing the graduation performance."

"I'm going to expel Deborah," said Harriet. "Someone from the second year can replace her." She went to the filing cabinet, pleased by his nod of agreement. "Where's Richard?"

"I took him home."

She flicked through the files. "You believe what he told you?"

"Absolutely."

She took out a file and handed it to him. "Our best second-year student – what do you think?"

He nodded and handed it back to her. "Fine."

Closing the drawer she went back to the desk. "Do you think we can keep this a secret?"

"Till after the performance?"

"For good," she said.

He looked at her in surprise. "I don't know – I hadn't thought of that. It's tempting. Apart from Deborah and Richard, only Phillipa, you and I know – and if you expel Deborah ... "

She opened the file. "Talk to Richard. I'll deal with Deborah."

Deborah walked down the corridor to the theatrette and tried to be pleased that she had found a place to live. Her saviour looked like a mouse, but he was better than nothing. He had believed her story about a man trying to rape her and had wanted to phone the police until she had explained that the culprit was her best friend's fiancé. He had taken her to hospital and waited while she was x-rayed and her broken fingers put in plaster. After driving her home he had gallantly put her in his spare room. His devotion was irritating her already.

Her fingers throbbed under the plaster in spite of the painkillers she had taken. As soon as she went into the theatrette Nicholas came over. "Miss Shaw wants to see you in her office immediately," he said curtly.

Harriet looked at her coldly as she entered her office. "I'm expelling you for attacking my secretary. Someone from the second year has been found to replace you, so the expulsion takes effect immediately."

Deborah was shocked. "Phillipa attacked me. She broke my fingers. Look." Deborah held out her plastered hand. "Are you going to sack her?"

"No. You tried to blackmail me into giving you a principal role and now you've attacked my secretary – I know why."

"You've only heard her side of – "

"Take my advice, Deborah, and change your ways, or goodness knows what will happen to you."

Deborah burst into tears. "Please don't expel me, please."

"You've had enough chances. I should have expelled you when you tried to blackmail me."

"Miss Williams said you were unfair to give me a minor role. I deserved a principal part. You've always hated me – I could tell by the way you used to look at me. Go on – deny it – deny that you've always hated me!"

"You're hysterical," said Harriet. "No, I don't like you. No one likes you. The men despise you and the girls loathe you."

"The girls are jealous. And you're jealous too. You're a merciless old maid. You hate me because I can get any man I want, and no one ever wanted to marry you!" She wrenched open the door of Harriet's office and ran down the corridor and out of the theatre.

The first phone call Vivien received in her office the following day was

319

from Deborah.

"I've got something to tell you about Harriet Shaw," she said.

Vivien, certain that Deborah's information was important, arranged to meet her for lunch in South Yarra. They met at noon in an expensive restaurant with lace tablecloths. Two hours later Vivien rushed back to the office and began typing.

Harriet Shaw Victimizes Talented Singer

When she finished the article she rang Nicholas. 'Just to make sure there's no chance of him having me back,' she thought remembering the letter she had received from Harriet thanking her for her piece in *The Australian Women's Weekly*. Hoping to keep Nicholas guessing, she had overcome the temptation to ring him.

"Hello, Nick," she said when he answered.

Expecting him to hang up she was surprised when he returned her greeting. His voice was cool, but at least he was speaking to her.

"Nick, could we meet – maybe for dinner?"

"Why?"

"I miss you." She bit her lip. She hadn't meant to say that.

"You should have thought about that before you went to Seamus O'Flynn," he said.

"You didn't let me explain – it wasn't – "

"All right, Vivien, explain."

She was startled. "I'd rather see you – it would be easier. I – "

"Presumably your story will be the same over the phone or in person."

"Yes, but … "

"Go on, I'm listening. Tell me how Seamus O'Flynn knew Aunt Harriet and I had disputes over modern opera."

"He guessed."

"Oh, so he's psychic now."

"Don't be sarcastic, Nick." She tried to remember Seamus's exact words. "He said Miss Shaw sacked someone once because they wanted to do a play she didn't like."

"You'll have to do better than that."

She imagined the shrug that preceded his words. "It's true!"

320

"Vivien, you were the only person I told about our arguments. Seamus doesn't know Harriet and he doesn't know me. I didn't tell him and neither did Harriet. So you must have told him."

"Nick, I promise I didn't."

"It's over, Vivien."

His neutral tone made her realize he would never change his mind, and his unreasonable attitude made her seethe. "All right, Nicholas. If that's what you want." She hung up.

The article was too controversial for *The Australian Women's Weekly*, but she knew Seamus would be interested. When she arrived home she looked for the photo of Harriet and Deborah she had taken at Harriet's party two years ago. It was missing. She searched in vain for the negative. She knew Nicholas was responsible. The lingering feelings of guilt about what she was doing vanished.

Chapter 28

'In mire my nest of love
they have been steeping!'

Tosca – Puccini

Nicholas took the mug of coffee Richard handed him and sat on the sofa. "Deborah's been expelled. The only way Natasha can find out is if you tell her."

Richard walked restlessly round his lounge. "I hate lying."

"You're not lying."

He stood by the window. "I'm keeping something from her, it's the same thing."

"What are you going to say? 'Natasha, one day I woke up in your bed with Deborah. We were both naked and I haven't the faintest idea how she got there.' How's she's going to react to that?"

"You believed me."

"I'm not emotionally involved with you. Some things are better kept secret. Don't tell Jacqui what happened either. The less people who know the better."

Richard frowned. "How's Philly going to explain her scratched face?"

"Good point." Nicholas thought for a moment. "Mozart got into a fight with another cat and she got scratched trying to separate them."

As Phillipa switched off the vacuum cleaner, she heard Jacqueline and Natasha calling goodbye to their parents. She opened the front door as their car drove away. "Hi. Welcome back," she said cheerfully.

"Gosh! What's happened to you?" asked Jacqueline.

"Mozart got into a fight and scratched me when I tried to rescue him." Worried that they would say they didn't look like cat scratches, she giggled nervously and looked at Natasha. "Just as well all this happened when it did – what with your face and my face, the wedding photographer would have run off with fright."

Natasha laughed. "Compared to me, you look like a model, Philly."

"Actually, I've had some bad news. Come inside." Quickly she told them about her aunt and began to cry when they hugged her sympathetically. Pleased that her tears would cover up her other lie she told them that Deborah had gone and left all her clothes behind.

Jacqueline looked at Phillipa in amazement. "How come?"

"She must have found a rich boyfriend," said Phillipa. "She's left opera school too."

Jacqueline went into the music room. "Her clothes are going to the church jumble sale." She opened Deborah's case and took out the fur coat. "But this is for Mozart," she said with glee. She went into the lounge and arranged it in his basket.

Phillipa found Mozart and put him in the basket.

Jacqueline bowed. "Oh, Mozart, does it suit you, my lord?"

Mozart sniffed the coat and stalked off.

Natasha laughed. "He doesn't like Deborah's perfume either."

Natasha, daydreaming about her wedding day, took a shirt out of the basket and put it on the ironing board. Her face was still swollen and the bruises had started to turn yellow. The gash on her forehead was hidden by her fringe. It itched and she longed to scratch it. As she was putting the shirt on a hanger the doorbell rang. She opened the door and saw Deborah. Thinking that she had come to collect her clothes, she smiled uncertainly, glad that Jacqueline was in the garden hanging out the washing.

"Hello, Natasha."

Natasha wondered how to explain that all Deborah's clothes had been taken to the jumble sale. "We thought you weren't – "

Before Natasha could finish Deborah came inside and kicked the door shut. "I've just discovered that I'm pregnant."

"Oh," said Natasha.

"And Richard Greythorn's the father of my child."

Natasha stared at her incredulously. "Liar. He hates you."

Deborah shook her head. "He pretended to hate me so you wouldn't get suspicious. We did have an affair, it lasted ages. Where do you think he went after he left you? Straight to me! That's why he was so angry about me moving in here. And when you were in hospital he came back here. I was alone and we spent all night in bed – your bed."

Natasha, hoping that she looked scathing, shook her head. "I was wrong about you. No wonder everyone hates you. Nick warned me, Jacqui warned me, but I was too stupid to listen. Get out." She went to the front door and opened it.

Phillipa was on the verandah looking through her bag for her keys. She looked up and saw Deborah. "What the hell are you doing here?" she snapped.

Deborah pushed past Natasha. "Ask your friend, Natasha. She found Richard and me naked together – in your bed, didn't you Phillipa?"

Phillipa turned bright red.

"Don't think you can get Philly to lie for you," said Natasha. Then she saw Phillipa's expression.

Furious with herself for not denying everything, Phillipa watched Natasha sitting at the kitchen table.

Her face was white with shock and her expression when she looked at Phillipa was accusing. "You should have told me."

Jacqueline stood behind Natasha with her hands on her rigid shoulders. "I just can't believe this. I can't believe it!"

"He was drunk!" cried Phillipa. "Deborah got him drunk on vodka and brandy. He didn't know he was drinking vodka."

Natasha stood up. "You should have told me, Phillipa. Why did he come here?" she screamed.

"To see me!"

Natasha pulled off her engagement ring. "Why did he stay when he knew you weren't here? The bastard, the bloody bastard!" She ran to the back door, pulled it open and threw the ring out into the garden.

Phillipa held the door so Natasha could not slam it. "Natasha, Nicholas doesn't think anything happened."

"Of course it did! Don't be ridiculous!" she screamed.

"Natasha, stop it, you'll hurt your voice," begged Jacqueline.

"To hell with my voice!" screamed Natasha even louder.

Jacqueline stood in front of her and grabbed her arms. "If you break your engagement to Richard your voice is the only thing you'll have left," she said desperately.

Natasha nodded. "You're right, Jacqui," she whispered. "I promise I won't scream any more, my voice is all I have left." She walked out into the garden.

Phillipa gave Jacqueline a push. "Go after her. I'll ring Nick."

Nicholas put the phone down.

"What's happened now?" asked Harriet.

"Deborah told Natasha what happened. That was Phillipa, she's distraught, it sounds as if they all are." He looked at his watch. "What the hell are we going to do? I've got a rehearsal of *The Flute* in an hour. Not only have we had to find a last-minute replacement for Deborah, *Tosca's* in turmoil. At this rate the whole performance is going to be a disaster. I should go to Gardenvale. Could we make it a music rehearsal instead?"

Harriet stood up. "I'll ask the conductor to polish up the boy's trio. It's quite valid, the new girl only stepped into the part last week. You go to Natasha."

Nicholas was surprised to find Natasha calm and reasonable. She was sitting in the garden in the dark. He sat on the grass beside her. "I'm so sorry, Natasha, I really am."

She didn't look at him but said in the same tone with which she could have asked him the time, "So you knew about it too. How many other people know?"

He saw no point in lying. "Harriet."

"And Richard and Deborah," she said.

"Natasha, I don't think anything happened."

She looked at him scornfully. "They were both stark naked in my bed."

He waited for her to say something else, but she continued to stare into space. "Natasha, you should cry."

"Why?" she asked in the same reasonable tone.

He thought how much easier tears were to deal with. Natasha's coldness made him feel redundant. "Because you've been hurt. You shouldn't keep things bottled up."

"Huh. I'm not going to waste my tears on him. He's not worth it," she said calmly. "All the time he pretended to hate Deborah. No wonder he was so upset when I invited her to stay with us. It would have stopped him going off to see her after he finished with me." She gave a little sigh.

"You can't believe that."

"Yes, Nicholas, I do. We both know he's a very good actor. You've praised his acting ability often enough. This is getting boring. I'm going to bed." She stood up and walked inside. He followed her. She went into the bathroom and shut the door in his face.

He stared helplessly at Phillipa and Jacqueline who were staring helplessly at him. "Go in after her, Jacqui, don't leave her alone."

Phillipa stared at him in anguish.

"Philly, heat some milk and put some brandy in it," he told her. "I want to knock her out for tonight. I don't like the way she's reacting."

Natasha came into the kitchen followed by Jacqueline. Her expression was blank. Nicholas stood up and took her arm and guided her to the table. She did not look at him.

"Natasha, drink this," he said firmly.

She picked up the mug. "Has it got poison in it?"

"No. Brandy. It'll help you sleep."

She laughed harshly. "Good. I'm going to be a famous opera singer."

They watched her as she drank. She finished and stood up. "May I go to bed now?" she asked politely.

He stared at her in dismay. "Do you need anything? Can I do anything for you?"

"Yes. Give me a real knife to stab Scarpia with."

Jacqueline hovered uncertainly as Natasha left the kitchen.

Phillipa put her head in her hands. "It's all my fault – I looked so guilty."

Jacqueline glowered at them. "Neither of you should have tried to cover it up!"

"I'm going to Richard's," said Nicholas. "I'll call in here on my way back."

Richard came to the door in his dressing gown. "Nick. Come in. I was going to have an early night."

326

"Deborah's told Natasha what happened."

Richard froze. "Oh, God. I'll go and see her and try to explain."

"I'm sorry, but it's much worse than that. Deborah told Natasha you've been having an affair with her for ages."

"She can't believe that."

"Unfortunately Phillipa arrived home at the wrong moment and when Deborah challenged her about finding you in bed together she was unprepared. Natasha's in a terrible state."

"I knew I should have told her what happened! Why did I listen to you?" He went into the bedroom.

Nicholas waited for him, wondering what would have happened if Richard had confessed to Natasha.

Five minutes later Richard strode into the lounge pulling on his jacket. "Where are my car keys?"

"I'll drive you."

"I can drive myself."

"Richard, you're in no fit state to drive anywhere."

"Go to hell. Where are my keys?"

He went into the music room, and Nicholas saw the keys on the mantelpiece. He picked them up, put them in his pocket, and waited while Richard searched the flat. Finally he admitted defeat.

"Shall I drive you?" asked Nicholas.

"I suppose so."

"If you're going to be obnoxious you can walk."

Richard shook his head. "Sorry. I'll kill Deborah!"

When Nicholas rang the doorbell, Jacqueline opened the door. Phillipa was standing in the hall.

"How could you, Richard? How could you?" asked Jacqueline furiously.

"Jacqui, please," said Nicholas. "Richard has to see Natasha – let's try and get this dreadful business sorted out."

Jacqueline slapped Richard's arm. "If you want your ring back, go and find it yourself, it's out in the garden somewhere."

"I don't care about the bloody ring, all I care about is Natasha."

"Do you?" said Natasha softly from the doorway of her room.

Desperate to let Richard and Natasha talk in private Nicholas put his hand on Jacqueline's arm. "This is between Natasha and Richard. Natasha, listen to what Richard has to say."

Natasha pushed back her hair and entwined her fingers in the strands. "I will certainly listen to his answer to my question, and I'd like you all to stay."

Phillipa edged towards the door of the music room.

"Philly, that includes you."

"Natasha, I don't think – "

"Nonsense, Phillipa. This won't take long. Now, Richard, did Phillipa find you and Deborah naked together in my bed? Just answer yes or no."

"Yes," said Richard steadily.

"Fine," said Natasha. "That's all then."

"I never had an affair with her."

"Liar." She turned to leave the room and then spun round, her polite facade replaced by fury. "I hate you!" Then she was gone.

Nicholas, angry with himself for his failure to control the situation, drove Richard home and made them both coffee.

"Do you think she'll ever forgive me?"

Nicholas put the mug on the coffee table. "Give her time. You're so right for each other. I'll get Aunt Harriet to talk to her."

When Nicholas told Harriet about Natasha's behaviour she was unnerved. 'She's reacting like I did,' she thought. Wanting to talk to Natasha in private she invited her to her house. When she arrived Harriet looked at her in concern. The parts of her face not affected by the fading bruises were white and her eyes were full of defiance.

Harriet took her into the lounge where she had tea and sandwiches ready. Faced with Natasha's aloof expression she was unsure of where to begin. "Natasha, please at least talk to Richard about it."

"No."

Harriet poured their tea. "I wish you'd believe it only happened once. Deborah's a liar. I'd stake my life on the belief that Richard hates her. She got him drunk."

"I've been drunk, Miss Shaw, but I've never been unfaithful."

Harriet picked up a sandwich. "I understand how you feel, but don't throw away everything you shared because of pride."

Natasha gave a false little laugh. "There was no need for him to sleep with Deborah. We were lovers. Does that shock you?"

Worried by Natasha's hostility, Harriet shook her head. "Just because I'm old doesn't mean I have narrow views. Just because I never married, doesn't mean I never loved."

Natasha lowered her head. "I'm sorry, Miss Shaw," she whispered.

Harriet saw that she looked ashamed. She took Natasha's hand and squeezed it. "Please talk to him."

"No."

Deborah ran up the steps to Richard's flat. The door was open so she went inside. He was sitting at the desk in the lounge writing. A record of Schubert Impromptus was playing on the stereo. Quietly she went into the room.

"Richard?"

He looked up. He stared at her. When he finally spoke his tone was weary. "What are you doing here?"

"I'm pregnant and you're the father. You've got to marry me."

"Why me, Deborah?" he asked dully. "Why did you ruin my life? I've always loathed you. You're vacuous and conceited. Your perfume gives me a headache – all your gestures are calculating. Calculated to attract men?" He shook his head. "They don't attract me – you don't attract me. Your face, figure, eyes and hair do not attract me. Understand? There's nothing natural about you – nothing spontaneous." He sounded bored. "If you're pregnant I'm not the father. Get some other idiot to marry you. What about the real father, or have you had so many men in such a short space of time you don't know who he is?"

He took some paper clips out of a tray and lined them up, concentrating on them, as if his life depended on getting them in a perfectly straight line. Not looking at her he continued speaking in a monotone. "Until now I had no idea how a man could kill a woman. I could kill you. If I thought I could get away with it I would kill you. It'd be easy to strangle or stab you. You're lucky I haven't got a gun because I'd shoot you. What would I do with your body?"

He rubbed his chin. "Koonya Beach. Yes, I'd take it to Koonya

Beach and throw it into the sea. It would be eaten by sharks. If it was ever found it'd be so battered it'd be unrecognizable. Of course it might never be found. Harold Holt's body never was and they searched for him a long time because he was the Prime Minister." He lifted his head and smiled. "But you're not important. No one would miss you, would they? You don't have any friends, do you?"

His smile terrified her. Stepping backwards she almost fell over the rug. Still smiling, he stood up. She turned and ran out of his flat. As she rushed down the steps she heard him laughing.

Two days later she had a miscarriage. She lost so much blood she collapsed and had to be rushed to casualty. The relief that she was no longer pregnant was marred by her exhaustion. After her release from hospital, she waited until the day of her singing lesson and went to see Ingrid Williams at the studio where she taught. By the time she had climbed the two flights of stairs her legs were shaking.

Ingrid opened the door. "Deborah!"

"I know you probably don't want to see me – "

"I've been trying to trace you, but no one knows where you live. Sit down. You look terribly pale – what's wrong?"

Deborah was surprised. She had been expecting Ingrid to refuse to teach her. "I've been in hospital."

"What happened?"

Ingrid looked concerned and Deborah decided to tell the truth. Not daring to look at Ingrid she stared at the piano pedals. "I had a miscarriage."

"Oh, Deborah, I had no idea you were pregnant." Ingrid's voice was sympathetic.

Deborah looked at her. "Didn't Miss Shaw tell you she expelled me?"

Ingrid nodded. "She also told me why. But I know she's treated you unfairly and I want to hear your side. Did Phillipa find you in bed with Richard Greythorn?"

Deborah nodded.

Ingrid looked disappointed. "Did you scratch her face?"

"Yes, because she pulled my hair." Deborah waited for the words of dismissal.

"Go on." Ingrid's voice was dispassionate.

Grateful she was being given a chance to explain she took a deep breath. "My mother threw me out of the house and I lost my job. I was frightened and desperate and I'd fallen in love with Richard years ago."

"Deborah, why didn't you tell me – you could have stayed with me."

"Thank you for not condemning me," Deborah whispered.

"Where are you living?"

"With a man who rescued me when Phillipa threw me out."

"Do you like him?"

"Not much."

"Will you listen to me if I give you some advice?"

Deborah nodded hoping that it was advice she would be able to take.

"Forget your singing career for the moment. Find a flat – "

"I haven't got any money or a job."

"Would you like to stay with me till you get a job? When you've saved enough money I'll help you look for a flat."

Deborah stared at her in gratitude. "Why are you being so good to me?"

Ingrid smiled. "You've had a rough life. Some of it's been your fault, some your mother's. I never wanted to get married, but I wanted to have children. I elected to do neither – having seen my parents constant quarrelling, marriage was too abhorrent to me."

Deborah felt a dart of hope as Ingrid continued. "Join an amateur operatic society. Sing for pleasure. Make friends. Stop looking on men as prospective husbands and women as rivals. Close girlfriends are valuable. Don't be eager to get married. I've never understood why girls want to rush to the altar."

"I want to be loved and taken care of."

Ingrid's smile was cynical. "So do most girls. But when they marry they do all the loving and caring. I've had many promising girls who give up singing because of their husbands, and many male singers whose wives make sacrifices so they can realize their ambitions." She gave Deborah some money. "Go to a cafe. I've got a student coming soon. Come back in an hour and I'll drive you to my flat."

Deborah smiled.

Ingrid looked at her in satisfaction. "You know, this is one of the few times I've seen you smile properly. Most of your smiles are mechanical."

"I've got a lot to learn."

"If you realize that, you're halfway there. Trust me."

"I do, Miss Williams."

Harriet got out of the shower, dried herself and wrapped a towel around her wet hair. The door bell rang and she pulled on her dressing gown, went down the hall and opened the door. First she saw Nicholas, then she saw his expression. He was carrying a newspaper and a new packet of cigarettes. "Seamus O'Flynn's on the attack again."

She unlocked the fly-screen door and pushed it open. He handed her the paper that was open at the page and they went into the dining room. There were two photos. One of her that she remembered Vivien taking when they first met, and a posed one of Deborah in an evening dress that had appeared in *The Australian Women's Weekly* a year ago.

Harriet Shaw Victimizes Talented Singer

Harriet skimmed over the first two paragraphs about the fight between Phillipa and Deborah, which questioned Harriet's reason for expelling Deborah, but not sacking Phillipa. 'Nothing that can't be explained there,' she thought. Then her heart raced.

> *Deborah tells a strange story about her first meeting with Harriet five years ago.*
> *'When Miss Shaw saw me, she looked shocked. I thought she was ill, she was so pale. I offered to change my audition, but she stared at me as if she hated me. She called me Annabel. I don't know why. I'd never seen Miss Shaw before. She refused to teach me and sent me to Ingrid Williams.'*

The piece ended with a question that made Harriet feel sick.

"Does anyone in Melbourne know about Annabel?" asked Nicholas.

"Not now. Hugh was the only person who knew."

Nicholas tore the cellophane off the packet of cigarettes. "How did he know?"

"I told him," she said, putting an ashtray on the table.

"So he didn't find out for himself?"

She shook her head.

"Then it might be all right."

She looked at his concerned face, pleased that he was with her. "As long as no one I knew in London is living in Melbourne now."

"Did a lot of people know about Annabel?"

She nodded, wondering what to say if he asked how many.

He lit a cigarette. "I'll lie for you."

She was surprised. "What about?"

"The scene in the theatrette – I'll say you were perfectly normal and didn't call her Annabel."

"Thank you, Nicholas. I don't deserve it. You were right. I should have given her a major part. I've brought this on myself."

The phone rang.

He stood up. "I'll get it – it's probably a journalist."

She heard him striding down the hall. Tempted to tell him about Annabel, she watched the smoke curling from his abandoned cigarette. 'But if I tell him about Annabel I'll have to tell him everything,' she thought. She tried to predict his reaction. 'He'd be sympathetic at first, but when he got used to what had happened he wouldn't respect me any more. I can't tell him – I'm too ashamed.'

He returned a few minutes later. "It was Jeremy Langford – a furious Jeremy Langford. He's going to issue a statement to the papers. He's worried about you."

"What did he say about the Annabel bit?"

He picked up his cigarette. "Nothing."

"Nicholas, you don't have to lie for me. I feel guilty about compromising your integrity. And everything Seamus O'Flynn has written, is right."

He looked puzzled. "Why the sudden pangs of conscience?"

333

"Because I'm old and my acts of good and evil might weigh against me when I die." She smiled grimly. "I'm frightened of going to hell – whatever form it takes. It never worried me when I was young, but it does now."

"Have you done anything so terrible?"

"I was unfair to Deborah. If I'd listened to you – "

"You could see what she was and I couldn't."

She smiled wryly. "No, I let my emotions get in the way of my judgment. She reacted to my unfairness."

"Would … no."

"Go on."

"How would Annabel have reacted?"

She stared at the ashtray. "Worse – much, much worse," she whispered.

"Let Jeremy defend you – he won't be lying. He said he'll tell them Deborah asked him to blackmail you into giving her Tosca. If asked, I'll say you felt unwell, but I can't remember you calling her Annabel."

It was not only Jeremy Langford who was enraged. Harriet had the support of all the third-year opera students who either rang the paper or wrote letters. Two days later *The Age* had a different point of view. Deborah was now immoral, a blackmailer and liar.

Vivien read the piece in frustration. When she got home that night after work she sat at her typewriter.

> *No one has heard Harriet Shaw sing since at least 1941.*
> *Why not?* She typed. *She was a brilliant singer who some*
> *said was better than Melba. She gave up. Why?*

As she lit a cigarette, she thought of something. Going to her desk she found the tape of her first interview with Harriet in 1971. Slipping it in the cassette player she fast-forwarded it and listened to the end of the interview. That Harriet had never returned to England had surprised Vivien then. Now she concluded that, given Harriet's wealth and the ease of travelling on a plane, there were deeper implications. She went back to the typewriter.

334

Harriet's sister has not seen her for over 40 years.
Her nephew, Nicholas, first met her when he was 26.
The singer – who never sings.
Is the person who runs the theatre really Harriet Shaw?
What happened to the Harriet Shaw who sang at Covent
Garden?

She stood up and paced excitedly round the room. The phone rang and she picked it up.

"Hi, Vivien, it's Seamus. A mate of mine is leaving *The Sun,* so there's a vacancy. Feel like escaping from the niceness of *The Women's Weekly* and doing some real journalism?"

"Yes," she said slowly. "I do. Actually – I've got something for a story right now."

"Harriet Shaw?" he asked.

She laughed. "Of course."

Chapter 29

'See the first tears that suffering
draws from me.'
Otello – Verdi

On the opening night of *Famous Scenes from Favourite Operas,* Natasha sat in the dressing-room having her hair done. Phillipa watched her expressionless face and knew that the hairdresser, whose attempts at conversation were rebuffed, was troubled. Emily, disturbed by Natasha's silence, had left the room.

"It'll grow back," said the hairdresser.

Natasha looked puzzled.

She pinned the first curl in place. "Richard's hair – that's what's upset you, isn't it?"

"No," said Natasha.

The hairdresser put down her comb. "I thought you were upset because I'd shaved his head – he's bald."

Natasha looked disdainful. "I couldn't care less."

"Oh." The hairdresser gave up.

Phillipa watched, feeling guilty for being happier. Nicholas telling her that he would commit perjury for her had made her think that, given the right circumstances, he might fall in love with her. Since Natasha's and Richard's broken engagement, the depression that had engulfed Phillipa for weeks had lifted. Previously she felt that she was the only person who was cursed with ill luck. Now that Natasha and Richard were plunged into misery she felt happier, but guilty. But guilt was preferable to misery.

Acutely aware of the lack of excitement in the atmosphere, Nicholas went into the dressing-room Richard shared with Frank and Guido. He stared at Richard's shaven head in astonishment.

"Like it?" asked Richard.

336

Nicholas shook his head. "But I'm not supposed to, am I? You look a lot older."

Richard put on his tie. "More sinister? A sadistic Nazi?"

"Yes."

"Now Natasha doesn't care, I'm sacrificing my hair for the opera."

Nicholas pulled out a chair and sat next to him. "Are you okay? Mad question. Sorry. Is there anything I can do?"

Richard shook his head. "At least Natasha doesn't have to pretend she hates me now." He laughed bitterly. "Do you think it's improved the performance?"

Feeling desperately sorry for him Nicholas said, "It doesn't need improving."

Richard pulled on one of his boots. "I was looking forward to this so much, now I'll be thankful when it's all over."

Nicholas stood up and patted his shoulder. "I'm sorry things have turned out like this. Break a leg."

"I wish I could break my neck."

Nicholas walked to Natasha's dressing-room and knocked.

"Come in," called Phillipa.

The room was full of flowers and good luck cards. A sheath of white roses lay on the floor and he picked them up.

"They're from Richard. Throw them in the bin," Natasha said harshly.

"Throw them in the bin yourself," he said, his calm voice belying his apprehension. He took out the card and read it then slipped it back into the flowers. "How are you feeling?"

She looked at him and her lips curved upward in a bright, false smile. "Wonderful, thanks. Excellent, never felt better. I know everyone expects me to be grief stricken, but I'm not."

He stared at her not knowing what to do. Her expression softened slightly as she stood up. She went to him and patted his arm in a gesture just short of being patronizing. "You look worried, Nicholas. Don't panic, I'm not going to burst into tears on stage."

Richard selected a cigarette from the box, lit it and leant on the table as Natasha began to sing 'Vissi d'arte'. Grinning, he drew on the cigarette, careful not to inhale, and blew out a plume of smoke. When Natasha made a strangled sound, he froze. He saw her cover her face with her hands. He glanced at the conductor, who looked alarmed but continued conducting. Wondering what to do, he decided to smoke and laugh till the end of 'Vissi d'arte' and see what happened. His intended roar of laughter sounded more like a bleat.

Willing Natasha to stop crying and begin singing again, he stood up and slowly walked towards her wondering if he should slap her face. It would be in Scarpia's character, but he had no idea how she would react. With dismay he saw that tears were pouring through her fingers and her shoulders were heaving. Listening carefully to the music he tried to plan ahead. The opera school training had prepared him for every conceivable emergency except this. His mind went blank and he could not remember what happened next.

With relief he saw the curtain fall. As soon as it touched the floor Nicholas ran onto the stage, helped Natasha to her feet and led her off.

The stage manager rushed up to him. "Go back to your dressing-room!" he snapped, grabbing Scarpia's jacket and tie off the back of the chair and thrusting them at him. As he walked into the wings he heard Phillipa addressing the audience from the other side of the curtain.

"We apologize for the interruption to *Tosca*. Miss Natasha Howard has been suffering from a very bad attack of the flu, but insisted on performing as her understudy was also ill. We will continue with the last act of *Rigoletto* as soon as possible."

He went into the dressing-room.

Guido was removing his costume. "You bastard."

Richard ignored him and began to undress.

Nicholas inwardly blessed Phillipa for her quick thinking as he entered Natasha's dressing-room. Jacqueline was standing stricken beside Natasha's chair. He saw with alarm that her face was twisted in distress.

Emily clucked in sympathy and helped Nicholas guide Natasha into the chair. "Can I do anything?" she whispered.

"Stay with her till I come back."

Frank put his head round the door. "What can I do?"

Nicholas gestured for him to come in. "Both stay with her, keep her here, don't let her leave whatever you do," he said softly.

338

Determined to prevent a disastrous *Rigoletto*, he grabbed Jacqueline's arm, pulled her out into the passage and led her onto the fire escape. He turned her to face him and put his hands on her shoulders. Her whole body shuddered with the crying she was desperately trying to control. He spoke slowly and calmly. "No, Jacqui, you're not going to cry. You haven't got time. You have to be on stage as soon as the set is changed. Take three deep breaths, come on, that's a good girl. One, two, three. Good. Well done."

Suddenly tears poured down her face.

Nicholas made a drastic decision. Pulling his cigarettes from his pocket he lit one. "Have you ever smoked?"

She shook her head and raised her hand to wipe her eyes.

Gently he took her arm. "Don't touch your face; you'll smudge your make-up." He placed the cigarette between her quivering lips. "Now, gently suck. Not too much, or you'll be sick."

She obeyed and he withdrew the cigarette. "Very gently, breathe in through your mouth."

She closed her eyes and did as he instructed.

"Now, exhale gently." To his relief she didn't choke or cough.

"Good, do the same thing again." She exhaled a column of smoke and he felt her body relax a little. "How do you feel?"

"Funny."

"Sick?"

She shook her head. "Just funny. An up in the air sort of feeling."

"One more puff, take a bit more this time."

She smiled at him through narrowed eyes. "Miss Shaw would kill me if she saw me now."

He watched her as she inhaled. "No, she'd kill me."

She handed him the cigarette. "I can see why people smoke, I feel calm – how weird."

He dropped the cigarette and ground it under his foot. "I'll send the make-up girl in to touch-up your face. See you in five minutes."

Nicholas and Phillipa stood nervously in the wings. Jacqueline sang her first line.

"She's going to be okay," he whispered.

"How did you achieve that miracle? She looked close to hysteria."

339

"I gave her a cigarette."

Phillipa gave a stifled giggle. "Good grief. It certainly worked."

His arm encircled her. "Oh, Philly, what a terrible mess this is." He kissed her cheek. "You were wonderful. It would have been much worse if you hadn't made that announcement."

Phillipa felt a thrill of pleasure and wished the moment could last for ever.

He gently withdrew his arm. "I'm going to take Natasha to my flat. She can spend the night with me; I'll have to take her to Aunt Harriet in the morning. We'll have to sort out what to do."

She frowned. "What about the party?"

"I'll ring Aunt Harriet later."

"Poor Natasha," murmured Phillipa.

"Come and help me."

She followed him, conscience-stricken because she was feeling happy in such awful circumstances.

When they walked into the dressing room Frank and Emily looked at them in relief. Nicholas leant over Natasha and put his hands on her heaving shoulders. "Get out of your costume – I'm taking you home with me," he said gently.

Emily helped her out of her dress and into her jeans and shirt.

"Sorry," gasped Natasha between her sobs. "I'm so – ashamed."

Nicholas held her tightly. "Don't worry about that now." He turned to Frank and Emily. "Can you bring her stuff to the car?"

Emily picked up the daffodil-yellow trouser-suit Natasha had been going to wear to Harriet's party and carried it to the car. They helped her into the front seat and Nicholas fastened her seat belt.

"Shall I come with you?" asked Phillipa.

Nicholas opened his door. "No, Philly. Tell Harriet, will you?"

Feeling rejected, Phillipa turned to Frank and Emily. No one spoke as they walked back to the theatre. Frank ran up the fire escape and opened the door for Phillipa and Emily. The flat feeling that had begun when Natasha and Richard broke their engagement had increased, and the gloomy atmosphere in the theatre was palpable.

As soon as they got to his flat, Nicholas took Natasha into the lounge and sat her in an armchair. He went into his bedroom and found

Algernon asleep on his bed. He stroked him and lifted him up. "Come on, Algie, your services are required." The cat purred loudly and settled into his arms contentedly. Nicholas carried him into the lounge and put him on Natasha's lap. She put out her hand and stroked him.

He went into the kitchen and poured her a glass of lemonade. When he returned she was sitting in the chair with her head leaning back on the headrest. Her eyes were shut and Algernon's head was resting on her shoulder. Her face was a mess of streaked and smudged make-up and under her swollen eyes were black rings of mascara. She looked utterly defeated. Kneeling beside her he covered her hand with his. She opened her eyes and he gave her the glass.

"Thanks. Am I going to be expelled?"

He shook his head.

"I've disgraced the school."

"Phillipa rushed out front and announced that you were suffering from a bad attack of the flu."

She chewed her lip. "Miss Shaw knows the truth. I won't get into the opera company now. I'll be lucky if she allows me to repeat the third year. My broken engagement shouldn't have affected my performance. As you're always saying, Joan Sutherland sang a performance the night her mother died. She sang when she had painful ear abscesses. I deserve to be expelled, I've let everyone down."

"Natasha, don't torture yourself. Harriet won't expel you."

"Why not?"

Nicholas thought about what to say. He was sure Harriet wouldn't expel Natasha because she was her favourite student and had a brilliant voice. But, as she had said herself, she had ruined the performance and her opera school training had drummed into her that whatever happened the show must go on. "If she does I'll defend you – wait and see what she says tomorrow. Now you've got to pick up the pieces."

She looked at him incredulously. "How? I've got no Richard and no career."

"You've got a career – even if Harriet does expel you – you've still got your voice. If you auditioned for the Australian Opera you'd get a principal part straight away."

"I don't want to sing with the Australian Opera yet – I want to stay with Miss Shaw." She pushed her hair back. "I'm dreading seeing her tomorrow. She had so much faith in me. Will you come with me?"

"Yes, of course."

"Who's going to do Tosca next week?"

"You."

Her eyes were wide with astonishment. "You'd trust me?"

"Yes. You've got tomorrow and Monday to recover."

"But I ruined the whole thing, I might do it again."

He shook his head. "You broke down tonight only because you refused to admit you'd been hurt. Instead, you became all frozen and then everything melted and burst out at the wrong time. Aunt Harriet will have to agree, but I don't think she'll have any objection."

She put her head in his shoulder. "Thanks."

He stroked her hair and suddenly longed to kiss her lips. Shocked by his reaction he pulled away and stood up. He forced himself to sound normal. "Now, what you need is a shower and a good night's sleep. I've put a clean towel in the bathroom. You can wear a pair of my pyjamas."

While Natasha was in the bathroom, Nicholas tried to unjumble his emotions. He tried to deny it, but he knew he loved her. He poured a brandy and lit a cigarette. Algernon jumped on his lap and he stroked him, his tattered thoughts whirling. 'I can't. Why not?' he mused. 'She's free, and so am I.' He lifted Algernon's chin. The cat looked at him adoringly as his purrs grew louder. Natasha came into the room dressed in his trailing dressing gown. Her wet hair hung round her shoulders.

She smiled slightly. "Why didn't you tell me how hideous I looked?"

"You didn't look hideous – just a bit messed up. Would you like a brandy before you go to bed? It'll help you sleep."

She nodded and sat beside him. Her presence, the fresh tang of her cologne and the smell of toothpaste on her breath unnerved him. The intensity of his arousal stunned him. He poured another glass of brandy and handed it to her. Not wanting to upset her he sat beside her again, trying to keep his feelings under control. They drank in silence.

"Nick, do you mind if I go to bed now?"

He stood up. "Your room's second on the right."

She put her arm round him. He held his breath.

"Thanks, Nick." She stood on tiptoe and kissed him gently on the lips. Forcing himself to return her chaste kiss he kept his mouth firmly shut. Unwillingly he released her and she left. He collapsed on the sofa, and Algernon looked at him in disapproval.

Profoundly relieved when the cast of *Rigoletto* took their curtain calls to prolonged applause, Harriet watched Jacqueline, who showed no feelings other than delight in the cheers that greeted her arrival at the front of the curtain. During the performance she had been terrified that Jacqueline would break down. Although anxious to get backstage as soon as the lights came up, Harriet decided it was more important to mingle with the audience.

During the interval between *Tosca* and *Rigoletto* she had resisted the temptation to escape from the auditorium. She had to face the audience and give credence to Phillipa's announcement that Natasha had the flu. To her surprise many people had not even mentioned the premature end, but had commented on the amazing production and asked when they were going to do a complete staging.

It was almost midnight by the time Harriet and Phillipa left the theatre. On the way to her car with Phillipa, Harriet saw Richard sitting on a bench in the tiny park by the side of the theatre.

"I'll be with you in a minute, Phillipa." She walked over to him. "Are you coming to my party, Richard?"

"No, Miss Shaw."

She knew that his confidence had deserted him. He now had the air of loneliness she had been aware of when she first knew him. "*The Friends of the Theatre* put a lot of effort into these parties, Richard. They've been at my house all evening cooking and preparing. They'll be disappointed if you don't come."

"I'm sorry, but I can't," he said dully.

She sat beside him. "Why not?"

He stared at the ground. "I'll be ignored."

"I'll speak to you. Phillipa will speak to you. Natasha won't be there, Nicholas has taken her home with him. Will you come?"

He shook his head. "I couldn't face it. Sorry, Miss Shaw."

Careful not to sound judgmental she said, "So, the youth who would have defied the Government over conscription, and didn't care what his colleagues said when he went on anti-Vietnam War marches, has become the man who won't come to a party because he might be ignored?"

For the first time since she had approached him, he looked at her. "I didn't care about the people at work and what they thought – I despised them," he said passionately. "But the people in the opera school were my friends."

She was pleased she had roused him out of his apathy. "Richard, it's important you don't hide away. In time your friends will ask you what happened and you can explain."

"I haven't got any friends now. They've all sided with Natasha – who can blame them? It's no good even thinking that they weren't real friends if that's their attitude – I'd side with Natasha if I was them. I've done something terrible – so naturally their loyalty is to her."

"Has anyone asked you to explain what happened?"

He shook his head. "I don't know what I'd say if they did."

"Tell the truth."

"What is the truth? I don't know, so how can I tell it?"

She placed her hand on his arm. "We don't know what the future is, Richard. You don't know what will or won't happen if you come to my party. I'm very fond of you. Will you come for me?" She held her breath.

"Okay," he said finally.

She stood up. "Good. Because if you hadn't I would have worried about you all night."

From her front window Harriet watched Natasha and Nicholas walk up the path together. Natasha looked terrified. 'She looks as if she's going to the scaffold. Am I such an ogre?' she thought. Nicholas held her arm as if providing physical and moral support. She opened the front door before they had mounted the steps to the verandah. Natasha looked at her and, although her mouth formed the words – "Hello, Miss Shaw," no sound came out. Harriet held out her arm to Natasha. "My dear child, I'm so sorry."

She saw Natasha struggling for control and she stood aside to let them enter. She followed them down the hall into the large sunny room

344

and they all sat on the yellow brocade sofa.

"Nicholas rang me this morning to tell me that he can see no reason why you can't do Tosca on Tuesday. I'll put you out of your misery by telling you that I agree."

"Thank you for having faith in me," Natasha whispered.

Harriet smiled. "Phillipa's announcement saved the show. Everyone believed her. Everyone who didn't know better, that is. Your parents were very upset. They thought I'd expel you. I have a notorious reputation."

Natasha opened her handbag and pulled out a handkerchief. "I would have deserved it. You're being very understanding."

"I've been thinking about next year. It's going to be very difficult if you and Richard have to work together so soon. I have no intention of expelling either of you, but nevertheless I think it would be a good idea if you went away to recover. I thought you might like to go to England. You were going for your honeymoon."

"You can still stay in my house," Nicholas said.

Natasha looked doubtful. "I'd never thought of going alone."

"Go for a holiday. Take trips to Europe, see a bit of the world," said Harriet.

Natasha bit her lip. "Is this a kind and tactful way of getting rid of me?"

"Kindness and tact are not my strong points, Natasha," said Harriet reproachfully.

Richard went through the gap in the curtain. The audience cheered. Briefly he felt happy as he acknowledged their applause before disappearing behind the curtain. 'At least I've got my voice,' he thought. After waiting for the applause to lessen, Natasha swept through the gap without looking at him. He heard the audience calling 'bravo' and stamping their feet.

"It sounds like a football crowd after someone's scored a goal!" whispered Guido.

Natasha reappeared.

"Right," said Nicholas. "Both of you now. Natasha, smile at

Richard when you go out."

She scowled.

Nicholas gripped her arm. "I mean it. Smile at him." He turned to Richard. "Take her hand – go!"

He grabbed her hand and led her through the curtain. The audience roared and stood up. She curtsied, made a gesture of thanks to the audience, and then she looked at Richard and smiled. It was an upward curve of the lips, and her eyes might have been dead for all the warmth they contained. Richard acknowledged the orchestra and conductor, and then they went behind the curtain. Natasha snatched her hand away. The stage hands rushed on to change the set.

Richard and Natasha walked into the wings. Nicholas shook Richard's hand and kissed Natasha. "Congratulations, both of you."

Backstage, Jacqueline hugged Natasha. "They applauded for ages. I'm so happy for you."

Richard heard Natasha say, "I'm grateful that I made it without breaking down again. The success doesn't matter any more. It's enough that I got though it. I hope I can keep it up for another four days."

Richard went into his dressing-room.

"Congratulations, Richard," Guido said formally.

Richard, used to Guido's anger, smiled in surprise. "Thanks, Guido. You too."

Guido looked at him coldly. "I'm not being friendly, Richard, just polite."

On the Monday morning after the final performance on Saturday, Jacqueline anxiously hovered by Phillipa as she opened *The Age* and searched for the review.

"I can't look," she said, turning away and going to the window.

Dramatically, Phillipa cleared her throat. "In an electrifying second act of *Tosca*, Natasha Howard sang with the passion of Callas and the purity of Sutherland."

"Wow!" Jacqueline ran to her side and read the rest of the review. "Fabulous. Let's wake her up."

They burst into Natasha's bedroom. "Wake up, you superb actress, you world class singer!"

Natasha rubbed her eyes, took the paper and read the review. She smiled. "Lucky they weren't there on the first night." She threw her arms round Jacqueline. "Congratulations, yours was fantastic too."

"I knew that would cheer you up." She sat on the bed. "Natasha, please don't go to England."

"I haven't made up my mind yet, Jacqui."

♪　　　♪　　　♪

"I can't comment till I've seen the article," said Harriet. She put down the phone.

When the fifth reporter rang, Harriet took the receiver off the hook. After having a shower, she went to the newsagents and bought the newspapers. *The Sun* was the only one running the story. She read it and laughed. "Well done, Vivien," she said.

As she prepared her breakfast, she considered confessing that hidden in the nonsense of Vivien's article, was the truth.

Switching off the kettle she put two spoons of Earl Grey tea in the pot. 'Nicholas, I gave up singing because I lost my voice.' As she spread marmalade on her toast, she tried to anticipate his reaction. 'He won't leave it at that, he'll want to know how – and I can't tell him.'

When she arrived at the theatre, Nicholas and Phillipa were waiting. Phillipa was fuming and Nicholas was looking ashamed.

"Aunt Harriet – "

"I know, I know, I've had reporters ringing me all morning so I took the phone off the hook."

He held the door open for her. "You'll have to sue."

"I can't."

Phillipa, who was walking in front of them down the corridor, turned round. "Of course you can. You must. She's lied."

"Calm down, both of you." They reached her office and went inside.

Nicholas shut the door. "Don't worry about my feelings, go ahead and sue her. I'm sorry I got involved with such a treacherous woman. I'm guilty of gross misjudgment."

Having prepared herself, Harriet felt in command. She smiled understandingly. "No you're not. I liked Vivien too, but she's one of these people who are vindictive when things go wrong. And she's a

347

journalist. Now that you're no longer going out together she owes you no loyalty. Just let it all die down, no one will believe her anyway."

"That's not the point, Aunt Harriet. She said you can't sing and that you're not Harriet Shaw. She's accusing you of being an impostor."

Harriet saw the conflicting reactions of relief, exasperation and puzzlement in his expression. "No, she's asking if I'm the same Harriet Shaw who sang at Covent Garden." She kept her voice gentle. "She's questioned, not accused. She's too clever for that. If she had stated I was an impostor, then I would sue. What I will do is issue a statement."

Phillipa grabbed her shorthand book and sharpened her pencil. "Good. Shall I begin, Vivien Anderson is a scurrilous liar?"

Nicholas grinned and sat down. "Yes."

"No, it's too emotive." Harriet had worked out what she was going to say while she was having her breakfast. "Right, here it is. Vivien Anderson's theory, that I am an impostor, is based on the fact that I refused to sing at fund-raising concerts for the war effort in 1941. I gave up singing to found a theatre and teach singers, and that is what I have done. To do something wholeheartedly, means giving up other things.

"In 1941 I was forty-seven. It is true that there are singers, good ones, who sing well into their sixties and beyond. I did not want to be one of them. I had no desire to play youthful parts in middle age, so I retired and made way for the young. I am now eighty. Like the rest of me, my voice has become creaky. No singer of integrity would inflict a creaky voice on her audience. No audience wants to see Mimi and Gilda played by a geriatric tottering round the stage." She saw Phillipa smile. "That is why I no longer sing. Not because I am an impostor who never could."

Part Four

FINALE

January 1974 to January 1975

Chapter 30

'Then it's over, all over?
You're leaving, my darling?'

La Bohème – Puccini

At dawn on New Year's Day, Natasha left the beach house and walked down the sandy track. She wanted solitude so she could think clearly. Although tempted to take Harriet's advice and go to England, the thought of going alone depressed her. Because Nicholas and Harriet would be casting the operas in the middle of January she had to make a decision quickly. Sitting on the top of the sand dunes she stared at the ocean and pushed memories of Richard aside.

'If I stay in Melbourne, I'll have Jacqui and Philly, my operatic career and my parents. But I'll see Richard.' She tried to think of other alternatives, but the only one she could think of was going to England and asking Jacqueline to come too. 'But if we both go, Philly will be alone.'

That night as they were getting ready for bed, she told Jacqueline.

Her stricken face almost made Natasha change her mind. "I don't want to be here on the day we were to have married." She sat at the dressing table and unwrapped the towel from her hair. "I'm going to stay for a year."

"Then I'm coming with you."

Not daring to look at Jacqueline, Natasha combed her wet hair. "Jacqui, I've got to get over this alone. I've always depended on you emotionally – but I've got to learn to be independent. You've got to go into the opera company, you owe that to Miss Shaw. A year apart will do us good, and we can't desert poor Philly."

"She can come too."

"Don't be silly, Jacqui. She wouldn't leave Miss Shaw for a year."

"She'll have to leave sometime. What if she gets married and has a baby?"

"That's different. I'll book my flight tomorrow – I'll probably be gone in a week."

Jacqueline chewed her lip. "A year's too long. I know you'll be living in Nick's house, but you'll be in a strange country with no family or friends."

"Anything's better than staying here and seeing Richard every day."

"He'll be in a different production. Miss Shaw would never put you together."

"I can't risk it. This time last year we were so happy – I never imagined things would turn out like this," Natasha said forlornly.

Trying to feel excited that in three days she would be in London, Natasha began to pack. Jacqueline helped her sort out her jumpers.

Phillipa came into the bedroom holding a letter. "It's from Richard."

Natasha slammed the drawer shut. "Throw it away."

Phillipa waved it at her. "Give him a chance to explain."

Snatching the letter, Natasha ripped it up and threw it in the wastepaper basket.

"You're your own worst enemy, Natasha," said Phillipa.

Natasha put her hands on her hips. "And what about you, Philly? You gave up Frank for some stupid reason. But Richard had Deborah in my bed. Not just any bed – my bed. So I don't want to hear any more about explanations." She picked up the opal pendant Richard had given her and held it out to Phillipa. "Would you like this?"

"Oh, Natasha, keep it."

"No, if you don't want it I'll throw it in the rubbish bin."

Phillipa took the opal. "You are one for throwing things away. Goodness knows what's happened to your engagement ring. I searched for it for ages, but I couldn't find it."

Jacqueline folded one of Natasha's jumpers. "Someone will probably find it in a hundred years' time and it will be worth a fortune."

"I hope it brings them more luck than it's brought me," said Natasha.

'This isn't really happening,' thought Natasha as Jacqueline parked the car at Tullamarine Airport. She watched her father taking her cases

352

out of the boot. 'I could back out – if I did everyone would be pleased. No one wants me to go and I don't want to either.'

They all went into the departure hall and Natasha stood in the queue in front of the QANTAS desk with her father.

"Dad?"

Her father looked at her. The queue moved forward and he picked up her cases.

'Miss Shaw suggested I go,' she thought. 'Maybe she does want to get rid of me – I wouldn't blame her.'

Her father put down the cases. "Yes, Pet?"

"Nothing."

When she booked in, Nicholas, Phillipa and Harriet arrived.

"We bought you a present," said Phillipa, thrusting a toy koala into her arms and bursting into tears.

Everyone else's self-control remained in place till her flight was called.

Nicholas put his arm round her. "I've sent my parents your photo so they'll recognize you at Heathrow."

Natasha hugged and kissed her parents, Harriet, and Phillipa, but broke down when she turned to Jacqueline. They flung their arms round each other and sobbed. Natasha disengaged herself and ran through the door of the departure lounge.

She had a window seat, and she looked at the crowd standing on the balcony waving handkerchiefs. She wanted to jump off the plane and join them, but it was too late. Wishing she had let Jacqueline come with her she ignored the safety demonstrations. Tears poured down her cheeks. The plane began to move along the runway and the waving mass of handkerchiefs became frenzied. As the plane lifted, Natasha looked down at the world she had left. "Richard," she whispered. "Richard."

14ᵗʰ January 1974

Dear Jacqui,

I'm now settled in Nick's gorgeous house in Kew. It feels strange being in the house where Miss Shaw grew up.

There are photos of her everywhere – she was stunning.
I'm surprised she never married – she must have had lots
of men interested in her. Maybe she was never interested
in them. I can't imagine her letting any man dominate her.
London's amazing – you need a map of the underground
train system. It's freezing, and my winter clothes are
inadequate so I'll have to buy a new coat and jumpers and
a hat! Don't laugh – you have to wear a hat or your ears
freeze.
Good luck with the casting – hope you get a good part.

"Come in, Richard." Harriet looked at his strained face. She had invited him to spend Christmas Day at her house with Nicholas and Phillipa, but he had refused, saying he could not bear the burden of pretending to be cheerful. For the same reason he had not attended the New Year's Eve Party in the theatre. "You've lost weight."

"Have I?"

She nodded. "Are you eating properly?"

"I suppose not."

"Grim Christmas?" she asked gently, thinking that to remind him about the importance of good nutrition would sound like a lecture.

"I spent it alone in my flat, cursing myself."

She lifted the lid of the piano. "I know it will take a long time to get over this. But your future's not bleak. Let's think about the good things in your life at the moment. Firstly, this is your last lesson as a student, next week you'll be a professional opera singer. We're giving you the role of Iago. Ah, is that a smile?"

"I didn't expect such a large role – thank you."

She opened his *Melba Method*. "We must build you up a good repertoire for Covent Garden. Goodness, I am doing well. You smiled again."

354

Phillipa wrote to Natasha as soon as the parts were announced at the beginning of February.

> *Jacqui's so excited! She's been given the part of the*
> *Mother in **The Consul**. Emily's got Queen of the Night –*
> *Miss Shaw wants to make the most of her before she's*
> *snapped up by The Australian Opera. We are also doing*
> ***Madam Butterfly**, because Harriet's worried about the*
> *financial aspects of **The Consul**. And for a change of*
> *theme – **Otello**. We're doing **The Consul** and **The Magic***
> ***Flute** in the same week with **The Consul** first, then the*
> *people with season tickets won't have to wait long before*
> *they're cheered up.*
> *Nick said that if **The Consul** fails he'll go crazy and need*
> *a psychiatrist. Harriet replied that he'll need a refuge*
> *from her rage!*

For two weeks Natasha explored famous sites, which, owing to the freezing weather, were practically tourist free. She had the Tower of London and Hampton Court Palace to herself and she enjoyed wandering through the parks with their herds of deer. Twice she was caught up in a bomb scare in Oxford Street and felt outraged with the IRA for targeting civilians. She liked writing letters home and made sure each letter contained different news. Although she found London enthralling, in many ways it shocked her. In a letter to Phillipa she wrote,

> *The underground stations are full of posters that say, **If***
> ***you're happy to be pregnant – fine. If not ring this***
> ***number.** Can you believe it? I nearly fell off the escalator.*

As the day of her skiing holiday approached, she realized that, for the first time since she had broken her engagement to Richard, she was excited about something.

Jacqueline opened the letter from Natasha. After describing the traditional Austrian resort and the chalet in which she was staying, Natasha continued:-

*Skiing is exhilarating. After only two days I can ski easily
down the nursery slopes. I wish I was with Richard
sharing the romance of the scenery, tobogganing and
moonlight sleigh rides.*

'Now you know how it feels, Natasha,' she thought. She frowned.
'What a spiteful thing to think.'
"What's wrong?" asked Phillipa.
"Nothing." She gave the first page to Phillipa.

Now I know how you felt when Max went back to his wife.

'Gosh, I'm a mind reader now,' thought Jacqueline.

*I'm sorry I wasn't more sympathetic. I remember how I
told you to stop wallowing and find another man. What a
smug creature I was. Philly was much kinder to you. I've
discovered how hard it is. If anyone told me to go and find
another man I'd feel like hitting them. Perhaps I needed
this to make me understand. I'm more mature now.*

Jacqueline smiled. 'We both are,' she thought.

"Frank!"
About to go into the theatre, Frank turned and saw Jacqueline and Emily running across the road. He put his arms round them. "Hi, Queenie and Mother. Next time we fill out a form that asks for our

occupation we can write 'opera singer'."

"Frank," said Emily excitedly. "Congratulations on Sarastro. Yes, we're professionals at last! You know, when we started opera school I didn't think I'd last the first term."

Frank opened the door for them. "Neither did I – I'd never seen anyone so nervous. Funny who's made it and who hasn't."

"I was certain Max would make it, Deborah too. And Natasha," said Jacqueline as they walked down the corridor.

Frank saw that she looked wistful. "Natasha made it. She's just away for a year."

Emily looked awkward. "There's Richard."

"Hello, everyone," Richard said cautiously.

Jacqueline ignored him and went into the theatrette. After a moment's uncertainty, Emily followed her.

Last time Frank had seen Richard his head had been shaved for Scarpia. Now his hair was almost back to its normal length, but Frank was shocked by the amount of weight he had lost. His unhappiness surrounded him and he seemed incapable of putting on an act. Knowing his situation was worsened by the fact that his friends had deserted him, he held out his hand. "This is all getting stupid, mate. I'm not going to ignore you."

"Thanks, Frank."

"Haven't seen you for ages. Why didn't you come to the New Year's Eve Party?"

"It went on all right without me."

"Natasha and Jacqui weren't there either. I missed you all. I feel I've lost all my mates. Well, maybe we'll make some new friends in the opera company."

Nicholas watched the new opera singers assemble in the theatrette, pleased to see Frank talking to Richard. Out of the twenty-four students who had begun opera school in 1971, only fifteen were left. Judy, because she had been ill so often, was repeating the third year. To Harriet's disgust, Faye had married her uncouth boyfriend and given up singing.

The first day was relaxed with no rehearsals. The morning began in the theatrette with a lecture for the newcomers. Then they went upstairs for a buffet lunch where they met the rest of the opera company and Isaac Goldstein, the new musical director.

When they were seated Nicholas stood up. "Welcome to your first day as professionals. In your three years at opera school you were taught the importance of humility. Things have changed for you now and it might be easy to forget that lesson. You'll be written about in the papers and magazines, and strangers will be interested in your life. When you leave the theatre after a performance some of the audience will be waiting for you, wanting your autograph. You will acquire fans. Having an adoring public can be very, very potent.

"But always remember that for every star there are at least ten unseen people who make it possible. Everyone taking part in a performance is important. An opera can't go on without the chorus, the set can't be changed without the stage hands and without lighting technicians you'd be fumbling about in the dark. For many of you this theatre is a stepping stone to The Australian Opera, Covent Garden and La Scala. When you make it – remember the lessons you learnt here.

"The lunch this afternoon is to welcome you into the opera company and give you an opportunity to meet everyone. The hard work begins tomorrow, so make the most of today."

"Can we take your bit again, Jacqui?" asked Isaac.

Nervous because she was unable to get the tune right and aware that the pianist was impatient with her, Jacqueline nodded. "Oh when will all this sorrow end? Damn you, you and all your friends! Why don't you men bring home some bread and not only fear and blood? A million dead cannot feed your child!"

"Better," said Isaac.

Finally the rehearsal ended.

"Are you coming to *The Scheherazade,* Jacqui?" asked Lois, who was playing the part of Magda Sorel.

Feeling that her operatic career was a disaster and that she must go home and practise, Jacqueline shook her head. With a wave of panic she saw Isaac coming over. 'He's going to tell me how hopeless I am,' she thought. 'He had to help me so much and everyone else sailed through.'

"You are worried, Jacqueline?"

She waited until every one had left the studio. "I don't think I'm doing very well – actually I'm doing badly."

He patted her arm. "Sit down."

'He's going to sack me.' Her heart raced.

Pulling out the chair, he sat opposite her. He smiled. "Don't look so frightened – everything's all right."

"It's not, I don't think I'm ever going to learn the music."

"Why?"

She rubbed her head. "It's all going so fast."

"Jacqueline, how many rehearsals have we had?"

"Three."

"And when did we start?"

"Three days ago."

"Do you know what I'm trying to say?"

Relieved he was not going to sack her, but still feeling a failure, she said, "But everyone else did well."

"You're the new girl – the only new person in *The Consul*. Everyone else knows each other and they have worked together before. And Lois has been dying to do *The Consul* for years – she knows the part already. Have you got a record of *The Consul*?"

"No, but I've ordered it."

"Had you ever heard the music before?"

"No."

"See? If you were Maddalena or Orpheus you'd already know the music and all the words – I'm right? As soon as you get the record you'll be able to listen to it and pick up more."

She nodded and smiled.

As he reached over and took her hand the sleeve of his shirt rode up. "You feel better now?"

Jacqueline, staring at the numbers tattooed on his wrist, was so shocked by the realization he had been in a concentration camp, she was unable to answer.

He pulled his sleeve down. "It's all right, Jacqui."

"I'm sorry, Isaac," she whispered.

He stood up. "Let's join the others in *The Scheherazade*."

359

When Natasha returned to Kew from Austria at the end of February she was lonely. Although the friendships made during the ski trip had been superficial she missed the company, the excitement of conquering new runs and the unpredictability of the days. Her life revolved around the frequent letters from home and if there were no welcoming letters on the mat in the morning she felt miserable. Although delighted that Jacqueline had been given a major part, her descriptions of the rehearsals made her envious. She wondered what part Miss Shaw would have given her and often felt that she had made the wrong decision in coming to England. 'I'm missing out on so much.'

3ʳᵈ April 1974

Dear Natasha

I'm loving rehearsals now, wrote Jacqueline. *As soon as I got the record and could listen to it every night things became much easier. Lois McPherson is Magda Sorel. She's thirty-four and Harriet calls her Mother Duck because she looks after all the ducklings like me. She's great to work with. The Australian Opera are always trying to get her to join them, but she hates travelling. Besides she's fiercely loyal to Miss Shaw.*
Here's a coincidence – she knew Max. They started opera school together. She went out with him for a month and then he dropped her. She was really upset at the time. So we've got something (or someone) in common.
The Mother is an emotionally demanding role and I come home exhausted. Even reading the score is traumatic. How Lois manages to sing some of her scenes without crying I don't know. Rehearsing full time is incredible – you progress so quickly.
Please be careful of the bombs, I worry about you.

♪   ♪   ♪

"Give me that handkerchief!" sang Richard.

The girl playing Emilia yelped as he grabbed it from her.

"Hold it," called Nicholas. "What's the matter with you all?" he snapped, although he suspected that Richard was making the others nervous. "Desdemona, if you look at Iago and Emilia during this bit the plot is lost. What's the point of the scene?" he asked, trying to curb his irritation. "All right, I'll tell you!" he said when no one answered. "Desdemona, if you see Iago grab the handkerchief, you'd say to Otello in the scene where he demands that you show him the handkerchief, 'But, dear husband, I saw Iago wrenching it out of Emilia's hands,' wouldn't you?"

The girl playing Desdemona nodded.

"And, Richard, you're supposed to pull the handkerchief out of Emilia's hand – not her arm out of its socket. Take it again."

"Give me the handkerchief or feel my angry hand!" sang Richard.

The girl playing Emilia forgot to come in.

Richard exploded. "For God's sake, get it right!"

Nicholas stood up. "Richard, I'm the director of this opera, not you. Okay, take a break, everyone. Richard, come here."

When the others had left, Nicholas said, "You're becoming a boor. I don't care what you do in private – but I do care about your behaviour when you're in this theatre. You're difficult to work with, you're making everyone nervous. It's because of you Emilia forgets her lines and can't get the moves right. You're erratic. The other day your portrayal of Iago was perfect. Today you're making him too aggressive and you've lost the disguised cunning that made him so credible."

Richard looked sullen.

"You've let your unhappiness change you," said Nicholas.

"I think I've got good reason."

"Really? You think you're the only person who's ever had a broken engagement? Far worse things have happened to people and you don't have to look far. Think of Phillipa – look at Isaac who spent two years in a concentration camp and lost most of his family. Think about them, Richard, and then see if you have the nerve to skulk around like a doom

361

laden prophet. Now go and apologize to everyone. Remember what I said on your first day? Continue like this and I won't be recommending a renewal of your contract."

Without giving him a chance to respond, Nicholas left the studio and went to his office, knowing that not so long ago he would have treated Richard far more gently. "I wouldn't have let it get this far, I would have tried to help, but we're in competition now, so he's on his own."

After the break, the rehearsal went well and it was obvious that Richard had apologized. But after the rehearsal Nicholas saw him going to his car instead of joining everyone in *The Scheherazade*.

The following morning Richard came into his office before rehearsal.

"Yes?" said Nicholas curtly.

Richard looked awkward. "I wanted to apologize. You're right, I'm sorry."

"That's okay, Richard. See you shortly."

Looking bemused by the dismissal, Richard nodded and left.

Thoughts of Richard haunted Natasha. She dreamt about him and woke feeling devastated. Awake, she imagined the things they would have done together and the wonderful honeymoon they would have been having. She decided to look for a job. Generally, the wages for clerks were appalling but it was not money she wanted, but something to fill her days. She started as a receptionist at Queen Charlotte's Maternity Hospital four weeks after she had returned from skiing. From Kew Gardens the train journey to Stamford Brook was only three stations.

As well as sightseeing and going to the opera, she spent her evenings and weekends listening to records, playing the piano, doing her breathing and vocal exercises and writing letters. The house became untidy and one night she looked around in dismay. The bookcase that had contained the scores was almost empty, scores and sheet music littered the floor and almost every record was out of its sleeve. 'Phillipa would kill me.'

Her first attempt to fit all the sheet music into the piano stool failed so she unpacked it completely. At the bottom lay an old scrap book. *Charlotte Shaw* was written neatly on the front. Inside were newspaper cuttings of Harriet's operatic career. The Sellotape securing them was brittle and some of them fell out as she turned the pages. The early ones described Harriet as a rising young star while later ones proclaimed her as Covent Garden's reigning Queen of the Night.

Fascinated, Natasha read the cuttings for an hour. Then, realizing that it was after midnight, she stood up quickly. Her cramped legs protested and she lost her balance. As her hand shot out to save her from falling, she knocked a large photo of Harriet off the piano. In dismay she heard the glass smash and limped over to pick it up. Carefully, she opened the catches and removed the backing, relieved that the silver frame was not damaged. Underneath was a wad of newspaper cuttings. She opened one.

Where is Harriet Shaw?

All her performances have been cancelled for this season and her family are refusing to say why. No one has seen her for weeks and her worried friends have no idea where she is.

Intrigued, Natasha unfolded the next cutting and stared at the picture in astonishment. 'Deborah?' she thought. Then she saw the name Annabel Nelson underneath. She read the piece. Aware that she had stumbled on a terrible secret she put it down on the piano. Conscience wrestling with her desire to know more, she wrapped the broken glass in newspaper. 'That journalist was right – there was an Annabel.'

She made a mug of cocoa and took it back to the drawing room. Giving into temptation she went back and read the other cuttings.

"I can't believe it," she whispered when she had finished. "But it does explain Miss Shaw's attitude to Deborah. Oh, Christ." She folded up the cuttings, noticing, but not caring, that her hands were blue with cold. Shivering, she sat in the armchair and wept.

363

Chapter 31

'To this we've come.'

The Consul – Menotti

After his daughter's death Max Carveth suffered from crippling guilt. Ever since giving up opera school and returning home two and a half years ago, he and Susan had fought constantly, often when Zoe was present. The memory of Zoe in tears, begging them to stop, haunted him. Only when her illness was diagnosed as cancer, did he and Susan stop fighting. He remembered that when he had heard of her conception, he had wanted her aborted, and how carelessly he had uttered the words. Remembered too, that in the weeks before their wedding he had longed for Susan to have a miscarriage.

'This is my punishment,' he thought.

For months he lived like a robot. He went to work, signed papers and spoke to no one beyond what was necessary. He and Susan moved round the house like separate entities, neutral to one another, each only vaguely aware the other existed. Then, gradually, he became aware of the outside world, and began to live and think as a participant of life, not a spectator.

One morning when he was reading the newspaper, he saw the heading,

National Theatre to do *The Consul* in May.

For the first time in almost a year he thought of Jacqueline. On Sunday he drove to St Kilda. As he stood in front of the theatre, nostalgia swamped him. He looked at the photos displayed in the windows, at first not recognizing the one of Jacqueline. The make-up and grey wig made her look at least fifty. He looked at the photos of Frank as Sarastro and Richard as Iago. 'If I'd stayed I would have been Pinkerton or Tamino,' he thought. 'Or maybe Otello.'

On Monday, he booked a seat for the opening night's performance. Zoe's illness and death had changed him, and for a year he had been careless of his appearance. It was Susan who made sure he showered and shaved every day, cleaned his teeth and used deodorant. He was aware that the prospect of seeing Jacqueline was turning him back to what he had been. He chose the suit, shirt and tie with a preference for the colours she liked. He bought a bottle of her favourite aftershave and splashed it on liberally.

He arrived at the theatre with a bunch of red roses. As soon as he took his seat, he opened the programme. The photo of Jacqueline made his heart beat quicken and he wondered what had happened in the years following his absence. The brief note about her gave him no indication of her marital status. 'For all I know she could be engaged or even married.'

From the moment the curtain rose on the grim set, Max was mesmerized. Jacqueline was so skilfully made up and her movements were those of a much older woman; he took a few moments to realize that it was her. She wore a shapeless brown cardigan with a grey skirt, and her thick black stockings had ladders and wrinkled round her ankles. When in Act Two she sang a lullaby to the dying baby, tears ran down his face, people in the audience wept and a woman, sobbing uncontrollably, stumbled out of the auditorium.

When the chief of police entered the man next to him whispered 'bastard, bastard!' and hit the arms of the seat with clenched fists. Max worried that he was going to start shouting.

As the curtain dropped on the final act and the cast took their curtain calls, all the main characters received a standing ovation. Cheering greeted the arrival of the conductor, Isaac Goldstein, on stage. Obviously emotional he put his arms round Jacqueline and Lois. It was a long time before the exhausted audience allowed the curtain to fall for the last time. Max had never experienced anything like it. As people stood up some were still crying.

His anxiety grew as he wondered how Jacqueline would react when she saw him backstage.

Feeling like bursting into tears and laughing in triumph, Jacqueline returned with Lois to their dressing-room, which was filled with flowers, good-luck cards and a telegram from Natasha. Isaac was waiting for them, but was too overcome to speak. Jacqueline and Lois kissed him.

"Oh, Isaac, you were fantastic," said Lois.

"Poor man," said Jacqueline when he left. "Tonight must have been really hard for him."

Lois hugged her. "It's one hell of an opera to make your debut in, Kid, but you were great."

Putting on a hair band to protect her hair, Jacqueline smeared her face with cold cream and wiped it off with a tissue.

Emily rushed in and kissed her. "You were both sensational! I've been bawling my eyes out. A woman near me was so upset she had to leave. I've just seen Miss Shaw with a crowd of emotional Jews, telling her how brave she is. She and Nick are surrounded by people. At this rate they'll never get backstage."

Jacqueline smiled introspectively. "It's weird being congratulated because you upset people. I had no idea it would be like this. Rehearsals are different – you don't get the feeling from the audience. I got a shock when I heard people crying – someone sounded hysterical."

Nicholas, Harriet and Phillipa came in.

Nicholas looked at Emily and grinned. "Enjoy it?"

"I'm glad I'm in *The Flute* – I couldn't cope with all this agony." She looked at them accusingly. "You both look very composed. How come you didn't cry?"

"We were too terrified," said Harriet as she kissed Jacqueline. "Are you coming back to my house for chicken and champagne?"

"Yes," said Jacqueline. "I'm starving. I was too nervous to eat before."

When Harriet and Nicholas left, Jacqueline dressed in a black trouser suit and a burgundy silk blouse.

Lois smiled approvingly. "That's a super outfit – I've never seen you dressed up before."

"Philly took me shopping – I hated it. She made me buy make-up too – that was more fun." She laughed. "I was going to wear jeans tonight, but she wouldn't let me." She picked up her sponge bag. "Just going to wash my face." She opened the door and stepped out into the passage. Max stood in front of her. She stared at him in astonishment.

366

"It's really me." He held out a bunch of roses. "Congratulations, Jacqui. You were amazing."

Jacqueline had fantasized about meeting Max many times. Her favourite scenario was leaving Covent Garden by the stage door after a brilliant performance of *Orpheus*, and being mobbed by her fans of whom Max was one. In her fantasies she was serene and beautifully dressed. Now, in reality her heart was pounding, and she knew that instead of looking beautiful and poised her hair was squashed and her face, shiny with the residue of cold cream, was turning scarlet. Momentarily paralyzed with shock, she gaped at him. Then she turned and ran down the passage and clattered down the fire escape.

Max caught up with her at the bottom and grabbed her arm. "Please, darling."

She spun round to face him. "Don't you dare call me darling!"

"Jacqui, please, we have to talk."

She grabbed the flowers and struck him with them. "Give these to Sue."

"Jacqui, please, something terrible has happened."

Her voice was shaking with fury. "Have you got someone pregnant – someone other than your wife?"

"Zoe died of cancer eight weeks ago."

She was horrified. "Max, I'm sorry – sorry. Oh, Max. Oh, God."

"Please can we talk, Jacqui? Let me take you for coffee somewhere."

"I can't, I'm going to Miss Shaw's."

"Don't refuse to talk to me. Have you got a boyfriend?"

She hesitated, she wanted to lie, but the ingrained creed of a lifetime was too much. Thinking that to let him know she was available would be foolish, she ignored the question. "Max, I'm sorry about your daughter, but I am not going to see you again – I can't. It wouldn't be right."

He began to cry. Dropping the flowers she put out her arm. He clung to her, great tearing sobs being wrenched from his body. She had never seen him cry before. She tried to understand what he was saying, but the only words she could distinguish were his distraught apologies.

"Max, I'll see you when *The Consul's* over, I promise. What about Wednesday in two weeks?"

"Yes, thank you, Jacqui, thank you," he spluttered. He drew away and wiped his face.

She saw tears trickling through his fingers.

He took a deep breath. "Sorry."

Chewing her lip, she watched him pull out a handkerchief and wipe his eyes.

"Shall we go to a restaurant in Fitzroy Street?" he asked.

She didn't want anyone she knew seeing them together. "No. We'll go to town. I'll meet you at seven in *Charley Browns*." She turned and ran back up the fire escape.

On the way to Harriet's, she was so preoccupied she nearly drove through a red light. At the party everyone congratulated her and she tried to concentrate on her triumph, not Max.

"Are you all right, Jacqui?" asked Nicholas. "You look distracted."

"I'm fine."

"You missed the autograph hunters. They were disappointed. Which way did you leave?"

"Autograph hunters?"

He handed her a glass of champagne. "You'll have to get used to being a star."

She smiled. "You've taught us humility too well. I didn't even think about autographs. Actually, I saw Max tonight."

He frowned. "I thought so. We saw him in the theatre."

"His daughter died of cancer."

Nicholas looked shocked. "Oh, hell. Are you going to see him again?"

She nodded. "I wasn't going to, but he started crying. I don't know what to do. Seeing him was a shock – I feel confused."

He put his hand on her shoulder. "I'd hate to see you hurt again."

"If I do get hurt it will be my own stupid fault," she said.

"Yes, it will," he agreed. "Is he still married?"

She sighed. "I don't know … I suppose so."

"Jacqui, remember what he put you through."

She nodded. "I'm not likely to forget."

"Are you over him?"

She ran her finger down the stem of her champagne glass. "No. Sometimes I kid myself and pretend I am, but I'm not." She felt close to tears. "Oh, Nick, I don't think I'll ever get over him. I go out with other blokes – nice ones and all I can do is wish they were Max. I know I'm crazy, but I can't help it."

"If you feel like that, do you think it's a good idea to see him again?"

"No. But I said I would so I can't back out now. I keep my promises."

"Does Max keep his?" He put his hand on her shoulder. "Did he have the decency to tell you to your face that he was going back to his wife?"

She shook her head.

"What's wrong, Jacqueline?" asked Harriet.

"Max," Nicholas told her.

"I see. What does he want?"

Nicholas told her about his daughter. Jacqueline saw that Harriet looked concerned and annoyed.

"I'm sorry about his daughter. I guess he'll want you to go back to him. This night was supposed to be your night, Jacqueline, and he's deliberately ruined it for you. Instead of revelling in your success you're upset and thinking about him. But you're an adult and there is only one person who can decide what to do." She swept away.

In spite of her turmoil Jacqueline smiled. "Well, I won't get any sympathy from her if Max hurts me."

"Do you think you'll deserve sympathy?" he asked.

"No, Nick. Not from you – not from anyone."

In *Charley Browns* in Exhibition Street, Max waited anxiously. Dressed in expensive new clothes, he had felt confident until he entered the restaurant and found Jacqueline had not arrived. When they had been going out together she had been punctual. 'She's not going to come,' he thought.

All week he had been planning their future and intended marrying her as soon as his divorce was absolute. He thought about where they would live and the children they would have. They would live and travel in luxury with nannies and servants. This time he would be a faithful and attentive husband.

369

As the minutes passed, his assurance trickled away. Not bothering to hide his agitation, he kept looking at the door. She arrived fifteen minutes late. Watching her coming over to his table, his optimism increased when he saw that she had taken trouble with her appearance and worn make-up. Fashionably dressed in a royal blue velvet trouser suit and a white satin blouse with pearl buttons, she was more beautiful than he remembered. Her black hair was well cut and shone in the candlelight. Gone was the girl who had dressed in jeans and cotton shirts. In her place was a dashing young woman. She was even wearing jewellery. He looked at the gold treble clef pendant on an intricate chain, wondering who had given it to her. Fear that she had a serious boyfriend dulled his relief.

He stood up and smiled. "I'm so glad to see you. I almost expected you to cancel."

She looked steadily at him as a waiter pulled out her chair. "I always keep my appointments, Max."

He forced himself to look at her hands, frightened he would see an engagement ring. Her fingers were bare. Happiness gave him confidence. "Jacqui, I'm sorry I hurt you. If it's any consolation those years have been hell. Have you forgiven me?"

"That's not relevant," she said briskly.

He felt less certain. She was more self-possessed than she had been three years ago. Then she had been easily persuaded. Now, she was independent and willful. She had achieved what she wanted. The critics had raved about her performance and the newspapers did a full page article about her, complete with photographs.

'She's an opera singer,' he thought. 'I'm still unhappily married. I still work at the same bank. I've achieved nothing. I am nothing. I have nothing.'

Jacqueline's expression was strange. It was almost cynical. "Lois was good, wasn't she?"

Feeling that the question was a trick, he looked at her blankly.

"Don't you remember her?"

"Should I?"

"Yes, you went out with her when you were at opera school the first time."

He put on a quizzical expression. "That was fourteen years ago."

370

"She remembers you."

He was about to say that he was a memorable bloke, but she was looking at him derisively. "Jacqui, I went out with lots of girls at opera school – you're the only one I remember. You're the only one who meant anything."

"And I'm supposed to be flattered."

He didn't know what to say.

"Are you still married?"

"Not for much longer." He realized that some people in the restaurant had recognized her. Typically, she was oblivious. "Jacqui, I missed you terribly. I went back to Sue because of Zoe. I didn't believe in fate before, but now … imagine how I'd have felt if I'd not had those last years with her."

She raised her eyebrows. "And has fate now decreed that you leave Sue and we can start where we broke off?"

He had thought she would soften, but her matter-of-fact tone made him feel he was at a business meeting. "Yes, Jacqui. Can't you see that?"

Looking intently at a drip of wax sliding down the candle, she shook her head.

He watched the sweep of her lashes. He had forgotten how long they were. He wanted her to tell him she understood, or start crying – anything but this coolness. "I've written to Miss Shaw about resuming my singing lessons, and I hope she'll let me start in the second year of opera school." He waited for her to say something, but she just nodded. "Jacqui, do you still love me?"

She traced the pattern in the damask serviette with her fingernail. "Max, when I look back over the time we spent together, I was hardly ever happy. I didn't deserve happiness. I'd taken you from your wife and daughter."

He was depressed that she hadn't answered his question. "I wouldn't have married Sue if she hadn't got … " He stopped awkwardly.

"Oh, Max, you haven't changed. Still the same – selfish and conceited – thinking only about yourself."

"Jacqui, I'm thinking about us – you and me."

The waiter came over and gave them the menus.

When he left, Jacqueline pulled a piece of warm wax from the candle. "You're thinking about yourself. If you had any feeling for me, you wouldn't have come near me. You would have felt too ashamed. I feel ashamed of the way I behaved. I committed adultery," she said softly. "I was wrong. I didn't care about Zoe and Sue and how they must be suffering. Natasha did, Miss Shaw did, my parents did, Nick did. Everyone did except me – and you."

"I cared about Zoe," he protested.

"What about Sue?"

"Not really," he admitted.

She rolled the wax between her finger and thumb. "You still have a wife, and if you and I went back to what we were, I would still be committing adultery. Sue's had enough unhappiness without me stealing her husband."

"Darling, I'm going to get a divorce – I want you to be my wife."

"Don't call me darling. You were going to get a divorce before, but you went back to Sue."

"You don't understand." He tried to explain. "I didn't go back to Sue – I went back to Zoe."

She touched the pendant, but said nothing.

"Jacqui, have you got a boyfriend?"

She shook her head.

"Who gave you the pendant?"

She looked amused. "Miss Shaw. She gives everyone gifts of jewellery to commemorate their debut. The women get pendants, brooches or earrings and the men get cuff links or tie pins. Emily got a marcasite crescent-moon brooch."

Relief made him smile. "I thought maybe a boyfriend had given it to you."

"Of course you did, Max. That's the way you think. Do you know what happened to me on the last night of *The Consul*?"

She looked so hostile, he felt too apprehensive to do anything but shake his head.

"After the performance, we had a party in the foyer. A man started talking to me. He was very interesting, good looking and was about thirty, I guess. He congratulated me and we chatted for about half an hour. Then some people wanted my autograph and he lent me his pen.

That's when I saw he was wearing a wedding ring. I felt disappointed. A while later he asked me out. I refused and told him he was lucky I didn't slap his face. I stalked off and when I was talking to Nick I proudly told him what I'd said. He was horrified and informed me that the guy's wife had drowned two years ago."

Max laughed.

Jacqueline looked angry. "It's not funny. I found him and apologized and told him I'd go out with him, but he said he didn't want to have anything to do with someone as hard and suspicious as me. That's what you've made me – hard and suspicious. And foolish. A married man on the prowl takes off his wedding ring, doesn't he, Max?"

He stared at the tablecloth.

"Doesn't he?" she insisted.

"Yes," he whispered.

She leant over the table. "Have you been celibate?" she whispered.

The question was so unexpected, he knew he looked guilty. "It's different for a man."

Her mouth twisted in disgust. "Who are the lucky women?"

"Sue. Only Sue." He took her hand and squeezed it. "But I think of you. Darling, I'm a man. You know what I'm like."

She pulled her hand away. "You think of me – well that must be just wonderful for Susan," she said slowly. "What would you do if she got pregnant?"

He stared at her. "She wouldn't."

"Why not? She's a woman – women get pregnant. She may be pregnant already. Stay with her. Whatever else your marriage lacks, you're certainly compatible in one respect." She pushed back her chair. "I wish you luck, and I'm truly sorry about Zoe," she said softly.

As she went towards the door an elderly Jewish man at a nearby table stopped her. "Excuse me. I think I recognize you from your photo in the programme. You were the Mother in *The Consul*?"

"Yes."

He looked emotional. "My wife and I ... we tried to get out of Germany, but we were too late. We were in the camps ... we never saw our daughters again. You were good ... you understood the desperation. I wanted to tell you that."

Max watched jealously as Jacqueline, looking slightly embarrassed, smiled and thanked him. She left the restaurant as the waiter arrived.

When Phillipa heard Jacqueline's key in the door she jumped off the sofa and went into the hall. "You're back early. What happened? Did he want you to go back to him?" she demanded anxiously.

"Yes," said Jacqueline.

They went into the lounge where Wagner's *The Flying Dutchman* was playing on the stereo.

Phillipa turned down the sound. "What are you going to do?"

Jacqueline stood with her back to the fire. "I refused. For lots of reasons. One was because of the trauma I'd go through with my family. I couldn't face all that again. They stood by me and forgave me."

Phillipa hid her relief. "What did he say to that?"

Jacqueline sat on the sofa. "I didn't tell him. I was going to, I planned it and I'd anticipated his replies. I thought he'd start with general things, but he ploughed straight in. He didn't ask after anybody, not even you or Miss Shaw. He's only interested in himself," she said miserably. "I've never got over him, you know, Philly. I've tried really hard. Sometimes I wonder if I'll ever be free of him. Seeing him tonight – I wanted him so much." She grinned. "I put on a good act though."

"Bloody man," said Phillipa. "He's unsettled you again. You know, I was sure you'd made up your mind to go back to him."

"Why?"

"Because of his daughter dying and because … well … those new clothes you wore to see him. You look so glamorous and beautiful."

Jacqueline smiled. "I wanted him to see me looking good. When he saw me after *The Consul* I looked a wreck. I want him to remember me for the rest of his life – I want my memory to haunt him. His haunts me, so mine can bloody well haunt him. He hasn't changed, you know – he's still as handsome as ever. He looked fantastic – grief's given his expression depth and made him look even more interesting. Why couldn't he have gone bald or got impetigo? Why couldn't he be fat?"

"Harriet will be pleased – she was worried about you. Is it okay if I tell her what you've decided?"

Jacqueline nodded. "He's coming back to the opera school."

"Is he? When? I didn't know anything about it."

"He's written to Miss Shaw. I suppose he'll start next year. I hope I don't bump into him too often." She put her head in her hands. "Don't ever fall in love, Philly. It's hell, believe me, it's absolute hell."

'I know,' thought Phillipa.

Max received a reply from Harriet, giving him an appointment to see her the following week. 'When I'm at opera school I'll bombard Jacqui until she cracks. She must still feel something for me otherwise she'd have a boyfriend. Whatever she tries to pretend, she's not indifferent to me, she blushed when she saw me after *The Consul*. Once she sees me surrounded by the girls in opera school, she'll get jealous.'

He noticed that Susan was charged with energy and had lost a great deal of weight. Even her double chins had disappeared. She appeared to hardly notice him. He concluded that this was a new ploy to interest him and supposed she had read about the tactic in one of the woman's magazines that were forever telling women how to get a man and how to hold onto him once they had snared him. He felt sorry for her. Poor old Susan.

"I was very sorry to hear about your daughter, Max," Harriet said, as he was shown into her office.

He swallowed. "Thank you, Miss Shaw."

"I could have put my decision in a letter, but I wanted to tell you personally. I've considered everything carefully, but you've let me down twice and I know that you would do so again."

He felt alarmed. "Miss Shaw, I wouldn't, I promise. No. No. I'm going to divorce Sue. I'm going to be free."

"Free from your marriage, or free from yourself, Max?"

"I don't understand."

"It's not freedom from your marriage you need. On two occasions you gave up your singing career, first because of your father-in-law and then because of your wife. You allowed these people to rule you. Most men faced with a father-in-law who told them to give up their singing career would have told him to mind his own business, but you obeyed him like a child frightened of the cane. You were seventeen when you started having singing lessons, you're now thirty-five and no further on than you were at seventeen."

"No. I've had two years at opera school – "

"You did the first year twice. On both occasions you didn't even finish the year. You haven't progressed to the second year yet."

"But I've had seven years of singing lessons. I thought you were going to audition me. I've been doing my exercises since I got your letter."

"One week of exercises in three years?"

"I've been under a terrible strain for the past year."

"I understand that. But did you do any exercises before then?"

He went red. "Sometimes."

"The places in the school are too valuable to waste on people who don't have the commitment. You don't. If I took you back there'd be another reason for giving up. You've got the voice, Max, but you haven't got the dedication or the strength of character. I doubt that you'll ever be an opera singer."

He leant towards her desk. "I won't let you down again."

"That's what you said last time."

"Please, Miss Shaw, please." He was terrified he was going to break down and cry.

"I'm not the only singing teacher in Melbourne."

"But you're the best." She did not reply. She looked regretful, but she was not going to change her mind. He stood up, wanting to leave before he started crying. "Thank you for seeing me."

He left the theatre and drove home. It had never occurred to him that she would refuse to have him back. Good tenors were unusual enough, tenors as tall and good looking as him were rare. "My life's empty," he said as he turned into the driveway. When he went inside Susan was waiting.

"Max, we have to talk."

He sighed and sat on the sofa. "What about?"

"I'm going to be a nurse."

Nothing she could have said would have surprised him more. "What? You can't."

"Why not?"

"You haven't worked for years and you're too old. Student nurses are all young."

She sat in the chair opposite him. "Most are, but there are some late starters. I'm only thirty."

"I don't think they'll accept you."

"The Royal Melbourne Hospital already has."

"Oh." He was confused. "What's brought all this on?"

"Zoe. The nurses were so wonderful to her, to all of us. Knowing they cared helped me. I've lived a parasitic life and I want to start again. I forced you to marry me. I naively thought that when we were married I could make you love me. When you fell in love with Jacqueline I should have let you go. I made you suffer and I made Zoe suffer – I'm sorry, Max."

"I'm sorry too. Sue, why don't we try again? Let's have another baby."

She stood up and went over to the window. "No. I was a manipulative wife and a useless mother. No decent woman uses her child as a weapon against her husband. Once our divorce is finalized we can go our separate ways. I've found a flat near the hospital. I'm moving out next Saturday."

"I don't want a divorce. Sue, please don't leave me."

She looked at him in disbelief. "Don't be silly, Max, of course you do. What's the matter with you? You're free now. You can go back to opera school." She smiled. "Jacqueline might still be single."

He began to laugh and found he couldn't stop.

When Susan's belongings were loaded onto the removal van, she went into the lounge where Max was standing staring out of the window. "Good-bye, Max." She held out her hand.

Astonished by her calmness, he stared at her. "Fourteen years of marriage, and we're going to shake hands like strangers and go our separate ways."

"We've always been strangers, Max."

"Sue, please give me another chance. I know it was all my fault."

She shook her head. "You only want me because I'm leaving." She went outside and got into her car. The removal van moved off and she followed it.

He roamed around the house. Susan had taken what furniture she needed and left the rest. The half-empty rooms looked stark. Going into the dining room he poured himself a glass of gin and sat at the plate glass and chrome table, crying. Tears dripped onto the shining surface of the glass Susan had always kept polished. He finished the drink and refilled his glass. He had eaten nothing all day, and its effect was immediate, manifesting itself in double vision. Unsteadily he stood up and gripped the table as the room swayed. The lonely atmosphere of the house overcame him so he picked up his keys and went outside, not seeing the light mist of rain.

He walked for hours, not knowing or caring where he was going. Eventually he wandered into a park. He stared up into the wet branches of the trees. 'I'll go to Sydney and audition for The Australian Opera. No, why bother with The Australian Opera when Covent Garden's waiting? I'll marry and have more children, and I'll be a good husband,' he vowed.

Filled with euphoria, he walked out of the park trying to work out where he was. 'I have to get home. There's so much to do. As soon as I've sold the house I'll go to England. I'll rent a flat and audition for Covent Garden. Miss Shaw's wrong – I am going to make it. I'll show her!' He stepped onto the main road.

He neither heard nor saw the lorry that hit him.

Chapter 32

'Racked is my heart!'

Parsifal – Wagner

"Hello, Miss Shaw."

Harriet smiled as Jacqueline entered her office for her first assessment as an opera singer, dressed in her favourite casual style of jeans and navy jumper over a white cotton shirt. But there were changes marking a growing awareness of her appearance. The jeans fitted well, the angora jumper looked expensive and she wore shoes of polished black leather instead of desert boots or sneakers. The gold treble clef pendant, that Harriet had given her on the last night of *The Consul*, added decoration.

"Sit down, Jacqueline. Nicholas and Isaac will be here in a minute. I wanted a private talk with you before they arrive. Phillipa told me about your decision about Max and that you were worried about him coming back to the opera school."

Jacqueline nodded. "I'm bound to see him around, but I'll avoid him as much as possible."

"You won't – I turned him down."

Jacqueline looked astonished. "But – "

Harriet waved her hand. "He's got a brilliant voice, etcetera, etcetera. But that's all he's got and I told him so. And, Jacqueline, you've proved yourself. I didn't want you disturbed by him. You've matured and you're a credit to this theatre. One day you'll be a credit to the opera world. People will be talking about you, and young contraltos will be modelling themselves on you long after you're dead."

Jacqueline touched her pendant. "Gosh. I was so sure you'd have him back."

Harriet nodded. "So was he."

When Nicholas and Isaac came in, Harriet said, "Now, this is the bit I've been looking forward to. Next season we're doing Gluck's

Orpheus – you are Orpheus."

Harriet had expected Jacqueline to either burst into tears or be too overcome to speak. Instead she jumped up and threw her arms around her. "Miss Shaw, oh, Miss Shaw."

Isaac laughed and Jacqueline hugged him too. "Oh, Isaac, thanks. Nick, you too. I can't wait to tell Natasha!"

"You deserve it, Jacqui," said Isaac. "You were a delight to work with."

She looked at Nicholas. "That's because of Nick and Miss Shaw."

Isaac nodded and looked at Harriet. "Never have I worked with such a lovely group as here. Your opera school has taught them well."

Nicholas went into the studio where Richard, Frank, Rhonda and Emily were waiting. He, Isaac and Harriet had cast the four relatively new singers in *Don Giovanni,* agreeing that their voices and professionalism outweighed the risks. Feeling it was important to have a session with them alone before involving the other principals, he had asked them to come in the day before the first rehearsal. Trying to disguise his feelings of rivalry towards Richard, he sat at the table. "Has everyone done their character analysis?"

They nodded.

"Right, Richard, we'll start with you."

Richard opened his folder. "Giovanni reminds me of Max so that made it difficult for me to do a sympathetic character analysis."

"Why?" asked Nicholas.

"Because I didn't like him."

Frank grunted. "Neither did I. I was glad when he left."

Nicholas held up his hand. "Hang on, Frank. So why, Richard, does that make it more difficult?" He saw Richard's hesitation. "Don't be embarrassed."

"Because it's hard to think about his good points," said Richard.

"Okay," said Nicholas. "But look at the positives. You've got a character you actually knew, who was like Giovanni." He saw Richard's pages full of neat writing and headings. He had obviously done a great deal of work. "Let's hear what you've got."

380

"Giovanni was indulged by everyone since infancy because he was so good looking," Richard began, sounding more confident. "His charm is natural. He could have been a good person, but he was corrupted by his father who introduced him to sex at an early age by having one of his mistresses seduce him. Because he could have anything he wanted, his nature, which could have been different had he been set a good example, became twisted and centred on sex and depravity. He's a fantastic lover who gives his conquests extreme physical pleasure – that's why they pursue him." He grimaced. "I can't really think of any good points to give him, but I thought it was important to try and work out why he's so bad." He looked at Nicholas questioningly. "Shall I go on?"

Nicholas, agreeing with his assessment, nodded.

Richard turned the page. "His formative years were spent without a mother. Either she died, or was exiled and not permitted to influence him. She'd been around in his early childhood so he missed her terribly. No one told him what had happened, perhaps they even told him she was coming back. When she didn't, he felt she'd betrayed him. Part of the reason he seduces women and leaves them in the lurch is because he is frightened of loving in case it is taken from him." He shrugged. "That's it. It's a bit superficial, isn't it?"

"Not at all," said Nicholas, wishing he could deprecate his reasoning.

"I think it's deep," said Rhonda. "I can imagine a heart broken little boy waiting for his mummy to come back. It's distressing."

Nicholas realized Rhonda was attracted to Richard. He assessed her potential as his future girlfriend. 'If he started going out with someone else, I might have a chance with Natasha,' he thought. Feeling encouraged, he joined in the praise and then turned to Emily. "What are your feelings about Donna Anna?"

"Confused." Emily consulted her notes. "In the introduction of the score it says that she refuses his advances, but the words she sings imply otherwise. She says she'll never let him go till he tells her his name and she calls him a vile seducer. That sounds as if she let him have his wicked way with her and then regretted it. In those days loss of virtue resulted in vendettas and duels."

Nicholas had expected her to blush, but she remained composed, and he marvelled at the difference in her. Over the years, the changes had been gradual. He felt that he and Harriet had achieved a triumph.

She looked at Frank. "And Leporello says, 'Ravish a girl then murder her father,' so I'm not sure what to think. Maybe I'm just infatuated, because he's told me I'm beautiful or something."

Richard chuckled. "I reckon I've had you, Emily. I think you should be chasing me round the stage in your nightdress, with me trying to get my clothes on." He looked at Nicholas. "That'd ensure queues down the street."

Tempted to tell him to stop fooling around, Nicholas checked himself, knowing that once he would have joined in the fun. It was a long time since Richard had joked and he wondered if it was a sign that he was getting over Natasha.

"Does it matter if he's had sex with her?" asked Rhonda. "It's set in a period and class where people were betrothed without even knowing each other, so if Giovanni talks about love to a girl, was it interpreted as lovemaking?"

Frank nodded. "Interesting point. When I say 'seduced' do I mean mentally seduced or in love with?" He looked at Nicholas. "Was kissing before marriage permitted then?"

Nicholas thought. "I don't know. With all the chaperones it probably wasn't – or if it was it would be very brief. But, good question. I'll see if I can find out about Spanish morality in those days and what was permitted and what wasn't."

"I've thought of something," said Richard. "If Giovanni had sex with all these women, some of them would be pregnant."

"Yes!" Rhonda laughed. "Oh, Nick, let me play Elvira pregnant."

Nicholas looked at her with mock disapproval. "Certainly not."

At the end of the session, he said, "I suggest you all get together and discuss your characters before tomorrow – group sessions are helpful."

He was pleased when Richard suggested that they all go to *The Scheherazade*.

As he watched them leave, he decided that Richard was not attracted to Rhonda. 'It'll be a long time before he allows himself to get involved with anyone else – he's still hoping that Natasha will forgive him,' he thought.

♪ ♪ ♪

20ᵗʰ June 1974

Dear Nick,

*I can't thank you enough for letting me stay in your
beautiful house. I know how lucky I am. I've made friends
with a girl at **Queen Charlotte's** and she invited me to her
place for dinner. She lives in a tiny bedsit and shares a
kitchen and bathroom with six people. I almost fainted
when she told me what the rent was. It's more than we pay
at Gardenvale. I couldn't manage if I lived here
permanently. The wages are terrible and the cost of living
is extortionate.
One of the registrars took me out for a drink in a pub after
work. His name's Calum and he likes opera. He's taking
me to Hever Castle at the weekend.
I'll never get used to going into a church that was built
during the reign of William the Conqueror.
Please tell Miss Shaw that I received her letter and will
reply soon.*

Love

Natasha.

By Natasha's request her letters were always passed around when they
arrived. It saved her having to write the same thing over and over again.
Nicholas finished reading Natasha's letter, wondering how interested
she was in the doctor. The fact that he liked opera was an added worry.
"What does he look like?" he wondered. He imagined them walking
round Hever Castle with Natasha awed by the history of Anne Boleyn.
Would Calum kiss her? Had he kissed her already? He shoved it back
into the envelope and put it in his pocket. When he arrived at the theatre
he went into Harriet's office and gave her the letter. "Natasha's latest –

it came this morning. Give it to Philly when you've finished."

She took the letter. "Oh good."

"I'll see you after the rehearsal."

"You look glum, Nicholas. What's the matter?"

"Nothing."

Everything went wrong in the rehearsal of *Don Giovanni* and he lost his temper twice. At the end of the day Harriet came into his office.

"What's the problem, Nicholas?"

"Nothing," he replied irritably.

"Then why are you shouting at everyone?"

"I'm not shouting at everyone. Frank forgot to come on and Isaac defended him when I rebuked him. It's going to look terrific if he forgets his entrance during the performance."

"For goodness sake, Nicholas, it wasn't a performance – it was a rehearsal – a very early one at that. It's far to soon for the principals to know all their moves. Shouting is unprofessional, you know that. You were rude to Isaac and he's upset."

Nicholas felt guilt-stricken. "I'm sorry. I didn't mean it personally."

"He took it personally. Apologize to him." She pulled out the chair and sat down.

"Yes, I will."

She opened her handbag and took out Natasha's letter. "Is it anything to do with this?"

He frowned. "Why should it be?"

"She seems interested in this doctor." Harriet took the letter out of its envelope.

"So? What's that got to do with me?"

"Everything, Nicholas." There was a long silence. "I've suspected for a long time how you felt about her."

He shook his head. "You can't have. It happened the night she broke down in the middle of *Tosca*."

Harriet smiled. "I think that was when you realized. But you've loved her a lot longer than that. Why did you conveniently fall in love with her as soon as everything with Richard was off? You met Natasha when she was an ugly school-girl and you have seen her mature into a delightful and interesting young woman. You rearranged a rehearsal when she found out about Richard and Deborah, and when she broke down during *Tosca* you took her home with you. Why? Phillipa and Jacqueline would have looked after her. You've loved her for a long time, but you denied your feelings. She was going out with Richard and you're an honourable man."

"An honourable man – like Brutus. My first conversation with Natasha was about Brutus."

"What are you going to do?"

"Wait until she gets back."

Harriet put the letter on his desk. "She might not come back. She might marry this doctor on the rebound. It would be dreadful if she married some stranger, she might give up singing."

"Thanks for your optimism. I've got a lot of work to do – at this rate I'll be here all night."

"All right. Good night, Nicholas."

When she reached the door Nicholas said, "You won't tell anyone, will you? About Natasha – I mean."

"Of course not. You should know by now that I'm very good at keeping secrets."

When Harriet arrived home she thought about her conversation with Nicholas. She often worried that he might marry a girl she disliked. Natasha was one of her favourite students. If they got married she would be delighted.

'Perhaps I'm being selfish. But I want him to stay in Australia. If he marries Natasha, he would have real ties here. I want him to help me run this theatre and take over completely when I'm dead.'

"Nicholas," she said the next day. "If I can find a temporary director, would you like to go home for six months?"

He looked at her in surprise. "Yes."

"Let's compose an advertisement. We'll put one in *The Age* and one in *The Herald.*"

They were besieged with applicants. The tenth person to be interviewed impressed Harriet and Nicholas with his passionate love and knowledge of opera, his enthusiasm and his youth. Harriet offered him the job immediately.

That night Nicholas realized that when he was back in England he could look through his grandmother's journals and see if she had ever referred to Annabel.

Natasha gazed round the low beamed restaurant. "This place must be awfully old."

Calum smiled indulgently. "It's only Regency."

"That was the bloke before Queen Victoria, wasn't it?"

He laughed. "The bloke! How disrespectful."

"He was only a man. The way some people go on about the monarchy you'd think they were gods. They eat, drink and reproduce the same way as everyone else, but in more opulent surroundings."

Natasha enjoyed the evening. They talked about the differences between Australia and England and she deliberately kept the conversation impersonal. When they arrived home he declined her invitation to come in for coffee. He did not attempt to kiss her and she realized with surprise that she wanted to be kissed. In bed that night, she lay awake wondering if she was getting over Richard. Finally she fell asleep but, when she awoke from a dream about Richard with a feeling of raw pain, she knew she was not getting over him at all. The next day, Calum invited her to *The Barber of Seville* at The English National Opera. She accepted with a feeling of excitement.

Natasha felt nostalgic as the curtain rose, and longed to be on the stage instead of in the audience. As the opera progressed she realized with surprise that Nicholas's productions were just as good. Afterwards Calum took her to supper.

"Did you enjoy the opera, Natasha?"

"Yes."

"You seem unsure."

She sipped her Viennese coffee. "No, it's just that – well, I expected it to be a lot better than anything I'd ever seen, but it wasn't. In fact in some ways it wasn't as good." Seeing that he was interested not irritated, she went on, "Nicholas would have had more interplay between the characters. I prefer our costumes – they're more colourful. Our wardrobe mistress makes and designs all the costumes – she won't have any synthetics – says they look cheap and don't fall and flow

386

properly. She only uses natural materials – silk, cotton, wool and velvet ... sorry, I really sound picky – I loved tonight and the singers were terrific."

"It's fascinating. Go on – I've never met an opera singer before."

She picked up her cake fork and sliced through the thick icing of her Sacher Torte. As she told him about Harriet and her singing lessons and Jacqueline and Phillipa she suddenly felt emotional.

"I can't understand why you're here," he said quietly.

Choosing to misunderstand him, she said, "Because you asked me."

"I mean in London. You don't want to audition for Covent Garden, so – was it a broken love affair?"

She nodded. He was so sympathetic she almost started crying. She shook her head and blinked. "Sorry. I get too emotional sometimes."

"It's understandable. How long are you staying here?"

"Another six months. I like England but I get terribly home sick."

When he took her home Natasha invited him in. They walked up the path to the front door. She looked at the crescent moon shining through the trees. A feeling of physical longing swept over her. "Kiss me," she whispered.

He put his arm round her waist and stroked her cheek. Then he kissed her gently. She returned his kiss fiercely.

"Goodness," he said breathlessly. "We'd better go inside."

She was shaking as she put the key in the lock. They went into the drawing room and she tossed the jacket of her navy linen trouser suit on the sofa. "Would you like coffee?" she asked mischievously.

He ran his fingers through her hair and put his arms round her. "I don't think so." He kissed her lips and neck. Shaking with desire she pulled him onto the floor. Calum undid the buttons of her emerald-green silk blouse and pushed up her camisole. Her breasts were bare, and as he stroked them she gave a cry of pleasure.

"Richard!" she gasped.

He froze. "My name's Calum."

Natasha was appalled. "I'm sorry ... sorry."

He sat up. "I think we'd better have that coffee," he said stiffly.

Trying not to think that in two days Nicholas would be flying to England, Phillipa had a shower. That night she, Harriet and Jacqueline were taking him to *The Cuckoo* restaurant in Olinda. After drying her hair and putting on her make-up, she dressed in a cream satin dress that reached her calves. In a moment of recklessness, she undid the top pearl button then immediately changed her mind and did it up again. She looked in the mirror and scowled. "You're pathetic, Phillipa Matthews, utterly pathetic."

"Why?" asked Jacqueline from the doorway.

Phillipa spun round. Jacqueline was looking at her in amusement. She blushed and shook her head.

Jacqueline smiled. "You look as if you've come out of *The Great Gatsby*."

"I wear dresses this length because my legs are so horrible."

"What's the matter with them?"

"I've got no ankles."

Jacqueline opened her handbag and took out the car keys. "Everyone's got ankles."

"Well, you can't see mine. My legs look like tree trunks."

"Mine aren't exactly model's legs either."

"Yours have shape. You can see where your calves end and your ankles begin. Mine look like trunks with feet on the end."

Jacqueline looked exasperated. "You're a specimen of misery and dejection tonight. Your legs are there so you can walk on them. Start complaining when they pack up and don't get you where you want to go. Now, shut up about your legs and let's go. Shall I drive?"

"No, I will," said Phillipa, thinking that the twenty mile drive to the restaurant and the negotiation of the hairpin bends on the mountain would take her mind off her unhappiness.

"I'm really going to miss Nick," said Jacqueline as they reached the restaurant.

Phillipa parked the car. "So am I."

"He's probably homesick. I hope he comes back – it'd be awful if he stayed in England."

Phillipa had not considered that. 'Oh, God,' she thought as she got out of the car.

They arrived home at midnight and when Phillipa went into the kitchen to make the cocoa, she almost trod on the remains of a chewed mouse. Spreading out an old newspaper she was about to pick up the mouse by its tail when she saw a photograph of Max Carveth. She knelt on the floor and read the article about his death. She whimpered and closed her eyes in horror.

"What's happened?" asked Jacqueline behind her.

Phillipa yelped. "You made me jump!" She picked up the mouse, threw it on the paper and screwed it up.

Jacqueline looked at her in concern. "What's wrong, Philly?"

"I feel sick. Mozart left a half-eaten mouse on the floor."

"Yuk." Jacqueline held out her hand. "I'll chuck it in the bin."

"No!"

"What's the matter with you, Philly? You're as jumpy as – as a kangaroo with a twitch."

Phillipa burst into tears. "I don't know."

"You're upset about Nicholas going to England," said Jacqueline reasonably.

In bed that night, Phillipa was unable to sleep. Finally she decided not to tell Jacqueline about Max. He had been killed three weeks ago and if no one had told her by now it was unlikely that anyone knew. Although a verdict of accidental death had been returned, the possibility that he had committed suicide had arisen and Phillipa was worried that Jacqueline might blame herself. She wondered if she should tell Harriet and decided against it. Harriet might urge her to tell Jacqueline and she felt that was something she could not possibly do.

The next day Phillipa, Nicholas and Harriet went to Tullamarine Airport. Harriet was surprisingly cheerful and Phillipa, expecting her to be upset and in need of comfort, felt at a loss. As he disappeared through the exit, tears poured down her face.

Harriet put her arm round her. "He'll be back. Look forward – he's gone now, so we can start counting the weeks to his return."

Chapter 33

'Mysterious, unattainable,
The torment and delight of my heart.'
La Traviata – Verdi

After spending a week with his parents, Nicholas caught a taxi to Kew from Victoria Station and thought about his mother's reaction when he had asked her if she knew who Annabel was.

At first she was silent. "What do you know about Annabel?" she had asked finally.

"Nothing," he admitted. "Harriet mentioned her. A girl at opera school reminded her of Annabel."

"Deborah," said his mother.

He was surprised that Harriet had told his mother about it. Whatever had happened over forty years ago had affected them so much that even a girl who looked like Annabel was important enough to be reported. "Are you going to tell me?"

"No. Her voice was strained and a pulse throbbed in her neck. "If Harriet hasn't told you then I'm certainly not going to."

'Aunt Harriet told me a crime was involved,' he thought as the taxi crossed Hammersmith Bridge. He tried to analyze the statement. 'She didn't commit a crime, so that means either Annabel or the doctor did. Or does it? Yes, it must mean that. What sort of crime? Annabel must have done something terrible. No, maybe the doctor did something terrible, maybe he murdered someone and Annabel found out and told the police.

"No, that doesn't make sense. Aunt Harriet's hate is directed at Annabel not the doctor. Or is it? Would she hate Annabel because she reported a crime? She might do – if Annabel falsely accused the doctor. Did he go to jail for something he hadn't done? Worse – did he hang for something he hadn't done? Did he take the blame for something she did? How can I find out? The papers. I know his name and I've got a

390

rough idea of the dates.' He remembered the page of the journal he had found. 'My mother saw something. What? Who? Annabel. It must have been Annabel. What was she doing?'

As the taxi turned into Lichfield Road, his thoughts turned to Natasha. He paid the driver and got out with his cases. Natasha ran outside, threw her arms round him and kissed him. "Nick, I'm so glad you're here!"

Characteristically, her feet were bare, and she wore a crisp white blouse with navy trousers. Her hair was twisted into a knot on top of her head.

"Oh, Natasha, I've missed you." He lifted her up and swung her round.

She laughed in delight and kissed him again. "I think we'd better go inside," she said breathlessly. "We'll frighten the neighbours."

He put her down. "Blow the neighbours."

She picked up his two smaller bags and ran inside and up the stairs and put them on his bed. As she ran out of the bedroom she nearly crashed into him on the landing.

He laughed. "It's good to see you're still as energetic as ever."

"Dinner's ready."

He looked at her in mock astonishment. "You've actually cooked something?"

She laughed. "No, it's too hot, so it's a salad and then strawberries and cream for dessert. I bought some wine too. Is it all right if we eat in the garden?"

"Sounds wonderful."

"Are you going to unpack now?"

Nicholas, eager to keep the happy atmosphere said, "I'll do it later. Let's eat."

They carried their plates of salad into the garden. Natasha had stuck candles in two wine bottles and put them on the cast iron table.

"I've taken the next three days off. You don't mind me hanging around, do you?" she asked doubtfully.

"I'm delighted, why should I mind?"

She looked shy. "You might think I'm a nuisance."

Wondering how much her joy at seeing him had to do with her desire for companionship, he smiled. "Silly girl. I've been dying to see you." He filled her glass with wine and kept his tone casual. "Tell me all about this doctor you've been seeing."

"He's cultured, intelligent and kind, but I could never love him."

He felt relieved. 'Only one rival and he's on the other side of the world,' he thought. He was uncertain about what to say if she asked him about Richard. If he told the truth and said he was miserable she might feel sorry for him, but if he said he was fine she might feel jealous. "How do you feel about Richard now?"

Natasha grimaced. "The same, damn it. I wish I didn't, but I do. You tried to persuade me that Deborah hated me, but I was too arrogant to listen. But sometimes I feel that I was right. I pulled through, and that's something. But all that aside, I miss him and wish he was here. I wish we were married. Stupid aren't I?"

Nicholas shook his head. "If Richard came over here now and asked you to forgive him, would you?"

"I'd be tempted. I'm so unhappy without him, but I don't know if I could forgive him. I'm not a very forgiving person." She sipped her wine and looked at him seriously. "The world is full of women more beautiful and fascinating than I am. I want a man who won't be lured by all the gorgeous women, who'll love me as I am. I don't want to sit in a restaurant with a man who's distracted and stares if a beautiful woman comes in. I want us to grow old together, and him to still love me when I'm faded and wrinkled. He must love me, what I am inside, my character, not my face or my voice, but me."

'I'm the man you need,' he thought. 'I'd never look at other women.' He said, "I challenge your claim that there are a lot of women more fascinating than you."

She stared at him in surprise.

"Shall we have our strawberries now?" he asked, worried that he had been too revealing.

Natasha had also bought fresh coffee and brandy, which they took into the drawing room when it got dark. They spent the rest of the evening sitting near the French windows. To the strains of Rimsky-Korsakov's *Scheherazade* they talked about what to do with the next three days.

"Can we stay away from London?" asked Natasha. "I'm fed up with having to watch out for abandoned luggage in case it's a bomb."

He agreed. "Tomorrow we'll hire a punt in Oxford and go up the river. We can take a picnic and when we see a good spot we'll stop. If it's raining we'll explore the colleges instead and go to an old pub for lunch. Have you been to Blenheim Palace?"

"No, that's where Churchill was born, wasn't it?"

"Yes. Right, we'll go there too."

For Nicholas the three days passed too quickly. Natasha was interested in everything and he enjoyed being her guide. When he was showing her how to punt, she got the giggles and nearly fell into the river.

"I'm sorry," she gasped when he pulled the punt safely to the edge and jumped out onto the bank.

Laughing, he took her hand and helped her alight. "I thought the whole thing was going to turn over." He saw the weeping willow and the soft grass. "I think this is the perfect place for a picnic." They spread the rug out under the tree and had their picnic enclosed by the cool green branches.

"It's great not having to worry about snakes," said Nicholas.

Natasha peeled an orange. "Everything in England's so green. The trees and grass are green together. At home the trees are green and the grass is brown in the summer and in winter the trees are bare when the grass is green." She lay on her back and wriggled her bare toes. The dappled sunlight glinted on her hair. Nicholas ached to kiss her and imagined unbuttoning her blue and white striped shirt.

"Wouldn't this be a divine place to make love?" she murmured.

He was startled

"With Richard, I mean." She nudged him. "Did you think I was propositioning you?"

When Natasha returned to work Nicholas began his search for information about Annabel. First he scanned the journals again. After years of frustration he was not expecting to find anything and was excited when he discovered that she was to have been one of Harriet's bridesmaids. Because his deductions about Annabel had been based on Harriet's hatred, the discovery that they had once been friends confounded him.

Remembering the stacks of old photograph albums in the wardrobe, he went up to the bedroom that had been his grandmother's. Identifying the newest looking one, he took it out and opened it. The photographs were affixed at all corners. He took out the first one and turned it over.

Harriet and Charlotte – Richmond Park 1920

Halfway through the album he saw the photo. 'Annabel,' he thought excitedly.

Harriet and Annabel. Christmas Party 1922.

'No wonder Harriet was horrified when she saw Deborah. They even have the same expression.'

He studied the two girls. Both had dark hair, but the similarity ended there. Annabel was conventionally beautiful but her expression was calculatingly sexual. Like many of the photos downstairs Harriet's face radiated excitement, joy and strength. Abandoning the newer albums he selected an older one. He studied every photo carefully and finally found what he had been searching for. A photo of Harriet and Annabel together as children. Doggedly he worked his way through every album until he found the earliest picture of Harriet and Annabel; a picture of his grandmother and another woman each standing with a pram.

Elizabeth and Celia with Harriet and Annabel 1894.

'Celia,' he thought. 'Grandma had a cousin Celia. If this is the same Celia, that means Annabel was Harriet's second cousin.' That Harriet and Annabel were related had never occurred to him. Taking the photo of Harriet and Annabel downstairs, he began to search through the earlier journals. Even his grandmother's references to Annabel as a child were not flattering.

> *Annabel is so conceited. She is always looking at herself in the mirror and today I heard her say to Harriet, "I'm prettier than you." Harriet laughed and replied, "But I've got more friends." Clever Harriet.*

394

I feel sorry for Celia. Annabel is a strange child and so inward looking. Her vanity is not entirely her fault. People gasp when they see her and then say to Celia, 'Oh, what a beautiful little girl!'

When he reached the journals written during the First World War, he lost track of time. There was a significant reference to Annabel at the funeral of her brother who had been killed in the Somme.

The funeral was held in St Anne's. So many maimed young men attended. This war is so mind shatteringly tragic. Celia was very brave, but so white I was frightened she was going to collapse. During the service Annabel became hysterical and had to be taken out of the church. She was absolutely no comfort to Celia. Yet I have the feeling that she was gratified to be the centre of attention. She is definitely unstable. The sooner she marries the better. But it will have to be to a strong man who can control her.

He heard the front door bang. He slipped the photo of Annabel and Harriet into the book and returned it to the shelf, as Natasha came into the room.

In spite of his successful career, Richard was unhappy. Although he never again made the mistake of snapping at his colleagues, and made the effort to appear normal, he suffered from loneliness. Every time he drove through Gardenvale on his way to the theatre he recalled the enjoyable times there and the holidays at Koonya Beach.

Reports of the IRA bombings in London worried him. When he heard that a bomb had exploded in The Tower of London, injuring many tourists, he rang Phillipa in a panic. To his relief Jacqueline had rung Natasha as soon as she heard the news, and she and Nicholas were alive and well.

He knew he should try and make new friends, but found the effort of going to parties and trying to appear happy too much. Jacqueline's hostility was natural, but it hurt. Nicholas's change of attitude was bewildering, and he came to the conclusion that, for some reason, Nicholas had decided that he had been guilty of having a long standing affair with Deborah. He wanted to ask him about it, but Nicholas's demeanour towards him did not encourage confidences. He was grateful that Phillipa still spoke to him and was pleased when she expressed the opinion that when Natasha had time to think, she would forgive him. He clung to that fragile hope.

At the end of Richard's singing lesson Harriet handed him back his score of *Don Giovanni*. "That was excellent."

"Thank you, Miss Shaw. Could I make an appointment to see you, please?"

She looked at her watch. "My next pupil is not due for an hour."

"Will you release me after this production? I want to go to England and see Natasha."

"Richard, I don't force people to stay, you only sign a contract for the duration of the production. I want willing singers, not ones here under duress. Have you heard from her?"

He shook his head. "If I went to see her I might be able to persuade her to forgive me. I want to make her believe that Deborah was lying about the other times. I was going to ask you for her address."

"I'll have to have her permission first. I'll ring her tonight. Come and see me tomorrow."

"Thank you, Miss Shaw."

When he had gone Harriet sat back in her chair remembering the day Natasha had burst into the theatre for her audition. 'I would never have guessed then that not only did the skinny, ugly little scrap have a divine voice, but that years later she would have two men loving her to distraction,' she thought.

Nicholas was tempted not to tell Natasha about Richard wanting her address. Harriet had rung just after Natasha had gone to work and his conscience tortured him all day. But, if he won Natasha, he wanted it to be an honest victory. When she arrived home exhausted after a frantic day, he made a pot of tea and they sat at the kitchen table.

"Aunt Harriet rang today. Richard asked for your address, he wants to come over. Harriet told him she had to ask you first. She didn't know if you would want him to know, so I told her I'd ask you and phone her tomorrow."

Natasha looked overjoyed.

He forced himself to smile. "I thought you'd be happy."

"Oh, Nick, I've missed him. I don't know if I can forgive him – but the thought of him coming thrills me. If he's going to sacrifice an opera season for me, he really must love me."

"He may be intending to audition for Covent Garden. Seeing you might just be something else on his agenda, so don't get your hopes up too much. Still, if he did that, you could go back and sing with Harriet for a few years. He's messed up your career long enough."

She looked puzzled. "You've changed. After it happened you were on his side."

He went over to the sink. "I could hardly believe what had happened. You weren't the only one in a state of shock. I've had time to reflect. You gave up everything, not Richard. He's a professional opera singer now and you're not. He was the one found in a compromising situation, not you. I believe he's innocent, but that doesn't mean he is."

She looked doubtful and he felt guilty. 'I'm an unprincipled bastard,' he thought. He sat next to her. "I'm not trying to spoil your happiness."

She put her head on his shoulder. "What am I going to do?"

"Natasha, I can advise you, but I can't tell you what to do."

"What do you advise then?"

"Remember how you felt when you got engaged?"

She nodded.

"Don't marry him unless you feel like that."

She put her arms round him. "Thanks."

Desire swept through him He forced himself to hug her casually and then pulled away before he lost control and kissed her.

Chapter 34

'Oh! Love's dire anguish!'

Parsifal – Wagner

Early in September the phone ringing dragged Nicholas from sleep. Switching on the bedside lamp he screwed up his eyes and saw that it was four in the morning. He rushed into the hall as Natasha hurtled down the stairs. She picked up the receiver and he heard the panic in her voice: "Hello!"

Praying that nothing had happened to Harriet, he held his breath.

"No it isn't, you moron!" She hung up and spun round. "He wanted a taxi – I thought something awful had happened at home."

He sighed in relief. "So did I."

She went back to bed, but Nicholas, knowing he would be unable to get back to sleep, put on his dressing gown and made a pot of tea. Taking it into the garden he sat on the bench and thought about the difficulties of living in the same house as Natasha. He did not ask her out; they simply did things together. There was a casual intimacy between them in that they unselfconsciously wandered round the house in their pyjamas and dressing gowns and had no hesitation in visiting each other's bedrooms. But there was no opportunity to ask her out formally and he wondered if, from her viewpoint, they were like brother and sister. He was normally asleep when she left for work at half past eight and he wondered if he should wake up earlier and take her in a cup of tea. 'I could make the breakfast this morning.'

Enjoying the peace and the scent of the air as yet unpolluted by traffic fumes, he listened to the waking birds. "Should I tell her how I feel? No. If she doesn't feel the same she'll be embarrassed."

When he went inside to make the breakfast there was a letter on the mat from Richard. Taking it upstairs he knocked on Natasha's bedroom door.

"Come in."

She was sitting on the floor putting on her shoes. "Hi, Nick."

"A letter from Richard." Stepping over piles of books and discarded clothes, he dropped it on her lap.

She looked at it. "Thanks."

He hesitated, hoping she would tear it up, but she opened it. Deciding not to bother about breakfast he went back to bed.

Natasha dreamed her way through the day and looked forward to meeting Nicholas in The White Cross pub in Richmond after work.

She was walking across Richmond Green when she saw Nicholas about thirty yards ahead. She ran after him and grabbed him round the waist.

"Natasha, you little devil, you scared the wits out of me!"

"Richard's leaving Melbourne the day after *Don Giovanni* finishes. He'll be here in eight weeks!"

"What are you going to do about Calum?"

"Oh, I don't know. I'd forgotten about him."

He scowled. "Go to the pub by yourself – see if you pick up another man and make him fall in love with you. Should be easy – London's full of lonely men."

Natasha looked at his retreating back in bewilderment. His anger dampened her elation. She walked along the river to Kew hoping that by the time she reached home he would have calmed down.

Nicholas arrived home cursing himself. Lighting a cigarette he stared into space while he waited for Natasha to return. He heard the front door open and went into the hall. "I'm sorry, Natasha."

"Nick, you were right."

"No I wasn't. Come and sit down."

They went into the drawing room and sat on the sofa.

"Nick, I've been thoughtless and self-centred. Ever since you arrived home, all I've done is talk about my feelings. We haven't talked about yours at all. It must be painful coming back. England must be full of memories of the girl you were going to marry, and all I've done is prattle on about me. I must have been so boring."

He shook his head. "I was in a foul mood and I took it out on you. My affair ended a long time ago. She was shallow and silly. No, that's unfair – she wasn't."

She lowered her head. "I feel shallow and silly sometimes."

He took her hand and squeezed it. "You're not." The urge to kiss her was almost overwhelming. "Richard can stay here if you like."

"He's going to book into a hotel in London and ring me. I'd rather he didn't come here. I don't know how things are going to turn out yet."

"You were so excited this afternoon, I thought you'd made up your mind to marry him."

"I've been thinking. I don't know if I can ever trust him again."

The spark of hope ignited. He smiled. "Shall we go out to dinner? There's a lovely place on Kew Green."

"Oh, yes. I'm starving. I'll just go and change."

Nicholas was ready before Natasha. While he was waiting he went over to the bookcase and took the photo of Annabel and Harriet out of the journal and stared at it. "What did you do, Annabel – what the hell did you do?" he said aloud.

"Nick?"

He turned and saw Natasha standing in the doorway. Feeling foolish because she had found him talking to a photograph, he slipped it back into the journal. "I didn't hear you come down. Are you ready?"

She looked uncertain. "Don't you know about Annabel?"

"No. Do you?" he replied half-jokingly.

"Yes," she whispered.

He shook his head. "We're not thinking about the same person." Something in her expression alerted him. "Are we?"

She bit her lip. "Miss Shaw's cousin?"

"Yes."

She came towards him. "Oh, Nick, I've wanted to talk about it ever since I found out. Please don't think I was snooping – I found them accidentally."

He stood very still. "What happened?"

"Annabel was in love with Miss Shaw's fiancé. They had an affair, but he still wanted to marry Miss Shaw. A few weeks before the wedding Annabel came here in the middle of a dinner party." Natasha shut her eyes. "Annabel ... shot herself in front of them all – your mother was only a child."

'That's what she saw,' he thought. He visualized blood and brains spattering the room. 'How hideous. How absolutely hideous.' He looked at Natasha. "How did you find out?"

"Newspaper cuttings." She went over to the piano and picked up a photo. "I dropped this and broke the glass. They were between the photo and the backing."

"But Aunt Harriet said that a crime was involved."

Natasha frowned. "It was suicide, wasn't it? We had a debate at school on whether it should be decriminalized."

"Of course." He was irritated with himself for not thinking of something so simple. "But I don't understand why she was so desperate to keep it secret. It wasn't her fault."

Natasha took a deep breath. "Nick, there's something else."

"What?"

Natasha went to the bookcase and took out an album of piano sonatas. She opened it, took out the cuttings and handed them to him.

He read them with a feeling of incredulity. He knew that the facts must be true but he had difficulty believing them. Shocked, he stared at the separate photos of Harriet and Annabel, understanding how Harriet would have felt if this had been made public. His first impulse was to ring her and apologize.

"Nick? Are you all right? You look as if you're all tangled up inside."

He folded up the cuttings. "I am."

"That's how I felt when I found out."

They stood in silence for a few moments, and then Nicholas looked at his watch. "Come on, kitten, get your coat."

"Are you sure you still want to go out?"

"Yes, we need a walk and food – and I desperately want a drink."

She went into the hall and put on her coat. As they walked out of the gate she slipped her hand into his and squeezed it. They arrived at *Pissarro's* on Kew Green and sat at one of the secluded tables in the area known as the stables. All the furniture was scrubbed pine, and the high backs on the pews made for intimacy. The menu was on a blackboard and had to be ordered at the counter. The wine bar's delicious food and relaxed atmosphere made this one of Nicholas's favourite places, but he was feeling so upset he was hardly aware of what he was eating or drinking.

For the first time he saw himself through his mother's eyes – curious about something that had nothing to do with him. Inquisitive, like a journalist digging out secret tragedies while caring nothing for the feelings of people whose lives he was so intent on prying into. He appreciated Natasha's silence and when they arrived home he felt less depressed. While he lit the fire, Natasha put on a record and poured out two cognacs. Replacing the fire-screen, he sat opposite her.

"I wonder if that man suffered as much as Miss Shaw did," said Natasha. "He probably married someone else and has grandchildren now."

He swirled the cognac round. "Did the photo of Annabel remind you of anyone?"

"Deborah. When I first saw the cutting I thought it was her."

He went to the bookcase and picked up the photo. "This is a better one."

Natasha took it. "God. It's Deborah in every way. The expression, the … everything. It's like she was an identical twin."

He nodded.

She gazed at the fire. "Sometimes when I feel really unhappy, I make myself remember her tragedy." She looked around the room. "I feel Miss Shaw's presence so strongly in this house. But strangely – she's young. It's as if she left something behind, and that's endured for all these years. Perhaps it always will."

A chill crept down his spine. "I used to feel her here too. You're right – she did leave a lot of herself behind. Almost everything."

On the train on the way to visit his mother, Nicholas thought about the scale of Harriet's tragedy. 'In one night she lost her best friend and her fiancé and discovered they'd betrayed her.' He wondered who had broken the engagement. 'Probably Harriet. Or it might have been both of them. Annabel's suicide would have destroyed Harriet's trust and poisoned the marriage.'

He found his mother in the greenhouse.

"Nicholas, what a surprise," she said. "You should have told me you were coming." Her smile faded. "What's wrong?"

"I've come to apologize."

She checked the temperature and shut the door of the greenhouse. "Apologize for what?" They went into the kitchen and she washed her hands. "Would you like some tea?"

"No. Sit down, Mother."

"This sounds ominous." They went into the drawing room.

Not wanting to involve Natasha in the discovery, in case his mother thought she was snooping, he said, "Last night I knocked the photo of Aunt Harriet off the piano and broke the glass. Under the backing were newspaper cuttings about Annabel's suicide – and – everything else. I understand why you didn't want to tell me and I want to apologize for my insensitivity."

"I put them there," said his mother slowly. "I'd forgotten all about them. Everything that was ever written about Harriet I kept in a scrap book, but these were too awful. But I couldn't bring myself to throw them away. I didn't want my parents to know I had them either, so I hid them behind the picture."

He put his hand on her shoulder. "I'm sorry. Thinking about it must be horrible, but I wanted you to know that I knew. I won't mention it again."

"I hated Annabel," she said, as if he hadn't spoken. "She treated me as if I was a pest. Harriet used to play with me, teach me the piano, help me with my homework and sing for me. When she became engaged she took me shopping and told me I could help with her babies when they came. I was so excited about being a bridesmaid. I liked Andrew too. When he came round it was fun, but when Annabel was there I hated it. 'Do we have to have that child tagging along,' she'd say in her bored voice. All those years ago, but I can remember that voice.

"When she shot herself I didn't know why. I remember her coming into the dining room and Andrew shouting 'Annabel,' and then there was a loud bang. There was a time when nothing happened … silence … no one screamed. Just silence. Annabel wasn't there anymore – just this – blood everywhere." She shivered. "All over Andrew, Harriet – we were all covered in it. I didn't understand … " She put her hand to her head and ran her fingers repetitively through her hair. "I almost laughed. For a few seconds I thought it was a joke – but my ears hurt and something smelt strange. Our housekeeper rushed into the room – it seemed like ages later, but it must have been less than a minute. Then everyone moved. It was like the game we used to play at school – the teacher would play the piano and we'd have to skip or jump and when the piano stopped we'd have to freeze and if we moved we were out. Then when she began playing the piano we all jumped about again – it was just like that.

"My mother rushed me out of the room and our housekeeper got me out of my bloody clothes, washed me and put me to bed. She was whimpering and wouldn't talk to me. She wouldn't let me leave the room. There was a lot of noise downstairs. Harriet was crying and I wanted to be with her. Doors were banging and there were a lot of strange voices – police and ambulance men, but I didn't know that then. Finally I must have gone to sleep although I tried not to.

"In the following weeks Harriet laughed a lot, but I knew she wasn't really laughing. She told everyone that she was bored with Andrew and had been about to break the engagement. I knew that wasn't true either. In those weeks she became like Annabel – hard and false. Then one Sunday when we were having lunch she picked up her plate and hurled it at the wall. Then she began screaming. She screamed and screamed and didn't stop – not even when some men rushed into the house and dragged her away.

"She was gone for two years. My parents told me she was in hospital getting better. One day I heard my father say to my mother, 'Don't let Charlotte see the newspaper.' Of course that made me want to see it. I looked for it but couldn't find it. Then a girl at school started teasing me. 'You've got a mad sister in the lunatic asylum,' she'd say. I didn't believe her, but she brought cuttings from the newspaper to school and showed me. She was going to show everyone else, but I took them from her.

"I missed Harriet so much. My parents were distracted, and the house was quiet. That's what I noticed most. There used to be so much fun. Then there was nothing. No parties, no wedding, no visitors, no Andrew. I never saw him again.

"Then my mother told me Harriet was coming home. I was so excited I didn't listen to her warnings that Harriet had changed. All I could think about was that she was coming home and everything would be like it used to be. When she arrived I didn't recognize her. She was thin and pale and her hair was white and very short. She was old. She looked at me without seeing me. For months all she did was sit at the window in the drawing room and stare into the garden. She didn't speak and she hardly moved. She wasn't my Harriet any more."

Her voice, that had been wavering, broke completely. Her mouth twisted as she screwed up her face. She put her hands over her eyes and cried. "I wanted to tell you when you were going to Melbourne. I wanted you to understand her, but Harriet made me promise not to tell you – she was so ashamed. Insanity. It's such an awful word."

He sat on the arm of her chair and tried to think of something comforting to say. He had rarely seen her cry. At her mother's funeral she had been strong while he had almost broken down. He took his handkerchief out of his pocket and gave it to her. She wiped her eyes.

He went over to the window. "I wish I'd known before I met her. I was too forceful. I would have been gentle with her. God. When we were arguing about Deborah I lost my temper and mentioned Annabel. I wish I hadn't."

She blew her nose. "Oh, Nick. Did you argue much?"

"Yes, didn't she tell you?"

"No." She folded up the handkerchief and looked at him accusingly. "Is that why you came back? To find out about Annabel?"

"Obviously, Aunt Harriet didn't tell you that, either."

She looked alarmed. "Nicholas, you haven't fallen out completely?"

"No. I've fallen in love with Natasha."

Chapter 35

'Have you no kindly word for me?
No look, no smile, no greeting,
not – one sign?'
Der Rosenkavalier – Strauss

When Phillipa returned from the airport after seeing Richard off, she was met at the front door by Jacqueline brandishing a magazine.

"I just can't believe this drivel!"

"Don't read it then," said Phillipa.

"Listen to this. I'm going to be sick."

"Are you going to tell me, or are you going stand there exclaiming dramatically all afternoon?"

Jacqueline followed her into the lounge. "Wait till you hear this."

"I am waiting."

"A honeymoon in Europe, follows the marriage of Deborah Ryland to – "

"What?"

"There's a photo," said Jacqueline. "They met in an amateur operatic company. They were playing opposite each other in *The Merry Widow*."

"It's a wonder they didn't have to change its name to *The Merry Tart*," said Phillipa.

"He's a solicitor."

Phillipa smirked. "Hope he specializes in divorce."

"He looks nice," said Jacqueline gloomily.

"He's too good for her then."

Jacqueline threw the magazine on the floor. "It's bloody unfair. She caused so much misery."

"Life is unfair, Jacqui. Perhaps he's a swine."

"He doesn't look like one."

Phillipa picked up the magazine and studied the photo. "He looks nice. And she looks beautiful," she said grudgingly. "A magnificent lace and satin gown – Ugh!"

"We sound like a pair of bitter old spinsters," said Jacqueline.

Phillipa grimaced. "We are bitter old spinsters – well, not old, just bitter. We sound horrible. Are we?"

"No. If we read about someone else getting married, we'd be pleased. We're just being human."

Phillipa grinned. "Yes, human and horrible."

Jacqueline sat on the floor. "Four years ago I thought I was going to be happy. If I'd been able to choose my destiny I would never have chosen this. Sitting here being bitchy, with Natasha in England equally unhappy. When I look back, I realize that the only time I experienced real, pure happiness were those first months of opera school. Everything was perfect. Then I discovered Max was married. I've never felt that type of happiness since. Isn't it awful that my pure state of happiness, when every single thing was right – adds up to a few weeks out of the twenty-four years of my life. Isn't that depressing?"

"Yes," said Phillipa. "My perfect state of happiness lasted ten days."

"After your sister was born?" asked Jacqueline softly.

She nodded. "I wanted a sister so much. Then I got her and ten days later I lost everything. I'll never experience perfect happiness again, but I hope you do, Jacqui."

"Oh, Philly."

The mood was getting too emotional. Phillipa went to the stereo and switched it on. "How would you define perfect happiness?" she asked.

"Having what you want and not wanting anything else," said Jacqueline.

"Yes," said Phillipa thoughtfully.

"When I started going out with Max, Natasha and I were doing what we'd always wanted. She was happy with Richard and I was falling in love with Max. We enjoyed our jobs, and opera school was exciting. Then I found out Max was married and everything changed. Natasha and I started fighting and I was jealous because my family liked Richard and hated Max. I know I behaved badly, but at the time I felt I was being persecuted. After Max went back to his wife I felt more at peace, but I was still jealous of Natasha and Richard."

407

Phillipa wondered if she should tell Jacqueline that Max was dead. She tried to gauge the reaction.

"Are you all right, Philly, you look a bit – strange."

Deciding she was not brave enough to break such terrible news, she nodded. Anxious to get off the subject of Max, she went back to the sofa without putting a record on. "It's good that you can look at things and see how they really were. You'll find someone soon. There are loads of nice blokes in the opera company."

"Why don't you go out with one of them then? I mean it, Philly – why?"

She shook her head.

"Do you mind if I say something?" asked Jacqueline.

"If you're going to go on about Frank, please don't."

"I've given up there," said Jacqueline ruefully. "Well, you're very attractive … but you're – I can't find the right word."

"Frumpy?"

"Don't be a dill."

"Aloof?"

"No, but that's sort of along the right track." She bit her thumb and concentrated. "You look as if you belong to someone."

Phillipa was startled. "No one should belong to anyone."

"I didn't mean it like that. You look as if you're – emotionally taken. I know you're not, but you look as if you are. Does that make sense?"

Phillipa laughed, to hide her embarrassment. "No, you idiot," she said. She changed the subject abruptly. "How will you feel if Richard and Natasha get back together?"

"I'll forgive him. If Natasha can, I'll have to."

Harriet looked at the letters from The Australian Opera addressed to Jacqueline, Richard, Emily and Frank. The one for Richard she gave to Phillipa, asking her to write and tell them he was in England, but that she would hold the letter till he returned. Guessing from experience that they were being offered roles, Harriet was pleased for them, but knew they would be a terrible loss to the theatre. She consoled herself by thinking that when Natasha came back she would have her for a year.

Hiding her regret when Frank came for his singing lesson she gave him the letter.

Frank read the letter and grinned. "Wow. They're offering me Méphistophélès in *Faust*."

She smiled. "You deserve it, Frank. I'll miss you, but I knew this was coming. Congratulations."

"You won't miss me, Miss Shaw."

"Frank, I will, very, very much," she insisted, surprised by his reply.

He shook his head and his grin widened. "You won't. I'm not going – I'm staying here."

She was astonished. "Why? Frank, this is an enormous opportunity for you. Australian Opera for a few years and Covent Garden after that."

"Miss Shaw, I don't want to sing at Covent Garden, I don't want to leave Australia. I want to stay here for ever. I don't want to travel. Europe holds no interest for me. I love it here – you trained me and made me what I am so why should I desert you? I want to live in Melbourne for the rest of my life. I can stay with you, can't I?"

Harriet felt touched. "Yes, of course, if that's what you truly want."

"It is, Miss Shaw, it is. Truly."

She smiled. "And I was preparing to lose you, Jacqueline, Emily and Richard all at once."

She was further delighted when Jacqueline and Emily turned down principal roles and told her that, while they wanted to sing with The Australian Opera and Covent Garden one day, they were going to stay with Harriet for another four years, because they owed their success to her and wanted to repay her.

In the eight weeks since Natasha had shown Nicholas the cuttings about Harriet, there had been an increasing rapport between them. They went to the opera and ballet at Covent Garden and the English National Opera and afterwards talked for hours, about the performances, productions and costumes. At weekends Nicholas took her sight-seeing or to visit his parents. One Saturday morning as he was sitting in the conservatory reading a book about Verdi, and enjoying the mild early November sunshine, Natasha wandered in, still in her dressing-gown. "The house is disgusting – we'd better have a clean up. We didn't wash-up last night and it's a month since we vacuumed."

"I hate cleaning. Shall we go up to Oxford Street instead?"

She giggled. "You're nearly as bad as I am."

"I'm worse. Get dressed and we'll go and do some Christmas shopping."

Oxford Street was crowded. "I've never seen so many people," Natasha complained.

They went into John Lewis and bought most of their Christmas presents.

"This is more fun than cleaning," said Natasha. "Let's go and have afternoon tea."

He nodded. "The pubs are shut, but I know a cafe nearby. It's down a side street, so it's not full of tourists."

They sat down thankfully, exhausted from struggling through the crowds.

Natasha picked up the menu. "Oh, fantastic," she exclaimed. "Cappuccino coffee. The things I miss in England are cappuccino coffee, malted milks and pavlovas. I'm going to have scones with jam and cream." She looked at him mischievously. "This will give us energy to do all the cleaning when we get home."

"Let's go out to dinner."

"Can we go to *Pissarro*'s on Kew Green?"

He nodded. "We'll go early so we can get a seat in the stables. It gets full on Saturday nights."

She grinned. "What about the cleaning?"

"We'll think about it next year."

They arrived at *Pissarro*'s early and got a coveted seat in the stables. Natasha had fish for her main course and Nicholas chose steak and kidney pie. They bought a bottle of red wine.

Natasha pushed her empty plate away and rested her elbows on the table. "I'm going to have chocolate mousse."

"The passion cake's delicious."

"Passion cake. That sounds naughty," she said suggestively. "What happened to you when you had some, did it make you feel passionate?"

He smiled at her through half closed eyes. It was the first time she had been provocative with him and he wondered if this signalled a change in their relationship. "Yes. I was with Sally. We'd just been to visit my grandmother to tell her we were getting engaged."

"Did Sally have passion cake too?"

"Yes."

"Did you have an enjoyable time afterwards?"

He laughed. "Extremely."

She raised her eyebrows and they smiled knowingly at each other.

"Nick, were you ever interested in Philly?"

He shook his head. "Philly's a bit dull. That might sound mean but she's always organizing and tidying. I always felt she was much older than me. She's so sensible. She even used to mother Aunt Harriet. If I'd wanted to marry a mother figure I'd choose Phillipa. But I want a companion, not someone who's always tidying up after me. Am I being disloyal?"

"No. I feel the same. Sometimes I used to feel on edge at Gardenvale. I know my untidiness must drive people mad, but she was worse than Mum. It hardly makes for wild romance does it? You never nag about my untidiness."

He laughed. "As I'm even more untidy than you, it would be hypocritical of me. I'll go and order our puddings."

She nodded. "I'm going to the ladies."

He had just ordered and was on his way back to their table, thinking about Natasha and hoping that tonight would change their relationship. She had teased him about the passion cake. 'What would happen if I kissed her when we get home?' he thought.

Someone tapped him on the shoulder. "Nick?"

He turned round. "Tanya!" he exclaimed throwing his arms round her. "You look well." He kissed her. "Being married suits you."

"You wretch, why didn't you write and tell me you were coming? I haven't had a letter for ages."

"Sorry, it was a sudden decision. What are you doing now?"

"I'm at Richmond Theatre all next week, I'm Anne, in *Richard the Third*."

"Congratulations."

"Are you back from Australia for good? I thought you were going to stay there forever."

"No, I'm on holiday. Listen, why don't you and your husband drop round after the show one night next week? I'd love to meet him. I'll make some supper and we can catch up."

She kissed his cheek. "I will. Love to."

He went back to their table. "Sorry I was so long, I bumped into an old friend. She's coming round next week for supper."

Natasha nodded and he saw that she looked shocked. "Are you all right? You look as if you've fallen face downwards in a bag of flour."

She took a deep breath. "I was just thinking about something." She sounded breathless. He filled her glass and wondered about her abrupt change of mood. The teasing intimacy had gone and an almost morose atmosphere had taken its place.

"Thank you for tonight, Nick," she said softly.

He raised his glass. "Here's to you and Richard. Good luck, Natasha. Are you excited about tomorrow?"

She looked at him intently. "No," she said deliberately.

He reached over and took her hand. He longed to tell her not to trust Richard; that he had been unfaithful once and might be again, but instead he said, "Don't be nervous, I know how you must feel, it's only natural. You haven't seen him for nearly a year." He wished she'd say that she'd changed her mind and had decided not to see him.

She said nothing. Dejected by the change in her, he released her hand. They waited in silence for their passion cake.

Natasha lay in bed. The curtains were open and the moonlight streamed in. She stared at the sharp black outline of the leafless trees silhouetted against the clear sky as she recalled the blinding revelation that had struck her in the restaurant. On her way back to their table she had seen Nicholas hugging an attractive girl. She'd felt as if someone had hit her over the head with a sack of wheat. She loved Nicholas.

The knowledge stunned her. Feeling panic stricken she wondered if the girl was his ex-fiancée. Nicholas was very definitely interested in her. Finally she fell asleep.

Richard rang the next day and she unenthusiastically arranged to

412

meet him in the foyer of his hotel on Monday evening at seven.

Natasha arrived home from work, feeling that her life was chaotically out of her control. She had a shower, washed her hair and rushed into her bedroom. As she put on the dress she had bought at Laura Ashley she realized that subconsciously she had bought it and the black high-heeled shoes with Nicholas in mind, not Richard. For Richard she would have worn a trouser suit.

"You look stunning," Nicholas said, when she came downstairs. "Nervous?"

She nodded and he took her hand. "You don't have to commit yourself, Darling."

Natasha looked at him. He had called her darling. The endearment had slipped out casually, but it made her want to fling herself in his arms and kiss him and have him kiss her back. Shocked, she imagined him undressing her, his hands caressing her bare flesh and his lips kissing her – not tenderly like Richard, but demanding and rough. 'What the hell's wrong with me?' she wondered angrily. 'I'm frustrated, that's what,' she admitted.

"Are you going to bring Richard back here with you?"

She shook her head. "I don't know."

He walked with her to the station and after she caught the train he went to the off-licence and bought champagne. Pessimistically, he put her odd behaviour down to nerves. He'd lost. She hadn't fallen for him even though they'd lived under the same roof for months. They'd laughed together, talked about their feelings, shared the pain of Harriet's secret and been untidy together.

She would come back with Richard tonight, starry eyed, and announce they were getting married. He had bought the champagne for them. He would congratulate them and smile. After they had finished the champagne he would go to bed and leave them alone.

Richard dressed in his best suit and was ready nearly an hour before Natasha was due to arrive. He had booked a table at an Italian restaurant just round the corner from his hotel in Kensington. She walked into the foyer wearing a stunningly simple dress in black velvet.

Long sleeved with a high neck it fell to her calves. She was wearing make up, and he felt dispirited when she did not return his smile, but stood in front of him rigidly.

"Natasha." He was furious with himself when his voice wavered. He meant to sound confident.

"Hello, Richard," she said. He was surprised to hear sadness in her tone, where he had expected to hear coldness.

He cleared his throat. "I've booked a table at an Italian restaurant round the corner. I hope you're hungry." He wished she looked more like the Natasha he knew. This sophisticated woman wearing high heels and sheer black hose was beyond his reach. "I wish you were in jeans," he blurted out.

"Why?" she asked coolly. "I thought you liked glamorous women. You always pretended you were above all that, but finally your true feelings for Deborah surfaced."

"That's not fair, Natasha."

"Isn't it?"

Anger replaced his misery. "My true feelings for Deborah surfaced – dangerously. She came round to my flat one day and tried to make me marry her and – "

"Did you have an ecstatic reunion?"

"No. I almost murdered her. She was terrified. If she hadn't left I would have strangled her."

"How melodramatic," she said indifferently. "Shall we go to this restaurant or not? I'm hungry."

They walked in silence to the restaurant. He was angry and hurt. When they sat down, he looked at her steadily. "Why did you let Miss Shaw give me your address? Did you want revenge?"

"Why did you sleep with Deborah?" She picked up the menu.

He stared at her. "I came over here to try and explain what happened, but if you don't want to listen, I'm not going to waste my time."

She looked confused and he decided to take the initiative away from her. He stood up. "You know the name of the hotel I'm staying at. I don't know the number but look it up in the phone book if you want to contact me."

She looked startled. "Richard!"

414

He ignored her and strode out of the restaurant.

The waiter hurried anxiously over to their table. "Is anything wrong?" he asked.

Natasha stood up. "Yes, everything, but not with your restaurant. I'm sorry."

She walked outside and hailed a taxi. "Kew, please," she said to the driver. She was too depressed to cry and stared out of the taxi window. The driver tried to make conversation but she didn't hear him. She felt so much worse than she had when her engagement to Richard was broken. Then she had been in control and could have chosen to forgive him. She had been surrounded by sympathetic people. Now she had no one. 'I wish Jacqui was here,' she thought. The taxi drew up outside the house and she rummaged through her bag searching for her purse.

"Don't worry, love, bad times don't last forever," said the taxi driver.

Natasha handed him his fare and a tip. "Thank you, but nothing will ever be right again."

She went up the path and fumbled at the front door with her key. She hoped Nicholas was not in, but even this wish was not granted.

He came into the hall and looked at her in astonishment. "Natasha, what's happened?"

"Nothing." She started to climb the stairs.

He followed her. "Did you see Richard?"

She nodded.

He tugged at her arm and pulled her round to face him. She was standing two steps higher and her eyes were level with his. "Darling, what happened? Tell me."

Angry that he had called her darling, when the endearment meant nothing, but was just used out of theatrical habit, she snapped, "I was horrible to him. I don't love him any more. I only realized the other day."

"Why not?"

"I love someone else," she said recklessly.

He looked angry. "Is it the doctor?" he asked, tightening his grip on her wrist.

"No, it's you. Oh, God." She shut her eyes in shame and lay down on the stairs and howled.

She was aware of Nicholas getting down beside her. She ignored him. He pulled her into a sitting position and cradled her in his arms. Too embarrassed to look at him she buried her head on his chest and said, "I'm sorry, I'm sorry. I wasn't going to tell you. It just came out."

He kissed her.

She pushed him away. "Don't feel sorry for me. Don't you dare – "

"Natasha, Natasha, Natasha, I've loved you for ages." He laughed.

Her eyes widened. "What?"

"I love you." He kissed her wet cheek.

"Really?" she whispered. "Since when?"

"Since the night you burst into tears during 'Vissi d'arte', perhaps before. That's why I'm here. How long have you loved me?"

"Only since last night when I saw you with that girl in *Pissarro*'s. That's why I've been so miserable. Thank heavens I told you."

Nicholas pulled her to her feet. "Thank heavens you did."

"Where are we going?" she asked as he put his arm round her waist and led her up the stairs.

He looked at her tenderly. "Where do you think we're going?"

"Your bedroom I hope," she murmured in his ear.

Natasha woke as the faint rays of the weak morning sunlight filtered through the ruby brocade curtains. She was curled up in Nicholas's arms and as she stirred he kissed her cheek. She opened her eyes and looked at him with a sleepy smile.

He kissed her lips. "Will you marry me?"

Natasha laughed joyously. "Yes, yes! When, where?"

"As soon as possible." He turned over and looked at the clock on his bedside table. "Who shall we ring first?"

"Miss Shaw," said Natasha promptly.

"What about an engagement ring?" he asked.

"I don't want an engagement ring. Can we be really wicked and stay in bed all day?"

He laughed. "What a splendid idea. I've just remembered, there's a bottle of champagne in the fridge, I'll go and get it."

She kissed him. "We're descending into the depths of decadence."

He pulled her into his arms. "Mmm, wonderful isn't it?"

Chapter 36

'My anguish gives way to despair,
as if an icy hand
had gripped my heart in torment!'

Eugene Onegin – Tchaikovsky

Phillipa vomited into the basin for the sixth time in an hour. She sat on the chair in the bathroom shaking.

Jacqueline appeared in the doorway. "What's wrong?"

Phillipa bent over as a spasm of pain gripped her stomach. "I must have food poisoning, it could have been the fish I had at the restaurant tonight." She jumped up and dry retched into the basin. "My ribs are hurting. I've got nothing left in my stomach to bring up."

Jacqueline disappeared and returned a minute later with a glass of water. She handed Phillipa the glass. "Drink this, then at least you'll have something in your stomach."

Phillipa took the glass. Her hand was shaking so much she spilled some of the water. "Thanks," she gasped. "Go back to bed, Jacqui, there's nothing you can do."

"I'm not leaving you like this."

Phillipa staggered to the basin and vomited with such force her eyes watered. Jacqueline went into the kitchen and got another glass of water.

Phillipa drank it gratefully. "That didn't hurt so much."

"It'll stop you from becoming dehydrated – hang on I'll get you another one."

In the early morning Phillipa was still vomiting, but the pains in her stomach were not as severe. The phone rang and Jacqueline went to answer it. Exhausted, Phillipa sat in the chair. She heard Jacqueline's joyful cries coming from the lounge.

"Natasha! That's wonderful news! I can't believe it. I'm so excited! Philly will be thrilled too!"

Despite the pain she smiled. Natasha and Richard must be back together and they were all coming home.

Jacqueline rushed into the bathroom. "Nick and Natasha are getting married! Natasha wants you and me to be bridesmaids."

Phillipa jumped up and vomited into the basin.

At last Jacqueline went to rehearsal, and Phillipa was alone. The last three hours had been purgatory, what with having to pretend she was happy about Nicholas and Natasha and cope with Jacqueline's delight. On reflection, she was pleased about her food poisoning, which had given her an excuse for her lack of joy. Now she was alone, the pains in her stomach competing with the pain in her soul. When the phone rang she nearly didn't answer it but its persistent ringing penetrated every corner of the house.

It was Harriet. "Jacqui's just told me how ill you are, darling. Have you got any brandy?"

"Yes."

"Good. Pour yourself a generous measure and drink it quickly, it will help kill the germs. If you don't feel any better in an hour ring the doctor."

"Thanks, Harriet," she said weakly. "Isn't it wonderful about Nicholas and Natasha?"

"We'll have to start organizing things." She could hear that the news had delighted Harriet. "They're getting married in England."

"Oh wonderful, I've always wanted to go to England." Her throat tightened and she gasped as the tears poured from her eyes. "Sorry – I'm going to be sick again."

She went into the kitchen, poured some brandy into a glass and drank it straight down. Half an hour later she felt much better. She went to bed and slept and did not wake until Jacqueline came home.

When Richard returned to the hotel after his disastrous reunion with Natasha, he decided that instead of waiting for her to contact him, he would distance himself completely and go to Europe. He went to a travel agent and booked an open plane ticket to Florence and a one-week stay in a hotel. From there he intended to travel by train to Rome, Venice and Milan and then onto Austria, Switzerland, Germany and France. 'I won't tell Natasha. Let her wonder. When I come back she might be ready to talk reasonably.'

Nicholas led Natasha down the lane in Petersham and into the small church of Saint Peter. She gazed enraptured round the old church. "It's perfect, look at these lovely pews."

"They're Georgian box pews," he explained. "In my last year at drama school, a friend of mine was married in this church and one of his brothers had a little girl." He reached over the side of the pew and showed Natasha the small sliding bolt that locked the door. "Well, she unlocked the pew, and her father, not realizing, leant on the door – it flew open and he fell out with a crash onto the floor."

Natasha laughed. "When shall we get married?"

"It depends on our guests, seeing everyone except my parents and a few of my old friends have to get themselves here from Australia. It's November now, we can't leave it later than February because we've got to get back to Melbourne for the beginning of the season. So I think it'll have to be as soon after New Year's Day as possible."

"What about the reception?"

"The Petersham Hotel, which is a short walk away. And it's where I'm going to take you for lunch."

Phillipa marvelled at her acting ability. No one guessed she was miserable, and Jacqueline's excitement was so infectious, Phillipa found herself swept along with the arrangements. The wedding had been fixed for the beginning of January, and Natasha assumed, without asking, that Phillipa would be the other bridesmaid. Quick phone calls replaced letters.

"Natasha said it would be better to buy the bridesmaids' dresses in

London," Jacqueline said after one phone call. "It'll be freezing in January, so what do you think about velvet?"

"I don't mind, you choose," said Phillipa, wishing she could miss the wedding. 'Maybe I'll be lucky enough to be struck down by another bout of food poisoning on the day,' she thought.

"No, you have to wear it too," Jacqueline insisted with maddening fairness. "And Natasha wants you to help her pick the wedding dress. Isn't it exciting?"

Phillipa dreaded having to meet Nicholas again, and hoped her stoical nature would see her through the day. She worried about breaking down in the church. There was no one to whom she could turn. She wished Richard was here. While she might not be able to bring herself to tell him she loved Nicholas, his unhappiness might make things easier for her.

She booked their flight and made appointments for rush vaccinations. She asked Emily if she would like to stay in their house while they were away and look after Mozart.

"Oh yes, I'd love to," said Emily. "I'm thinking of moving out of home and trying to be more independent – this might spur me on a bit. Who's looking after Algernon?"

"Harriet's next door neighbour. Emily, do you remember what you told me years ago?" asked Phillipa hesitantly.

"About loving Nicholas?"

"Yes. I was, well wondering – "

"If I was upset?" said Emily helpfully.

"I just wondered if you still loved him."

Emily nodded. "Thanks for keeping my secret for all those years, Philly. I know I can trust you. I was upset. I thought Natasha would pine for Richard for years. This happened so suddenly, it was unexpected. A few years ago I thought he was going to marry Vivien. When they broke up I had fantasies that he'd ask me out, but he never did. I wish he'd chosen me, but I knew he'd never love me. Whoever he loved would have to be very special, and Natasha's special."

"So are you."

"I'm not his type, I'm too shy. I'm only vivacious when I've had something to drink. I often envied you and Jacqui and Natasha, you were so confident and independent. I used to watch you all and wish I

420

was like you. I envy Natasha, but she deserves him. I hope they're happy. I really do."

For two days Phillipa was given a reprieve from everyone's rapture, which melted dramatically when they had their cholera and typhoid injections. Everyone reacted badly and Jacqueline's arm swelled up so badly her hand turned blue. Harriet had to spend two days in bed, while Phillipa, although in agony, soldiered on, thankful she did not have to appear excited and happy all the time. A fortnight later the injections were repeated, and everyone, except Phillipa, was dreading them. She welcomed the excuse for a few days' respite from everyone else's happiness.

Their suitcases were ready in the hall. Jacqueline and Phillipa checked each other's bags to make sure the passports and tickets were safely inside.

"I hope the plane doesn't crash," said Jacqueline, as she peered out of the window, waiting for the taxi.

"You're so cheerful," said Phillipa.

"Planes do crash you know," argued Jacqueline.

"Jacqui!" said Emily.

"Not one QANTAS plane has ever crashed," said Phillipa.

"Really?"

"Yes really. Why do you think I booked us on QANTAS?"

"Truly?" said Jacqueline in admiration.

"Yes. I'm not particularly keen on flying either, but we're more likely to be killed on the way to the airport."

"I suppose there's always a first time," said Jacqueline gloomily.

"Shut up, Jacqui," said Emily. "You'll upset Mozart."

Jacqueline turned from the window and ran into the hall. "The taxi's here," she shouted.

Phillipa hugged Emily. "Bye. I hope Mozart's not too naughty."

When they arrived at Tullamarine Airport, Jacqueline's parents and Harriet were waiting.

At Heathrow, Phillipa steeled herself to meet Natasha and Nicholas. They collected their cases and walked past the excited crowds in the arrivals hall. Phillipa hung back pretending she was having a problem with the wheels of her trolley. Natasha, glowing with radiance and dressed in a green cashmere coat and matching hat, flung herself into Jacqueline's arms, then Harriet and Nicholas were hugging each other. Finally it was her turn.

She hugged him. "Oh, Nick, it's wonderful to see you again, we've all missed you."

He kissed her. "I've missed you too, Philly. And don't think you can lark about sightseeing – you're coming shopping with me. I need you to help me get a suit."

"Great," she said turning away and gritting her teeth.

Natasha threw her arms round her. "Philly, it's smashing to see you! Nick and I really missed you. It's taken us four days to clean and tidy the house."

Although Natasha's tone was facetious her words pushed Phillipa's spirit lower. 'Is that all I'm good for? How boring. Am I like an old woman – always fussing and tidying?' She pointed to the cases. "There are so many wedding cards in there, it's a wonder we had any room for clothes!"

Nicholas organized the exodus from the airport, and outside they piled into two black cabs.

Harriet knew as soon as she saw Nicholas and Natasha at the airport that they had found out what had happened. Natasha had always looked up to her in respect and admiration, but at the airport she looked at her with sympathy. Nicholas's embrace had not been only that of a nephew, she had felt his pity. In Melbourne the prospect of being in England for the first time for over forty years had frightened but excited her at the same time. Now she felt betrayed. Nicholas had found out about her past and had told Natasha. 'Of course he told her,' she tried to reason with herself, 'he's going to marry her. How did he find out?' she wondered.

Nicholas put a comforting arm round her shoulder. "Are you all right?"

She nodded and took a deep breath. 'He would never have done that before – he would have assumed I was all right,' she thought. 'Now he knows I'm vulnerable. I'm no longer his tough, fearless Aunt Harriet.

I'm a pitiful creature who went mad and was committed to a lunatic asylum. I've lost his respect. We will never work together as equals again. He may never say it to my face, but he'll think I'm unbalanced.'

"Has it changed much, Aunt Harriet?" Nicholas asked as the taxi turned into Lichfield Road and pulled up in front of the house.

She looked out of the window. "It looks just the same – except for the blocks of flats on the corner. The trees are bigger."

"What a divine house," said Jacqueline.

"It's beautiful," agreed Phillipa.

Nicholas picked up Harriet's cases and carried them up to her room. She followed him and walked over to the window.

He shut the door. "Aunt Harriet, we might not get another chance to be alone and I wanted to tell you something. When I went to Australia, I had no idea, but when I came back here I – a photo of you fell off the piano and broke and underneath were newspaper cuttings about … " he faltered uncertainly.

"You found out what happened? Yes – I know you have."

"I feel guilty about the way I treated you – if I'd known – "

"You would have been sympathetic? I can't stand sympathy."

"Not sympathetic perhaps – more understanding."

"Hugh knew. I realize that his knowledge blighted our relationship. He treated me gently and let me get away with things that you didn't. The theatre is better as a result, and so am I. I'm a nicer person now than I was when you first met me. I'm more understanding and I listen to advice, something I never did before. Now that you know, don't sympathize with me – I'd hate it. Natasha knows too doesn't she?"

"Well – yes. How did you know?"

"I saw pity in her eyes. I wish you hadn't told her."

"Who wouldn't feel pity? She admires you – you're her inspiration. Actually, I didn't tell her – she told me. She broke the photo frame and found the cuttings. She was devastated when she found out and so was I. You're a great woman, Aunt Harriet. You always will be."

She didn't want him to see the tears gathering in her eyes, so she looked out of the window. "Great women don't go mad, Nicholas." Her voice was husky and gave away the fact that she was crying.

Nicholas crossed to the window and stood next to her. "You didn't go mad – you had a breakdown – hardly surprising after what you went through."

"People have endured far worse and survived. Look at the war – some women lost their husbands and all their sons."

"Yes, but it was happening to everyone. Women could share their grief. You endured the betrayal of your best friend with the man you loved, witnessed her suicide and had a broken engagement. Your parents comforted you, but they didn't go through it too. Aunt Harriet, you lost so much in such a short time."

She nodded. "I never saw it like that before. Thank you, Nicholas. I'm very happy for you and Natasha – you know that don't you?"

He handed her a handkerchief. She took it and wiped her eyes. "I think I need to be fortified by a drink before I go downstairs."

"Brandy?"

She nodded and he went down to get it. Harriet looked round the room aware of the sounds of excitement from downstairs. Nicholas returned with the brandy.

Taking the glass she raised it in a gesture of a toast. "Wonderful stuff brandy." She threw it down in one gulp. "I'm ready to go down now."

He held out his arm. "Don't start helping me round as if I'm a geriatric. I've walked unaided all my life and I'm perfectly capable of still doing so."

He grinned at her. "Yes, Aunt Harriet."

She grinned back. "That's better."

Natasha was showing everyone to their rooms. "Jacqui, you're sharing with me, Philly you're in this room. Where are Mum and Dad?"

"Downstairs," called Jacqueline, her normally low voice high pitched with excitement. "Mum, let me help you with that case."

Harriet stood in the doorway of her bedroom and looked up at Nicholas. "Everyone's so excited – your wedding day is going to be quite an event."

He led the way downstairs. She entered the drawing room and sat in one of the arm chairs. Feeling strange, she sat in silence for a few moments. 'The years in Australia might never have been,' she thought. 'The room's hardly changed, even the drapes and upholstery are the same colour.' She stood up and crossed the hall into the dining room. The image of Annabel was vivid. Then Jacqueline, Phillipa and

424

Natasha came into the room and the sensation passed.

"Miss Shaw – " began Natasha.

Harriet put her arm round her. "As you're going to be my niece by marriage you'd better stop calling me Miss Shaw. Why don't you just call me Harriet?"

Natasha shook her head. "It would sound disrespectful. You've always been Miss Shaw to me."

"Well, what about Aunt Harriet then?"

Natasha smiled. "Yes, I could call you Aunt Harriet, Aunt Harriet."

"Philly, I want to buy Natasha an exotic night-dress for her wedding night. Will you help me choose one?" asked Jacqueline.

"Yes," replied Phillipa, her smile belying her feeling of dread. The last thing she wanted to do was imagine Natasha dressed for her wedding night. Going shopping for the wedding dress and Nicholas's suit had been enough of an ordeal.

Nonetheless, she accompanied Jacqueline to the lingerie department of Dickens and Jones in Richmond.

"Look at these," said Jacqueline, carefully pulling a white silk night-dress off the rail. "What do you think?"

Phillipa nodded. "Although I don't think she'll be spending much time in it, do you?"

"Philly! You don't usually come out with remarks like that." On their way to the cash desk, she nudged her. "But you're right, she probably won't even put it on."

Outside, they looked at the dark grey sky. "I hope it snows," said Jacqueline. "Let's go and have lunch."

They found the Refectory Restaurant in a little lane, opposite a church.

"This is lovely," said Phillipa as they walked through the courtyard. "Typically English and old."

After ordering, Jacqueline said, "Shall we ask Emily to move in with us when we get back?"

Phillipa, remembering her conversation with Emily before they left, agreed. "The house is too big for two and three will be more fun."

"Oh, listen!" said Jacqueline. "Nick's booked into an ancient hotel

425

for their honeymoon, and their room has a four-poster bed. Natasha doesn't know – it's going to be a surprise." She sighed wistfully. "He's so romantic. He'll be a wonderful husband, don't you reckon, Philly?"

"I don't know," she replied offhandedly. "I've never thought about him like that."

Harriet sat in the first-class compartment and tried to read the magazine Nicholas had bought her on the platform. She looked out of the window at the misty landscape and the frost encrusted trees. In an hour she would see Charlotte again for the first time in forty-six years. When Charlotte was eighteen she had been planning a trip to Australia but then she had met and fallen in love with her future husband. When Nicholas had been born the years had passed too quickly. Harriet had wanted their meeting to take place alone, not amongst the hustle of Heathrow Airport with everyone watching.

Now Harriet was going to spend three days with Charlotte and her husband. As the train pulled into the platform she picked up her case with a shiver of nervous excitement. She opened the door and stepped outside. The first thing she saw was Charlotte walking down the platform towards her.

Chapter 37

'We have drunk from the cup of affliction
And have shed bitter tears of repentance,
Oh, inspire us Jehovah with courage,
So that we may endure to the last.'

Nabucco – Verdi

Jacqueline ran to the window. "It's here, it's here!"

Phillipa gathered up the wide skirt of her lilac velvet bridesmaid's dress, and opened the door. A shining black carriage driven by a man in a scarlet coat and drawn by two chestnut horses drew up outside the house.

Natasha looked at them in delight. "Whose idea was it?"

"Your future husband's," said Jacqueline.

"I'm going to cry," said Natasha.

"No you're not," said her father, holding out his arm for her to take.

The driver helped them inside, where they sat on the blue velvet seats, and looked out of the windows.

"It's snowing!" said Jacqueline.

As the carriage drove through Richmond, people waved and called out good wishes. "I feel like a princess," said Natasha as she waved back.

'Oh, God,' prayed Phillipa. 'I know I've hated you, but help me survive this day without breaking down and making a fool of myself.'

Natasha sat opposite her. Dressed in a heavy satin bridal gown that had a high neck and long puffed sleeves, she looked beautiful. Red curls fell over her shoulders and her sheer veil was held in place by a circle of gardenias and violets interlaced with delicate fern. Looking at her radiant expression Phillipa felt that life was kinder to Natasha than she deserved. 'You've been blessed with loving parents, a twin sister, a superb singing voice, and Nicholas,' she thought. 'Once you were unattractive and skinny. Now you're stunning. Jacqui's never recovered from Max, but you got over Richard in less than a year.' At that moment Phillipa hated her, then hated herself. 'I'm a bitter old maid,' she thought.

"Philly, you look sad," said Natasha.

'Hell,' she thought. "I suppose I am a bit," she said, deciding to blur the edges of truth. "I feel a bit weird. This was … all so sudden. I was just thinking that so many people are missing out. Emily – "

"I know," said Natasha. "We thought about getting married in Melbourne, but decided too much would be the same. Same church, bridesmaids, guests, just a different groom."

Phillipa nodded. 'Things could be worse,' she thought. 'Millions of people are dying of starvation or cancer. Through the centuries people have had to endure worse than this. I could be riding in a cart to the guillotine with crowds jeering and throwing garbage at me. I could have been going to be burnt at the stake like Joan of Arc, or waiting to have my head chopped off like Anne Boleyn or Lady Jane Grey. That would be much worse than going to Nicholas and Natasha's wedding,' she thought as the carriage went up Richmond Hill.

As she entered the church behind Natasha to the joyous strains of Handel, she saw Nicholas turn and smile. Thankful that the layout of the church meant she was spared a long walk up the aisle, Phillipa lowered her head and stared at her bouquet. 'Oh, Nick, why did you have to be so decent, so good looking, so talented and fascinating?'

She took a deep breath as the organ played the opening bars of 'Oh Perfect Love'. Terrified that the beauty of the hymn would make her cry, she dared not sing, but mouthed the words. Tightly clutching her bouquet, she lifted her head and looked at the gold stained glass window, trying to think of something neutral. She couldn't. 'I'll play a game with opera titles. A is for *Aida*, B is for *The Bartered Bride* … no that's too easy, it won't count if it's got *the* in front. So B is *Boris Godunov*, C is for *Carmen* … D is *Don Carlos* … no that doesn't count. D, D, D … *Dido and Aeneas*."

When the hymn ended she was filled with relief that she had managed to stay composed.

Her throat tightened as they took their vows. She swallowed hard and stared at the window. 'H is for *Hansel and Gretel*, I … is for, for what? What starts with I? There must be one, yes, I know there is. What

428

is it?"

"I Natasha Rose, take thee, Nicholas Peter, for my wedded husband."

Phillipa bit her trembling lip, and tasted blood in her mouth. She licked her lip and hoped the blood would not pour down her chin. 'Maybe, in twenty years' time, I'll remember this day and be able to laugh about how I felt. I'll tell my children about it, to inspire them when they feel unhappy,' she thought.

When Natasha lifted her veil and Nicholas kissed her, Phillipa shut her eyes. She got through the next hymn, 'Love Divine all Loves Excelling', by continuing the game. 'I is for ... oh, forget I. J is for *Jenufa*. K ... no skip to L – *Lohengrin*! Yes. M, easy, *Manon*. N for *Norma*. And Nicholas ... '

Finally the ceremony was over and they went to sign the register near the pulpit.

Nicholas kissed her. "You look ravishing, Philly."

Dressed in the navy suit she had helped him choose, with his hair cut, he looked sophisticated and handsome. She could smell his aftershave and the perfume from the white carnation in his buttonhole. Her eyes filled with tears. "Weddings are so emotional aren't they? Everyone feels like crying with happiness! Gosh, I'm frozen!" she babbled, trying to stop her tears. She gritted her teeth and wished Nicholas would go away. To her relief he went over to Jacqueline and put his arm round her. "Hello, sister-in-law," she heard him say.

Phillipa smiled brightly at Harriet. "It was a beautiful service."

Harriet squeezed her hand. "Yes, it was. Very moving." She put her arm on Phillipa's. "I think you're almost ready to go. I'll see you at the reception. You did very well, my child. Very well indeed."

Harriet resumed her seat and Phillipa stood next to Jacqueline. As the organ began to play 'Trumpet Voluntary', they left the church and strolled back to the carriage.

'Now there's only the reception to get through,' thought Phillipa. To avoid looking at Nicholas and Natasha, she watched the snow, which was getting heavier.

"Wow!" she heard Jacqueline say as the carriage turned into the drive of the Petersham Hotel. "Is this where we're having the reception?"

"Yes," said Natasha. "Gorgeous, isn't it?"

Phillipa leant over Jacqueline to look out of the other window.

"Wait till you see the view," said Nicholas.

The photographer took their photos as they stepped out of the carriage. "I don't want you posing, just look natural."

Phillipa forced herself to smile. 'Everyone back home will look at the photos and no one must ever guess how I feel.'

Inside, they joined the guests who were gathered at the windows, transfixed by the view from the Nightingale Room. For the first time that day, Phillipa's smile was genuine, as she gazed at the River Thames, silver in the reflected light. Patches of green on the slope leading to the river were disappearing under the snow.

Jacqueline tugged her arm. "Come and sit down."

Reluctantly Phillipa followed her to the main table. She wanted to sit next to Harriet so Nicholas would be out of her view, but the name place had put her opposite him. It was a small reception with twenty-five people, mostly family and Nicholas's old friends.

When the sun shone through a break in the clouds, the photographer rushed everyone outside. "This is one of the most famous views in England," he told them.

"And you're photographing one of the most famous opera singers in the world," said Jacqueline, pointing to Natasha.

He looked startled.

"No, Jacqui," said Phillipa. "He's photographing two of the most famous opera singers in the world!"

Jacqueline whooped and threw her bouquet in the air. She failed to catch it and it hit her father on the head.

Phillipa burst out laughing. The photographer pointed his camera at her. She heard the shutter click. 'Good shot,' she thought.

At five in the evening Nicholas and Natasha left for their honeymoon in Devon. Trying not to think about the bridal suite with the four poster bed, Phillipa watched them going to the car Nicholas had hired. Natasha wore a green velvet trouser suit and cream angora jumper. Riding boots in black leather, which she had pulled over her trousers, completed the outfit.

"If she had a hat adorned with ostrich feathers she'd look like a

430

cavalier," said Harriet.

Afterwards everyone went back to Nicholas's house. When the last guests left, Jacqueline and her parents went to bed. Phillipa made hot chocolate for herself and Harriet, and they sat by the fire in the drawing room.

"I think you're in the wrong job, Phillipa," said Harriet quietly. "You should have been an actress."

"I'd be a terrible actress. I can't act."

"Your performance today was remarkable."

Phillipa felt uneasy. "Performance?"

"How long have you been in love with Nicholas?" Harriet asked gently.

Phillipa blushed. "A few months after he started at the theatre."

"And you say you can't act. I only guessed when Nicholas and Natasha kissed at the altar. I saw you shut your eyes and when you opened them I saw your pain. I never suspected anything before today. I knew you were very fond of him. Don't be a sour old spinster like me, Phillipa."

"You're not a – "

"I am. Do you know why I never married?"

Phillipa shook her head.

"Funny, how for over forty years I've kept this secret and now that Nicholas and Natasha know I've got this urge to tell you – I don't want you finding out from someone else. I was engaged. My cousin was going to be my bridesmaid. She fell in love with Andrew and burst into a dinner we were having for my mother's birthday and shot herself."

Shocked, but suddenly understanding, Phillipa looked at her. "Annabel?"

Harriet nodded. "When I first saw Deborah it was like seeing Annabel. She even wore a jaunty little fur hat, just like Annabel used to. When we were children we were like sisters. She didn't have any wish to be anything other than a wife and mother. Her only specifications were that he had to be handsome and rich. Andrew was neither. He was a dedicated doctor and it wasn't his looks that attracted me, it was his character. He was intense, but had a sense of humour. He didn't try to rule or dominate me and didn't care that I made more money than he did. Annabel never envied my success either, she loved

431

having a famous cousin. My mother thought Annabel was superficial and vain and she worried because we were so close.

"Then Annabel changed. During the depression she became very serious. She sold her fur coats and jewellery and gave the money to my mother for the soup kitchen. Then she began attacking me for doing nothing for the homeless, when I did a great deal. I gave concerts and all the proceeds went to charities, but she said that I never got my hands dirty. She went to the soup kitchen with my mother and then announced she was going to train as a nurse. The family were amazed.

"It was Andrew's influence, but no one realized then. I should have known. I knew Annabel so well. Whenever she was interested in a man she became like him. If he was an aristocrat she'd talk to him about shooting, riding and hunting and estate management. If he was an actor she read all the new plays and memorized bits of Shakespeare. If he worked in the city she talked about interest rates and the stock market. She was a perfect chameleon. When she started being concerned about the poor and ill I should have guessed. But I trusted her and when she wasn't around I missed her.

"When they began their affair I have no idea, but I knew nothing about it till the night she shot herself. He broke our engagement, he didn't tell me to my face – he wrote to me. I never saw him again. I pretended I didn't care. Then I went mad and had to be committed to a lunatic asylum. I screamed so much I lost my voice. I can't remember much about it. Then they brought me home and when I saw myself in the mirror for the first time, I wanted to die. My hair was white and I looked old and thin and ugly. I'd lost the man I'd loved, my singing voice and my lifelong friend.

"For months I indulged myself in grief. In a perverse way I enjoyed everyone worrying. One day my father took me to the East End and made me watch the queues of hopeless men who'd lost everything because of the depression, and told me how selfish I was being. I realized he was right and I felt ashamed. A month later I went to Australia."

Tears rolled down Phillipa's cheeks, making trails in her make-up. "It must have been dreadful for you, coming back here."

Harriet nodded. "I can't wait to get back to Australia. I have so many regrets about my life."

432

Phillipa looked at her anxiously. "But what about all the things you've achieved?"

"I would rather have married and had children." She glanced around the room. "All those years ago I should have left here as a bride, instead I left to be committed to a lunatic asylum. I had another chance to be happy, but I threw it away. I wish I'd married Hugh. He told me he would love me till the day he died, and he did. I loved him, but I was frightened that if I'd admitted it, he would stop loving me, or something dreadful would happen – like last time. When I met him I was still young enough to have children. I gave him nothing. He was too gentle with me. He should have demanded more. I'm a failure and a fraud."

"No," protested Phillipa.

"Yes. I didn't give up my singing career because I wanted to help young singers – I gave up because I couldn't sing any more. All these years I lied about my motives and pretended I was philanthropic. Vivien Anderson was very astute, right from the beginning she knew I was lying. I was terrified she'd find out and I'd lose my credibility. I was glad when she and Nicholas broke up." She smiled. "But so were you, I suspect."

"Yes." Phillipa swallowed. "Whatever your motives, Harriet, you've been courageous. You built a new life. You founded a successful opera school and theatre. I love you, Nick and Natasha love you and everyone thinks the world of you. You're not a failure or a fraud." Her voice cracked and she wiped at the tears running down her cheeks and splashing onto her dress.

Harriet stood up and put her arm round Phillipa. "Today you passed a test of endurance and courage. You've survived with your pride and integrity intact."

Phillipa felt a frisson of guilt. 'You don't know about the letter I destroyed,' she thought. 'It might have brought Nick and Vivien together again.'

"Why don't you stay here for a while and have a holiday, Phillipa? I'll miss you terribly, and I'll have to find someone temporary to replace you, but I'll keep your job open for you."

Phillipa blew her nose. "I don't know. I hope I can act normally when Nick and I have to work side by side every day."

"Your relationship with him will remain unchanged except for your hope for the future. He was a very good friend and he still will be. Now you're emotionally free."

"Thanks, Harriet. I'll let you know as soon as I decide."

Harriet walked over to the window and gazed out into the street. "Phillipa, something strange has just happened."

Phillipa joined her at the window and looked out, but could see nothing strange in the amber glow of the street lights. "Where?"

"Hugh was the only person I ever told. I didn't tell him the way I told you. I gave him the bare outline when I turned down his first proposal of marriage. I thought it was only fair to tell him. I've always heard that it helps to talk about things, but I didn't know till now how true it was."

She smiled and Phillipa was startled by the depth and warmth in her eyes. 'I've never seen her smile like that before,' she thought.

"I began to hate Annabel when she shot herself. Usually when people die we feel guilty and only think about their good points. We imbue them with qualities they never had. I did the opposite with Annabel. I hated her. Hated her for ruining my life. When I saw Deborah it was as if Annabel had come alive again. I treated Deborah unfairly. I didn't give her a chance."

"You don't feel guilty do you?"

Harriet shook her head. "I've seldom felt guilty. Some people feel too much guilt – I don't feel enough."

"You said something strange had happened," prompted Phillipa.

"I don't hate Annabel any more."

Natasha, her cheeks flushed with happiness, walked into the dining room with Nicholas. "What a super place!" she exclaimed looking at the ancient timbered walls and ceiling.

He pulled out a chair for her. "I thought you'd like it. Are you sure it's old enough for you?"

"I hope it's not so old it falls down. Can we buy a four-poster bed?"

He laughed. "I take it you like it?"

"Very much." She licked her lips. "Shall we skip dinner and try it out again?"

"No. I'm hungry."

"So am I."

"Natasha, stop looking at me like that or we'll be asked to leave."

"Good."

He put a velvet box in front of her. "I know you didn't want an engagement ring, but I saw this in an antique shop and couldn't resist buying it."

She opened the lid and her eyes widened in delight. Taking out an amethyst ring surrounded by alternating emeralds and diamonds, she slipped it on her finger. "Purple and green – my favourite colours."

"I've got a surprise for you," he said after their main course. "By popular demand we're putting on *Tosca* in May – the modern production. Would Miss Howard like the part?"

First she looked elated, then her smile faded and she shook her head.

"Richard won't be Scarpia," he said lightly, to hide his hurt that her thoughts were with him.

She looked solemn. "Miss Howard can't accept the role. She wants it to go to Mrs Forrester."

Nicholas laughed. "I'd assumed you'd want to keep Howard as your professional name. You can if you'd rather."

"I'll think about it." She smiled slyly and scanned the pudding menu. "I can't see anything that I like."

He tried to look serious. "You love chocolate mousse."

"I've gone off it."

"Treacle tart?"

"I've gone off that too. And apple pie."

"Have you ever had sticky toffee pudding?"

She pulled a face. "It sounds horrible."

"It's delicious. You'd love it. I'm going to have pudding and cheese. And coffee and cognac and after dinner mints."

"I'll watch you."

"Unfortunately I can't stand people watching me eat – it gives me indigestion. So, we'll have to try out the bed again," he whispered.

435

Jacqueline hung up her bridesmaid's dress and put on her pyjamas and dressing gown. She felt detached from everything and the events of the day had the haziness of a dream. Tomorrow she and her parents were going to Cornwall for a week. Her handbag was on the floor and she took out Max's letter. It was almost torn in half from her constant folding and unfolding. She read it, as she had for nearly every day since she had received it. It was the only memento she had of their time together.

My Darling Jacqueline,

Sue has found out about you. She will take Zoe away and I will never see her again, unless I return home, give up my singing lessons, opera school and you. It breaks my heart to do this. I'm sorry that my love proved less worthy than yours. I will always love you. You had an innocence, purity and integrity I could never have matched. I wish you every happiness.
                    Yours forever in my heart,

                         Max.

Every time Jacqueline read that letter she cried. Tonight, for the first time she noticed that he had written: Sue has found out about *you*, not, Sue has found out about *us*.

"And I wasn't innocent or pure, Max. I didn't care about your wife and daughter, and I lacked integrity too. This letter's sloppy nonsense. And for years I've been thinking it was tragic and romantic."

She went over to the window and drew back the curtains. A flurry of snowflakes drifted into the room when she pushed up the window. She tore the letter into tiny pieces. Sticking her head outside she flung the bits up into the air, where they drifted to the ground with the snow flakes. Deliberately she pictured Max with Susan. There was no pain. She thought about Max and Susan with a new baby. 'Nothing,' she thought. She imagined Max happily married to a new and attractive wife. 'Still no pain. I'm free.' She shut the window and climbed into bed.

♪   ♪   ♪

Richard arrived back in England that night. His plane had been delayed at Pisa airport for five hours owing to the snow at Heathrow. He landed at midnight, grateful he had the foresight to book a room in his old hotel before he left Italy. He caught a taxi to Kensington and as soon as he was in his room he had a hot shower and fell into bed and slept soundly. He woke the next morning just in time for breakfast.

After breakfast he went into the foyer to the phone. English phones infuriated him and he felt he could never have a decent conversation while he was expecting to be interrupted at any moment by the phone noisily demanding more money. His nerves jangled with tension.

'Perhaps I should visit instead, or write,' he thought. 'But if I write she might not answer. If I visit she might be out. If she's in, she might shut the door in my face. On the other hand she might be delighted.' He picked up the receiver. Perhaps Nicholas would answer the phone. His hand hovered over the dial. Finally he dialled the first three numbers, but his courage ran out and he slammed down the receiver. He spent the morning in a misery of indecision. Deriding himself for his cowardice he went to South Kensington Underground and caught a Richmond train. On the journey to Kew he tried to plan what to say to her, and then gave up. 'After all, she might be back in Australia,' he thought, almost hoping that she was.

As he walked down Lichfield Road, he saw a girl walking cautiously down the icy footpath towards him. Enveloped in a grey voluminous coat with a hood she looked like an actress dressed for a role in *Doctor Zhivago*. As he got closer he stared at her in amazement. "Phillipa?"

"Hello, Richard," she said solemnly.

His first frightened thought was that Harriet Shaw had died and had been buried in England, and that Phillipa was here for her funeral. "What's wrong? Has something happened to Miss Shaw?"

"No." Her expression was grave. "Richard, I'm sorry. Nick and Natasha got married yesterday."

He felt light headed with shock.

She put her hand on his arm.

437

"Well, she didn't waste much time finding herself another man," he said bitterly.

She shook her head. "I know how you feel."

"Oh, sure you do."

"I feel the same way about Nicholas as you do about Natasha."

"What? Since when?"

"Six years."

He stared at her. "Six years? Ah … is that why you ditched Frank?"

She nodded. "When he and Vivien split up I thought I had a chance."

Feeling sorry for her because she had thrown so much away for nothing, he said sympathetically, "This must be agony for you too."

She nodded. "Natasha was cruel to you, Richard. She wouldn't let you explain."

"How could I explain being with Deborah in Natasha's bed? God, I don't want to think about it." He saw her shiver. "Where are you going?"

"The National Gallery."

"Let's go and get drunk."

Phillipa shook her head. "Pubs shut at three and don't open till five. Come with me."

When they arrived at The National Gallery Phillipa took off her coat and gave it to the cloak-room attendant. Richard saw the blue and green opal set off perfectly by Phillipa's white polo neck jumper.

She looked guilty. "Natasha gave it to me."

"I didn't think you'd stolen it. Opals are unlucky."

"Rot," she replied scornfully.

They spent the afternoon wandering round the art gallery. When they found themselves in front of a painting of the execution of Lady Jane Grey, Phillipa smiled. "I got through yesterday by thinking of all the dreadful things that could have been about to happen to me. Being beheaded was one of them. But I gave myself away. Harriet guessed. It was a relief to finally talk about it. If I hadn't told her I wouldn't have told you."

"I'm glad you did. I don't feel so alone now."

"Neither do I. I'm glad I met you, Richard."

"When are you going back to Australia?"

438

"Harriet said I could stay here and have a holiday, but I don't know. I'm toying with the idea of going back home and seeing how I cope with Nick and Natasha as a married couple. If it hurts too much I'll come back here and have a long holiday. What about you?"

"I'm tempted to stay here, but it would be more sensible to go back and sing with Miss Shaw for a few more years – I owe her a lot and I'm not ready for the English National Opera or Covent Garden yet. Having you around would help."

"Oh!" she clutched his arm. "I've just remembered. *The Australian Opera* wrote to you at the theatre – they must be offering you a part."

"They might just want me to audition."

Phillipa shook her head excitedly. "They offered Frank, Emily and Jacqui principal roles – they got their letters at the same time. They're not going though – they want to stay with Harriet for a while."

"I did too. But I don't know how I'll manage with Nick and Natasha around. Philly, if they do offer me a main part I think I'll accept it."

She nodded. "You should. I'll miss you – we could have helped each other."

"Oh, Philly, what a vile year this has been." He looked at his watch. "It's after five. Let's go and get drunk."

They collected their coats and went out into the snow covered, floodlit Trafalgar Square. When they reached the fountain Phillipa stopped and looked at the ice encrusted water. "Are opals really unlucky?"

"As soon as I bought it the bad luck started. I was warned, but I took no notice. Natasha gave you the opal before she came to England. What luck has it brought you? None. Throw it away."

She pushed back the hood of her coat, pulled off her gloves and handed them to Richard. Removing her scarf from inside her coat she fumbled for the clasp.

"Let me do it." He undid the clasp and pulled it from round her neck. He took a pen from his coat pocket and looked at the frozen fountain. He stabbed at the ice until it broke. Phillipa pulled off the chain and dropped the opal through the hole. She pulled her hood up. "'Vissi d'arte' – 'Love and music, these have we lived for, nor ever have we hurt a living soul'. What did we do, Richard? What did we do to deserve this?"

He put his arm around her. "I don't know. Let's get drunk."

They found a pub next door to the English National Opera. He pushed open the door and they went into its warm and smoky depths. They sat in leather chairs beside a blazing fire.

"I'm going to get champagne," said Richard.

"Isn't this an expensive way to get drunk?" she asked when he returned to the table.

He put the glasses down and sat opposite her. "Phillipa," he said earnestly, "we've just finished an episode in our lives. For you, it's the end of the Nicholas chapter, and for me, it's the end of the Natasha chapter. We've both been to hell. Now we're on our way back." His voice became husky. "It's no bloody good. If I ever see Deborah again I'll kill her."

"She's married – Jacqui and I saw it written up in a magazine."

He scowled. "I hope he's unfaithful. I hope he beats her. I hope he's got syphilis. I hope he makes her as miserable as she's made me." He raised his glass. "To Deborah's unrelenting misery, bad health and terrible luck."

Phillipa was about to agree when she remembered her talk with Harriet the night before. 'She made the past shadow her life – I'm not going to do that and neither is Richard,' she thought. "Will that make you feel better?" she asked slowly.

He took a large gulp of champagne. "You bet it will."

"Richard, all this acrimony is futile." She put down her glass. "If Deborah's unhappy – that's not going to make you happy. Instead of cursing her we should be thinking about how to find happiness ourselves. The first thing you've got to do is forget Deborah."

He looked at her incredulously. "Forget her? She wrecked my life – she'll haunt me forever."

"Only if you let her. She hasn't wrecked your life – only you can do that."

"Philly, she – "

"Listen, Richard, you've got so much – your voice, your good looks and your health – don't waste it on self-pity and hate – that's not going to change anything. You're going to be a famous opera singer. You're going to meet someone else and marry them. Right? You're going to be happy in spite of Deborah – not miserable because of her."

440

He put his glass down and looked at her intently. Finally he smiled. "Philly, you're right."

"And another thing, Richard, we're not going to waste time and money getting drunk," she said firmly. "Let's go and have some fun – let's go to the opera. *Faust*'s on at Covent Garden."

"Okay." He stood up. "We'll see if we can get some really good seats."

She pulled his arm. "Wait – finish the champagne." She raised her glass. "Here's to Natasha and Nick and their long and happy marriage."

"Nick and Natasha," said Richard. "And to you, Philly," he whispered.

She swallowed hard. "And you, Richard."

It was midnight when Phillipa arrived back at Kew. She and Richard had enjoyed *Faust* and she felt reborn. Getting off the train, she walked out of Kew Gardens station into the heavily falling snow. Watching the whirling flakes caught in the light of the street lamp, she smiled as she felt the snow settling on her face. She walked carefully down the deserted street, revelling in its beauty and listening to the squeak of her boots as they made tracks in the previously unblemished whiteness.

'When I get back to Melbourne I'm going to tell Frank the truth and ask him if we can start again. He might not want me – he might even have met someone else, but if he has I'll wish him luck and the next time I meet someone like him I won't mess it up,' she thought as she walked down Lichfield Road.

Expecting Harriet to be in bed, she was surprised to see the lights shining through the drawing room window. She went up the path to the front door. Through the open curtains she saw Harriet playing the piano. Opening the front door, she stepped into the hall.

She closed her eyes in anguish.

Harriet's broken voice, crackled as she struggled to sing, 'Oh sleep, why dost thou leave me?'

Thank you for buying this publication.

POPHAM GARDENS PUBLISHING

If you would like to find out more about

Popham Gardens Publishing

visit our web site at:

www.publishingforyou.com

or e-mail us on:

enquiries@publishingforyou.com

If you have enjoyed this novel and would like to recommend it to a friend, it is available as a paperback from Amazon CreateSpace or as an e-Book from the Amazon Kindle web site.

30048420R00250

Printed in Great Britain
by Amazon